MADE & MARRED

THE FATED CREATIONS

BOOK TWO

SAMANTHA R. GOODE

First published in the United States of America 2023
First edition

Samantha R. Goode, LLC
P.O. Box 581 Columbia Station, OH 44028

Internal design © Ari Annachi/Samantha R. Goode, LLC
Cover Design © Moonpress, www.moonpress.co
Artwork © Etheric Tales & Edits/Saumyasvision
Typeset by ProDesign, Etheric
Edited by Ari Annachi

ISBN: 979-8-9867539-5-9

For my readers, who have absolutely changed my life.
I am forever grateful.

Author's Note

Please read content information (TW) at www.samanthargoode.com/made-and-marred **before** reading this book.

You can also submit a suggested content note (TW) to the **Submit a Content Warning** button.

For more information on this series, including playlists, glossaries, pronunciation guides and more, please visit www.samanthargoode.com/the-fated-creations.

Wicket Mountains
Correnti
Madierian Sea
River Brawn
Neomaeros
Merwinan
Mad Strait
Widow
Rominia
Srotian

ASSILLION
MORTITHEV
TUS
VESTARIA
KROMEAN SEA
BLUSH BAY
PLAINS
EA
LEGEND
KINGDOMS
ROUTES

In Case You Forgot

A Summary of Bound & Barbed

While attending the local street market in the Kingdom of Kembertus, on the two-year anniversary of her father's death, Evaline Manor was searching for targets to pickpocket. Her mother had died in childbirth, and since the rulers of the kingdom were her aunt and uncle, they were her guardians. Though she was twenty-four and capable of living on her own, she was a member of Kembertus's ruling family, and her aunt and uncle, Lady Therese and Lord Elijah, planned to marry her off in a political marriage. They had taken all of her weapons the moment she arrived in the kingdom. Now she planned to use the money she stole to purchase a dagger; she wanted to flee as soon as she possibly could. It had taken so long to save enough, though, as she donated many of the proceeds to the local orphanage, where one of her closest friends, Jacqueline, worked.

Soon after she found the perfect target and picked his pocket of a heavy sum. Then she made her way to the Kembertus Orphanage to make a donation to Jacqueline, discreetly. They shared a conversation about Evaline's hard day with the anniversary of her father's death, and her friend sent her off with roses for the honorary resting place of his that she went to visit after.

Maddox Vicor and Wyott Whitlock were finishing up dinner at a tavern in Neomaeros just before they began their journey to Kembertus. Maddox was the son of Kovarrin Vicor—the leader of the Kova people. The Kova are a species of immortals that were gifted their power by the Gods. They had better senses of hearing, vision, and scent, than humans, and increased speed and strength. In order to sustain their abilities, they had to drink human blood.

The Kova's mortal enemies were the Vasi, their twin species. Alike in every way but two; the color of their eyes, and the way they fed. Where the Kova had gray eyes, the Vasi had red. And while the Kova did not kill to feed, the Vasi did. Vasi thrived on the fear and pain of their victims and had no conscience to hold them back.

Maddox and Wyott were sent on a special mission by Kovarrin. The two men were to make their usual stops around the Madierian Kingdoms to check in, then go to Kembertus. Since the Madierian Kingdoms (Correnti, Neomaeros, and Merwinan) were aligned with the Kova, the immortals offered them protection. But the Kromean Kingdoms (Kembertus, Vestaria, Arlomandrah) were, at one time or another, aligned with the Vasi. Vestaria still was, but the other two were not. The ruling families of each kingdom were some of the few humans who knew of the immortals, and they passed that knowledge down to their heirs, to carry on the alliances. When Arlomandrah's ruling family was slaughtered, and their kingdom was taken over by the killers, their alliance died with the rulers, as did Arlomandrah's knowledge of the immortals. Kembertus was the only kingdom to ever condemn the alliance. Wallace Manor, Evaline's father and heir to Kembertus, was a soldier who traveled throughout the kingdoms. When he was in Neomaeros, long before Evaline was born, he met two Kova, Maddox and Wyott, and fought with them to protect Neomaeros from a siege attempt from the false rulers of Arlomandrah. He saw the difference between the Kova and Vasi, and when he got back to Kembertus after his father's death, he broke the alliance with the Vasi and renounced his claim to the throne. He took his pregnant wife (Alannah Manor) out of the Kromean Kingdoms, and allowed his younger brother Elijah to rule, and never told his brother of the immortals.

Later that night Evaline had a nightmare about her father's death, as she did most nights. Her father was killed when the two of them had been traveling to Kembertus to help Elijah. They were attacked by a lone Vasi, and when the immortal fed from Evaline, Wallace stabbed the Vasi in the back, despite his own fatal injuries. When the Vasi stumbled away from Evaline, she saw her opportunity. She climbed atop the immortal and decapitated him. After, she held her father as he died. He said that there was much he hadn't told her about her life, and how the rest of it may look; that there was more at stake than she knew. He begged her to be happy, and then he passed.

After she woke from her nightmare, Evaline went to the boutique to see her other closest friend, Aurora. Aurora and Jacqueline were married, and Aurora owned the best boutique in the kingdom. When she got home for dinner, her aunt and uncle discussed the Ball and expressed concern that the owner of the inn, Nathaniel, would be overrun with guests. Evaline offered to go see him the next day and make sure he had everything he needed.

That night, while Maddox and Wyott were traveling, they heard a young girl scream and ran to help. They found a Vasi holding a young red-headed girl in his arms, while her father begged on his knees for her safety. Maddox and Wyott fought off the Vasi and protected the humans. Just before Maddox killed him, the Vasi asked whether their First sent them to Kembertus to look for something, too. Maddox asked why Vasier sent him, and the Vasi looked at Maddox and asked if Kovarrin was still choosing to keep his people in the dark, even his own son.

The next day Evaline went to the inn to speak to Nathaniel. Once inside she nearly walked into Maddox's back. She felt an odd sensation when she was near him, and noticed all the weapons he wore. Convinced he was just another rich man who wore weapons for fashion and not function, she decided to pickpocket one of his daggers on her walk out of the lobby. As soon as her hand landed on his weapon, his hand grasped at her elbow. He taunted her, and when she looked up, he knew they were mates, and she knew that he was a Kova. She told him as much, and he was surprised. She fled to her father's grave. Maddox tried to chase her but let her go. He asked what her name was, and a man standing in line outside of the inn told him that she was Evaline Manor.

As Maddox and Wyott walked into the forest, he questioned why the Goddess of Fate would mate him to the daughter of his friend then grew concerned that the Vasi they killed the night before was looking for her to get revenge on the Manor's for breaking their alliance.

Evaline spent the next few days in the castle, afraid of running into the Kova again. She tutored two young girls from the orphanage, Priscilla and Megin. After the lesson she went back to her room to count her savings and realized she had enough money to buy a modest dagger and holster.

Maddox and Wyott scouted Kembertus to ensure no Vasi came back looking for Evaline and Wyott suggested that they send a raven to Neomaeros, so that the Lord of Neomaeros could send a white raven—the only way the Kova communicated with the mainland—to Kovarrin and tell him about the Vasi they'd encountered. It was revealed that Wyott hates the First Vasi because of something he did to Wyott's father.

That night Evaline had a nightmare about the night after her father died, when she was traveling to Kembertus by herself. She was attacked by two men who planned to torture and kill her. She tried to escape, and one grabbed her braid and yanked her down to the ground, where she broke her wrist in her fall. They picked her up and carried her away toward their camp. As they got closer, she heard a voice in her head as a heat filled her body. She couldn't name the voice, but it was chanting the word "no" again and again. The voice screamed through her mind, her hands flung open against the restraints, and pain seared her palms as she felt wind against them. One man dropped her, and she realized that the man was dying, she assumed from a heart ailment. He scratched at his throat, and the other man called him Lonix. When Lonix died, the second man looked at her. It had been too dark to see their faces before, but now his face glowed in a faint blue light, contorted in fear. He ran away.

Evaline got ready for the market after waking up the next morning, dressing in oversized clothing and boots to disguise as a man at the Blacksmith's tent – since women couldn't own weapons. She braided her silver-white hair and wove in a gleaming strand of silver barbed wire and then hid the spikes. After the men had yanked her back and attacked her, she vowed she would never be pulled by the hair again.

When she went to the market and picked out a dagger, the Blacksmith accused her of being a woman. Maddox came up behind her and informed the Blacksmith that she'd been buying the dagger for him. She fled while Maddox bought the dagger. He caught up to her and they bantered, and finally he confessed that he knew her father. She had to get back to the castle, and he gave her the blade and holster. She tried to pay for it, but he refused.

Evaline went to her room in the castle and practiced with her new dagger. She felt a new confidence with the blade that wasn't there when she sparred with her father. The shadows in the room seemed to shudder, but she ignored it. Her aunt came in the room and Evaline barely hid the dagger in time. Evaline and her aunt got into a fight about the Ball and how Evaline needed to meet new men, and her aunt threatened to arrange a marriage if she could not find a suitable husband herself.

The next day Evaline went to see Aurora at her home and they discussed Evaline's fight with her aunt, and the Spring Solstice Ball. Finally, Aurora told Evaline that she was trying to open a boutique in Neomaeros, but that her application wouldn't be reviewed by the Lady of Neomaeros until it was too late to open the boutique for the next spring's courting season. Evaline offered to ask Therese to send a raven to ask the Lady of Neomaeros to move Aurora's application up in the queue, because Evaline wanted her friends out of Kembertus as soon as possible. After she left Aurora's house, she could feel Maddox's presence behind her, and they spoke. After she departed from him, he went to the inn and Nathaniel informed him of the Spring Solstice Ball occurring the following night, and Maddox decided to attend.

After Evaline got back to the castle, she had dinner with her guardians. They implored her to search for a husband at the Ball, and they discussed how their son Gabriehl needed to come back from traveling and find a wife, too.

On the night of the Ball Therese came in and did Evaline's makeup and hair and told her about how much her parents loved each other and how eerily similar she looked to her mother. Before Therese left, Evaline asked her to mail the Lady of Neomaeros for Aurora. She agreed. At the Ball, Lady Therese told Evaline that there was someone they wanted her to meet. She recognized the man—Bassel—as the second man who attacked her two years prior.

She tried to stop the panic attack she felt at seeing him, but all the horrible memories from that night flashed back. But finally, she realized that he did not recognize her, and that she had to be the one to stop him from hurting any other women. She agreed to dance with him, but while she did, the feel of his hands on her was too much and she began to have another panic attack. Maddox stole her from Bassel mid-twirl, and they danced together. She found herself calming in his arms as Maddox told her that her eyes reminded him of the Madierian Sea. He said that it was rumored that the Goddess of Seas, Merwinna, had eyes the same shade, and colored the ocean the way she did as an act of vanity.

He offered to train her. She was offended and he told her that she needed to find someone to train with because it had been two years, without training, since her father died. She grew overwhelmed and fled the Ball.

The next day Lady Therese came by to tell Evaline that she had sent the postage to Neomaeros for Aurora. Therese also informed Evaline that she was betrothed to Bassel, that he came to Kembertus under the notion that they'd be wed if he fancied her. Evaline refused, and Therese slapped her and informed her that the wedding would be in one month. After Therese left, Evaline dressed and scaled the wall outside her bedroom and went to the inn. Evaline finally accepted that she needed to get revenge on Bassel for what he did to her, and to stop him from hurting anyone in the future.

Maddox let Evaline into his room at the inn and in the firelight, he could see a red welt on her cheek. He became enraged, but she refused to tell him who did it to her. She asked if his offer to train was still available, and he said yes.

A few days later Maddox went to the stables to ride and take his mind off Evaline, when she arrived with Priscilla and Megin. Maddox helped Evaline teach the girls to ride. After they dropped the girls off at the orphanage, they continued to walk toward the main street and they talked more about how old Maddox was—one hundred and eighty-nine—and the rate at which Kova mature. He told her that Kova mature slower than humans, so they're children (human ages from infancy to nine years old) for about fifteen to twenty years. Adolescents for fifteen more, and are usually mature like Maddox by age forty. Evaline confessed that her father did not die by bandits, but by a Vasi. Maddox asked if she'd been bitten, and she showed him the scars from the Vasi's bite.

The next night was their first training session and the first time that she formally met Wyott. She asked why Maddox had a hatchet on his hip, and Wyott told a story about their childhood. He told her that when the Kova were young, Maddox was smaller and weaker than the rest. So, when they trained, he couldn't use the weighted training weapons, and could only use the nearby lumber axe. Since he'd throw a tantrum when he was weaker than the rest, they gave him a nickname that corresponded to his real name. Mad Axe. After, Maddox and Evaline sparred. She was faster and stronger than Maddox anticipated, and she was surprised by how quickly and easily her skills came back to her even though she hadn't used them in a long time. After they dropped her off at the castle, Wyott and Maddox walked back to the inn and Wyott asked Maddox when the last time he fed was. He confessed that it had been about two weeks, and Wyott became angry. He lectured Maddox that even though drinking from someone other than your mate became unpleasant after meeting your mate, he still had to feed. After Wyott stormed off, Maddox went out to try to feed. But when he did, the human's blood was like molten metal in his mouth and he had to cough it up to get rid of the burning sensation. He didn't understand why he was unable to drink from any human now that he'd met Evaline.

The next morning Evaline's body was sore from the exercise the night before. Eventually her aunt came to her room and informed her that they would be dining with Bassel that evening. After dinner Bassel stood and asked her to join him on a walk. They went to the courtyard and strolled through it before he proposed.

Maddox had snuck into Evaline's bedroom and was waiting on her bed for her return. He surprised Evaline, and they bantered about training. He asked if she wanted him to massage her muscles to soothe the ache, and she agreed that he could massage only her back, since she couldn't reach there. When she nearly fell back in relaxation and threw her hands out to catch herself, he saw her engagement ring.

He was enraged at the sight and when she told him it was an arranged marriage and that she didn't love the man, he asked her to let him take her away and she agreed. He wanted to leave that night, but she said they had to wait until the wedding in one month. He asked where the proposal happened, and she informed him it was in the courtyard. When he landed outside of her window a mixture of rage and fear swirled inside of him. To quell the anger, he decided he needed to destroy something, and headed to the courtyard.

Evaline woke to her aunt's screams, and Therese dragged her to the courtyard to see the destruction. Evaline realized that it was Maddox's doing and was touched. Therese made Evaline clean it up.

That night at training Maddox showed Evaline his Rominium dagger, made of the element that comes from the volcano—Mt. Rominia—on the island that the Kova are from, and Evaline was horrified when they explained what a volcano was. While they sparred with daggers, she confessed that she knew Maddox was the one who destroyed the courtyard, and when he was surprised, she tackled him with a dagger to his throat. After they dropped her off at the castle, Wyott questioned whether Evaline was strong and fast enough to take Maddox down by her own merit, or if it was because he was malnourished. Maddox confirmed that she was stronger and faster than any human they'd ever seen before.

After a four day break from training (to give Evaline time to rest), Maddox and Wyott spent the day in the castle's library looking for information on other non-human beings to try to figure out what Evaline could possibly be, because they were confident she was not human. Maddox and Wyott ruled out several beings because she didn't match their qualities. This included ruling out Sorcerers because even though they could wield one of the elements (Air, Terra, Water or Fire), they weren't abnormally strong or fast like she was. They were thankful she wasn't a Sorceress because their existence is illegal. In the Kromean Kingdoms whenever someone is found to have magical abilities, they were executed. Before doing so, the rulers would send a raven to the First Vasi and explain what element the Sorcerer wielded, what they looked like, and whether they were a man or woman. Each time they'd wait for a raven back from the First Vasi, and the parchment always said one word; execute.

Evaline came into the library and Wyott told her that Maddox loved to read romance novels.

Later that day Evaline had to go back to the library to wedding plan with her aunt before Therese explained what would happen during her wedding night.

The next night they had another training session and Maddox asked what she would like to train. She asked for a lesson on getting out of holds, and Maddox and Evaline practiced how to escape several different positions. On the last one, she spun out of his hold and her barbed braid slapped him in the face, drawing blood. Wyott immediately realized she had a weapon in her braid and found it incredibly cool. They finished training for the night and Evaline asked them about their home, and they told her that it was in the Madierian Sea. She confessed that she'd always wanted to see the ocean.

A few days later, Evaline was in her wedding dress at Aurora's receiving a fitting. After she took the dress off, the two started drinking, and Evaline told Aurora about the unpleasant conversation she had with her aunt about sex. She didn't realize how much she'd been drinking and became drunk. Aurora took Evaline to the inn so Maddox could help get her home without anyone seeing, and Maddox took care of Evaline. She tried to seduce Maddox, but he refused while she was under the influence.

The next day Evaline didn't remember what happened with Maddox. Soon, Bassel and Therese barged in and asked her to go to the market with them. She saw Maddox there and seeing him brought back all the memories from the night before—she was horrified. After Bassel bid the two Manors goodbye, Therese dragged Evaline to her room and asked who Evaline was ogling at the market and then accused Evaline of having relations with Maddox. They got into a fight and Therese confessed that it was embarrassing for her that Evaline was not yet wed. Before Therese left, she forbade Evaline from leaving the castle for the next week and a half until the wedding.

Maddox and Wyott were in the woods waiting for Evaline for hours and Maddox was growing increasingly worried. Maddox apologized to Wyott for keeping him away from his mate for longer than they anticipated, because now he understood how agonizing it was not to know whether something was wrong. Wyott consoled Maddox, and then they headed to the castle to see if Evaline was okay.

A few nights later Maddox and Wyott came for training. They practiced decapitating Vasi, and Evaline confessed to them that she was the one who killed the Vasi that attacked her and her father. They were both impressed and shocked.

The next day Maddox and Wyott went to the Blacksmith's store to pick up the custom ordered Rominium dagger he had made for Evaline. Wyott asked to get one made for himself, and Maddox forbade him to because he wanted it to be a one-of-a-kind piece for his mate. On their walk home, Wyott was angered when he discovered Maddox had still not fed, and Maddox finally confessed that he could not feed on anyone besides Evaline. Maddox made Wyott promise him that if something did happen to Maddox, Wyott would get Evaline back to Rominia and keep her safe, and Wyott promised.

A few days before the wedding, Evaline got to spend time with Aurora and Jacqueline. That night, she went to the cemetery to see her father's grave in the dark, and Bassel, along with two friends, walked by the cemetery and spotted her there and attacked her. She accidentally used the bond to communicate with Maddox and he heard her scream.

He got there just as one of the men was strangling her. Maddox killed two of the men but got stabbed in the process. When Maddox tried to kill Bassel, Evaline begged him not to. She wanted to be the one to kill Bassel, not Maddox, and she convinced Maddox to compel Bassel. Evaline and Maddox went back to the inn so she could help with his wound. In doing so he noticed the bruises on her neck from the man who strangled her, and realized she was in pain. He told her to drink his blood, because Kova blood could heal her. Maddox made her hold her dagger in case he lost control and accidentally hurt her in the process. She drank a lot of his blood, and he kissed her neck, but before they could go any further Wyott barged in and stopped them. He was angry that Maddox almost let Evaline drain him, which would kill him, and he left to get Maddox some human food to get back some of his strength.

A couple days later Evaline anxiously awaited her training session with Wyott and Maddox, but only Wyott showed up. He told her that Maddox was saving his strength, and they discussed their escape. He said that they would meet at five o'clock the night of the wedding by the wall that surrounded the kingdom. Wyott got back to the inn and saw that Maddox had recovered and allowed him to leave. Maddox went to the cemetery to take the locket on Wallace's grave, which had Evaline's mother's picture inside of it. Evaline had confessed she wanted to take it with her after her attack at the cemetery.

The night before the wedding Maddox came to Evaline's bedroom to see her. She apologized for hurting him, and asked whether there was something wrong with her because his blood tasted sweet to her. He told her there wasn't, but he didn't understand why she'd find it sweet. He saw her dress hanging behind her and again asked to make sure that Evaline was not going through with the wedding, and she said she was not. She didn't want to tell Maddox her real plan, afraid he'd be disgusted with her and try to stop her, or back out of their arrangement. Evaline asked him to help her compel the people she loved so that they wouldn't be implicated in her escape. They went to Aurora's house to compel Aurora, then the Orphanage to compel Jacqueline, Priscilla, and Megin to forget that they were friends with Evaline. Maddox compelled them to only remember if he said to.

The next day was the wedding. When Maddox heard the wedding bells, he ran to save her, convinced they were forcing her into the wedding. But he watched in horror as she willingly went through with the ceremony. At the reception, he showed up and summoned her to the kitchen, and was clearly hurt by her lie. She felt guilty but tried to convince him that she would meet him at the wall when she was done, but he didn't believe her anymore. He gifted her the Rominium dagger he had made for her, nearly kissed her, and left.

Evaline left the kitchen and found Bassel, ready to get her revenge. She and Bassel went to their suite, and she pretended to seduce him before impaling his hand on the wooden post of the bed. She waited until he remembered her, but first he asked how she discovered his ruse and the real reason he came to Kembertus to marry her. They were both confused by what the other had said. She told him that she was attacked by him and Lonix. Bassel became afraid, claimed that she killed Lonix that night, and fought back. He said that he would kill her, Vasier's orders be damned, but she was stronger and faster, and killed him first.

After, she went to her uncle's study to retrieve her father's sword hanging above the mantle and went to meet Maddox at the wall. He was happy to see her, but immediately saw the blood on her brow—an injury sustained from killing Bassel—and he wanted to go kill Bassel. She begged him to stay, and finally had to reveal to him that she killed Bassel. Maddox was in awe of her, and they kissed and were intimate for the first time.

During their travel Maddox and Wyott told her about Kova. That Maddox's father was the first of their kind, and so they called him the

First. They explained how they fed and that their saliva healed small wounds, like the pinpricks they left behind when they bit someone. They explained that Kova and Vasi could be born or created; they could be the product of two full blooded immortal parents, or one full blooded and one mortal, or they could be created via the change. All immortals that went through the change first become a Kova, and only became a Vasi if they drained a human. They told her that they'd never known anyone that changed into a Vasi. Wyott explained that since a Vasi's soul was already damaged, they couldn't go back to being a Kova after becoming a Vasi. Evaline asked about humans changing into a Kova, and Wyott explained that it could be done by a Vasi or Kova drinking the blood of the human, and then the human drinking the blood of the immortal. The mingling of their bloods was what caused the change, so it was a time-sensitive procedure. Before they could continue, they were attacked by a group of human bandits. The trio killed them all and continued on until they made camp for the night.

Maddox took the first watch while Wyott and Evaline slept and then shook Evaline out of a nightmare. She was dreaming of her attack from Lonix and Bassel, and when she woke up she had a panic attack. Maddox helped her through it, but demanded to know what the nightmare was about. He said that he cared about her, and that he only wanted to help her. She finally told Maddox about her attack, and about Bassel's role and why she had to kill him. Maddox confessed that he was glad he didn't know, because he would've tortured and killed Bassel himself. They kissed, and Evaline considered that she might be falling in love with Maddox.

The next day, they continued traveling when Wyott accidentally brought up that he had a mate, and that Maddox had one too. When Evaline realized that Maddox had a mate, and thought that he had been cheating on his mate with Evaline, she was enraged. When they made it to the next town she ignored him and flirted with a man at the tavern. Maddox became enraged and pulled her up to her room at the inn, and they got into an argument. After she discovered she was his mate, she was even more angry that he'd lied to her the entire time they'd known each other.

Finally, he confessed that he loved her, and that it was the reason he didn't tell her. He wanted to give her time to adjust, with the wedding and her escape, before he threw this on her too. They had sex for the first time and vowed that they both loved each other, until the end of their days, and in the Night that followed.

The next morning Maddox told Evaline more about the bond, and that she used it the night of her attack in the cemetery. He told her that mates could send thoughts, emotions, and even images, down the bond. Wyott, antsy to get back to Rominia, to his mate, now that Evaline was aware of the bond, called Maddox to go get some horses for the rest of their travel. Once Maddox left, Evaline had a panic attack. She was worried that Maddox would force her to live in Rominia, or be a part of their ruling family, and was concerned that she just fled one prison to end up in another. She gathered all her belongings and left the inn. Once she got to a creek in the woods she calmed down. She realized that Maddox would never make her do something she didn't want to, and that she should give him the opportunity to explain. She remembered that she loved him.

When she turned to head back to the inn, she found that her cousin Gabriehl was behind her, and he quickly made it clear that he was aware that she killed Bassel, who was his friend. A man grabbed her from behind and six more appeared. She recognized one as the man who flirted with her at the tavern. They knocked her out and abducted her, but not before she dropped her Rominium dagger for Maddox to find.

When Maddox got back to the inn, he was devastated when he realized that Evaline had left him. But he pulled himself together, determined to find and protect her, even if she chose not to be with him; he couldn't let her die in the woods. When they found her Rominium dagger, they knew she had been taken and had left it behind for them to find. Maddox screamed in anguish, determined to find her.

Chapter One

Evaline

"Good morning, sunshine."

The voice filtered through my dreams. I almost smiled and sighed in contentment from waking up beside Maddox. But before my eyes could flutter open, before I could anticipate seeing the glow of the morning sun cascade over his bare chest and touch the olive skin that stretched over the tight muscles on his torso, I felt an ache in my lungs. It was sharp and rhythmic, easing for one moment before crashing back down on me again—reminiscent of the stories my father would tell me of the waves that crashed on the Madierian shore.

I tried to groan, but realized I couldn't make any sound at all. Air evaded my compressed lungs, and pain pulsed with every attempted breath. The discomfort stretched to my chapped lips, behind which my tongue lay lifeless in my dry mouth. I tried to wet it, to close my mouth and swallow, but was hindered by a cloth that was shoved inside.

Tears stung the edges of my eyes as I opted to take deep breaths through my nose, but still, only the faintest amount of air flowed through. My clothes were damp, my hair stuck to my face, and I knew that we must have traveled through a storm.

When I opened my eyes, the ground was a blur beneath my face, and I had to concentrate to recall the recent events.

Maddox and I were mates.

I'd panicked and fled.

Gabriehl found me.

And now he was taking me…Gods knew where.

I winced as the horse I was slumped over jolted forward.

The ache in my lungs reverberated through my ribs. How long had I been draped here like this?

"There she is," Gabriehl remarked from a nearby horse.

I stilled.

I didn't bother trying to speak, just listened to the stomp of hooves around me, straining my eyes to look around, despite my limited visibility with my head angled toward the ground.

A voice rumbled through the thighs that braced my body in place. "That must've been some dream you were having."

My eyes widened as I knew exactly what he was talking about—my dreams of my last night with Maddox—and I bit back the tears that threatened to fall.

I didn't know how long I'd been knocked out, but I knew we'd be hours ahead of Maddox.

What had he thought when he got back to the inn and realized I was gone?

He probably thought I left. I had, but I could never truly leave him. Not anymore. I'd fled as one last act of selfishness. My last effort at protecting my own heart. His confession could have gone a thousand different ways, but in each of them, I would have gone back. I *was* going back when Gabriehl stopped me.

I had just needed a few moments of clear air, of being alone with my thoughts. Of being away from Kembertus, Therese, Bassel. Even Maddox. I needed one moment where the only person I had to answer to was myself, where there was no pretending, no lying about my plans, or maintaining the walls that I tried so hard to hold steady around my heart.

So much had happened in the last month, and most of it was jammed into the last week alone. I'd just needed time to process it. But I was happy Maddox and I were mates. I loved him.

Realization hammered through me as I remembered the bond. The bond that I could talk to Maddox through. I squeezed my eyes shut and searched in my mind. I had no idea what I was looking for, but I searched nonetheless. It was as if I was crawling through the darkness of my head, my hands outstretched, searching the ground for that tether. As if it were a physical chain I could find and tug.

After several minutes of finding nothing, I could've cursed myself.

I should've at least asked how the bond worked before I ran away. I only knew that I somehow used it the night Bassel and his friends attacked me in the cemetery. I squeezed my eyes shut once more, trying to remember what I'd done that night.

I had tried to escape, to flee into the happy memories of my mind. I'd pictured Maddox sitting on his bed, the way we'd been the night I was drunk and he took care of me. The night he said no to me, even though I begged. When he chose what was best for me over what he wanted.

I'd reached out to him then, as if I could touch him through my memories, and he'd heard me. I steadied myself, trying to stop the slight tremor that had started rolling through my body, and tried to replicate what I'd done then.

I pictured the two of us last night, when he'd proved his loyalty. I pictured the way he looked at me as if I was a portrait of divinity, how he promised to love me even when we were dead. I replayed those moments over and over, reaching out again and again, and waited to feel that same stir in my mind that I had the night I used the bond.

There was nothing but static.

The horse jostled me roughly again and I nearly slid off before the man's hand came to grip my waist. I squeezed my eyes shut as he held me against him.

I took a deep breath, or as deep as my bondage would allow, and tried to clear my mind and think of what to do. I didn't know how long I'd been knocked out, but I knew we'd be hours ahead of Maddox. I still had the dagger hidden in my boot, but I could no longer feel my father's sword at my hip. I could at least fight with the dagger when the time came. For now, I just had to focus on surviving.

"When are we going to stop for camp?" asked a man behind me, interrupting my thoughts.

"We can't risk the men she was with catching us. If they found she was gone and picked up horses, they could be right on our tail. We have to push through the night." I heard Gabriehl say and noticed for the first time the orange swath of light that coated the land below me. It was sunset.

I'd been gone for hours—nearly the entire day—and Maddox was nowhere to be found. Heartache settled in my chest as I realized he wasn't coming for me.

From the moment I'd met him, I'd feared trusting him. I pushed back against his attempts to get close to me, refused to show him who I really was, to let him love me. Afraid that it'd be a mistake, that it'd leave me vulnerable to being hurt. Being betrayed.

But my greatest mistake wasn't trusting Maddox, it was leaving him.

"How would they catch up to us? We're heading southeast and they're heading either east or northeast. We're far enough now that they would've diverted their path." The man whose lap I was on rumbled above me.

I stilled and felt my already dry mouth desiccate.

Southeast. Why did that strike such fear within me?

My fatigued brain wracked through every map I'd ever seen throughout my life, picturing the small town Maddox, Wyott, and I had been in between Kembertus and Neomaeros, right on the cusp of the River Brawn. What lay southeast of it?

Not Arlomandrah, that was south. Not Vestaria, thank the Gods; that was straight east.

And definitely not Kembertus which was where Maddox was likely headed—something these men already thought.

"I'd rather be safe than risk having to deal with any more interruptions in this deal. Bassel dealt with most of the details, I don't want to risk being late for the exchange," Gabriehl snapped at the man.

I thought back to the history lessons my father taught me about who resided near the oceans. The Kova and Vasi didn't live on the mainland, at least not the majority of them. They lived on their own landmasses.

"Humans don't believe in the monsters who lurk in the night." My father's voice filled my head with a lesson he'd given me once. "But they do fear those that lurk in the depths of the oceans. Sea monsters don't exist, but take the blame for Vasi bloodshed." Tears stung my eyes. "The island where the Vasi reside is in the Kromean Sea. They overtake pirate and trading vessels, drain those aboard, then make their way to Brassillion and dock the stolen ships in a port south of Vestaria. They kill so frequently there, that at certain times of day, in certain shades of sunlight, the color of the water is altered by the blood. One day, the humans named it accordingly." His words echoed in perfect memory in my head, and I realized that silence had fallen over the men around me as Gabriehl had been sharing a similar story.

"Have any of you ever been to Blush Bay?" one whispered.

I gritted my teeth, doing my best to ignore the way they sank into the fabric in my mouth and the dank, vile taste of it.

Why would Gabriehl take me to Blush Bay? It was a major Brassillion port, but what did that have to do with me? I'd never been before, and my father never mentioned going either. I just knew the lore that surrounded it; that Vasi roamed there.

Gabriehl was taking me to someone, collecting a bounty for him and his posse. But who would want me in Blush Bay?

My skin paled, my heart felt as if it stopped even as I jostled atop the horse's back, as every thought, interaction, memory I'd ever had regarding the Kova or Vasi flashed through my head at once.

My attack, my father's death, the stories he'd told me as a child, the information I learned of the Kova from Maddox and Wyott.

No. My voice was but a whisper in my mind. *Please, Gods. No.*

Maddox's father's name was Kovarrin. He was the first Kova to ever exist.

My eyes widened, I stared at the shifting ground below me, as my heart raced, realizing that the immortal species was named after the First, after Maddox's father. It seemed so obvious now, but I'd never considered it. Maddox had never mentioned it.

I tried to calm myself, to think through the information logically, but another memory flashed forward faster than the former and all I heard was Bassel's threat during our fight the night I killed him.

"I'm going to kill you, you fucking whore. Vasier's orders be damned."

For the first time since I'd woken up slung over this horse, I throttled myself. I shifted my body and attempted to roll off my mount. I shrieked and screamed as much as my parched throat would allow. I swung my head and bit down against the dirty cloth in my mouth.

"I'll be damned." Gabriehl chuckled from his horse. The laugh grew louder as I thrashed, and I knew he had turned to face me. "I guess she does know whose bounty we're collecting."

Bassel wasn't supposed to kill me, but he had been willing to defy orders to survive.

Vasier's orders.

Vasi.

CHAPTER TWO

Maddox

I'd lived nearly two centuries and had never known greater stress than in these last few weeks with Evaline.

I knew it was because of the bond, because of the deep love I had for her. It had grown since the moment I saw her and swelled with each witty remark she threw my way, with every swipe of her dagger through training, and from the smiles that infrequently graced her face.

I'd lived nearly two centuries having to only worry about keeping myself, and sometimes Wyott, alive.

But then there was Evaline. The person I'd waited my entire existence for, that I had begged the Gods for.

Once, the thought of losing her had been the greatest torture I could imagine. But I'd give anything to trade *that* anxiety, the fear of something that hadn't happened yet, with the reality of losing her. The pain that radiated throughout my body and hummed in my ears was the worst I'd ever endured.

Wyott was beside me on a horse galloping to keep in stride with my own. We had let the third steed loose hours before. We couldn't keep dragging it along at the pace we were trying to keep.

"We could run faster than this," I growled low against the wind.

I saw Wyott's head flick toward me out of the corner of my eye.

"You're beyond malnourished, Maddox. You can't afford to keep expending your energy until you feed," he said, his voice stern, before turning back. "*When* we find Evaline, you're going to need your strength to save her. You can't waste it now."

I released a ragged breath through my gritted teeth.

We were hours behind them—whoever they were. Who knew how far ahead of us they had traveled. Who knew how long she'd been gone by the time I discovered her empty room at the inn.

Wyott and I didn't speak as we rode, and it took every ounce of my control not to vault off the horse and sprint to her. To my Evaline.

As soon as we'd found her abandoned dagger, the one I'd gifted her, and realized she'd been taken, we'd immediately ridden east.

As our horses' hooves pounded the ground and the sun beat on my neck, the idea of who might've abducted her ravaged my thoughts and possible routes traced through my mind.

We could go to Kembertus. It seemed that the most likely scenario was that Evaline's aunt and uncle discovered Bassel's body and sent a retrieval team out on their fastest horses to come find her. She'd embarrassed them and committed treason. They would execute her—whether she was family or not.

But Bassel's family would be angered, too. They'd lost their heir to Vestaria, they'd want to spill the blood of the person who did it. Especially since she was a woman. The implication that they were involved in Evaline's abduction chilled my blood. The thought of her being taken back to that kingdom, the methods they'd undoubtedly find for torturing her until she begged for death, scared me far more than the idea that she simply left me, or that she didn't love me at all.

But I tried to calm myself. While they certainly had reason for abducting her, their involvement was unlikely. It seemed implausible that Vestaria would've had the time to discover Bassel's death and send a team all the way out here to get her in the few days we'd been gone from Kembertus.

Out of the two, Kembertus seemed more feasible.

But there was another option.

It seemed as if a lifetime had passed since Wyott and I had saved that man and his daughter from the Vasi the night before entering Kembertus.

That Vasi had been looking for something.

Once I'd met Evaline, once I learned her last name and knew she was the daughter of my old friend Wallace, I'd worried that the Vasi had gone near Kembertus to look for her. His presence near the kingdom, and her father's previous snub of the Kembertus-Vasi alliance, seemed too related to be a coincidence.

If that Vasi was lurking on the outskirts of the kingdom, who knew how many more were just waiting for her to leave the safety of the walls?

My anger flared at the thought that I'd taken her out of one harmful situation, only to steer her into a worse fate.

I warred with myself for a few more miles, up until the point where there wasn't any time left. The fork in the road split my choice into two paths.

The left, for northeast. For Kembertus. For the family she scorned.

The right, for southeast. For Blush Bay. For the Vasi who could be looking for her.

"Which way?" Wyott asked as we stormed toward the fork.

I couldn't be wrong. We couldn't be wrong. If we went the opposite direction as her captors, I'd never save her in time.

"Maddox," Wyott said again, his voice urgent, as we headed straight for the tree that split the road.

Her aunt and uncle would kill her, no doubt. Would the Vasi? Why would they even want her?

"Pick!" Wyott shouted.

As we had mere seconds to divert, the thoughts, the options, the stakes, the consequences flashed through my mind in bursts. But amidst the chaos of this internal war, the sound of the horse's hooves, the thunder above, and the patter of a squirrel's feet on a tree branch a few yards away, I remembered the most important fact. The most vital aspect of this entire situation, of this decision, that I'd been forgetting: Evaline and I were mates.

I surged for the bond, but there was nothing. I was too far.

I gritted my teeth, sent a prayer to Rominiava, and clenched my eyes shut to focus. I felt out into the air around me and tried to remember the way the pull felt when she was near. The way it reminded me that she was close, begged me to seek her.

I couldn't feel it, there was no trace of the bond. Too many miles separated us.

But there was a feeling. The slightest hint of intuition that whispered through my mind.

And Gods, who knew what caused it? Who sent the thought rustling through the depths of my mind?

The Goddess of Fate? Wallace? Evaline's mother?

My eyes flashed open and I jerked the reins to choose a path. As Wyott and I turned down it, I could only hope I'd picked correctly.

I'd had a lot of firsts with Evaline, and here she was, taking me toward another.

I'd never seen the east coast of Brassillion before, never been so close to Blush Bay.

Chapter Three

Evaline

Water rushed down my windpipe and caused a piercing pain in my lungs. I coughed, sputtering to clear my airway.

"Hurry up," the man above me snapped. His hand clenched harder around the canteen that he'd been tipping into my mouth. "I'm not going to stand here all day."

I coughed again and spit out some phlegm. Despite my pride, I tilted my head back. I knew I needed to drink as much water as I could, Gods knew the next time they'd offer again.

For the first time since I'd woken up, we'd stopped traveling to give the horses some rest. We'd ridden through the night and although I tried to sleep as much as I could during the travel, my bumbling on top of the horse wouldn't allow me to.

I'd given up on trying to fight my way off the horse after I realized where they were taking me, *who* they were taking me to. I'd only fall off and kill myself in the process. Breaking my neck or being trampled by the horses along the way would be less than ideal. If I wanted to have any chance of getting away, I would have to utilize one of the rest stops they took but I knew this wouldn't be the one. I was so thirsty that my mouth was cracked and all I could do was desperately guzzle water down as fast as it streamed into my mouth.

My wrists ached from the rope tied around them, but I was thankful they were still in front of me and that my legs were unbound.

"That's it," the man grumbled out as the stream of water ended.

I lurched forward just as he stepped out of reach.

"I need more. Please," I begged. I had to squint against the midday sun to look up at him, and a pulse of pain radiated through my skull.

He rolled his eyes, slamming the cap back onto the canteen before turning away from me.

"And I need a satchel of gold, but here we are," he said.

He strode toward a group of overturned logs, where the rest of the men sat and had begun to unpack various rations. I couldn't tell what they had from where I had been dumped, but my stomach grumbled for it all the same.

As I watched them stuff pieces of food into their mouths, I realized it had been two nights since I had eaten—at the tavern when I'd been angry with Maddox. I had hardly eaten, just pushed my food around my plate. I could have cursed myself.

Stupid, stupid girl.

I swallowed my annoyance and did my best to send with it all the thoughts of what my father would say if he could see me now—how I always needed to be nourished in case something like this happened, how misguided I was by leaving the safety of the inn at all.

I leaned back onto my bottom and welcomed the cushion of grass as I pulled my legs out from underneath myself to stretch. I took a deep breath. I didn't dare speak anymore or ask for food. I was thankful the man had left the gag out of my mouth, and I didn't want to risk him replacing it.

I looked to my right, past the horses, to the path we'd been traversing. The road we had traveled led miles and miles back to the town where I'd been abducted, to the town where I left Maddox and Wyott behind. Back to the inn where Maddox had finally torn all of my walls down. Where I *let* him tear them down. Where he said he loved me.

Tears misted my eyes and I didn't bother blinking them away. I *deserved* each and every one of them, I *deserved* the ache in my heart, and I *deserved* to torture myself with thoughts of what Maddox must've been thinking when he returned to the inn and saw that I'd left. For all intents and purposes, I had left him. For one moment, I turned my back on him—on both of them. They'd been more of a family to me than my aunt and uncle had, and still I had walked away.

He cared for me. I should've realized sooner that his feelings were true. I should've known how much I meant to him based on everything he'd done for me. How he'd armed me, trained me, and rescued me from Kembertus. It didn't matter that we were mates. He loved me.

But I'd still doubted him and left when things became confusing. Would I run every time there was a potential for pain?

Even if he forgave me someday, even if he found the dagger I left behind and realized I was kidnapped, even if he was barreling down the forest paths to get to me, to save me *again*, he wouldn't be headed this way. He'd go back to Kembertus, maybe Vestaria, where he must think I was taken.

He'd never guess that I was headed into the waters of Blush Bay, to whatever land the Vasi resided on.

A shiver wracked my spine despite the heavy heat of the sun on my skin.

I turned back toward the small group of men and tried to gauge whether or not they knew who they were working with. If they did, they were fools. If they didn't, they were unfortunate.

They seemed afraid of Blush Bay, but when Gabriehl told them about it he never mentioned the Vasi. Only the lore of the sea monsters.

I was willing to bet that whatever deal Vasier made with them would be promptly ended once Vasier had what he wanted. Once I was in his grasp, I wagered that he would kill all the bandits who delivered me to him.

I hadn't known the Vasi even had a leader before learning of Firsts from Maddox and Wyott, but I didn't peg him as a man who fulfilled his promises.

My eyes drifted to Gabriehl. I scanned his wide shoulders and red-tinged hair that flopped over his pallid forehead. Did he know of the

Kova and the Vasi? If he did, he didn't let on. I doubted he could hold his own against one. If any of the men knew of Vasi, I didn't know. The one who'd flirted with me in the tavern had seen Maddox's eyes—I suppose if he'd known they were Kova, he would've said so by now. Gabriehl would've been far more concerned with staying on the path, too, if he thought immortals that could run far faster than these horses were on our heels.

If they were on our heels.

My heart did another painful thump and I clenched my jaw. But as if Gabriehl could feel my gaze, as if he could hear my thoughts, he turned to me.

"You'd think you'd mind your business over there instead of staring at me like you want me to shove that gag back in your mouth," he said, his eyes cutting between mine.

I didn't know if I should speak. I didn't want any more humans in this world knowing about Kova—it could put Maddox and Wyott in harm someday—but I didn't have to mention the benevolent immortals.

Besides, if he didn't listen to me, he'd likely be dead in a few days' time.

"Do you know who you're taking me to, Gabriehl?" I asked. My voice was calm and even and only slightly raw from my still-dry throat. He opened his mouth to respond, but I cut him off. "Or should I say, do you know *what* you're taking me to?"

He narrowed his eyes. I shrugged in response.

"You think you can scare us into turning around?" He laughed a short humorless laugh. "Come on, Evaline." He stood and took a step toward me. "You're the daughter of the mighty Wallace Manor. I thought you'd have a bit more fire in you." Another step. "More fight." Another. "You're settling on words? On empty threats? On old myths?" By the end of his tirade he was standing in front of me.

My eyes were on his boots when a smile stretched across my face. A sharp, wicked, smile.

I had to tilt my head all the way back, painfully so, in order to meet his eyes. But when I did, his own smile faltered at the sight of mine.

"You're right. I am the daughter of the mighty Wallace." I cocked my head, smile still wide. "The one he taught how to fight. The one he taught how to kill." The other men had gone silent, all of their faint chatter had ceased as they turned to us one by one, listening to my words. "The one he taught about the monsters who look human but drain the blood of their screaming victims in the dark."

Gabriehl rolled his eyes, trying his best not to look terrified, judging by the pursing of his lips.

"If there were beings like that, surely between the eight of us, we would've seen one in our lifetimes," he said, raising his eyes to look over his men, nodding to them.

"Nine."

Gabriehl's head snapped back in my direction. "What?"

I kept my head tilted back to keep eye contact with him. Even if it hurt, even if the muscles in the back of my neck begged me to release tension. Even if there was a drop of sweat sliding from my forehead into my hairline.

"You said eight. There are nine of us here."

Gabriehl was quick to roll his eyes again before he turned his back to me and walked away, waving off my remark as he did so.

"Doesn't make much difference."

I watched him walk off, the ache in my neck grateful for the release. But I couldn't contain myself, and he didn't get far before I spoke again.

"It makes all the difference," I started. "Because it renders your statement false." He stopped short of his men, back still to me. "Perhaps between the eight of you, you've never seen a Vasi."

His shoulders tightened at the name of the immortals I was trying to warn him about. As if giving them a name made them more real, as if assigning them a title made the beings stand up from my words and forced them into existence.

"But when I'm added to the count, it changes."

Gabriehl slowly turned to face me. "Shut your mouth, before I stick the cloth back in it," he growled. "You can't scare us with your childish stories."

I continued as if he hadn't spoken.

"The count changes because I've seen a Vasi in my lifetime. The one that killed the mighty Wallace Manor," I said, and ignored the pain that leaped through my chest at the memory.

His eyes widened and I saw the slow bob of his throat as he swallowed. He kept his stance wide and rigid, and none of the men behind him saw the flash of fear he displayed. They, too, showed signs of concern. A flexed jaw, a worried brow, a clenched fist.

I tilted my head and smiled at them again, and did my best to make it terrifying.

"No doubt you grew up hearing about your big and strong Uncle Wallace and all of his accomplishments on the battlefield. Do you want to know who killed the Vasi? Who killed the very immortal that defeated Wallace Manor?"

As if he knew my next words Gabriehl stalked toward me again, this time faster, with a purpose. I knew what it was, so I forced my words out quickly to ensure they'd make maximum impact.

"*I* killed that Vasi, the monster that drank my blood and tried to kill me." He was halfway to me. "*I* cut his head clean off his shoulders, with a measly dagger no less. And I'm not afraid to meet them again," I taunted as he drew closer. "I'm not afraid to see them when we get to Blush Bay," I lied, my voice rising. "Because out of all *nine* of us, I'd say I have the best odds." I roared.

Gabriehl stopped in front of me, his chest heaving with anger, and looked down at me.

"Stop talking," he barked.

"How many Vasi have you killed, Cousin?" I asked with a grin.

The last word hardly left my lips as the back of his hand came down and connected hard with the side of my face. There was only a second's worth of pain before darkness encroached on my vision.

Chapter Four

Wyott

Maddox wasn't with me the day my father died.

No one was.

My father and I, along with a few other Kova, had been on a trip when the Vasi found us—when Vasier found us. When he took away the last family I had left.

A week later, by the time I made it back to Rominia I was a malnourished, weeping mess.

And even though his home was too far from the port to hear me coming, and though there was no possible way he could've known I was on a ship pulling into Rominia's port, Maddox stood on the creaking wood of the dock, waiting for me.

I learned later that he'd been there every day, waiting for me to come back. He'd stop by after training, sit on the dock between meals, run down before bed, waiting for my return.

We were brothers before we were brothers.

That day when I stepped off the ship, when he ran up to me and saw the grief on my face and the bags beneath my eyes, he didn't ask what happened. He didn't ask where my father was. He didn't ask why there was blood coating my clothes.

He simply wrapped his arms around me, lowered us to our knees, and let me sob.

I cried for what felt like hours. I cried until my throat was raw. I cried until my tears made their way through the cracks of the dock, and joined the salty waters of the Madierian Sea. Until Kovarrin and Rasa came to find us.

And throughout those hours, never once did Maddox's embrace falter. Never once did he straighten out of our uncomfortable position, never did he ask to get off our knees that were bruising beneath our weight.

He listened. He held me. And he cried, too.

Maddox was there for me on the worst day of my existence. And so I was there for his.

The hours since we'd gotten back to the inn and found Evaline missing passed in a blur. They consisted of mostly silence between us as our horses ran, but I knew there was a war raging in his mind. He was struggling with which direction to choose, then even after he chose, I knew he feared he'd made the wrong decision. He was worried that he couldn't save her in time; concerned with what they'd already done to her.

"We'll make it in time," I yelled over the wind rushing past us.

I tried to force him out of his fear, remind him that nothing was accomplished by his torturous thoughts, but even as I said the words, I knew he wouldn't heed the advice.

If this was Cora missing, if I was in Maddox's position, I'd be just as enraged as he was—just as devastated.

So I did what I could do. I reminded him that she was powerful, that she was quick and strong. That we'd prepared her for these types of situations. I voiced that she was stronger and faster than any human we'd ever fought with, or against. That she could do more than either of us truly knew, and that it would only help her survive. After a few hours of reminders, his shoulders seemed to loosen.

But beyond that, there was nothing I could do for him.

What was worse than not being able to help, any more than I was, were the words I knew I had to say next. He'd be angry or think that I didn't have his back. But even if he didn't want to hear them, he'd have to listen.

"Mads," I started, and his eyes flashed over to mine, head still facing forward. "We have to stop."

His jaw clenched and I heard his heart rate jump.

"No, they can handle a bit more," he said, his voice gruff.

I took a quick breath and reminded myself to be as kind to him as I could.

"No, they can't. You know that."

His hands tightened on the reins but after a moment he pulled to slow the mare until we were both stopped. We jumped off and led them to a nearby creek to rest and graze.

The horses were tired. We'd stopped several times already for brief breaks, but never long enough. Maddox wasn't allowing them to get the rest they needed, he was too desperate to get to her.

Which was how I knew he'd hate this.

"This is it for the night. We're camping here." I set my saddlebag in the grass and began to loosen the tack buckles.

His head snapped toward me so hard I was afraid he'd hurt himself.

"No we're not," he argued.

"You know we have to," I said, turning to face him. "They need rest. They can't keep up this pace. Stopping for a bit at a time is doing nothing."

His brows furrowed as he glared at me, as if his stare alone would change my mind. When I didn't budge, he let out a shaky breath.

"I am not stopping. I'll continue on my own if I have to."

I shook my head and stopped myself from rolling my eyes.

"You know you can't do that. You're not strong enough right now." He opened his mouth to argue, but I cut him off. "Mads, you know I'm right. Trust me, no one hates that I'm saying this more than me. But I'm only doing what's best for you, and for Evaline."

He scoffed and backstepped a few paces, as if he was so disgusted with my words he needed to put space between us. "It's not exactly best for Evaline if they're killing her right now, as we're wasting time at this fucking creek."

"And what's the alternative?" I barked back at him. "Running there and expending all your energy so that by the time we get to her, you're too weak to save her?" I finished, then added. "Or worse."

I thought his eyes would've softened at that. I thought he would understand my fear, what I was trying to protect him from—Kova didn't turn to Vasi by accident often, but it wasn't impossible. If he drained a human, he'd make the change and be gone forever. His rage alone could push him over the edge, and the risk was only worsened by the fact that he was already weeks past when he should've fed. He was strong, but not invincible.

He took a step toward me. "You made a promise to me once—to do whatever it takes to help her, even if it meant leaving me behind."

I took a step toward him, too, appalled that he'd throw that in my face.

"Of course I did, because I would do anything to help the both of you. But you *know* this isn't the same situation. I told you that I would protect her if you were taken, if something happened to you. This isn't me breaking that promise, this is me avoiding having to keep it. Nothing has happened to you yet and I refuse to let it."

He growled and turned from me, pacing away before turning back again.

"I don't know what you can't understand about this," he said, and his clenched fists shook at his sides. "But I don't matter anymore," he croaked, flexing his hands. "Only she does. And I can't fucking sit here and wait to go to her, knowing she could be hurt right now, screaming my name."

I forced the frustration away, forced the muscles in my face to relax, to drop the anger etched there.

"So you'd rather that she watch you die?" I asked. As the words left my mouth images of watching the Vasi kill my father, and drag him away, entered my mind and my eyes fell to the ground. "Or watch you turn? Either way, she'd lose you forever. I'm trying to prevent that."

I shrugged and lifted my gaze again, and found that Maddox's shoulders hadn't loosened, his face hadn't calmed. His chest heaved, and fists clenched as he snapped at me.

"So that's it then? Every day, you're ready to go find Vasier and get your revenge. Every day, you hope you'll be the one to end him. Just not when it's for Evaline. Not when it's for me."

I winced at his words, at the accusation in them. As if they were that very hatchet on his belt, and he'd just flung it at my face.

I took another deep breath, a slow swallow, and pictured the two young boys holding each other on that dock.

"She has already watched one person she loved die in front of her eyes," I started.

As I said the words, I regretted never confessing to her that we had that in common. I felt a twinge of guilt for not sharing with her sooner that I knew the pain she felt. For a moment I felt the urge to go after her just as Maddox wanted. To go get the woman who had so quickly fit into our family and become a little sister to me.

But I shoved it away and focused on logic.

"I refuse to let that happen to her twice," I vowed.

Maddox's shoulders softened, and I knew he finally heard me. My words had finally broken through his haze of anger.

I strode closer and put a hand on his shoulder. "You can only control what's *in* your control. What's happening to her is not. Resting now is. You can rest, and let the horses do so, too."

Maddox looked at me out of the side of his eyes and I saw tears there. His frustration had given way to sorrow, and I realized that it was probably the first time he'd allowed himself to break down since he discovered that she was gone.

And so, I did what I knew he needed. I wrapped my brother in my arms and let him cry.

CHAPTER FIVE

Evaline

The night was unusually quiet. I sat up from where I laid back on the grass and cracked my neck before squinting around. The only light I had to see by was that from the full moon, which broke through the canopy of trees above me. For a moment I thought we'd stopped for the night, that I'd been dropped here from a horse and left. But as I looked around at the hazy landscape, I realized that I was dreaming.

I stood and rubbed my unbound wrists.

I stretched, surprised I felt the urge in my dream state. I was even more surprised when my joints cracked.

My brows furrowed. Usually, when I was aware that I was dreaming, I didn't feel discomfort or pain.

"Evaline," I heard a soft voice whisper.

I whirled to face it but was only met with the wind that swept past me and rustled the leaves. Shadows stretched and danced along the ground and I spun back again, searching for the source of the voice.

Dread crept up the back of my neck, spiking my heart rate, and I was reminded of the nightmares I'd had growing up; the ones that I never remembered, but that always sent a deep fear radiating through my bones.

The trees shifted around me. Despite the moon's brightness, the shadows on the ground seemed to slither around. Goosebumps rose along my skin as the shadows writhed and crawled up the trunks, stretching to fill every bright space. An odd humming noise filled the silence that the halting wind left behind.

I'd always dreaded these nightmares as a child—I woke up more scared than I could voice to my father. I knew that I was dreaming but couldn't break free, and when I did wake, I couldn't explain what caused my terror. Only that I felt it.

But as I spun on my heels, looking for an escape from the shadows, the soft whisper of a voice spoke my name again. I tried desperately to find its source in the dimming light. No one appeared, and my heart raced. As the throbbing darkness grew around me, it sung, and I found myself rooted in place, unable to move or call out. Darkness wove through the branches above my head, and I wondered, briefly, if this was what I'd always been scared of—what all children, all adults deep down, are afraid of—the deep trill of darkness. And being alone in it.

Much to my displeasure, I did not wake with the ability to stand and stretch like I could in my dream. I was slung back over the horse, braced between the thighs of the man who'd flirted with me in the tavern.

They stopped the horses shortly after I woke, once the sky turned a soft orange that melted away into the deep blue of late evening. I wasn't sure how much time had passed while I was unconscious—it could've been a few hours, or a day and a half.

I took a deep breath, happy for the chance to expand my lungs, and was looking forward to an entire night of it.

At least until they dragged me over to a maple tree and tied me to its trunk.

I tried to ask if they were fucking kidding me through the cloth in my mouth, but only an unintelligible string of groans came through. The two men pinning me to the tree laughed and tied the ropes so tight around my chest that I found myself missing the horse.

They didn't bother unbinding my wrists, but instead looped rope around the trunk and my torso until there were rows of it down my chest and over my arms. They confined me in a standing position against the bark, which only allowed my knees the slightest bend. They left my ankles free, but it didn't much matter in this position. I could kick until I was exhausted but that wouldn't loosen the ropes.

I could feel the weight of my dagger in my boot and tried to remain hopeful that somehow during their slumber I could reach it and cut myself loose. It'd be extremely difficult but the moment they all fell asleep, I'd try.

They setup camp in the clearing by erecting four separate tents and building a fire. A few of them disappeared into the woods that encircled camp and when they came back, I could see that they'd hunted for dinner. They never offered me any water or food; I was forced to stand against the tree watching them drink and finish their roasted rabbit and squirrel.

My eyes drifted to the stars above, which were only just beginning to peek through the darkening sky, when a man addressed me.

"Hey, murderess." My eyes snapped over to his. "Why'd you do it?"

He sat and waited for a response. Either he was drunk, or he forgot that there was a gag in my mouth.

"I asked you a question," he said, his tone harsher this time.

"Cradley." Gabriehl rolled his eyes. "She still has the rag in her mouth, you fuck."

Cradley narrowed his gaze toward my mouth and finally saw the cloth. He ambled over, nearly tripping, despite there only being grass beneath his feet, and ripped the cloth gracelessly down my chin. I spat the taste of the rag to the side and wet my lips. They'd been dry and cracking for hours.

"There, now you can tell me why you killed Bassel," he said, bringing the bottle he was holding to his lips. I watched a dribble of it fall down his chin before I met his eyes.

"I tried to tell Gabriehl before you abducted me," I snapped, throwing a glare at Gabriehl over Cradley's shoulder. "Bassel was a monster. After my father died, when I was traveling to Kembertus alone, Bassel and another man attacked me in the forest."

Gabriehl straightened at my words and looked toward me.

"Bassel never mentioned that he knew you before your betrothal."

I shrugged as much as the rope would allow. "He didn't remember me, it must've been too dark that night."

"What happened to the other one?" Cradley asked.

I furrowed my brow. "What?"

He waved his bottle in the air. "You said Bassel and another man attacked you. What happened to the other one?"

I raised my chin. "He died." There were a few murmurs amongst the men before they looked back to me. "I don't know what caused it, maybe a heart ailment."

Gabriehl bent an elbow to prop his hand on his knee. "So you survive Bassel that night and go to Kembertus. Then two years later Bassel arrives to marry you, and you recognize him," he said, and gave his head a slight shake. "And, so what, you decide to get your revenge?"

His eyebrows furrowed and I knew why. He couldn't fathom a world in which a woman would get justice for herself. And that arrogance only fueled the rage that had been growing in my chest since the moment they took me.

I ground my teeth. "I *decided* that he wouldn't hurt any other women the way he'd hurt me. I decided that I'd been given this life for a reason, and on the day of our wedding, it was to rid the world of monsters like him."

Cradley bellowed a laugh. He was so close that I felt the spray of his spit. My nails were about to draw blood from how hard I clenched my fists. He raised a brow and turned back to the men behind him.

"So she fancies herself a hero, then." The group burst into laughter and the clink of their bottles filled the air. Cradley reached out a hand and dragged his knuckles down the ropes that covered my chest. "Some savior you are."

I narrowed my gaze at him. "I never said I was a hero."

He shrugged before putting his dirty fingers on my face, shoving the cloth back in my mouth. Once it was in place, he patted my cheek with two rough strikes and gave me a lopsided smile.

"Tell me, what do they call a hero who can't save themself?" He cocked his head and I had to fight the tears from coming on.

I opened my mouth, as if I could respond with the fucking gag, but before I could Gabriehl sounded from the campfire.

"Cradley, leave her alone," he commanded.

Cradley gave one last wink before stumbling back to the group.

Gabriehl stood up and addressed all of them. "That goes for the rest of you. No one messes with her tonight." He made a point to look each man in the eye and waited for their nod of understanding. When his gaze landed on Cradley, the latter only raised his bottle in acknowledgement, then Gabriehl turned toward his tent. "Put that fire out when you go to bed, no reason to signal our location more than necessary." He looked around camp warily, eyes coasting over the tree lines. "We're close to the drop off location for tomorrow morning, and I don't want any surprises or delays. Get to sleep at a reasonable hour."

Then, he disappeared into his tent.

Hours had passed since they'd all retired for the night and put the fire out. I should've been cold, and I might've been, if I hadn't spent an hour twisting my body in an attempt to grab the dagger from my boot.

My ribs ached from the dig of the ropes and a sweat had broken out on my forehead. I was doing my best to bend my torso and raise my ankle up close enough to my hands. The dagger was holstered inside my left boot, a few inches below the opening. If I could get it up close enough to reach it, I could cut my way out of these bindings.

And what will you do once you're free?

The worries were already plaguing my thoughts. If I freed myself, where would I go? I had no home anymore. No one to run to.

I pursed my lips and blinked away the tears. For now, I would steal one of their horses and flee as fast as I possibly could.

The bark of the tree bit into my back as I straightened to take a breath. My chest heaved at the effort and bile rose in my throat as the memories of Bassel and Lonix flashed through my mind.

Here I was, again, stuck in the forest, pinned to a tree. A lifetime seemed to have passed since the two men had me in this same position two years ago.

My lungs filled as I took a deep breath and shrank again as I forced every ounce of air out. I needed to make my chest as small as I could against the bindings to allow the ropes some slack. I bent forward, and down, as far as I could, stretched my fingers, and lifted my left leg up at an awkward angle.

I'd failed so far on every attempt. Each time I only grazed the butt of the dagger, unable to wrap any fingers around it to pull it free. But time was running out. Gabriehl said the drop-off was scheduled for the morning, and I didn't know how early that meant. I didn't know when they'd wake, so I had to make every moment count.

My hand was too far below me to see where I was reaching, so I clenched my eyes shut to focus on my sense of touch. I twisted my leg up and crawled my fingers down until they found the opening.

I slipped my fingers under the lip of the boot. They palpated down until I felt the cool stone of the dagger's handle.

I paused to take the tiniest breath and calm myself. I shoved my right foot into the ground while I pushed my chest against the bindings in one big thrust and clenched my fingers.

My breath stuttered as I barely grasped the blade. A drop of sweat slid down my nose and I froze, scared I'd lose my hold, but my middle and ring fingers were locked on either side of the handle. Slowly, so slowly, I eased it up. It felt like ages, but was only seconds, until it was free of the holster and my boot.

I straightened but kept my grip on the dagger firm as I tilted my head against the tree and took a full, deep breath.

I looked up to the waning moon shining down on me.

"Thank the Gods," I whispered so quietly that only the wind could hear me.

My hands were shaking from the exhilaration but I forced them to calm as I twirled the dagger in my hand until I could tilt the blade up toward the bindings on my wrist and moved the blade back and forth against them. It was painfully slow, but I didn't have a choice. If I dropped the blade I'd be fucked.

Just as the dagger bit through one of the ropes around my wrists, I heard a rustle. Instinctively, my eyes snapped to the tree line, but then flicked to one of the tents whose flaps were being moved aside.

Fuck.

I couldn't drop it, and I didn't have time to put it back in my boot. So I did the only two things I could.

I twisted the blade to nestle between my hip and left arm, and clasped my hand completely around the butt of it.

And I prayed.

Please, Vestari. Please don't let them see the dagger.

Cradley's head popped out from the tent just as I finished securing the blade. I did my best to even my breathing as he headed straight for me.

"Why so sweaty, lovely?" he crooned as he stepped in front of me. I didn't respond, I couldn't with the gag, so I just stared at him. "I couldn't sleep, too busy thinking about what I'm going to spend that bounty on once we hand you over tomorrow." He swayed slightly as he stood, and I knew that he'd continued drinking once he'd gone into his tent. "A new horse. A new pair of boots. A night at the tavern." He shrugged. "But you know what I won't need to buy?"

My composure was locked down like a vice around my neck. I stared at him as he spoke and kept my hand clenched around the handle of the dagger to keep it pressed against me.

"I won't need to buy a new sword," he said, and I nodded. Anything to appease him until he grew bored of me and went back to his tent. But his lips drew into a malicious smile. "Because once we deliver you tomorrow, I get to keep yours."

My eyes widened, jaw tightened, and I had to concentrate not to let the dagger fall from my grip.

His smile grew at my reaction, and I tried to wrangle my composure back.

"But who knows, I could just melt it down, forge a new weapon." He shrugged. "Or a set of horseshoes." I strained against the ropes holding me back, trying to launch myself at him.

I hadn't seen my father's sword since I was abducted. I wasn't sure if they'd left it behind. I had hoped so, because that would mean Maddox could have it. That he could keep my father's memory alive wherever he went in the world.

If my father was here, he'd say that I was letting my emotions get the best of me; that it was just a sword. I knew I shouldn't fall into Cradley's trap, but the more he spoke, the more difficult it was to control myself. The thought of my father's sword in the possession of the men who were no doubt aiding in the death of Wallace Manor's only heir, enraged me.

I clamped down on my anger, on my hate, but it didn't matter, because Cradley looked down, narrowed his eyes at my wrist.

"What the fuck?" he said as he leaned closer to me.

His hand reached for my dagger but before he could get it, I cocked my head back and thrust it forward, head-butting him as hard as I possibly could in the nose. He hissed and stumbled back, and my vision spun for a moment.

I'd hoped it'd knock him out, or that he'd stumble and fall and hit his head. After a moment he straightened and touched his hand to his nose. I caught a glimpse of the blood that soaked his fingers when he pulled them back into view.

"You stupid bitch," he snarled as he came toward me.

He grabbed my dagger and ripped it from my grasp before the other hand grabbed my jaw. I hissed against his harsh grip but he only tightened his hold. He was faster and stronger than I thought a drunk man could be.

"You better thank the Gods the bounty on you requires your life intact, because that would've been your fucking death sentence." He cocked his head and a vicious smile lit his face before he shrugged. "Then again, it only stipulates that you must be alive, not unharmed."

I cried out as he sunk my own dagger into my left side. The pain was unlike anything I had ever felt—white hot and searing, as if a fireplace poker was jabbed through my skin.

"Not enough to kill you, just to hurt real bad," he mocked in my ear.

He pulled the dagger out slowly, making sure to twist it on its path, and I screamed again, tears pricking my eyes. My shouts died in the cloth shoved into my mouth. When he pulled the blade out completely, he wiped my blood on my pants and took my dagger with him.

Before he walked too far away, he threw one last taunt over his shoulder, quiet enough so as not to wake the others. "Your blood, for mine."

CHAPTER SIX

Maddox

It'd been too long. Too much time had passed since the last time that I saw her, since she went missing, and I was so afraid of what that passage of time meant. What could they be doing to her right now? What had already been done?

We'd ridden hard all day, and Wyott was right. Letting the horses get rest last night was necessary. But now we were hours into another dark night. The shadows were playing in the leaves of the passing trees as the horses rode, slower than I could stand, and I had to remind myself to breathe.

Prayers slipped through my mind and to the Gods every few minutes, the repetition of words were a comfort as I did my best not to fall apart.

Please Gods, keep her safe. Please Vestari, Mortitheos, Rominiava, Correntan, Arlomandric, Merwinna, Neomaeries, Kembertic.

I addressed prayers to every God. I needed the help of them all. For Vestari to help her fight her captors. For Mortitheos not to take her into the Night. For Rominiava to spark our mating bond as soon as we were close enough to use it. The other five didn't have dominion over anything that could help her, but I prayed to them regardless.

"We're getting close to Blush Bay," I called to Wyott. "Either we're going to be too late and they're already on a ship heading to Mortithev or we're going to stumble upon them any moment."

I was too afraid of the former to give it much more thought, and instead opted to feel for the bond, to scream down it and hope with each breath that I'd hear her reciprocation.

Ev–, I started to say down the bond, but was hit with something. Not the feel of the bond, but something else. Something worse.

The scent of blood.

It coasted through the air and ripped into my senses. It was minimal at first, just a hint, but definitely blood. I kicked the horse into a sprint without a second thought and turned to speak to Wyott, to tell him that we must be getting close. Just as I opened my mouth, a new scent hit me. Still blood, just not from the same source as before.

That blood was ordinary, it could have belonged to any man or woman in any kingdom. But this blood I knew.

Evaline! I screamed down the bond and slipped from the horse without telling Wyott why. I knew he'd understand the moment I sprinted away and the scent hit him. I heard his horse's hooves pick up in speed just as I broke out of earshot from him.

But I didn't care that I couldn't hear Wyott anymore, I wasn't listening for him. I was straining to hear any indication of the bond, any sound from the woods I was tearing through.

The scent of Evaline's blood grew stronger and I wasn't sure if it was because I was getting closer or because she was losing more.

As I ran, I dodged the trees that stood in my path and hurtled those that were fallen across it. I noticed that each stride felt slow and difficult to make, as if I was running through mud instead of twig littered dirt. I knew it was because I was malnourished, but I tried to force the worry out of my mind. The worry that I should've fed from her sooner. The worry that waiting might have cost me more than I could've imagined.

A few more steps and I broke through what felt like a fog, but there was nothing in front of me. No low hanging clouds or even smoke. The fog wasn't physical, it was mental. It was as if I'd walked directly through the veil that separated this world from the Night.

As I hit the odd boundary, I reached out.

Evaline? I called down the bond and without pause I felt the swell of it, of her response, and it replenished my strength. A smile lit my face as I pushed to run faster.

Maddox! Evaline shouted through my mind and I could feel her relief, but then there was a sear of pain.

A growl ripped through me at the confirmation that she was harmed. *Are you okay?* I asked. I knew I was getting close.

I felt her sigh through the bond, try to calm herself, before she answered. *Yes. Yes I'm fine. Thank the Gods you found me.*

Brief, ever brief, tears flowed through her voice and I knew without a doubt that I'd made the right decision to come for her. I wanted her to know that I'd *always* come for her.

I should be there soon. Are you near any landmarks? Any water? I took in a breath, hunting for her scent, and altered my course toward it.

Not really, just in a large clearing.

There, just ahead, I saw a break in the trees, with the faintest hint of moonlight tunneling through the leaves.

I think I see it. One more minute, Eva. I'll be there, I promised.

Thank you. Thank the Gods. Thank—. But she didn't continue.

Eva? I asked and concern laced my voice.

Before she could speak, I knew what she'd say. Because I heard them, smelled them, just as they'd smelled her blood. They'd been farther away, camping closer to Blush Bay, I assumed, but at the scent of her sweet blood they came running as fast as they could. It was the most decadent I'd ever encountered and I knew the Vasi would go feral for it.

They're here, we whispered together.

I pushed even harder and broke through the throng of trees surrounding a clearing that housed a few tents to find the love of my life strapped to a thick tree. She was in the center, facing me, and a hundred paces away.

But just as I broke through, so did they.

The two Vasi locked eyes with me and without another breath all three of us sprinted for the center.

Her eyes flashed between the three of us in the second it took us all to reach her. She met my gaze before one of the Vasi blocked her from my vision.

A roar ripped through my chest as I halted behind him. I seized the back of his neck before his mouth reached her shoulder and threw him as far as I could behind me. The second Vasi appeared and he stretched both arms between us, but he was deep in bloodlust and made the mistake of keeping his eyes on her.

I snatched the arm reaching for me and wretched it behind his back until he crumbled to the ground in pain. The other Vasi landed on my back at the same moment I tore the throat out from the one I had on the ground. I hissed at the impact and the world flashed as I spun and planted my hands against the chest of the Vasi behind me so, again, he was launched to the other side of the clearing.

"Pests," I snarled.

I glanced at the Vasi on the ground before turning toward Evaline. Although he was gasping for breath and still far from death, her fear was plain on her face. She was my first concern. I took a step toward her, but froze as humans began stumbling out of their tents.

The entire interaction between the Vasi and I had only taken a few breaths. The sounds had probably taken longer to break through their haze of sleep. My poor Evaline had likely just been watching in horror, unsure of what was happening since her eyes wouldn't have been able to keep up with all the motion.

I ignored them as I started to rip the ropes from her. There were so many strands, and I almost got through all of them before I heard the footsteps from the Vasi I'd thrown behind me. I let out a frustrated groan and glanced at her furrowed brow. There were still a few ropes around her hips and wrists, but I had to leave them and spin to catch him as he leaped toward my neck.

Just then I heard Wyott break through the brush. The sound of hooves was missing as he sprinted and I wondered if he'd heard the Vasi and left the steeds to run off.

Just as our eyes met, the humans barreled toward him.

"Fuck," I murmured.

The Vasi yelped in pain and I realized my hand was clenched firmly around his throat. I didn't understand where my strength was coming from. It was as if being near Evaline fueled me. As if she gave me all the strength I needed to protect her. I tightened my grip further, ready to decapitate him, when sharp fangs sunk into my calf. I hissed and jerked my leg away from the Vasi on the ground. I reached down for his neck too and slammed their heads together until I heard a satisfying crack. I felt Evaline's fear ripple through the bond, heard her struggling against the ropes, trying to free herself. There were too many left, too tight, she wouldn't be able to wriggle out of them.

The Vasi recovered quickly. I wasted no time and plunged my hand through the chest of the upright one. The other was still bleeding badly from his throat, and I reached down, baring my fangs to finish his decapitation. He flopped sideways, dead, and the Vasi whose chest my hand was buried wrist deep in let out a cry of pain. I finally ripped his heart from his chest, and he fell beside his companion.

Ideally I would've kept them alive in order to question them, ask what their orders were, and why were they supposed to take Evaline. It seemed rather clear at this point that it was the case, but I had no choice. They were too deep in bloodlust—far worse than any Vasi I've ever seen. I wondered for a moment how long they'd gone without feeding. I'd seen Vasi hunt humans bleeding far worse than Evaline was, and they didn't act half as crazed as these two had.

I tried to turn back to her, but a human ran up behind me yelling, "She's *our* bounty!"

I turned, and the sight of him stopped me in my tracks; fresh blood trickled from his nose and dried blood rested around it. Bruises marred his pallid face.

Understanding hit me—it was his blood I'd smelled first back on the horses, before Evaline's. The knowledge that she had likely caused that wound on his face, and what he clearly had done to her in retribution snapped the hold on my willpower. The Vasi were already dead. Wyott was taking care of his last two humans, and all I could focus on were the eyes of the filth that had injured Evaline. My Evaline.

The world broke out into shades of black and red, and I reached forward and locked a hand around his throat. His eyes widened as I jerked him toward me. A growl ripped through my throat as I dug my teeth deep into his neck.

In that moment the pain of the burn didn't matter. The sear of his blood down my throat was merely an inconvenience as I took drag after long drag. I wanted him to suffer. I wanted him to hurt. He had harmed the only person in this life who mattered, who would *ever* matter, and he deserved to suffer for that.

His arms flailed against me, and I grabbed at them. My fingers grazed a blade, and while my teeth sunk deeper into his neck, I wrenched the dagger free from his hand and sunk it into his shoulder. His arm went slack and I continued to feed.

Evaline screamed against her gag behind me, and I heard Wyott, too. But really, it didn't matter. Because I'd made up my mind, I'd made it up the moment I saw this man. I knew he had to die. I briefly considered using the knife, but instead my mind tossed with the understanding that the only way this man could die was by the bite of my jaw.

That's what he deserved.

Some small voice deep within me started to surge, gruff and low. I recognized it as my own, but it was barely discernible and sounded as if it were speaking to me from behind a barrier. It urged me to continue. Not to stop. To keep going until this man was gone.

You're underfed, the voice whispered. *You need this. You deserve this. He took her from you.*

With each sentence he muttered, my head gave a nod. Because I agreed with him. This man did deserve it, and as I felt his heart begin to race, another voice broke through.

"Maddox, stop!" Wyott screamed from across the clearing.

Of course he'd try to stop me. He didn't understand. Cora had never been taken from him.

I took another drag, felt the man below me start to go limp, and heard Wyott again.

"Maddox!" he begged.

I froze as another voice entered my senses. A whisper fluttered down the bond and it swelled into a tidal wave of emotions as Evaline opened the bond up entirely and forced the image of what she was watching down it, into my own mind.

And I saw myself hunched over this man. I saw the rage that coiled my body. I saw the pale face of the human below me.

But what I felt was worse. It was rage, too.

Evaline was furious, screaming for me, screaming *at* me, begging me to stop. This entire time I hadn't heard her down the bond, hadn't felt her. I'd been so focused on avenging her that even she herself had disappeared from my conscious. And the more she pushed the images—her rage—through, the fainter that voice in my head had become. Until it sounded as if a thousand walls were constructed between the two of us, and he went silent.

I tore myself away from the human and bent to wretch up all of the blood I'd drank. I'd ignored the pain while I fed, but the longer it sat in my stomach the hotter in burned.

The human's heartbeat was faint, but still there. I hadn't ended his life. But as I threw up the last of the man's blood, Wyott finished the job with his blade.

I turned to Evaline, an apology on my lips, but it died at the sight of her.

Evaline, still tied to that massive tree, stood in rigid silence with wide eyes. It wasn't because she was afraid of me, or angry, but because there was a dagger pressed to her throat. My eyes rose to the man standing beside her, his blond hair fluttered over his pale forehead. His hand trembled where it held the handle of the blade.

Wyott and I stood silent, waiting for his next move. He seemed uneasy, as if he wasn't sure if he was willing to kill her, but would do so if it meant staying alive. There was a rustling in the tents beside us and his arm twitched.

Maybe he was protecting his friend, or leader, who still lurked in a tent?

"Don't do anything stupid," I said.

There was a fair amount of distance between us, and I gauged how quickly I could move to him.

This wasn't like when that Vasi had the young girl in his arms. He hadn't used a blade, just his teeth as the intended weapon, and we'd been able to distract him. This man held the dagger with force against Evaline's skin. Rage crawled through my body as the bite of the dagger drew some blood from her neck.

He opened his mouth to speak but then closed it again, his eyes flashing to the tent beside us. Clearly, he was concerned for someone in that tent, but Wyott and I didn't dare move. If he was willing to kill for this person, surely he'd do so before we got very far.

My eyes flashed to Evaline. I saw her chest rise and fall rapidly and knew she was panicking again.

I reached down the bond that she'd slammed wide open for me, and felt everything. I felt the anger and the fear, the love and the hate. I felt the way her hands flexed and her body buzzed with an otherworldly heat as it flooded her senses and coursed through her veins.

My eyes widened as I stared at her, and her own eyes looked back at me.

And deep within them, there was light.

Dim at first—like the rising of a midnight moon—but then brighter, clearer. It darted forward like a shooting star, and the clearing lit. Light flooded through every nook, every crevice. Shadows dispelled and the dark of night evanesced. Not the warmth from a fire, or even the cool, consistent light from the moon. But a bright, blinding Madierian Sea Blue swept over us and buzzed with energy.

It was a light that demanded attention, that demanded obedience. A light that came straight from my mate's eyes.

"What—" Wyott murmured beside me, but his words were cut by a loud crack akin to the sound a ship makes when it collides with rocks. My head snapped up as the tree above her began splintering.

The man didn't have time to react or even comprehend what was happening when the tree came to life, when it lowered one of its thick branches to reach down and seize him. A moment later, its rugged branch was around his throat before it tugged him against the trunk, hard.

The tree limb tightened as the man's feet kicked beneath him until his body stopped thrashing. His face turned blue, a much duller version of the color emanating around—from—Evaline.

And I felt all of it. The swell of her magic, the confusion in her mind, the searing pain in her side. But most of all, I felt her energy diminish. I felt that burst of magic use up what was left of her, what was left of the blood she still had circulating in her veins.

So when the man dropped to the ground, dead, the light faltered until it extinguished, and she collapsed against the few ropes that held her.

I ran to her and ripped the ropes off, catching her as she collapsed forward.

"Eva," I whispered and knelt to the ground as I turned her over in my arms so that she faced me. Her head fell back, limp, and I pulled the gag from her mouth.

"My Eva," I croaked, brushing my thumb against her cheek. I heard her heartbeat, but it was so faint, so weak. What if she had already died? Was that a phantom heartbeat I was hearing? My heart sunk further with every moment her body was limp in my lap.

I heard Wyott talking to someone, and knew he'd grabbed the other man in the tent. Heard him compel the man to sit still and be quiet, before running over to stare down at Evaline over my shoulder.

"Maddox," Wyott urged. It was all I needed to rip myself out of my thoughts.

My teeth sunk into my wrist before I lowered it to her lips, but she didn't stir, didn't wake and wrap her mouth around it as she'd done the last time I'd healed her.

"Evaline!" I screamed, shaking her. My blood only trickled down her cheeks, past her lips. No amount of it could heal her if she didn't drink it.

I heard her heart rate slow and held her tighter. My head fell to rest against hers, forehead to forehead as I rocked the two of us and ignored the tears that fell from my cheeks onto hers.

I gave up on words and reached down the bond.

Eva. My Eva, please come back.

I begged her. But I could feel the fatigue within her, how tired she was from fighting, how much pain she bore. The loss of her father, never truly knowing her mother, the trauma of what Bassel and Lonix tried to do to her, all lurked in the depths of her mind.

She was too tired to continue.

Eva. Please, sweetheart, please, I begged down the bond, straight into her mind, to her soul. Bargaining with it. Pleading with it. *I need you. I need you and I know that's selfish. I know you're tired, but I need you to wake up. Because I can't live in a world where you don't exist, I won't.* A sob worked its way up my throat and my blood still trickled past her lips.

You are the strongest creature I've ever met, and I need you to be strong now. Be strong for me now and I'll spend the rest of my existence making up for it. I'll be strong for you so you never have to do it again.

I pictured home. I pictured the two of us walking down the beach in Rominia, hand in hand, as I'd done a hundred times before. I pictured showing her my house, all my friends, my parents. I sent all the images down the bond, showing her the life we could have together.

I can take you home to Rominia. Where you can feel safe. Where you can be whoever you want to be. And we can start over, there, together.

I kissed her forehead, her cheeks, her eyes, her nose.

Please, please, my Goddess. My mate. I love you. Until the end of my days.

It was faint at first, the slow stir at the other end of the bond. It ebbed and flowed like the Madierian until it was stronger, until I knew she was coming to.

A sob of relief burst through my lips as a gasp tore through hers. She took in a harsh breath and I pulled my head back to give her space. Her eyes remained closed but she tilted toward me. I put my wrist near her lips again, and she took a gulp.

And in the Night that follows.

Even down the bond her voice sounded raspy but Gods I'd never heard anything so beautiful.

Thank you. Thank the Gods. Thank you.

I repeated over and over, and wasn't sure if I was sending the thoughts in a prayer to the creators or down the bond to my mate. But it didn't much matter, because she was here. She was alive. I didn't lose her.

Wyott's hand fell onto my shoulder and I looked up through my tears to see his eyes held his own.

"Thank the Gods," he said as if he'd heard my thoughts.

I looked back down at her. She took another drink and I nodded.

"Yes, yes, sweetheart," I encouraged her. She'd need a lot, and I didn't care how much it took. I felt Wyott's presence behind me, knew he was leaning over to see how much she was taking. I knew he'd be worried that I was malnourished, but she could have it all if it would keep her safe.

I reached down the bond. Her pain was weakening. The healing power of my blood tingled as it healed her wound. Heat started to return to her fingers and toes.

But her drags slowed and I felt her fatigue start to return.

She pulled away and rested her head back down on my arm.

"No, keep drinking," I urged. "It's not enough."

There was no response as I felt the bond quiet. It wasn't gone, but she was unconscious again.

"It's okay," Wyott said behind me. "She got enough to save her, let her rest. It'll only help."

I took in a shuddered breath but nodded. It would have to be enough.

Chapter Seven

Evaline

I don't know what I was expecting to find when I opened my eyes, but it wasn't a man dying on the ground below me. The last thing I remembered was the sound of Maddox's voice as he begged me to feed from him. I was so tired, but I'd done what he asked.

Now, I was dreaming again. The hum of the darkness around me confirmed it, and so did the feel of the man's blood running through my fingers.

"Hold on," a soft voice said, and I realized that it came from my lips. "Please, you have to hold on."

But the voice wasn't mine. It was familiar, and feminine. I swore I'd heard it before, but it wasn't mine.

I looked down at my blood covered hands and pushed them harder against the wound at his neck. His eyes were wide, and a dull blue that was probably brighter when he had life left in him. His hair was brown and his jaw strong. I knew him from somewhere, I was sure of it. I just couldn't place him.

"Not like this," my lips said, but I wasn't in charge of them. It still wasn't my voice, and the more I looked at the hands staunching his blood, the more sure I became that those weren't my hands, either.

Whatever nightmare this was, whatever vision I was witnessing, it wasn't my own. I was viewing it from another woman's eyes, yet I felt her pain and knew her thoughts as if she and I were one.

Desperation swelled in her chest as she felt the rush of his blood against her fingers slow. The tears that fell down her face landed on his cheek. I watched them slide down his jaw until they mixed with the blood from his wound.

He reached up a hand and she felt the soft caress of his thumb wipe away a tear.

"I love you," he whispered as much as he could through the blood that filled his mouth. "I always have."

A rush of guilt swept through her at the words. She knew he loved her with his entire heart, his entire soul. He wanted to marry her and spend the rest of their lives together, but she didn't return the feeling. She loved him like family—like the brother she'd never been blessed with. Like the best friend she'd ever had.

But he loved her in a way that she could never reciprocate, and here he laid, exhaling the last few moments of life, because he'd saved hers.

I didn't know what had happened to him, but her thoughts mixed with mine until I wasn't sure whose were whose.

She watched as he closed his eyes and sobs wracked her body until he was still below her.

She was responsible for the loss of a man who deserved more than she could have given him, *had* given him. The guilt suffocated her until it was too much.

Until she was sobbing and fumbling through her mind for words, any words, until she remembered those forbidden words, and uttered them. It was one phrase she repeated over and over. She grabbed the dagger that had fallen to the ground beside him and split her palm open.

She blinked hard to clear the tears in her eyes and bent over him again, placing the fresh wound directly over his. She continued to mumble the words I had never heard before and didn't understand. The wind ripped around her and she felt the buzz of energy rush through her veins. The longer she spoke, the harsher the wind became, and the hotter the blood felt coursing through her body. Her hair twirled from the wind around her, lifted off of her shoulders, and stray white strands whipped in front of her face.

The pain in her blood rushed to her chest and heat burst through it with every beat of her heart, seared its way to the edge of her skin, as if her blood was boiling her from the inside out.

But she bit the words out past the pain and focused on his closed eyes, and the curve of his jaw.

The wind, the pain, the scream of the shadows around her came to a peak, and then the world went still.

And slowly, so slowly, she felt him stir.

She removed her hand and saw that his wound was gone. She held her breath and watched as his eyes fluttered.

When they opened, gone were the beautiful blues his eyes had been only seconds before. They were just as soft, but this time colored a dark, steely gray.

He stared up at her, brows furrowed in confusion. He was so familiar, and Gods I couldn't understand where I knew him from.

"Alannah?" he whispered, looking deep into her eyes and sitting up to take her face into his hands.

My thoughts stilled.

Alannah?

But a groan rose behind her, and they both snapped to look at it.

Another man laid in the clearing with blood blooming from his chest, his face covered in it too.

The man she'd just saved braced himself beside her, while the one lying on the ground stirred again, and her throat felt as if it collapsed. She was afraid of him.

It was in that moment that she understood her mistake. Perhaps the gravest in her lifetime, in her family's history.

Her eyes moved down to peer at her hands, to the palm she'd cut open. It was covered in blood—both her blood and the blood of the man with blue-turned-gray eyes.

Suddenly, memories flashed through her mind and she showed me what happened minutes before I'd entered this dream.

The man on the ground was standing over her, screaming at her. His hands locked around her throat, tightening until she couldn't escape. He had suffocated her until she nearly died, but she'd fought against him. Her hands swiped at his face, her nails clawed down his cheeks and left bloody tracks. She tried everything to free herself, but amidst her defense, her hands had become covered in his blood.

No, she thought, as realization hit.

No! What have I done?

She was screaming in her own mind. Rage and guilt and fear settled deep within her as she looked back to her assailant and watched his eyes flutter, too.

They squeezed, and then opened, and he turned toward her.

Red.

And they looked at me. At *me.* Not the woman—Alannah—whose body I was in. But to me, Evaline. My own fear unfurled through my body, into my mind, in cold tendrils.

"Evaline," the woman's voice echoed into the night, and the shadows swirling around the dream jolted as I entered my own body again. I still kneeled on the ground in the same clearing from the dream, but the men were gone.

"Evaline," she said again.

My spine straightened. I recognized it this time. It was the same voice of the woman I'd been hearing for weeks now, and the more I thought about it, perhaps my entire life. It was the same voice that had coaxed me down from a tree when I was eight—I'd climbed too high while my father hunted and was afraid of falling down, but she'd talked me through my descent.

And when I was sixteen, when I awoke from a horrific nightmare, I'd heard her soothing voice sliding through my mind, too.

She was there the night Bassel and Lonix attacked me.

And so many other times since then.

Alannah…

In an instant I knew why her voice sounded familiar, why it was so soothing and why it stirred nostalgia, that feeling of coming home, through my chest.

Of course, I was pierced with surprise when the man with gray eyes called her by that name, because the only Alannah I'd ever heard of in my twenty-four years was Alannah Manor.

I stood and turned slowly to face her. The dark shadows that writhed around us contrasted harshly against the stark light of the moon pouring down.

She stood in a white linen dress. I could see where the front of it opened, how it tied to the side; a birthing gown. Though she'd died in it, the gown was still pristine, as if she'd just put it on for the first time.

"M-Mother?" My voice came out so much weaker than I intended, so frail and vulnerable.

She looked as if she'd nearly collapsed in on herself from joy, her balled hands flattened over her chest. She nodded and tears began to fall down her cheeks. "Yes. Evaline. Yes, my baby."

She rushed forward and I leaned into her embrace when she gathered me in her arms. I wasn't afraid that this was a trick, or that it was only a dream. It felt too real to be anything but exactly what it seemed. I had never felt more safe than I did right now, in the arms of the mother I never got to know.

I felt her tears slide into my hair, and knew mine were drenching the shoulder of her gown. How strange, to love someone you've never met.

Even stranger to not cower in fear at the sight of your dead mother.

A thought struck me then. The blood drained from my face and I pulled away from her. Before, with Maddox and Wyott, I'd had a dagger at my throat when the clearing was flooded with light that came out of nowhere.

"Have I died?" I looked around us. "Is this the Night?"

She pulled back, hands grasping my shoulders, and shook her head violently.

"No, you haven't died. You are just sleeping. Unconscious and recovering from your attack. And thank the Gods," she said with a deep breath, then gave me a small smile. "You have no idea how long I've been trying to make contact."

I furrowed my brows. "What do you mean?"

She squeezed my shoulders then slid her hands down, clasping both of my hands in hers.

"Since you were old enough to communicate, to have memories, I've been trying each and every night to coax you out of your dreams."

I squeezed my eyes shut, shaking my head. I couldn't comprehend any of what was happening. I still was not completely convinced that I wasn't dead.

"How? Why?"

Her mouth turned down in a frown and worry wound through me.

"There is so much about your life that you don't know, and I'm so sorry I wasn't there to tell you any of it." She pulled me to a few large boulders on the edge of the clearing and we sat. "But I need you to listen, because I don't know how much time we have left. In all these years I've never made direct contact with you and I don't know how long it will last." She squeezed my hand. "I just pray to the Gods that you remember this when you wake."

I opened my mouth to speak, but closed it. What could I say? I didn't understand any of this, but I didn't want to waste the time I had with her admitting that. I just nodded for her to continue.

She pursed her lips. "Do you understand what you just watched? The memory I showed you?"

I gritted my teeth. Now that I was in my own head again, in my own body and out of the memory, it was clear.

I'd just witnessed the birth of the Kova and the Vasi.

"Yes. I think so," I said and took a steadying breath. I knew the Kova had looked familiar and the reason why only hit me now that I'd been pulled from the memory. He looked familiar because Maddox bore a striking resemblance to his father. "That was Kovarrin and Vasier."

A wave of shame coasted over her features. "Yes. The night they changed."

I looked over the grass, where I'd seen the men lying only minutes prior. They'd been dead, both of them. I'd felt Kovarrin's heartbeat stop against his neck.

I looked up toward the dark sky and the full moon, as if the Gods might present themselves and tell me what happened, what they'd done. But I knew they wouldn't, because what I'd learned to be true, hadn't been. What Maddox and Wyott had grown up knowing, the birth of their species, was all a lie.

"The Gods didn't give them their immortality," I stated, then turned to face her. I could almost hear the echoes of her chant in my head and feel the heat of her blood below my skin. "You did."

She nodded and her brows knit together as she trained her eyes on me, gauging my reaction.

A thousand thoughts flew through my mind, but I stopped on a couple in particular. How could she have created two entirely new species? How could she have known Kovarrin and Vasier if they were centuries old?

I clenched my eyes shut and shook my head. "How old are you?"

She pursed her lips. "I'm similar in age to Kovarrin and Vasier. We're all nearly eight hundred years old—or I would be, if I was still living."

I pulled my hands from hers and slid them across my cheeks, up into my hair. My eyes were wide as I tried to understand.

"Are you immortal?" I asked, then corrected myself. "Were you immortal?"

"Not really. It's not that simple." She paused as if to search for the words to continue but I cut her off.

"How did you do that? How did you turn them—create them?" I asked.

My heart started to beat painfully against my chest. I grabbed ahold of the slick boulder beneath me and I looked toward the ground to steady myself.

She reached out to touch my knee lightly. "I'm a Sorceress," she said. A beat passed between us and I looked up to find her gaze fixed intently on me. "You are too, Evaline."

I shook my head and stood, moving a few paces away from her. My throat was starting to close, my chest felt tight. The dark forest around us hummed and the image of my mother in front of me began to waver.

Her eyes widened and she stood. "No," she croaked, then reached out and grabbed my wrists, squeezing them for my attention. "Listen to me," she said in a rush.

I tried to focus my gaze on her as the world around us started to fade into darkness. Shadows crawled around her, shading the clearing.

"Vasier… You saw him in the dream?"

I nodded and gasped for breath, straightening my spine to open my lungs. I knew I should ask what Vasier wanted with me, why he'd paid Bassel and Gabriehl to abduct me, but I couldn't form a sentence.

"He felt your magic the moment it awoke that night with Bassel and Lonix, and every time since."

Tears stung my eyes and I wasn't sure if it was from my fear, or my inability to breathe.

"He knows you're here. He knows that your magic is awake." Her voice quaked and her hands tightened around me. "He won't stop until he has you."

I tried to take a breath in, but there was no space.

The world shifted and the shadows began to devour her. She was yanked from me as the world faded away and her shouts sounded like a whisper.

"You're the only one who can stop him. It is your fate."

The world was suffocatingly dark, and then it was blindingly bright.

I jolted forward as I came out of the nightmare and nearly fell off the horse I was riding.

"It's okay," Maddox said as he tightened his arm around my waist and pulled me back into his chest.

I stilled and tried to breathe, but just as it had been in the nightmare, my throat was constricted. Despite the safety of his embrace, I tried to pry his arm off of me. It only felt restrictive to my breathing.

I tried to speak, but only gasps escaped me. He pulled the horse to a stop below us. Without waiting for him to help me, I slid down. He had to move in a blur to catch me as I stumbled and nearly fell.

"It was just a nightmare," Maddox said as he pulled me to the ground to kneel with him. He placed his hands on my shoulders. "Everything is okay."

He could say that all he wanted, but it didn't make it true. How could everything be okay?

Sorceress.

Creator.

Immortal.

"What can I do?" Wyott said from somewhere beside me.

Maddox ignored him. "Eva, breathe for me. Just like last time, remember?" His voice was soft.

I stared at the grass that stood between our knees, and tears stung my eyes as I felt myself growing faint again. My chest was both moving too fast and not fast enough. There was no room for the full, whole inhale I so desperately needed.

"Please, sweetheart," Maddox said again. I felt his hand close around one of mine. He moved it, and placed my hand on his chest. A moment later I felt his hand on my chest, and I jolted back; the contact startled me. I didn't want any more pressure on my chest but I couldn't force any words out. Even my blouse felt too tight.

"I'm sorry," he said softly, but I understood what he was doing now. He faced me and held my palm to his chest while he flattened his own over mine. I could feel the difference in the way our chests moved. The rapid rise and fall of mine was shocking compared to the calm and consistent grace of his.

"Feel my breaths. We're going to slow yours too," he said. I stared at his chest, at the sight of his large hand covering mine. "Look at me, Eva."

This wasn't like last time, my breaths didn't calm as quickly, but I had far more to fear now.

"Evaline," Maddox said, but I could only focus on my mother's words. That it was my fate to stop Vasier. What was I supposed to do against him?

Maddox's hand squeezed mine and he held it tighter to his chest. He didn't press his hand against my chest in the same way, though. And thank the Gods. I think if I had an ounce more of pressure I'd stop breathing completely.

How could it be my fate? How could I—

Sweetheart. Maddox's voice filled my head and my eyes snapped up to his. His voice mixed in with my thoughts. I'd nearly forgotten that was something we could do together.

I looked into his cool gray eyes and he smiled at me.

It's okay. He kept his steady gaze on mine as he communicated through the bond, and I nodded. *Everything is okay. You're here. I'm here. Wyott's here. Nothing will ever separate us again.* My chest loosened a bit. I had been abducted, but I wasn't anymore. He was right, we'd all survived.

My heart slowed down the smallest increment, and Maddox smiled.

Yes, Eva. That's my girl.

I nodded at his words, and at the thoughts I checked off in my head. My reminders.

Gabriehl abducted me.

Maddox and Wyott saved me.

We all were okay.

We were together again.

My breathing slowed another fraction, and Maddox's hand squeezed mine briefly.

Keep going. You're doing so good.

My free hand fell beside me and I wrapped my fingers around some grass.

I thought I'd die with those men or that I'd die with the Vasi. But I didn't. They'd come to save me. My boys had come to save me. My family.

My breathing slowed further and I noticed that the difference between mine and Maddox's wasn't so drastic anymore.

I looked over his face, remembering that there was a time that I didn't think I'd ever see it again. I wanted to remember everything about it. The cool gray of his eyes, the scar that nicked his eyebrow and the other that etched his lower lip.

My eyes wandered up to the dark black curl that flopped over his forehead. The same one I'd seen a dozen times and would never get sick of seeing ever again. Because I'd never leave again. Gods, why had I done that?

It was a moment before I realized that I was breathing normally. That Maddox and I kneeled together, knees almost touching, with our hands pressed against each other's chests as if our arms were the bond that linked us instead of the one in our minds.

Tears pricked my eyes as I met his gaze and I was reminded of the most important part.

They'd *come* for me.

I launched my weight forward and Maddox caught me in his chest without effort. I wrapped my arms around his neck and started to shake with sobs.

"You came for me," I said as his arms tightened around me. He pulled me onto his lap and I buried my head in his neck. "You came for me," I cried and I felt love and happiness and relief flood down the bond.

"Of course we came for you, Evaline. We always will. I *always* will."

I shook my head against his neck and continued to cry. "I thought you wouldn't, or even if you did that you'd go to Kembertus." I pulled back from him, just far enough to look into his eyes. "I thought I'd never see you again," I said, then looked up to where Wyott stood beside us. "Either of you." I reached up to squeeze Wyott's hand as he stood beside us. "Thank you," I said as I looked up at him, then back to Maddox. "Thank you for finding me."

Maddox looked up at Wyott and gave him a look, and Wyott nodded. "I'll go tie up the horses and hunt for some dinner," he said looking around. "It looks like we're camping here tonight."

Maddox reached up and held my face in his hands as Wyott walked away.

"I'm so sorry," he said low and my brows furrowed.

"Why would you be sorry?" I asked, shaking my head. "I'm sorry. I'm so fucking sorry, Maddox." I reached up to hold onto his wrists. "I just needed to breathe, I needed to have a moment to myself. So much had happened." Tears began falling down my cheeks again. "But I was coming back. I promise, I was coming back when Gabriehl took me."

Maddox kissed a tear as it slid near the corner of my mouth.

"Don't be sorry, Eva. *I'm sorry*. I'm sorry I didn't stay with you that morning to discuss what it all meant. That I didn't stay to remind you that nothing had to change, and that we could do this at whatever pace felt comfortable to you. That I would go anywhere in the world as long as it was with you."

My chin quivered as he spoke. Even in the few days since I'd been abducted, I'd forgotten how well he knew me. That he understood I'd fled in panic at the thought of being tied down to another set of expectations, whether they were his, his family's, or anyone else's.

"Will you forgive me?" I asked, searching his eyes.

He smiled gently. "Only if you'll forgive me," he said before leaning forward and kissing me.

When we pulled back I flattened my hands over his chest. "I love you. Until the end of my days."

Maddox's thumb caressed my cheek. "And in the Night that follows. I'm so, so thankful that you're safe. You have no idea how out of my mind I was when you were gone."

"Yeah he was an asshole," Wyott called from where he was tying the horses up to graze.

Maddox smiled as I laughed and looked back to him. "I was."

As he said the words I remembered the look on his face when he'd first stepped through the tree line. His eyes had been fierce and his chest rose and fell nearly as rapidly as mine had with my panic attack.

But that memory only brought on another, of the Vasi that he killed. I wrung my hands in my lap.

"I have something to tell you," I said softly.

Wyott was there in an instant, moving across the grass in a flash of speed.

"You're a Sorceress, we know."

My mouth gaped as I looked between them. Wyott chuckled and I snapped it shut.

"How do you know that?" I asked as I stood.

Maddox rose and took my hand gently in his. "We watched you use your magic to kill the man who had his dagger to your throat."

I tilted my head back. "What are you talking about?"

Maddox and Wyott looked between each other.

"You used Terra, the element you have the ability to manipulate," Wyott said. "You used it to kill that man. You made the tree strangle him."

I shook my head. "I only remember a loud noise, and a bright flash of light."

"That light came from you, Eva. From your eyes," Maddox said.

I laughed, but he didn't. My smile dropped. "Oh, fuck. You're serious." I looked between the two of them. "Is that normal for Sorceresses?"

Wyott shook his head. "None that I've ever heard of."

Maddox shot him a look and he raised his hands in innocence. "What? She asked."

I looked to my mate. "Is there something wrong with me?"

"Nothing wrong, but perhaps something extraordinary," he said before he tilted his head. "When Lonix died, what happened?"

I let go of his hand and crossed my arms. "What do you mean? He died of some kind of heart ailment or something."

Maddox pursed his lips. "You said it was like he was suffocating. That he was clawing at his own throat."

I nodded. "He was."

Maddox nodded slowly and looked at Wyott.

"Oh, shit," Wyott said as his eyes widened.

"What?" I snapped at them.

"Did you feel anything when Lonix was suffocating?" Maddox asked me.

I flung my arms out in annoyance. "I don't know," I scoffed, but of course I did. I'd never forget. I took a deep breath. "I mean, yes. I guess. I remember my hands tingling with wind."

Maddox smiled. "I think you used your Air abilities that night. I think you might've killed Lonix by pulling the air from his lungs, without realizing that's what you were doing." He looked to Wyott. "It would make sense, both times she used her powers were in times of survival."

Wyott nodded, his eyebrows raised as he evaluated me. "I knew you weren't human, but I didn't expect you to be so powerful."

I let out a long breath of annoyance. "If someone doesn't explain what you two are talking about right now, I will get violent."

Maddox smiled softly at me and stepped forward. "You're clearly a Sorceress, yes. We witnessed that. But Sorcerers and Sorceresses traditionally only have the ability to manipulate one element. Air, Terra, Water, or Fire. There's never been a Sorceress who can wield more than one in any histories I've ever read."

I flicked my hand at him and raised a brow. "Continue."

Maddox laughed. "Evaline, you have more than one element. You used Terra and Air, Gods only know if you have the ability to use the other two." He shrugged. "But if you can use two, it doesn't seem out of the realm of possibility that you can use all four."

I looked between the two of them, waiting for them to tell me that this was a joke. When neither of them moved, I turned away from them.

"Gods-dammit," I said with annoyance, stifling the tears trying to fill my eyes.

"It's okay, we'll figure it out. If you want to go back to Rominia, we have resources there that can help," Maddox said, wrapping a hand around my shoulder in comfort.

I shook my head and looked down at my boots. "It's not that," I said, then rolled my eyes. I turned around to face them again and felt a brief pang of worry come down the bond. "I mean, yes. Obviously, it's that. But it's more. I knew I was a Sorceress before you told me that because, while I was unconscious, my mother visited me."

I proceeded to explain to them that I'd seen my mother in a dream—or a nightmare—I still wasn't sure. I didn't tell them about Kovarrin as that seemed like a secret a father should share, not me, and I knew they didn't know the truth behind how their species was created because they'd already confirmed that the Gods had gifted the Kova their powers.

Maddox's brows were furrowed and his arms were crossed by the time I'd finished.

"And you think it was really her?" he asked.

I took a deep breath. "I really do. I can't explain how I know, but I just do."

"I'm sure that was scary, or confusing at the very least. Are you okay?"

That was a weighted question, and so was the response. "I'm alive, and with you guys, and that's all I can focus on right now. But there's something else." I twisted the end of my braid and looked up at both of them. "My mother told me that Vasier knows about my magic."

Wyott straightened.

"She said he knows that my magic is awake, that he felt it, and he won't stop until he has me."

Maddox's jaw clenched and he took a slow breath. He swallowed, and opened his mouth to speak, but then shut it again.

Wyott looked sideways at Maddox and then turned to face me.

"We figured that much was true. We knew when we went to Blush Bay, when there were Vasi there. We knew that Gabriehl was taking you to Vasier."

Unease crawled through me at the mention of my cousin's name.

"Gabriehl wasn't the only one working for Vasier. Bassel..." I started, and Maddox's eyes snapped to mine. "He planned the entire thing with Gabriehl. When I killed him, he mentioned Vasier's name. That he didn't care about Vasier's orders, and he was going to kill me. He asked me how I'd figured it out, and I think he meant the scheme. That he went to Kembertus to marry me, to take me to Vasier. I just didn't understand at the time."

Maddox was quiet for a moment, and I wished I knew what he was thinking. I felt down the bond, but he must've blocked me from being able to sense his full worry.

Maddox turned to Wyott. "We need to get to Neomaeros as quickly as possible."

"And then Rominia," I interjected. Maddox turned and I saw the hope blossom in his eyes. "I want to go to Rominia as soon as we can."

Chapter Eight

Evaline

We didn't stop to camp, but let the horses graze for about an hour while I ate and drank nearly an entire canteen myself. In the daze of everything that had happened, I'd forgotten how malnourished and dehydrated I'd become.

Maddox sat beside me, staring down at his hands, lost in thought. Wyott tried to maintain cheerful conversation, but his chatting dwindled after a bit.

After the horses had some rest, we continued. They said I'd only been unconscious a few hours, so Maddox was too worried about more Vasi in the area to stay so close to Blush Bay.

They'd taken three horses from Gabriehl and his men so that I had my own, and tents, too. I'd been afraid to ask what had happened to Gabriehl. Despite what he'd done, and what my aunt and uncle had done and the bounty they put on my head, I felt guilty at the thought that Maddox and Wyott had killed Gabriehl.

But they must have noticed my worry, and as we rode through the night, they explained that they hadn't killed him. He was more valuable alive. Instead, they compelled him to forget that he'd seen the Kova and the Vasi. He would go back to Kembertus and tell his parents that he and his friends had found me and were bringing me back to Kembertus to collect their reward. He'd tell them that they were attacked by a group of bandits on the way. Ironic, considering that's what his group had been. Gabriehl was compelled to tell my Uncle Elijah and Aunt Therese that the other men and I had been killed in combat, and he'd narrowly escaped with his life.

I should breathe easier knowing that there was one less enemy out there looking for me. But I'd rather fight for my life against the humans than Vasier.

"We should stop here," Wyott said the next evening, nodding to the creek that ran to our right. "The horses can rest and we can refill our water."

It was late by the time we finished tying the horses up and setting up camp. Wyott volunteered to keep watch so that Maddox and I could get some rest.

The tent we ducked into was small, but it was warmer than sleeping beneath the stars.

Maddox had already laid out two small sleeping pads he must've also stolen from Gabriehl's camp. The couple inches of padding would do wonders against the hard knots in the ground. With the blanket and pillows he tossed onto it, it almost looked like an actual bed, and I was grateful.

I moved to my side of the mats and kneeled down onto them before I noticed that Maddox still stood just inside the tent's flap.

"What are you doing?" I whispered.

He gave me a small smile. "Do you want me to stay in here with you? I don't have to."

My brows furrowed. "Of course I want you to stay with me, Maddox. Why wouldn't I?"

"I just want to make sure we're taking this at a pace you feel comfortable with," he said, his eyes cast down.

I shook my head and crawled until I could reach for his hand and pull him to me.

"That's not what I was worried about," I said. The guilt was immediate in my stomach. "I just didn't know what all of it meant. I didn't know if I'd be free to do whatever I wanted, travel where I wanted, being mated to the son of the First."

"I understand." He took a deep breath. "I would love to take you to Rominia, because I know we'd be able to keep you safe from Vasier there. We have protective wards around the island, and in all the Madierian Kingdoms. Vasi can't get in, and we could do whatever we wanted there. But if you wanted to travel farther, we could." A dark look passed over his eyes. "We'd just be cautious."

I smiled. This was the conversation I should've waited around for. But I tried not to be too hard on myself considering everything that had happened in the last few weeks.

"Sound good?" Maddox asked.

I nodded. "Of course."

He smiled and caught my chin in his large hand, ducking to kiss me.

"Thank the Gods," he whispered as he pulled away.

He fastened the flap of the tent shut while I sat back and started removing my boots. I threw them in the corner and then moved to unfasten my holsters, but my hands froze.

"Do you know what happened to my father's sword?" I asked Maddox as he crossed to his side of the mats.

He started removing all the weapons strapped to his back and hips. "Wyott has it. He carried most of the extra supplies on his horse after we left." He motioned to my calf where the empty holster for my silver dagger sat. "I didn't realize that dagger was missing. We didn't look for it." His eyes flashed to mine and I could see the apology in them. "I'm sorry, it must've gotten left behind. We can get you a new one."

I sighed. "It's okay, maybe it's better off anyway. It was the first and last dagger I bought in Kembertus and that part of my life is over."

Maddox nudged my shoulder as I reached for the empty holster on my thigh. I smiled when I saw he was holding the Madierian Topaz crested Rominium dagger.

"Thank you," I said and grabbed the dagger to re-holster it.

"Thank you for dropping it for us to find. It was quick thinking. Your father would be proud," Maddox said.

I only nodded and started removing my braid and barbed wire. I didn't want him to see the tears that filled my eyes at that. Because he was right. My father would've been proud of me for thinking to drop it, even if he would've probably chastised me for getting abducted in the first place.

But that thought triggered another. My father had known I was a Sorceress and never told me. He had the chance that night he died, but I remembered every word he spoke instead. He'd said that he and my mother had discussed what they would tell me about my life, and when. That there was more in the world, more at stake, than I knew. At the time I didn't understand what he meant, but it was clear now that he had been speaking of Vasier.

Maddox lowered to the mats behind me and removed his own boots. I tossed the wire away and ran my fingers through my hair to try and remove any tangles.

I hadn't undone my braid when we'd camped just after fleeing Kembertus, but between the two Kova with me, and my newly discovered but poorly understood magic, I felt safe enough to now. I wouldn't sleep soundly if I rolled over in the middle of the night and stabbed myself.

My spine popped as I laid back onto the mats and I sighed in contentment as I finally had the chance to fully spread out. Maddox laid on his side, propped on his elbow. With his hair falling around his face as he looked down at me, he caressed my cheek with his thumb.

"I don't think I'll ever get used to how breathtaking you are," he said softly.

I snorted. "I'm a mess, Maddox."

He clicked his tongue. "There isn't a time of day, in any state, that you are anything less than perfect, Eva."

He bent to kiss me. His hand fell from my face and trailed down until it landed on my waist.

I hissed from the pain that his touch caused and he jerked his hand back. He removed his lips from mine with blazing eyes that shot to my side.

"I'm sorry," he whispered, but his voice sounded surprised. I followed his gaze and saw that the source of the pain was covered by a blossomed rose of blood-stained fabric. He lifted it up slowly, and I think he was afraid of what he'd see.

There wasn't a wound anymore. Only dried blood remained.

"It shouldn't still hurt," he ground out.

"It's okay," I whispered. "It'll heal."

He moved to the satchel that sat just off the mats and grabbed his canteen and a shirt, which he tore in two.

"Maddox don't ruin a shirt, I'm fine."

He was silent as he wet it and gently dabbed the blood until my skin was clean. And there, in the center of where the blood had been, was a plum-purple bruise with a small scar adorning its center.

He cursed under his breath, stroking his thumb over it gently.

"I'm so sorry, Evaline," he whispered, his voice hoarse as his eyes drifted up to meet mine.

I shook my head. "Why are you sorry? You didn't cause this."

"Because I was too late. And you couldn't drink my blood fast enough to heal yourself."

I raised my hand and drug it through his hair.

"You healed me enough to save me. If all I have is a bruise and a small scar, I'm happy." His jaw tightened and I sighed. "Would it make you feel better if I drank more now?"

His eyes were hard.

"You can't, it's too late. Kova blood can only heal the initial wounds. Once the body's own healing takes over it no longer works." He nodded to my wrist. "That's why your wrist never got better when you drank from me the first time. It had already healed."

I shrugged. "Like I said, it's just a bruise."

He shook his head. "And a scar."

"I figured you'd find those sexy," I said, my voice sultry. Maybe flirting with him would distract him from his anger.

But he didn't bite. "Not when I'm the cause of them."

I huffed. I'd had enough. I reached up and gripped his face with both hands to turn him to face me.

"Stop. Stop blaming yourself for what happened. It was my fault. I'm the one who ran. It isn't as if I don't deserve this—"

"You don't deserve this." His voice was sharp.

"You know what I mean. All of this, it was my fault. Not yours. And I won't heal any faster with your guilt looming over me. Please," I whispered, searching his eyes. "Let's forget all of it. I'm safe. I'm here, with you. I love you."

His eyes finally softened.

"I love you." He dipped his head to move his lips over the newly formed scar on my side. "Since the moment we met," he whispered against my skin, moving my shirt up with his other hand as he trailed kisses up my torso. "Even if you were pickpocketing me."

The fabric bunched near my breasts, and he kissed the hollow between them while I laughed.

He pulled away and dragged my shirt back down to cover me.

"What are you doing?" I asked.

His eyes flashed to mine and I could see the obsidian swirling beneath them, ready to make its ascent to the surface.

"What do you mean?"

His low voice told me he knew.

I grabbed the collar of his shirt and tugged him until he laid on top of me and between my legs. His lips met mine for a kiss, a real kiss, not like the brief ones we'd shared since I'd woken up. I wanted the kiss he'd given me against the wall and when we made love. The kiss that swallowed every piece of who I was and put me back together again.

He moaned softly against me as I tried to deepen it, but pulled away, leaving a hand to grasp my hip.

"Evaline." His eyes were black. "You need to rest." But his eyes didn't leave my lips as he spoke.

"No, I need you," I whispered.

The hand on my hip tightened and he took a shaky breath.

"Wyott is right outside," he whispered, eyes flashing to mine.

He didn't care about that, not really. In two hundred years of friendship there was no way they hadn't overheard each other in an intimate moment.

But he thought I'd care. And maybe I should've. Maybe it should bother me that I could hear the scrape of Wyott's blade against the rock outside. But it didn't. Because I'd gone my entire life without feeling the way Maddox made me feel, and I'd almost lost it.

"I don't care."

A wicked smile lit his lips. "That's what I was hoping you'd say."

His lips crashed down on mine once more.

The scraping of Wyott's blade outside stopped, and I knew he'd taken a walk to give us privacy.

Maddox's mouth on mine was intoxicating. More than the wine I'd overindulged in at Aurora's house. Because every kiss, every touch of his skin on mine, felt like bolts of lightning striking between us. My heart thudded against my chest as he slipped his tongue into my mouth and tugged my hips against his.

My hands fumbled down his front, until they were at his waistline and hauling his shirt out of its tucked position.

He lifted himself off of me to pull it over his head and threw it to the side. He captured my mouth with his again quickly as his hands held my hips and we rolled so that I lay on top of him. The movement startled me and a surprised gasp left my lips, and he took the opportunity to flick his tongue against mine.

I ran my hands over his bare chest and shoulders as I straddled him. I moaned at the way they rippled below my touch, tightening as his arms did so around me. I raised one hand to grasp his jaw, angling it to the side and dragged kisses down his neck. He groaned beneath me, hands moving down to cup my ass, pulling me even closer as he ground his hips against mine. I moaned into his neck at the feel of his cock against me and his hands tightened, moving me against him once more.

I sat up and pulled my own shirt over my head, tossing it beside me, as I watched his eyes take in every inch of my skin. They glistened in the night but even with the darkness around us, the glow of the fire outside our only light, I could see the black swirling there.

"My Goddess," he whispered, and I smirked down at him.

"Are you going to worship me, now?" I let my hands graze over his chest as I said the words.

He growled and sat up with me, hands on my back as his mouth attached to my skin, dragging his teeth down my chest until my nipple was in his mouth.

I moaned and tangled my hands in his hair.

"I live to worship you, Eva," he mumbled against my skin.

"Don't ever stop," I moaned breathlessly, my head falling back in pleasure.

"Never," he growled and moved to the other breast.

It was good, so good, but it wasn't enough. Not now that I knew what he felt like inside of me. I rolled my hips forward, over him, and he groaned against me.

I pushed away, standing up from him as he watched me unfasten my pants, letting them fall down my hips and pile on the floor. His eyes watched me hungrily as I stepped back toward him, raking over every inch of me, each part exposed.

He raised his hips and kicked his own pants off when he realized that's what I was waiting for, then raised a welcoming hand toward me. I stepped forward and took it and he tugged me onto him again, catching me in his arms as he kissed me. I pushed him down until he laid back and he brought me with him. But this was too slow, and I needed more.

I sat up and felt for him until his hardness was in my hand—soft but strong.

My hand froze and my eyes widened as a realization lit my mind. We'd already been together once and hadn't used any form of contraceptive. I had no intentions of having children anytime soon, and panic beat through my chest.

Maddox raised on his forearms. "What's wrong?" he asked.

I looked up to meet his eyes. "I just realized that we haven't used any method of preventing pregnancy," I said, shaking my head. "I don't want to get pregnant."

A smile twitched up on his lips despite the heat that still smoldered in his eyes. "Eva, I've already taken an elixir that prevents that."

My brows furrowed. "You have?"

He nodded. "Of course. A century ago. Our physicians make it."

I pursed my lips. "Do I have to take it too, for it to work?"

He shook his head. "No, once I drank it, it sterilized me. If I ever want to be fertile again, I just take the reverse elixir."

A deep sigh of relief shook through me as I pushed him back down to the bed. "Thank the Gods."

His breath hitched as he watched my movements, hands stilled on my thighs. I raised my hips, one hand on his chest to balance me as the other lined him up.

Maddox, I whispered through the bond, and his eyes flicked up to mine.

Yes? And Gods, even his voice in my head sounded breathless.

But I'd gotten what I wanted. Because I wanted to lock eyes as I sank down over him, and that's exactly what I did.

He groaned as I moved. Still slow, wanting to feel every inch of him as I sank down.

His head fell back onto the pillow when our hips met. "Fuck, Evaline," he gasped.

I sucked in a breath. Out of all the positions we'd been in the night we made love, this was one of my favorites. Having him below me made me feel powerful, as if his world started and ended with me, as mine did him. Above him like this, I had control and I could do as I wished.

And the thoughts had my heart quickening, had the throb between my legs pulsing harder.

I rose and fell, watching him the entire time. Drinking in the way his eyes fluttered shut, how he bit his lip and the way his fingers curled into my hips as I moved.

I rose again, faster this time, and again, and again.

His chest heaved beneath my hand and I could feel his heart beating fast, knocking against my palm in rhythm with my pumps. As if to say *yes, yes, yes.*

At this angle he hit a spot inside of me that tightened my core with each stroke until I was bouncing above him in desperation, moans loosing from my lips faster than my breaths.

His hands on my hips helped me move as groans shook from him.

I could feel myself winding up, tighter and tighter until I knew I'd unravel.

"Look at me," I commanded.

His eyes flashed open, meeting mine. They were fierce, and I knew why he'd had them closed. I could see the lust in them and knew he was fighting for his own control.

But I wasn't afraid, I knew he'd never hurt me, and a part of me liked seeing this side of him—this feral part of Maddox that crazed for me.

So I swirled my hips as I moved and he shuddered. He sat up again, meeting me as one hand caught the back of my neck and pulled me in for a kiss. Maddox's teeth pulled at my lower lip before his tongue slipped past and took my breath. He dropped his mouth to my nipple again, his hand coming up to the other that ached for attention.

And this closeness to him, this power I felt above him, the spot he hit deep within me, had me inching closer and closer to that precipice. I moved faster and he guided my hips as my moans grew louder, helping me to stay on track as I faltered above him, so close.

My head fell back, hair falling behind me as I moved, as he kissed my chest. My hands grasped at his shoulders and I shivered at the feel of his body against me hard and strong.

"Tell me you love me. That you'll never run again without giving me a chance to explain." His lips moved over my breasts and his hands tightened around me.

"I love you," I gasped and had to take a steadying breath to get the words out. "I'll never run again. It's you and I, always."

The words had him biting down on my skin harder than I expected and I screamed his name, coming undone around him.

"You and I, always," he repeated.

He flipped us before I knew what was happening, and I was limp below him as he thrusted inside of me. All energy had drained from my muscles at the release, but his movements quickly relit the fire.

"Oh Gods," I groaned and covered my face, the ecstasy overwhelming.

"No," he said above me. "Don't cover yourself. I want to see every second."

I gasped for air as I moved my hands, letting them fall into my hair, pulling at it as he moved inside of me. I met his eyes then. And they were blazing, a molten black flame engulfing them.

I found my strength finally and raised my legs to wrap around his hips, allowing him access to a deeper part of me, my hands moving to clutch his back.

He shivered above me and lowered his mouth to mine. It was rough and sloppy and we were both edging toward the cliff.

And his hips moved so naturally, so expertly, but I needed more.

Harder, I said down the bond, as my lips were taken over by his.

He groaned against me and followed my command, hips meeting mine in a delicious rhythm.

Don't stop. Don't ever stop, I pleaded again.

Never, he promised.

He hit that spot inside of me, and I unraveled for the second time, biting his lip as I did so.

He cursed above me and I knew he was hitting that high with me this time. He only stopped when both of us were a pile on the ground, breathless and blissful.

Chapter Nine

Maddox

I hardly slept, and I knew the insomnia was going to become an unwelcome guest in my life. At least until we could get to Rominia. I'd almost lost Evaline once and couldn't risk a recurrence.

Each time I began to drift into sleep, the images of her below me, nearly lifeless, would flip in front of my eyes like the pages of a book. Turning so quickly that they came to life, moving in real time so I was forced to watch as the blood leaked from her body.

And each time this torturous story played out for me, I'd wake, eyes blazing and heart hammering.

But then I'd look down at Evaline lying across my chest, clutched in my embrace. Each time I was surprised that the frantic thud of my heart against her ear didn't wake her and I'd focus on loosening my grip on her, assured she was still alive. I'd stroke her hair and listen to her light breathing, enjoying the tickle of breath against my chest with each exhale. Her sleep would lull me, rhythmic and entrancing until I fell back into darkness, where I watched the pages flip once more until I woke again.

Over and over.

All night long.

But now it was morning and she was braiding her hair, eyes focused on the ground in concentration as she did so. She sat on a log in front of the fire beside Wyott, who sat ready with her wire. His leg bounced in anticipation as he watched her weave the pieces from the crown of her head until she only had the three bunches of hair left.

She draped them over and between different fingers to separate them with her left hand, and shook her right arm.

Wyott presented the wire, his eyes alight.

Evaline laughed. "Give me a minute."

She switched hands in order to shake out the left and rolled her shoulders.

Wyott quirked a brow. "You can take down a Vasi and kill a man twice your size—Gods, even wield magic—but your arms hurt from braiding your hair?" His voice was incredulous.

She cut him a look, her mouth dropping open in offense. "You hold your arms above your head and meticulously braid your hair, then tell me it doesn't hurt. I could be the world's strongest being and braiding my own hair would still make my shoulders scream."

He just held the wire up once more, ignoring her explanation. "Are you ready now?"

She rolled her eyes and took it. "Yes," she said spreading the three bunches between both hands again.

Wyott watched her fingers weave the wire in her hair. From where I sat across from them I couldn't see, but based on his facial expressions Wyott was thoroughly engrossed.

When she finished, she tied off the end and flung it over her shoulder, onto her back.

Wyott shook his head. "That's very impressive."

Evaline snorted and flicked her eyes over to me. "Are we heading out soon?"

I shrugged. "How do you feel?" I knew riding a horse for so long could wear on her body, leaving sore spots over her legs and bottom.

"I feel fine. I think getting a good night's sleep on solid ground was exactly what I needed."

A wave of relief hit me. I desperately wanted to get to Neomaeros as quickly as we could to get her within their wards and keep her safe, but didn't want to push her.

"Good, we should be there by late afternoon."

Evaline nodded and stood. "Perfect."

Wyott stood beside her and adjusted his swords on his hips. Evaline saw the move and turned to face him with a bright smile on her face and her hand outstretched.

"I'll take my father's sword now."

He grabbed it for her but as soon as it touched her palm she spoke again. "And as long as we're handing over weapons, if you wanted to give me that bandolier of throwing knives, I'd be all set."

I had to bite back a laugh as I watched his face fall into a mask of annoyance. "Not this again."

She shrugged and added Wallace's sword onto her hip holster. "Didn't you miss me?"

He turned and walked to his horse. "I can't remember why," he grumbled below his breath, but by the wicked smile that lit Evaline's lips, I knew she heard him.

The moment we passed through the gates of Neomaeros later that day I let out an audible sigh of relief.

Wyott and Evaline both looked over at me at the sound. Evaline furrowed her brows. Wyott only nodded. He understood.

But where I felt relief, Evaline felt grief. It came down the bond immediately, she wasn't trying to hide it from me.

And I understood.

Guilt struck me in the gut; this would be the first time she'd been here, in the kingdom where she grew up with her father, since his death.

Fuck. I felt like a prick.

I tried to look at her through my peripheral. She hated being checked up on, so I hid it. But I wanted to gauge whether I should say something. Sometimes the last thing Evaline wanted was attention brought to her emotions. Other times, she wanted someone to see her.

By the tight clench of her jaw and the way she sat straight as a board on the horse, I knew it was the former.

Unfortunately, Wyott didn't know my mate as well as I did. And before I could warn him with a look, he opened his mouth.

"How is it that you survived the events of the last few days fine but preparing to meet with Lord and Lady Hohlt has your heart running a mile a minute?"

She whipped her head to him. "How is it that you've lived several human lifespans but never learned to keep your mouth shut?" she snapped.

She faced away from me so I couldn't see her face. But from the way Wyott paled, I was sure her expression was lethal.

He flicked his eyes to me over her head and I gave him a solemn look.

"Evaline grew up in Neomaeros," I said.

I didn't elaborate. I knew Wyott would know the entirety of what that meant—that this was where she grew up with her father, and she was returning without him. I didn't want to say the words out loud. Evaline didn't want to hear them.

I'm here, was all I said down the bond.

She took a steadying breath. *I know.*

We left the horses at the stables and made for the castle. I put a hand on the small of Evaline's back as we walked, and moved my thumb back and forth in an attempt to soothe her. A cobbled path led us from the stables to a grand spiral staircase at the base of the castle. It wound until we were several dozens of feet in the air in front of strong mahogany doors that were guarded by two men.

"What business do you have here?" asked the one on the right. He looked to his companion before settling his eyes back on us. "It's rather late."

I nodded. "I know, I'm sorry for the inconvenience, but we just got in and we're friends with the Lord and Lady. Can you tell them Maddox, Wyott, and Evaline Manor are here?"

He nodded to his partner, and then cocked his head toward the door.

The second man disappeared inside to relay our message. I didn't recognize either of them, so they must've been new to the castle, or new to the kingdom.

My father was friends with Lord Peder and Lady Margot, Evaline whispered down the bond. Even though she didn't speak the words aloud, I could hear the tears in it.

My hand slid to rest on the crest of her hip, and I tugged her into the crook of my arm. *I'm sorry we had to come here. You and I can go somewhere else while Wyott fills them in, if you'd like.*

She looked down at the stone beneath our feet. *No, it's okay. It's been two years, I should've already contacted them while I was in Kembertus. It's time.*

Okay, I said back. *But it's your decision. We can leave whenever you'd like.*

She nodded, and just as she did the second guard came back to his post. He reclaimed his position and started to speak.

"They'll be here short—"

Before he could finish the doors swung open and we were met with the sight of Lord and Lady Hohlt.

Lady Margot's eyes landed on Evaline immediately and widened. Without a word she stepped forward and wrapped my mate up into her arms. Evaline's eyes flashed up to mine and her brows furrowed before she wrapped her arms around Lady Margot, too.

I looked to Wyott, who was taking in the scene with the same confusion as I, and then we both swung our heads to look at Lord Peder.

"It's been a long two years," was all he said.

Chapter Ten

Evaline

Lady Margot's welcome was kind, but it had me confused. My father had been acquaintances with them, but I didn't recall them being close enough for her to have this kind of reaction to seeing me.

"Evaline, we have been so worried about you," she said in my ear as one of her hands stroked down my back. She pulled back and gave the same greeting to Maddox and Wyott. When she was done hugging the three of us, she turned toward the door and motioned for us to follow.

As we passed Lord Peder in the doorway he nodded to me, and shook both Maddox and Wyott's hands.

She led us through the lower floor of the castle into, what I assumed was, the Lord's study. We passed a few sitting rooms along the way, though they lacked the privacy of a closed door, so when we reached the office I knew they likely wanted a report on what Maddox and Wyott had found during their travels in Kembertus, and conversations like that couldn't happen in the open.

When we made it to the study she turned to the guards that had been trailing us.

"Please give us some privacy."

They nodded, spun on their heels, and disappeared down a corridor.

Lady Margot took my hand and led me into the room, straight for the two parallel chaises that sat next to the fireplace.

"Peder can you…?" she said to her husband as he closed the door behind the Kova. She motioned to the fire and he nodded and moved to add a few logs.

I hadn't spent much time in the castle, and had never been in this room, but even in the couple years I'd been away I'd forgotten how kind the Lord and Lady were. They often excused their servants from their duties, and still paid them. Seeing them today, hearing their soft voices, reminded me of the time Lady Margot helped me up during one of their Balls when I was young.

I'd tripped over my flowery dress while dancing with a few of the other young girls and had fallen into a heap of tulle. Some of the kids started to snicker, and while I searched the room for my father, nearly in tears, it was Lady Margot's hand that stretched toward me.

I felt Maddox's hand on my knee and realized I'd been staring into the flames and hadn't heard them saying my name. I jumped and turned to Lady Margot, who sat on the chaise across from me. Her hazel eyes furrowed in concern and the light from the fire danced across her russet skin.

I shook my head. "I'm sorry, I didn't hear that."

She gave me a small smile even though I could see the pity in her eyes.

"Evaline, we are so sorry for your loss," she said in her light voice, and Lord Peder came to stand by her side, putting a hand on her shoulder.

"Your father was an honorable man. It is a shame that he was taken too soon," he said above her.

"Thank you." I gave them each small smiles, but sweat started to bead on the back of my neck.

I didn't like being here. Not because they weren't kind, but because being in this castle, walking the streets of Neomaeros, reminded me too much of him.

More than that, I hated the sorrow that their pity was dragging up. The way their words called my tears closer to the surface.

Maddox and Wyott must've sensed my discomfort because the former enveloped my hand in his and the latter plopped down onto the chaise beside the Lady and cleared his throat.

"So we bring along an addition this time and all of a sudden the Kova aren't the most interesting guests anymore?"

The Lady playfully rolled her eyes and swatted at his leg and the Lord laughed. I smiled at Wyott when his eyes fell to me. I knew he felt guilty about his comment earlier, and I didn't want him to be.

"Evaline's not a guest," Lord Peder said as he turned toward me. He fixed his brown eyes on me and the ochre skin around them crinkled from his smile. "She is a Neomaerian."

A flutter burst through my chest, because his words reminded me of who I was before all the horrors that I faced since the last time I'd been here. That I wasn't an orphan who was mistreated in Kembertus, but a strong woman raised by a strong father from a free city.

"Thank you," I said, nodding to both of them.

Lady Margot sat forward and she looked at me with wide, earnest eyes.

"Evaline, you must know that we were unaware of your father's death until very recently." The words rushed out. "He'd told us he was traveling there to deal with some issues regarding Elijah's succession. It was a year before a passing traveler spread the news of his death here."

And they passed it to my father. It's how the Kova found out he'd passed, Maddox's soft voice said down the bond.

"I understand, I'm sorry I didn't think to send the news over."

I looked toward the fire. I'd never considered writing them after I was in Kembertus, never thought they'd want to hear from me.

"A lot of that first year was a blur." I swallowed the lump in my throat. "I didn't leave my room much."

"Please don't apologize, I only mean to tell you that we didn't know you were in Kembertus, alone with them, for a year. And when we found out, I wrote to you. But you never responded, so I assumed you'd found some sort of happiness there with your family."

My head snapped toward her. "What?"

The top half of her long black braids were pinned up, but those that fell down her back slipped over her shoulder as she looked up at her husband, then back to me.

"I wrote you several times over the last year, to ask if you were okay, if you were happy there. I offered to send guards to escort you back." She shrugged. "We knew your father hated the idea of you living in his home kingdom, based on the few conversations we had with him about it, so I was prepared to send a few guards to bring you home."

"There were several times she wanted to go get you herself," the Lord said. "But we didn't want to disturb you if you preferred Kembertus."

I shook my head and pulled my hand from Maddox's. I looked down at my hands in my lap. They shook for a moment, so I clenched them into fists.

"I never received any letters."

Anger, that same sweltering rage that my aunt and uncle constantly stoked in me, started to simmer deep and low. I clenched my jaw and took a shaky breath. I wasn't sure if I was upset because I could've been living safely in Neomaeros for the last year, or if I was only angry that my aunt and uncle had, once again, taken a choice from me.

Maddox spoke so I didn't have to. "Lord and Lady Manor did quite a lot to maintain control over Evaline in her time there."

I felt their eyes on me, but didn't raise my head. I only tried to focus on not breaking down. Because I was so tired, and so sick of discovering new information about myself, my life, that I just wanted to be done with this conversation. I wanted to take a bath. I wanted to stab something.

"Which included forcing her into an arranged marriage with the heir to Vestaria," Maddox continued.

Lady Margot gasped and Lord Peder cursed. Hearing their reactions to that news, what my guardian's reactions should've been at the prospect of that arrangement, tore me from my rage. I wasn't with them anymore, I wasn't locked in Kembertus. I was in the place I was born. Where I learned to walk and to ride horses. I was safe, from my aunt and uncle at least, and I didn't need to be angry at them anymore. I needed to let them go.

I raised my head and met the Lord and Lady's eyes briefly.

"It seems word hasn't spread here yet, so I should inform you." I took a deep breath, and for a moment felt a swell of pride down the bond from Maddox. "The man they married me to had attacked me once before. On my trek to Kembertus, the day after my father died." Peder's jaw clenched and Margot's brows furrowed. "He didn't remember me, but on the day of our wedding I killed him so that he'd never hurt anyone like that again. I just thought you should hear it from me."

Lady Margot stood and moved to sit on the arm of the chaise beside me and placed her hand on my back.

"Evaline, you don't have to justify what you've done. Peder and I are well aware of the atrocities that are allowed in the Kromean Kingdoms. We're just thankful you made it out safely." Then her eyes flicked to Maddox and Wyott before her spine straightened. "How did the three of you come together? Last we heard, you two were heading to Kembertus to check on something for Kovarrin."

Maddox and Wyott explained what had happened, how they found me, that Maddox and I were mates, and that they had helped me escape. They explained my abduction, that Vasier was looking for me, and theorized that I was the very thing that both Kovarrin, and Vasier, were looking for in Kembertus.

I bit my tongue while Maddox spoke about Vasier, and out of the corner of my eye I could tell that Wyott was just as uncomfortable as he leaned forward with his elbows on his knees. From his glower at the floor past his balled fists, he seemed angry, while I was just uneasy.

We talked to the rulers for a few more minutes, but then it was time for us to leave. Lady Margot spoke as we all stood. "You know where the guest rooms are," she said to Maddox and Wyott, and they started to thank her.

I grabbed Maddox's hand, squeezing it. "Actually, is there room at the inn?" I asked Lady Margot.

She cocked her head. "I'm sure there is, but the Kova always stay in the castle when they're here. We're happy to have them, they're honored guests."

"I just..." I pursed my lips.

It's okay, sweetheart. She'll understand, Maddox said down the bond.

I gave Lady Margot a smile. "I appreciate it, I just can't stay here. Or the home my father and I used to live in. Or on the street I grew up on. It's all too painful, and I don't want to spend the night somewhere where the memories will drown me. I'll have nightmares." I knew it would be that same one from the night he was killed.

Her face crumpled and she nodded, then pulled me in for a hug. "I understand. I'm so sorry Evaline."

"It's okay," I whispered.

"His belongings are still here. We've preserved the home you two shared. One day, when you're ready, it'll be waiting here for you."

I clenched my eyes shut and despite my efforts to hold them back, a few tears slipped through. I nodded against her shoulder. "Thank you," I said. "For all of it. For thinking of me last year. And for the letters. It means so much."

When we pulled back and bid the rest of our goodbyes, Maddox informed the Lord and Lady that we'd be out of the city early the next morning, to head back for Rominia. I was glad for it. I loved my father, I loved the kingdom where he raised me, but Gods knew the pain of it all was suffocating me. I needed to be outside of these walls.

Maddox warned them about Vasier and told them to keep their eye out for any reports of Vasi outside of the walls of Neomaeros.

We thanked them for their hospitality as they walked us back to the door, but before we could leave, I remembered something.

"Wait," I said, turning in the door's frame. "Lady Margot, you recently accepted a business license for review for my friend Aurora. She's opening a boutique here next summer."

Her eyes lit with recognition. "Yes, her business looks quite profitable and her designs are beautiful."

I nodded. "It is, and they are." I reached for her hand, pulled her close and whispered in her ear so the guards wouldn't hear. I told her that Aurora and Jacqueline were my best friends, that they had no memory of me due to compulsion. She nodded as I spoke and patted the top of my hand as I uttered my request. "Please keep them safe."

"Of course, Evaline," she whispered back.

As the two Kova and I walked away, and we exited the castle and descended the stairs, I realized that the rulers cared far more about me than I ever imagined. More than my own guardians did. I regretted not mailing Lady Margot myself about Aurora's application. At the time, I'd never considered that she would take my inquiry seriously. I thought that it would require another ruling Lady to move Aurora's license review up the queue, but perhaps my guardians had done more than imprison me. Perhaps their lack of concern made me forget all those that cared about me, even if it was from afar.

Chapter Eleven

Wyott

The wind hit us as we walked down the steps of the castle and headed for the inn, but before we could get too far Maddox turned to us.

"I need to go run a few errands," he said to Evaline, then flicked his eyes over her head to me. "You both go do something fun. We'll meet at the inn and I'll have dinner delivered to our rooms so we can get to bed early."

They kissed goodbye and he turned to cut down an alley. Evaline turned toward me, her brow cocked.

"I don't want to go shopping at the Blacksmith's."

I over exaggerated a sigh and threw my arms up as we started walking.

"You never want to do anything I want to do," I whined, but then a small smile slipped on my face and I grew somber. "I know you don't—the memories," I said softly.

Her brows twitched toward each other, and I knew she was surprised. I diverted our path to a patch of woods that fell within the city's walls.

"I have a better idea anyway."

She didn't respond with a snarky comment and that's how I knew that this was exactly what she needed. We were a lot alike, and when I needed to fight the grief that wracked my mind often, I stabbed things.

"Where are we going?" she asked as we entered the woods.

I turned to her with a sly grin on my face.

She quirked a brow. "What?"

I flipped one of the throwing daggers from the bandolier on my chest and pointed the blade toward her. "Want to learn how to throw daggers?"

She gave me a coy smile and nodded.

This was one skill that Maddox and I hadn't taught her during our midnight training sessions back in Kembertus. It had never come up, which was how I knew she didn't know how to. Her father had trained her in several combat skills, but not everyone had the gift for dagger throwing, so I assumed he wasn't skilled enough at it to teach her.

We found a spot in the woods where the setting sun filtered through enough of the canopy for Evaline to see, and I pointed out a particularly wide tree.

"That should give you a big enough target to aim for."

She nodded and I handed her one of my throwing daggers before pulling one out for myself. I stood beside her and staggered my feet.

"Your footwork will be similar to throwing a punch. Your throwing leg should be back, and you move your weight forward onto the leading foot as you throw." She nodded, so I continued. "Then you hold it back like this," I said as I bent my elbow and reared my forearm back. "And extend."

I demonstrated and the dagger drove home in the tree's rough bark. Evaline nodded vigorously.

"Some people prefer to flick their wrist, and others don't," I said as I walked to retrieve the blade. "You can also get a feel for it and decide if you want to hold the dagger by the handle, or on the blade."

I came back to stand by her side, and threw another one that dug itself deep into the middle of the trunk.

"I think I got it," she said.

She threw one, but her wrist twitched awkwardly at the end, and the handle hit the tree where the blade should've dug in.

"That was a good first try," I said as I jogged over and scooped up the fallen dagger. "I know it's hard to understand when you're just starting, but you want to have the perfect rotation on the knife." I stood and grabbed the handle of the blade still in the tree to yank it out. "And you don't really know it until you feel it for the first time." I walked back toward her and handed her both knives. "Here, try again."

Evaline threw them. Both drove into the tree this time, just at two complete opposite ends of it.

"That's good!" I said, throwing her a smile.

She jogged forward to grab the blades.

"I think I should practice with some targets," she said as she pulled the knives from the tree.

My eyes widened at her confidence. Throwing knives was hard enough; hitting targets took years to master.

"I don't think we should skip to skilled shots yet. Let's focus on the basics."

She rolled her eyes as she walked back toward me. "Oh come on, Wyott. What's the harm?"

I laughed and shook my head. Of course she wanted to try trickier shots. I'm not sure why I ever thought she'd listen to me.

There was a large maple leaf on the ground at the base of the tree we were aiming at. I found some sap leeching from the bark and stuck the leaf to the trunk. I turned toward her and waved at the leaf.

"There, now you have a target. But I still think you should focus on the fundamentals."

She smirked and fell into her stance, so I walked back to stand beside her. She pulled her arm back to throw, but then turned her head to me.

"What do I get if I hit it?"

I snorted. "The honor of hearing me lecture you on how it was a fluke."

She shrugged. "I feel good about this. Let's make a bet."

I narrowed my eyes, considering. I didn't know if learning she possessed magic was making her delusional, but there was no way she'd ever beat me throwing knives. I've been doing it for over a century. She'd been doing it for five minutes.

Or perhaps she was just trying to have fun, to take her mind off her father.

"Fine. What are the terms?"

Her eyes lit up as she thought about what she wanted. "If I hit the leaf, I get one of your bandoliers."

I raised my eyebrows.

"Daggers *included*," she added.

That didn't seem likely, but I did love this bandolier and these daggers. It'd taken me years to find a set of such quality that fit my thick chest and long torso accordingly.

I pursed my lips. "And when you don't hit it, what do I get?"

She cocked her head. "What do you want?"

My eyes fell to the dagger at her thigh, the one Maddox had gifted to her.

"I won't ask for your actual Rominium dagger, because Maddox would gut me, but when I win I want to have the Blacksmith make me one just like it."

Her brows furrowed. "That's it?"

I nodded. "Maddox told me I wasn't allowed because he wanted a one-of-a-kind dagger for you." I shrugged. "But Maddox respects the terms of bets."

She nodded and setup again and a thought hit me. "No take backs and no arguing after, okay? I take gambling very seriously, and the first rule is to never take a bet you know you can't win."

I saw her smile out of the corner of my eye as she nodded. "I respect the terms of bets, too. Don't worry, we're just having fun."

I crossed my arms and nodded, turning toward the tree.

Evaline raised her arm, extended it, and flicked her wrist. The dagger sliced through the air before driving deep into the very center of the leaf. It dug so far that from here I could see the sap beginning to seep out.

What the fuck?

Her smile was wide as she turned to me and held her hand out for my bandolier.

Fuck!

My jaw clenched and I narrowed my eyes as she spoke.

"You know what my first rule of gambling is, Wyott?"

I took a deep breath and sighed, dropping my crossed arms. "What?"

"If a gamble seems too good to be true, it probably is."

I cut my head down toward her. "You could've just told me your father taught you."

"Where's the fun in that?"

I rolled my eyes. "No one likes a hustler."

She raised up on her toes before dropping back down on her heels. "And no one likes a sore loser, so…" she trailed off, raising her hand higher.

I huffed and pulled the bandolier over my head. As I dropped the leather into her hand, I felt a physical pain shoot through my chest. I loved that fucking bandolier.

Evaline squealed and I knew it was because she'd finally gotten what she wanted, she'd been asking for the damned thing since we left Kembertus. She pulled it over her head but I couldn't bear the sight and walked toward the tree, removing the blade.

"If you're so good at throwing knives, let's make it interesting, let's—"

She cut me off. "More interesting than taking one of your bandoliers?"

I sighed and wondered idly why I helped Maddox save her. "Yes."

She finished tightening the straps around her and faced me again. "Okay, what?"

I put my back to the tree. My body took up most of the space, so there was only a little bit of room on either side of my head.

"Don't hit me."

She rolled her eyes. "Is this another bet?"

I shrugged. "If you want it to be." I tried to remain nonchalant. I was sure if she knew how badly I wanted my bandolier back she wouldn't make the gamble.

She pondered for a second.

"If you win," I started, hoping my offer would entice her. "You can have another one of my weapons. If I win, I get my bandolier back."

She narrowed her eyes and paused to think about it.

"Deal."

I tried to hide the glint in my eye. She got into position, balancing her weight between both feet.

I almost felt guilty—for several reasons. I knew she'd just played me and there was nothing holding me back from playing her, but this was different. I wasn't just playing a silly game, I was divulging a secret. She squared up, cocked her hand back. She reared back, aimed, and brought her arm forward—

"Maddox needs to feed," I interjected.

Her wrist stuttered at the release of her throw and it aimed right for my head. I struck my hand out to catch it by the handle and stopped the tip of the blade an inch from my nose. I pulled it away, a wry grin lighting my features.

"Now that's fucking cheating," she snapped, pointing at me.

I shrugged and walked toward her.

"No more cheating than hustling somebody."

She crossed her arms and scoffed. "Oh, I beg to differ."

I stopped in front of her with my hand out and knew an arrogant smile adorned my face.

Evaline huffed and handed it to me. After donning the strap back on, my features turned grim.

We'd had our fun, but I did have a real reason for coming out here. Besides helping her get her mind off her father, I needed to tell her this information where Maddox couldn't hear us. He was clear across town.

Maddox would be angry—furious—with me, but he knew how worried I was about him, and this had been eating at me since the moment I found out. It was irresponsible to keep it from her any longer. Not when it put him in danger, not when she already watched him almost turn.

"I was being honest, Evaline," I started and her brows furrowed. "He's severely malnourished." I moved to stand beside her, aimed for the tree and hit the maple leaf at one of its points.

"What do you mean malnourished?" She crossed her arms beside me. "How often do Kova need to feed?"

"Normally, once a week. We can go longer, but it gets uncomfortable. After one week without food, it'd be similar to you after not eating for one day. I've gone two weeks before." I ignored the pang in my gut, that was when my father was killed. "But it's not good for us. And the longer we go between feedings, the more irritable we can be. The weaker we are, and the more likely we are to snap."

"What do you mean 'snap'?"

I tilted my head down toward her slightly and met her eyes.

"You know what I mean."

I saw the thoughts racing through her mind. I knew she was recalling when we'd saved her, how Maddox nearly drained that human of all his blood.

Her features darkened and she swallowed. "Okay. Why are you telling me this?"

I sighed. "Maddox hasn't fed in over a month."

Her jaw dropped and her eyes flicked between mine. "What? Why?"

My hand dragged down my face and then smoothed over my beard. I was sorry to be the one that had to share this burden, but so relieved that I'd have her on my side, that she'd help me make him feed.

"He fed the day before he met you, but then he saw you and the bond snapped into place."

She nodded, urging me to continue.

"Normally mates feed from each other. Cora and I for example—" I swallowed. Saying her name sent a wave of longing through my spine, and the thought of feeding from her sent blood somewhere else entirely. I shook the thoughts away. "But it's a preference, not a requirement. With Maddox, it's different. After he met you he became unable to feed from anyone else."

Her eyes narrowed. "What do you mean?"

I told her about his experiences trying to feed in Kembertus. How it felt like he was drinking molten metal. By the end her eyes were wide with horror.

"Why do you think that is?"

I shrugged. "It could be because you're a Sorceress. No Kova has ever been mated to any being other than a Kova."

Her brows unfurled as that sunk in.

"I need to let Maddox feed from me." She didn't pose it as a question, but her eyes lifted to mine anyway, waiting for an answer.

I gave a curt nod. "Yes. The sooner the better."

She took a deep breath and mimicked my nod.

"Okay, I will. Tonight."

Relief sagged my shoulders, the weight of worry I'd been bearing for my brother finally dissipated.

Evaline's eyes softened and I knew she understood. "Is there anything I should know?"

I turned to throw another knife, anything to take my mind off the fact that Maddox was going to murder me for telling her all of this. But it had to be done.

"Nothing in particular. It shouldn't hurt because he'll be gentle and with mates it's usually arousing instead of painful." I gave her an appraising look. "Although things may be different. Nothing with you two seems to be normal." I shrugged. "But I'll be there if you need anything—"

Her scoff cut me off. "No, you won't."

I opened my mouth to speak, but she cut me a glare that made me rethink my words.

I sighed. "He won't agree to that."

The words accented the sound of the dagger I'd just thrown as it landed in the tree.

"He'll have to." She took one of the blades from my hand and threw it. It hit the point at the top of the leaf. "And when he does, you'll be in the other room. If I need you, I'll scream."

My cheeks heated as unwanted images flashed in my mind. I cleared my throat. "If you need me, yell my name. Like I said, feeding on a mate is arousing. I don't want to run in there for a different kind of scream."

Her eyes narrowed as she looked up at me.

"Wyott, keep talking like that and next time you're up against that tree you won't be able to catch the dagger I throw at your face."

I shot her a grin. "We both know that's not true."

CHAPTER TWELVE

Maddox

Where are you, my Goddess? I asked down the bond as I walked down the tavern stairs after setting up the surprise I'd gotten Evaline.

We're heading toward the inn, she responded.

My hand pushed against the rough wood of the door and I walked out of it, felt the way my heart fluttered when I turned the corner to see her walking up.

"Where have you two been?" I asked, flicking my eyes to Wyott.

"Just practicing throwing knives," he said and I could tell he seemed unlike himself. It had to be Cora, and that same guilt I'd felt every time I watched him pine for her hit me. But I tried to ignore it as he tilted his head. "Did you know your mate already had that skill?"

I laughed and reached forward to take her hand in mine.

"I did not," I said slowly, handing him his room key.

Wyott sighed. "Yeah, well neither did I." He stepped forward and clapped a hand on my shoulder. "A piece of advice, don't make bets with her," he said before walking into the inn.

I swung around to smile at Evaline. "It sounds like you hustled him." I couldn't help the laugh that filtered into my words.

She grinned. "He needed to be reminded not to underestimate me."

My hand slipped from hers and into the dip in her waist, tugging her closer.

"What did he lose?" I asked.

She rolled her eyes. "Nothing for very long. I immediately lost it back to him. He's a cheater."

I smiled, lowering my lips to her forehead. "Then it sounds like you both learned a lesson in gambling today."

We walked inside and I led her straight to our room. We could order dinner to be delivered, and I wanted to show her the surprise.

"Where did you go today?" she asked.

"To get you a gift."

She whipped around to face me, sending her braid flying over her shoulder.

"What?" she asked, as I shut the door.

I nodded toward the bathroom and followed her in. Surrounding a steaming tub of water were candles that flickered as we entered. Beside it sat a table with the assortment of soaps I'd picked up for her. The smells of lemon, rose, and lavender filled the air.

"This is for me?" she asked.

"I just wanted you to have a nice, relaxing bath after everything you've been through." I shrugged. "The inns never have the good stuff."

A beat passed before I reached a hand toward her hip.

"Do you like it?" I asked in her ear.

She nodded and turned in my arms. "Thank you," she said as I leaned down to kiss her.

"You're welcome."

I could hear her emerge from the water in the bathing chamber. I imagined the way the water would slide down her naked body before she was able to dry it. I almost stood, waltzed into the room and fucked her against the wall.

But I couldn't. I was quickly falling into malnourishment, and the hold on my control was slipping. When we'd been together in that tent I'd fought every second to keep ahold of it. Each rise of her hips drove me closer to that edge. But I hadn't had the capacity to tell her no, not after the fear of nearly losing her had rested so freshly in my gut. Not when I wanted to feel her around me, watch her come undone, if only to commit the look of her, the feel, to memory.

She walked out of the bathing room, toweling her quickly drying hair, in nothing but that Gods forsaken pale blue silk robe. The tie was fastened around her waist, her hips wide in stark contrast just below.

She smiled at the way I watched her from where I sat on a chair beside the dining table, facing the fire.

"What?" she asked.

I shook my head. "Nothing, just admiring you."

She blushed and shook her head, hanging the damp towel over a hook on the wall. She bent then, flipping her hair over her head and gathering it into her hands, pulling a hair tie around until her long white hair was in a bun on top of her head. I tried to ignore the way her robe slid up when she bent over.

I made a sound of approval at the hairstyle.

She laughed and walked toward me.

"You like it?" She stood in front of me, between my legs, and rested her hands on my shoulders.

"Mhm." I reached forward and rested my own hands on her hips, tugging her closer. "I've never seen you wear your hair like that before," I said, looking up at her, a lazy smile on my face.

She shrugged. "I've never let anyone feed from me before."

Every muscle in my body hardened at the immediate realization of what had occurred.

"I knew I shouldn't have left you alone with Wyott." I straightened.

Of course that would be the first thing he'd say to her the moment I left. I understood that he cared for me, but he needed to respect the boundaries I was so desperately trying to set for her.

"Don't be mad at Wyott," she said softly. "He's just concerned." She raised a hand to brush the hair from my face. "So am I."

I shook my head. "Don't be, I've survived far worse. I'll be fine."

Her grasp on my shoulders tightened. "Why won't you let me do this for you?" Her voice was hard, and I knew this was going to be a battle.

"Evaline, I am malnourished right now. I don't trust myself not to hurt you accidentally."

She shook her head, "I trust you enough for the both of us."

I gripped her tighter and pleaded her with my eyes. "Don't."

Her mouth set into a hard line. "And what's the alternative? You slowly become more and more malnourished until you snap, drain someone and become a Vasi?" Her hands held my face, pulling me closer. "And I lose you forever?" The words were a whisper.

I clenched my jaw. I knew that she was right, that Wyott was right. I needed to feed, but I didn't want her to feel rushed into it.

"I don't want you to feel obligated." My voice was tight.

She rolled her eyes before snapping them back to mine. "I don't feel obligated, Maddox. I want to help you and I know I'm the only one who can. So just do it already," she said.

I let out a long sigh before moving to stand, but her hands flew to my shoulders once more, pushing me down.

"What are you doing?" I asked.

She shook her head. "Wyott will not be joining us."

"The fuck he's not." I scoffed and her hands tightened.

"He's not. I already talked to him. I told him this was going to be intimate, just you and I."

It was my turn to roll my eyes.

"There is no way in the name of the Gods that I am going to feed from you in this state without Wyott here to interject if things go badly."

"Maddox, I don't want him here." Then her voice softened. "Isn't feeding from a mate intimate?"

I begrudgingly nodded.

"And isn't the first time that happens special? Is it a crime that I don't want an audience for that?"

I stared at her a long moment. "Have I ever told you how truly stubborn you are?" I asked, my hand trailing upwards to cup her waist again.

She smiled and her grip on me loosened. "Maybe once or twice."

"Well I think it's time for another reminder."

She laughed and shook her head, tilting her head slightly to expose her neck. "No, it's time for something else entirely."

My gaze fell to her neck, and down to her cleavage, following the trail of the silk down the length of her body.

My hand moved to tug the hem of her robe. "You're not wearing this."

She laughed, as if I was joking, before realization flashed through her eyes.

"Why? I can only carry a couple changes of clothes, I'd rather my night clothes get ruined than the others."

I shook my head. "We can buy you more clothes if needed. You can't wear this."

She scoffed. "Why?"

I wrapped my hands around her hips once more and raised my eyes to meet her gaze.

"Because all I can think about right now is bending you over this table, and that is not the mindset I want to have when feeding from you for the first time in this weakened state."

I watched as the blush blossomed on her cheeks, traveling down her neck and onto her chest. Her throat bobbed as she gulped.

"No," she whispered. I swallowed a growl as I squeezed my eyes shut. "Nothing bad will happen."

I swiped her dagger, still sheathed in its thigh holster, from across the table and held it out to her.

"And I'm not holding that like you made me when I fed from you. It's not necessary."

"Evaline," I warned.

"This isn't a negotiation!" she snapped, her eyes hard and unmoving.

I stared at her a moment before reaching out. She gasped when she felt my hands moving the holster over her thigh, so, *so,* close to that sweet part of her, before fastening the dagger there. I looked up at her as my hands worked blindly. Her wide eyes met mine.

"This *is* a negotiation," I said, low. "And this is my condition."

She just nodded, her jaw clenching.

I took a deep breath as my eyes coasted over her neck.

"If you start to feel weak, or too cold, do whatever you need to do to put me down," I advised.

"I understand."

I swallowed, my mouth beginning to water at the thought of tasting her, something I'd thought about since the day we met. Since I smelled her blood when she tried to pickpocket me. So sweet and decadent, calling out to me, made for *me.*

I took her hands from my shoulders and laid them by her side. "Keep them here."

I cut her a look, urging her not to argue, and watched her swallow whatever retort she'd been ready to sling back at me.

I reached for her, steadying my hands on either side of her rib cage, to hold her still. She cocked her head, exposing her neck to me, as she looked toward the ceiling.

I readied myself as I stared at the vein I could see pulsating beneath her silky flesh. I eased closer and felt her hold her breath.

My lips brushed her skin and she straightened in my arms, waiting.

"If it hurts, tell me," I whispered against her skin. I felt her nod.

I took one last deep breath, and sank my teeth in.

I paused as Eva gasped from the contact, waiting for her to push me away. But she didn't, only rolled her head back slightly and relaxed into my arms.

The rich, sweet taste of her flowed effortlessly past my lips and my grip on her tightened. It was perfect, she was perfect. So decadent and sweet, tasting of molten dark chocolate, just barely bitter.

All of me fell victim to the bliss, and something inside stirred awake. I felt a pulse deep in my head, as if someone were banging against a door. I squeezed my eyes shut as I focused on shoving walls between the sound and I, until my hands didn't shake where they held her, and I had a grasp on my control.

And for a moment that worked, and I relished the feel of her in my arms, the taste of her down my throat, the softness of her skin against my lips.

Evaline moaned into the air. The sound answered something deep in my soul, and her hands raised to loop over my shoulders.

I didn't have the capacity to make her put them back down to her sides, not when her hands were grasping at me, her breaths coming faster, and I knew she was feeling what all mates felt when they fed from each other; ecstasy.

I took a long pull from her, the warmth spreading through me so quickly I groaned at the feeling. That pulled a reaction from her and she threw her head back further, nails digging into my shoulders through the shirt I wore.

"Maddox," she moaned and I couldn't take it anymore. I couldn't take the distance between our bodies.

My hands slid from her sides to her back, and I pulled her flush against me.

That pounding in my head started again and I was so focused on pushing it away again that I couldn't stop her when she raised one leg and wrapped it around my lap, then the other until she sat down on me completely, immediately rolling her hips against mine.

I growled against her neck as the arousal I was trying so hard to damper hit me full force.

With my hands back on her hips, I pulled them against mine and the feel of her pussy rubbing against my quickly hardening cock snapped something inside of me.

She gasped and the sound brought me back to reality, back from the taste of her blood, from thoughts of burying myself inside of her, from what it would feel like to feed from her while I did so.

I removed my mouth, flicked my tongue over the wound out of reflex to heal it, and pulled away to look at her. My hand raised to the back of her neck, angling her down to look at me.

"Why'd you stop?" she whispered, breathless.

The oceans in her eyes were churning, undulating with passion, with arousal, and it took every piece of my strength not to unfasten my pants.

"Did I hurt you?"

She shook her head. "Of course not."

I'd let myself go too deep, get too worked up, and had been afraid I'd hurt her, maybe scared her, when she'd gasped.

I took a deep breath. "Good."

Her eyes fell to my mouth, and I licked my lips, realizing there was likely remnants of her blood there.

"Aren't you going to continue?" she whispered.

I shook my head. "No, I had enough." A lie, but we didn't need to press our luck the first time.

Her hand slid up my face, her thumb stroking just beneath my eye. My jaw clenched.

"You're lying."

The bags beneath my eyes were clearly still evident.

"I'm fine. Let's not move too fast."

She moved closer, leaning into my chest as she stared at my lips. The sight tugged at me, begging me to take her, but I couldn't.

"You need more. And I want you to get enough." Her voice was low, laced with lust.

My hands on her hips tightened.

"I'm fine. You're feeling the effects of the bond, the arousal, urging you to let me finish. It's the instinct of the bond, but I don't need any more right now. I promise."

Instead of responding, she closed the distance between us and crashed her lips onto mine. Immediately my bottom lip was locked between her teeth as she pulled.

I groaned, my brows furrowing, but didn't make myself pull away. Instead I kissed her back, parting my lips for her and feeling the sweep of her tongue against mine, the sweet taste of her still lingering there. Her hands moved up, into my hair, tugging it as she kissed me fiercely. My hands roamed up her back, until I had one wrapped around her neck, holding her to me.

She moaned into the kiss, rolling her hips over mine, and I nearly gave in.

I pulled her back slightly as we heaved for air, her eyes wild with lust and I knew mine matched.

"I don't care whether it's the bond or not, I don't want you to stop."

Her hand fell between us until she palmed my groin, and I felt my jaw slacken.

I clenched my eyes shut, trying to focus on silencing the throbbing in my head, removing my hands from her and fisting them at my sides.

"I can't. I'm barely hanging on, I don't want to lose control."

She straightened in my lap. "You won't hurt me."

I heard a sweep of air, and when I opened my eyes she was removing her robe completely, letting it fall to the floor.

I groaned.

Her nipples were already taut, as I knew they'd be. Her chest was heaving for air. I watched as her hands rested on her thighs, saw the peak between them and how it glistened.

It was *painful* to hold myself back like this. When all I wanted was to ravish her.

"What are you trying to do to me?" I gasped, my hands folding over my face.

"I think it's pretty clear." Her voice was husky. "We both want this, Maddox. You don't need to be afraid."

I slid my hands down my face, not letting them touch her.

"Of fucking course I want this, Eva. There isn't a moment in the day when I don't want you."

She shrugged. "So have me. Feed, and have me."

I shook my head violently. "I don't think I could fuck you right now without losing control, let alone feed, as well."

Based on the uptick in her heartbeat, I knew the words excited her.

"Wyott's in the other room, if I get scared I'll scream his name. That's what we agreed to earlier."

Hearing another man's name on her lips, when she was undressed and turned on, had rage flowing through me before I could stop it.

It was Wyott, my brother, someone I knew would never take Evaline from me but it didn't matter in my current state.

My hands found her then, clenching around her waist.

"I don't like hearing you say another man's name when you're naked in front of *me*."

A smile tugged at her lips, sultry and calculating.

"Then do something about it," she whispered.

I growled as I stood, and her legs wrapped around me as her lips crashed onto mine. I kicked the chair out from behind me, heard the splintering of wood, and knew it'd broken against the wall. I turned, sitting her on the edge of the table, breaking our kiss for one second to sweep my arm across the rest of it, sending the various holstered weapons thudding to the floor.

She pulled my face back to hers. Her strength would never cease to amaze me. Her legs unraveled from around me and spread open between us, until she was exposing herself to me.

Her scent immediately hit me, and I dropped to my knees before her.

She gasped as I pulled her to the edge of the table, her hands planting on the top of it to catch and prop herself up.

I looked up at her, the sight stole the breath from my lungs.

A Goddess.

She looked down at me with wild eyes, her hair falling from its bun in a mess of tendrils. Her breasts heaved with her chest for air and her nipples went taut, begging for me. The only item she wore was the dagger strapped around her thigh.

My lips started there, trailing the edge of the holster around her thigh, my hand following until it was wrapped around her leg. I moved to the other side and did the same until I pulled both legs over my shoulders.

She gasped, staring down at me.

I continued trailing my lips up her thighs, kissing every inch of skin *except* the exact spot that shined in the light for me, the wetness increasing every second I didn't kiss it.

She whimpered above me, "Please Maddox."

"Mmm," I mumbled against her skin. "Maybe this is your punishment for teasing me."

She groaned, dropping her head back with the sound.

"That's not fair," she gasped.

I looked up at her as I continued trailing my mouth lightly over her skin. I felt her legs twitch slightly around my head and the move hardened my cock even more. How badly she wanted me, how much she needed me, would never get old. The firelight glowed around her body, kissing her skin just as softly as I was. My eyes continued trailing up until they got to hers; I hadn't even noticed she'd straightened.

With her eyes locked with mine, and after seeing how deeply the colors within them swam, I gave her what she wanted—what *I* wanted.

She gasped when my lips touched her and moaned when my tongue dipped inside. Her sweetness filled my senses and the beast within me raged again.

Moans fell from her lips like a melody as I continued and her arms shook below her before she let them slide out and her head disappeared from my view so all I could see was the crest of her arched abdomen, and the profile of her breasts against the quickly darkening room.

I couldn't resist and didn't break my rhythm as I placed my palm on her stomach and moved it upward until it reached her chest, moving to her breast and then over her nipple.

"Maddox," she hissed, the word barely escaping between moans.

Hearing my name from her mouth, knowing I was the only man who would *ever* make her feel this way, locked the vice around my cock harder and loosened the reins on my control until I was moving faster, my tongue moving over her delicious skin until all I could taste—*smell*—was her.

I brought my hand back down and let one finger slide inside while my tongue moved up to give sole attention to her clit.

Oh, fuck, she nearly screamed down the bond as she arched even farther, and I saw her hands reach out, grasping the edges of the table on either side of her until her knuckles turned white.

Tell me what you want, I replied, never removing my mouth from its work to drive her closer to that edge.

My finger curled inside of her and I knew it wouldn't be long by the way she tightened around it.

I want you.

I chuckled against her skin and she shivered. *Want me to what?*

As she came closer to her precipice I came closer to losing control. But I couldn't stop now, not when she wriggled beneath me so, not when the most powerful drug in this world was her screaming beneath my mouth.

I want you to fuck me.

The words filled my head and stole my breath. I'd been expecting her to say something similar, but hadn't expected those words.

And they affected me. Drove me wilder than I'd already become, and I growled against her skin, letting my teeth graze her.

She jolted and came undone around me, screaming my name inside and out as she did so, but I moved as she rolled through her release. I stood, ripping the fastener of my pants away until they fell to the ground, and reached for her.

Her wide eyes stared at me as my arm snaked beneath her, slipping in the arch of her back, and pulled her up until our lips locked together in a frenzy.

She moaned into my mouth and I deepened the kiss, not daring to hesitate. Her hands found my hair, tugging on the strands as she tried to pull me closer.

Shirt, too.

The command had my lip twitching up into a smirk and I broke the kiss long enough to rip it off over my head before grabbing her neck and bringing her lips back to mine. I felt her smile against my mouth as I lined up, grasping onto the remainder of my control as I eased inside instead of the rough motion that I would have preferred. Regardless, she gasped and I wondered if I'd ever tire of eliciting that reaction from her.

She wrapped her legs around my hips as I moved and pulled me against her, her hands still tangled in my hair. She let out a loud moan and her head fell back, causing more of her long waves to fall down her back, feathering against my arm that still held her there, my other hand with a firm grip on her hip.

She arched further and my lips dropped to her neck, kissing along it. I heard her take a breath to speak and I knew what she was about to say by the uptick in her pulse as my lips moved there.

"Drink, Maddox."

My hands tightened around her but I didn't dare stop my rhythmic thrusts.

"No." It was resolute, no room for retorts.

"But—"

"No," I said harder, in time with a thrust.

She gasped and pulled my hair until I was looking at her.

"You want to, I want you to, please. You need more."

My jaw screamed in protest as I clenched it so tight I thought it would shatter. I wanted to so fucking bad. But I was so afraid that I'd lose control, so afraid I'd hurt her or worse.

Don't be afraid, she whispered down the bond, no doubt feeling the fear that swept through me.

My rhythm slowed for a second as I considered, but shook my head.

"It's not worth the risk."

Her annoyed sigh filled the room but I ignored it and caught her lips in mine, this would have to be enough for now, even though I knew I desperately needed more.

She kissed me back, fiercely, but as if she was distracted. Was she angry with me?

I deepened the kiss, desperate to show her how much I wanted her, how much I loved her, afraid she took my hesitation as a disregard for her.

And I was so distracted by that thought that I hadn't noticed the soft swipe of her blade as it was removed from its sheath, until the scent of her blood hit the air.

I froze, removing my mouth from hers as I looked down.

She'd made a small slice in her neck, not big enough to harm her only deep enough to draw blood, to bait me.

I growled with the effort to control myself, and without consciously telling them to my hips began thrusting again, hard.

She moaned and exposed her neck to me further.

"Evaline," I warned, but my voice was so uncontrolled we both knew I was close to breaking.

"It's okay," she whispered as she tightened her legs around me, her hands moving to grip my shoulders roughly. "I trust you."

It was all it took to shatter my remaining control. I growled and moved forward, latching onto her neck so quickly I was afraid I'd hurt her, but she just moaned in my ear and clutched me tighter.

I grabbed her hips and pulled her closer to the edge of the table, closer to me, as I increased my rhythm.

I took a pull and the cells in my head felt as if they'd exploded in unison. The feel of her around my cock, the taste of her cascading down my throat, her moans echoing through the air so loud there was no doubt every room around us could hear. It was all too much and not enough, something I'd been afraid to take but desperately needed. It was everything and nothing all at once, and when her hips started moving to meet mine I nearly broke.

"Don't stop," she begged, and I didn't have it in me to say anything in response, only moving harder against her, dragging more of her blood between my lips and eliciting a scream from between hers.

She shivered in my arms and groaned so deep I felt the vibrations through her neck echoing down around me until I was done, propelling over the edge so fast, and so hard, and unlike anything I'd ever experienced before.

She bucked against me, squeezing her legs together and screaming as her nails dug into my shoulders and I knew she drew blood. Her heart rate increased in a surge and her blood rushed past my lips.

Our movements slowed against each other as we rode our highs until we were still, except for the heaving of our chests against one another. I slowly pulled my mouth away, removing my fangs, and flicking my tongue over the wound to heal it. She shivered at the touch.

I rested my forehead against her shoulder as I tried to regain my composure and rein in my control.

A contented sigh sounded through the air as she relaxed against me.

"Wow."

And the word reminded me of what we'd just done. What *I'd* just done. Lost control, gotten too rough too fast, fed from her when I shouldn't have.

I ripped myself away, hands finding her jaw and tilting her up to face me.

"Are you okay?" I breathed.

Her brows furrowed. "Of course I am."

My eyes searched hers for a lie, then tilted her head and examined her neck. It was fine, healed from my bite and flushed from the scrape of my facial hair, but fine. I released a sigh of relief and pulled away from her, removing myself as we both shivered at the cold that hit us.

I met her eyes as she stared up at me.

"There we go," she whispered, her hand raising to caress my cheek, just below my eye. "No more bags."

I tried to be upset with her, but I couldn't.

"You shouldn't have done that. The risk wasn't worth the reward."

She snorted. "Maybe from your point of view."

My eyes leveled with hers and she dropped the jovial demeanor.

"Nothing bad happened. And if it had, Wyott was in the other—"

I rolled my eyes and pulled away from her, redressing.

"If it *had*, then he would've been too late. Don't you realize it would only take a second for me to kill you? Sorceresses aren't human, but they *aren't* immortal. You can die just like any plain being."

She crossed her arms over her chest.

"Why are you getting upset over an outcome that didn't happen?"

"Because I'm upset that I let myself lose control, Evaline!" I shouted and immediately regretted it from the way she winced. I moved toward her, enveloping her in my arms. "I'm sorry," I said, taking a deep breath. "I'm just afraid of losing you," I whispered.

She looked up at me and in those eyes I saw the life we could have together, the years spent in each other's arms exactly as we were now, and I so desperately needed to hold onto that.

"I love you," she whispered back.

I rested my forehead against hers and closed my eyes. "I love you, you stubborn Sorceress."

And only the sound of her laugh filled the room.

CHAPTER THIRTEEN

Evaline

The next few days passed quickly. We rode the horses hard and arrived in Merwinan as the sun prepared to set.

It wasn't until we crested the hill on the outskirts that I saw the entirety of the castle's walls before us and what stretched behind it.

Eternity.

Or that's what it seemed like.

The grass below us stretched to the walls of the kingdom and beyond Merwinan's western most wall the grass turned to sand, and then into ocean.

It was sprawling and wide and teal—a deep turquoise that was unlike anything I'd ever imagined.

"Wow," I whispered and felt Maddox's hand brush my knee.

"The Madierian Sea," he said softly from the horse beside me.

I looked up at him, eyes wide. "This is the Madierian Sea?"

A stupid question. I'd seen the maps before and knew that Merwinan sat on the ocean's coast.

The shock in my voice wasn't because I didn't know where we were, but because of what Maddox had said about it before.

He turned to me then, raising a thumb to brush the corner of my eye.

Madierian Sea Blue, he whispered down the bond.

He'd compared my eyes to the water below us once. Butterflies fluttered in my stomach at the recollection of when he'd said the words to me. When he knew we were mates. When he loved me, but couldn't tell me, because he wanted to give me time.

How had we gotten from there to here? I was a world away from the woman I'd been, and it had only been a handful of weeks, but the transformation felt like years had passed.

Maddox bent forward and kissed me softly.

We turned our horses down the hill with Wyott ahead of us and bursting at the seams—to get to Cora, I assumed.

Maddox's mood began to change too. He and Wyott were both giddy as we turned past Merwinan's walls toward the stables off the beach, and I had to hold back my laughter at how boyish the two of them were acting.

But, of course, I knew what caused it. They were almost home after the better part of a year of being away. They were close to seeing their friends, their family, to being in a city where they weren't 'other' anymore.

Something was changing in me, too.

The closer we got to the water, the stronger the feeling became. Power. Strength. The feeling buzzed through my veins until I felt it settle in my heart. With each pump that beat through my chest, the feeling flashed through my blood.

I was so entranced by the water that I didn't notice that Maddox was guiding me toward the docks until I felt the sand I walked along change to hard, creaking wood.

"I was wondering when you two would be heading back home," a voice called in front of us. I finally pulled my attention away from the ocean. "Maddox." A tall man clapped a hand into my mate's and shook it. "I never thought I'd see the day."

"Saxon, this is my mate, Evaline," Maddox said, placing an arm around my waist.

Saxon's green eyes shifted down to mine.

I smiled and extended my hand to his. "It's nice to meet you."

"It's lovely to meet you," he said, raising an eyebrow. "I'm glad Maddox finally found you, he's been rather torturous about it for as long as I've known him, and I'm only thirty. I can't imagine how insufferable he's been for the previous lifetimes he's lived."

My expression must have given away my confusion. Maddox squeezed my hand and spoke down the bond.

He's a close friend so he knows about us. He's considering turning.

"Yeah, yeah. She's new. But we all know you missed me the most," Wyott's voice boomed over my shoulder.

I laughed and caught myself against Maddox's chest as Wyott moved past me and wrapped Saxon into a hug.

The smile on Saxon's face widened and his eyes crinkled as he hugged Wyott back.

"Of course, of course," he said before the two pulled apart and Saxon ran a hand over his short black hair. "Are you lot looking to go home tonight?" he asked, then looked to the skies.

I followed his gaze to the spot where the sun was arcing down to the horizon.

Wyott shifted his weight from one foot to the other beside me. "Is that possible?"

The hope in his voice sent a flash of warmth through my chest. Gods, even I was ready to get him back to Cora and I'd never even met the woman.

Saxon cocked his head. "Are you doubting me?"

"I just don't want you to make the trip if you don't feel the conditions are right. We can wait until morning, if needed," he said. His voice shook with anticipation.

Saxon laughed. "Gods, no." He waved a hand over Wyott's form. "You're clearly excited to get home. And trust me, Cora's ready too."

Maddox laughed but Wyott straightened at the mention of her name.

Saxon turned to Maddox. "It seems we've both been enduring their heartache."

Maddox shook his head slightly. "I'm sure I don't know what you mean," he said, his tone light. "Wyott has been the perfect traveling companion."

Wyott shifted his weight again. "Yes, yes, I miss my mate." Then he looked between the two of them and his words became rushed. "Are you going to keep hassling me about it or are we going to sail this ship and cure it?"

Saxon nodded. "You might be worse off than she is."

He raised a hand toward the ship beside us and I looked up at it for the first time. I'd never seen a ship before—I'd grown up inland—so I wasn't sure if this vessel was large or small in comparison to any other, but it seemed massive as it rocked in the water.

"We have less bodies than we normally would, only enough to man the ship. I didn't expect anyone to cross the Strait tonight, but we can make it. The weather is fine, it'll just be a dark start." Saxon turned back and addressed me. "Luckily it's a straight shot made up of nothing but clear water, we won't have to worry about any rocks. We've sailed this route more times than I can count."

We traversed the gangway and I tried not to look over the edge, afraid I'd fall into the water and hit the side of the ship. I followed Saxon and Wyott's lead and jumped down onto the ship, but the rock of the boat immediately disrupted my balance. I tottered but Maddox landed behind me and slipped an arm around my waist to pull me into his chest.

"You don't have to hold me up, I'm plenty capable of learning to balance," I said, rolling my eyes.

"Who's to say I didn't just feel like doing this?" he asked before dipping his head to kiss me.

Behind us Saxon cleared his throat and we turned. A blush heated my face.

"If I see a second more, I'm going to get sick and it won't be from the waves." He and Wyott exchanged a look.

"Exactly," Wyott said, shaking his head. "You're all giving me shit for missing Cora but I've been dealing with this," he said, waving his hand at us. "Try being stuck in the room beside them when—"

A furious blush erupted in my cheeks, and I yanked my dagger from its holster, whipping it through the air toward his chest before he could finish his sentence. He snapped his mouth shut in an effort to catch it and his brows shot to his forehead.

"That was uncalled for."

I scoffed. "I beg to differ."

Saxon cleared his throat and coughed as Wyott handed me the knife back and the three of us turned to the captain. The evening sunlight fell over his deep brown skin as he tried to erase the amused look on his face and exchange it for a serious one.

"We'll set sail in a few. It'll take about a day and a half to get there, as usual. I know you've traveled quite a ways already so feel free to take a couple of the rooms below. They're nothing fancy, but there's a bed."

"Thank you so much," Wyott said and reached a hand out to shake his again.

"It's no problem," Saxon said as he shook it and walked a few steps backwards. "Besides, I'm going to remind Cora about this when I look to join Rominia's Navy," he said with a wink, before walking up deck to check the ropes under a large sail.

I turned to both Kova and asked, "What does that mean?"

Wyott thrust his chest out with a wide grin as he spoke. "Cora is the leader of our Navy."

A surprised laugh burst through my lips. "Really?"

They both nodded and I tried to hide the grin that crept across my face. It was so refreshing to know that Rominia was so different from Kembertus. While Neomaeros may have allowed women in the military, it felt like so long since I'd experienced such equality.

I composed myself and shook my head in disbelief. "That is amazing."

Wyott opened his mouth but his sentence was lost to a smile as he knelt down onto the deck. A second later, a flash of white and black fur pounced on him.

"Oscar!" Maddox and Wyott shouted in unison.

"This is Saxon's hound," Maddox said to me as he started petting the dog over Wyott's shoulder.

I bent to run a hand over the dog's thick fur. "He can handle being on the water?"

Wyott snickered as Oscar tried to lick his face. "He has remarkable sea legs for an animal that was never meant to cross an ocean."

Maddox nodded. "He lives wherever Saxon does."

The dog seemed to notice me then and turned away from Wyott to stand on his hind legs and wrap his front paws around my torso. He had long white and black speckled fur that must've knotted easily because the more my fingers brushed through it the more tangles I broke past.

"Oscar!" Saxon shouted from behind the helm. "Don't trample our new guest."

The dog took off in the direction of his owner and I tried to brush off the hair that clung to my clothes in his wake.

"You get used to it," Wyott offered, then looked around to all the water around us. "Do you feel any different out here?"

Maddox leveled his gaze on me then. He already knew the answer.

I nodded. "Yes, definitely. I don't know why. I just feel all this pent-up energy, like I drank enough coffee and tea to power me through the next week without sleep."

Wyott bounced on his toes and looked to Maddox.

"Can I?"

Maddox laughed and rolled his eyes. "It's not up to me."

"What are you two talking about?" I asked, crossing my arms.

Wyott turned to me and clapped his hands together. "We're headed off home soon, we're sitting here with nothing to do, *and* it's been days since we got you back from Gabriehl. You're rested and we're bored." He rubbed his hands together. "Let's see that magic."

The laugh that bubbled up from my mouth made his smile fall. "I can't just summon it."

He pulled me closer to the edge of the boat. "Sure you can, you're a Sorceress. That's literally what they do."

He held onto my shoulders and positioned me so that my back was against the edge of the boat.

I huffed. "And while I'm sure that's true, I only discovered this magic recently. I think I've only used it twice."

He stepped a few paces back from me while Maddox stood beside him, an amused look on his face. "You just have to learn how to access it," he said. "Wyott is right, you should be able to use it whenever you desire."

"I still don't even know why I have more than one element," I whispered at them.

Wyott pulled something out of his pack and turned toward me. "Well until then you're going to try the other elements. Think fast!" he said before jerking a canteen toward me. A stream of water arced through the air.

I sidestepped and watched the water barrel over the edge of the boat, and heard it splash into the ocean below us.

My eyebrow cocked as I looked back at him.

"What the fuck was that supposed to do?"

He rolled his eyes. "You're no fun. You didn't even try."

I narrowed my eyes at him. "Try what? Getting drenched?"

Maddox laughed. "He wanted to see if you could stop the water in its path."

I leveled Wyott with my gaze. "Maybe a better way to test that theory would have been to use your words, instead of assuming I could read your mind."

He waved his hand. "Fine, fine. Here, try to wield the water like you did the air and tree."

He recapped the canteen and handed it to me.

I ripped it from his grasp. "Can you keep your voice down?" I snapped. "I don't need everyone here knowing."

Maybe where they came from this was completely natural, but it wasn't for me. I'd only just discovered I had magic; I didn't want the entire world knowing. Especially considering I'd spent the last two years in Kembertus where being a Sorceress was illegal.

"What don't you understand when I say I can't just summon it?" I said to Wyott.

He crossed his arms. "Well you'll never learn with that attitude."

The canteen flew through the air so fast that he barely ducked out of the way in time. Maddox's hand shot out to catch it. My heart rate spiked as I remembered that all the humans on the ship could see us.

Wyott straightened and grinned, ignoring the heated look I shot at him. I looked around and realized that no one was paying any attention to us as they prepared the ship to depart, and I remembered what Maddox had said about Saxon thinking about becoming Kova. I crossed my arms and took a breath. Of course everyone here knew what they were, and no one would notice or mind their fast movements.

Wyott took Saxon up on his offer to nap while we sailed. Maddox didn't, likely because I wouldn't, though he probably needed to as well. He disappeared into Saxon's office while I remained on the deck with Oscar.

I felt guilty that I was keeping Maddox up, but I knew there was no way I could lie down right now, let alone sleep. And if I tried I would just end up continuously turning over and disturbing him out of sleep, anyway.

There was no way I'd get any slumber when I could feel my magic building, amplifying, and sucking energy out of thin air.

The night was dark, with only a few lanterns on the ship to light our way. The deck had grown quiet. Most of the men no longer needed to man the sails as we drifted further away from land. They drew about lazily on the deck, dozing off or playing cards. The only noises to be heard were Oscar's panting, the thump of his tail against the deck, and the slow slap of water on the ship below us.

I took in the black night. The sky was devoid of any stars; they must've been covered by clouds too far away for me to see.

I couldn't shake the odd feeling buzzing through me.

Suddenly a chill coasted through my body and I bit my lip. I wore a long-sleeved tunic and pants. The climate before we set sail was humid, I shouldn't have been this cold. But as another shiver wracked my spine, my hands stilled in Oscar's fur.

Something was wrong.

I stood and turned to face the side of the boat. The edge was only a few feet from me, but beyond it was a void of black, so thick and so intimidating. It seemed to crawl closer to me and I took a step back.

My ears strained for any sound. I didn't want to disturb Maddox and Saxon or wake the sailors or Wyott based on a feeling.

There was still only the slapping of water against the wood below us. I cocked my head as I realized the slaps seemed to be coming faster now, rolling against the ship in quicker intervals than they had been the entire voyage thus far.

My eyes widened. Were we close to a land mass? Nearing a crash?

I turned toward the captain's quarters, mouth dropping open to call for Maddox, but was interrupted by a vicious, shrieking bark.

Oscar jumped to his hind legs, shoving his front paws on the ledge of the ship, and barked violently into the dark.

My heart sank in my chest as his barks confirmed my fears.

I reached for Oscar and wretched him back away from the edge. He continued barking at the wall of night before us but didn't turn his aggression toward me as I dragged him away.

I heard the door to the captain's office slam open and snapped my head toward it. Time slowed as I saw Maddox step out of the room, his hand pressed against the center of the door.

Maddox's eyes were wild and landed directly on me as he screamed my name. The hair on my neck rose.

Before I could turn, I felt a blow on my chest, knocking me back until my head slammed onto the deck and Oscar pulled himself from my grasp.

I don't know what happened then. Maddox might've moved, might've run toward me or away, to get Wyott. The men sleeping behind me may have risen, Saxon may have drawn a sword.

All I could see were dozens of men swinging from ropes onto our ship, seemingly from out of nowhere, the wall of darkness was still thick enough to hide the ship that must now be beside us.

It was then that I remembered to breathe, and then that I realized I couldn't.

The blow to my chest had knocked the wind out of me and I turned over, tears stinging my eyes as I gasped for air.

Move. Get up. Fight, I urged myself, willing my lungs to expand, to accept the air and to *move.*

Oscar's bark broke through the wall of chaos around me, closing me in, and I snapped back into time.

I jumped up, whipping to face the onslaught of men landing on the ship. I saw Saxon to my right, already fighting. Maddox was fighting past a few men to get to me, and I heard him scream for Wyott.

I'm fine, I told him through the bond. *Don't worry about me.*

I drew my sword in one hand and the Rominium dagger in the other. I couldn't tell if Maddox responded because my mind was whirling with thoughts, with noise. The world around me was just as loud as that within. I knew it was my magic surging, screaming in my ears.

I tried to ignore it as a man grabbed my arm from behind. I turned, swiping my sword out and stabbing first. There was no time to consider who was the enemy and who was not. We were severely outnumbered as dozens more men flew over the deck.

The man choked on the blood that filled his mouth, with my blade buried in his throat, and fell. His grip loosened off me as I turned to face two more.

"Calm down. We don't want to hurt you," the one on the right said, too sweetly.

"I can't say the same," I said as I took a step back from them, crouching down.

"Just come with us. There's no need for violence," the one on the left said.

I scoffed as I heard the clanging of swords around me. "Tell that to your comrades."

The one on the right moved, and I swiped my sword out. He dodged but didn't parry, only reaching out to try and grip my arm.

They weren't lying.

My eyes widened as I bent on one knee, dodging his fingers and shoving my dagger into his heart from under his ribs.

They wanted to kidnap me. And that could only mean one thing.

"He won't stop until he has you." My mother's words slammed into my mind.

My heart raced in my ears, the thrumming of it blaring through my mind, as I whipped around and dodged the second man's reach, bringing my sword up and plunging it into his jaw. The heavy smell of his blood filled my nostrils as I ripped it out and moved away.

Vasier had sent them. But these weren't Vasi; they were human men.

I whipped around looking for Maddox and Wyott.

Maddox stood near the captain's door ripping through a few men at a time. Wyott, who had barely made it up from below deck was shredding through enemies. I turned back around to see that Saxon's crew were holding their own.

A pit formed in my stomach as I realized that these pirates knew who Maddox and Wyott were, and they were intentionally going after them, to kill them first.

They were leaving me, standing alone now, unharmed.

And that was exactly the point.

"Sweet thing, your brain is working so hard I can see the gears moving." I straightened as a cool, low voice drawled behind me.

I turned until I faced a mountain of a man. Similar in size to Maddox, but his hazel eyes gave him away. Human. I released a small breath of relief.

"You know who sent us." He smirked at me, taking a step closer.

He had long black hair, scraggly from months aboard his ship, I was sure. The pirates hat he wore was tilted forward on his head, the front pointed at me as if revealing his target.

"Yes," was all I said as I took a small step back.

He cocked his head and flicked a dagger around in his hand.

"He's rather desperate to find you." His eyes glittered as he looked at me, and I noticed a scar tracing the length of the left side of his face. It arced over his brow, barely missing his eye, and stopped just above his lips.

He might've been handsome if I wasn't so acutely aware that he was a sell sword.

"I'm sure he is" I responded as I tried to evaluate my surroundings. We were a foot away from the edge of the ship, and I'm sure if the sun was shining, I'd see his boat beside us. He was the captain, no doubt, and that meant he had experience in battle.

"Awfully peculiar that I'm sent off on errand to capture such a pretty little thing like yourself." He tipped the blade of his dagger toward me, motioning up the length of my body. "Let alone one who can fight."

A smirk of my own lit my face then as realization struck. A laugh bubbled from my lips.

"You don't know why he wants me, do you?"

I saw suspicion flash over his eyes. He didn't know, which meant he didn't know who I was, and he didn't know about my magic.

"It's not my job to know why my clients want someone. Only to deliver their package in one piece, dead or alive, however they request." He took another step toward me. "Now be a good girl and don't make this harder than it has to be," he said, and I could sense the urgency in his voice that he tried to cover with arrogance. I watched as his eyes flicked over my shoulder to where Maddox still fought, then over my other to Wyott. They were both still alive and likely shredding through his crew.

"You don't have much time," I said, coolly.

His eyes returned to mine and this time he smiled. It was so wide and so true, that it sent shivers down my spine.

"Sweetling, pirates may not be the most loyal of men, but what we are loyal to, we'll die for." He smirked before he rushed me. I backed away until I stood facing that darkness, facing this man as the wall of black swelled up behind him and fear rose in my throat. This was what

I imagined Mortitheos resembled, and for all I knew the man before me wasn't a man at all, but the God himself. The God of Night.

I swallowed the fear and adjusted my eyes back to his. "And what's that?"

The smile he wore grew, his eyes seething in the lantern light. "Coin."

Another barrage of men flew out of the nothingness and landed on the ship. Some swarmed Maddox and Wyott, others ran to Saxon's crew.

My brows knitted together as I looked around us. Maddox and Wyott were fighting a dozen men at a time, each, and Saxon's men were desperately fighting for their ship, their captain, to defend themselves from these pirates.

Because of me.

I focused my gaze on the captain before me and began to run different scenarios through my mind, grappling for what I could do to save us.

"I don't make a habit of running off with men whose name I don't know." I tried to keep the words casual, to deflect any suspicion from the thoughts racing through my mind.

He took a step toward me.

"Captain Brentyn." I saw his smirk but ignored it.

Goosebumps pricked my skin. I didn't turn, but somehow knew where each enemy was on this ship. My brief glances before were not really enough to go off of, but something inside of me knew where they were, how they were moving, and I trusted that.

I heard the shouts of the men fighting for their lives. I heard Oscar's growl as he had his teeth wrapped around an enemy's leg. Heard Maddox screaming at Wyott to get to me.

I'd pushed the magic down, hid it within myself since the moment I knew it was there. I shielded it away because each time I used it, I was a beacon; a light in the middle of the dark sea for Vasier to find. I felt it moving now, flexing within me, pulsing as it knew my intention.

"Captain Brentyn," I acknowledged him, taking a deep breath to calm my erratic heart. "You should know that whatever he was paying you to capture me?" I felt it rush through me, to my hands, behind my eyes, building up and up until I loosened the valve that held it there.

"Yes?" He narrowed his eyes, seeming uneasy.

One single, dry, laugh erupted from my mouth as I smiled my own sick, true smile at him. The same smile I'd given Bassel. "It wasn't enough."

With the widening of his eyes, I screamed. The rush of my magic in this amplified state was overwhelming. It buzzed in my palms and the boat below us teetered in the water. I knew with an undoubting certainty that I knew what to do, how to do it—as if the knowledge had been placed deep in my mind before I was ever born, and only revealed itself now that I'd called it forward.

The ship fell silent, and all fighting stopped as the area around us burst into light that matched the color of the very ocean we sailed. The light emanating from my eyes ripped through the darkness and brought the ship beside us into view.

Gasps fell from the men around us, along with curse words and prayers, as they saw what else lurked in the darkness.

Two giant waves of water, one on each end of the boat, rose dozens of feet into the air. The men strained their necks in order to view the top of the waves.

The captain turned back to me and I watched as true fear passed over his eyes.

"Now you see why he didn't tell you who I was," I whispered and cocked my head. "But as long as we're being honest with each other, know this," I hissed at him, low.

My muscles ached with the effort of holding the waves where they hung but I narrowed my eyes and spoke through gritted teeth.

"I am the light you see; I am the wind you breathe; I am the land you walk. And tonight, I'm the water on which you've sailed your entire life. The water that you thought you knew, that you trusted, that you conquered." He angled his blade toward me and I smiled. "And you've made yourself my enemy."

"It is an honor to die in the sea," he hissed at me and took a step.

I flung my outstretched palms inward, bringing my hands together and only stopped just before they met, and we all watched as the waves mimicked my movements—falling in on each other and breaking the ship beside us in half.

The cries of the men still aboard lingered in the air above the striking sound of splintering wood. Our own ship bobbed as the water level changed, and then righted itself.

I settled my gaze back on Brentyn as he turned to me. I moved my hands in front of me once again, bringing a wall of water up before us. I flicked my wrist forward and the water punched out a stream of sparkling turquoise and pulled two of his men into it.

He set his jaw and straightened his spine, leveling his eyes with mine. "I've fought each day of my life. I am not afraid to rest."

The water took a few more men and he cringed.

I flicked my other wrist as the water again snapped out and grabbed two more men. They squirmed in the wall of water, drowning in plain sight. I heard a few men drop to their knees and pray louder.

"I think when you go into the Night, you'll understand," I began and sent multiple streams of water plunging out, grabbing the rest of his crew and pulling them back in. "There is no rest for those like you."

He pursed his lips and opened his mouth to speak, but a fist of water grabbed him, too.

Chapter Fourteen

Evaline

The air was still misty as I fell to one knee, my hand clutched to my chest, which heaved from the effort I'd just put forth.

A shrill, bright, ringing filled my ears and muted the rest of the world as I focused on catching my breath.

I felt every stare from every man aboard the ship. The tension was palpable, curling through the mist. If I looked up, I might have even been able to see it.

But before I could, I felt the air shift around me, and knew Maddox had run to my side. I felt his arm around my back before the other curled beneath my legs, and in one swift move he had me in his arms. He moved across the deck without a word and my cheeks flamed from the stares of the men around us.

I looked around, eyes landing on Wyott standing with a dozen men at his feet. His eyes were wide and for a moment I thought I saw fear in them, but I didn't get a chance to look again before Maddox was plunging us into the darkness of the staircase below deck.

In the shield of the dark, I finally took my first deep breath.

"I'm fine," I said softly, placing a hand over his chest. "I'm okay, really."

I looked up at him for the first time and realized only then that I'd been scared, too. I'd been afraid that I'd look up and see fear, to see disgust or rejection. I was afraid that in one display of violence and fury, I'd lost the man I loved forever.

His jaw was set, so hard I could see the muscles within it twinge in the effort. His eyes showed nothing, staring ahead as he made his way toward one of the rooms Saxon had offered us.

"Maddox?" I whispered.

But he didn't break his pace or divert his eyes to mine. My heart quickened in my chest. This was it. This was the end. I'd known this had all been far too good to be true. He'd loved me more than I deserved, for longer than I knew possible.

He kicked open the door in front of us and walked through the threshold. It was a decent sized room with one large bed in the back corner. There was no other furniture, no decor, aside from a lone pillar in the center of the room to hold up the deck above us.

A shiver wracked my frame and I realized for the first time that I was soaked. The water had doused me when the wave crashed down. Maddox was wet too. His hair and his skin were coated in fine droplets, but his clothing was only damp.

He set me down in front of the door and I crossed my arms around myself. If he was going to do this, to break my heart and leave me here, I wished he'd hurry up.

But I watched as he shut the door, locked it, and turned back to fix his hard gaze on me. I barely had enough time to look up at him before his hands were clutching my jaw, my neck, and his mouth was on mine.

A gasp fell from my lips as I felt a weight lift from my heart. My hands met his wrists and he shuddered beneath my touch.

He pulled away and tilted my head up to scan my face, his eyes wild. "Are you hurt?" he asked in a shaking voice.

The evidence of his worry for me clutched my heart and I shook my head quickly.

"No, I'm fine."

His brows furrowed as his eyes scanned my face once more. He moved forward then, slowly, until I felt my back meet the door behind me. His hands dropped, running over my body. My arms, my torso, checking for injuries.

"Maddox," I said, reaching a hand up to clasp his cheek. "I'm okay." His wide eyes didn't soften. "You'd smell blood on me, remember?"

"You don't have to be bleeding to be injured," he said quietly, and raised a hand to trace over my chest, my collar bone.

A sharp hiss slipped from my lips at his gentle touch. I looked down in shock.

He pulled the collar of my tunic back slightly to reveal a purple bruise in the center of my chest, at the base of my collarbones—exactly where I'd been booted in the chest by the marauders.

"It might be broken," he said, and I could hear the pain in his voice, the hatred at the thought that I was hurt.

Without a word, he bit his wrist and turned it toward me, holding it to my lips.

I paused and stared at the wound. "Won't drinking our mingled blood cause me to change?"

That's what he and Wyott had said caused a human to change into a Kova. Did it work the same for Sorceresses?

An emotion I couldn't name passed in his eyes before he smiled. "No, it's been too long. It would have to be in the same day I fed from you."

I closed my lips over the wound and my eyes widened at the sweetness that filled my mouth. His own darkened as I took a long drag and his muscles tensed as he watched me. The warmth spread to my chest quickly, and a tingle covered my skin as the healing began.

I took another drag and Maddox grunted, falling forward slightly and bracing his other hand against the door above me. His eyes drew black and trained on my lips.

I took one last drag and watched as his chest moved unevenly, as he tried to control his breaths. Upon feeling the pain over my chest ease, I pulled away.

His eyes focused and he swallowed before asking, "Was it enough?"

"Yes," I whispered, pulling the front of my shirt forward to show him that the bruises had faded away.

He nodded, pursing his lips.

"And there's no pain?" He tapped along my collarbone and I held still while he prodded. "You're not drained, physically or mentally, from your use of magic?" His eyes were scanning my face and landed on my lips when I shook my head.

"No, I'm fine."

"Good," he said, his voice stern, before a hand clasped over the back of my neck and melded my lips to his.

It was not gentle this time, as it had been minutes before, and his entire body pressed me up against the wooden door. My hands moved up, looping around his neck and pulling him closer to me. He pulled me closer to him by the waist before sliding his hands over my ass, pulling at my thighs.

A soft moan escaped me from his touch, and I realized how much I needed this. How much I needed this affirmation that he still loved me despite my darkness; despite my magic.

He slipped a hand between my arms and tilted my jaw up to deepen the kiss before pulling away just enough to speak.

"For the second time I've put you in harm's way." He spoke against my mouth. "For the second time you've been hurt, because of me." His hand on my jaw tightened and his teeth grazed my lips in a kiss.

"I'm okay. I can—"

He cut me off, moving to rest his forehead against mine. "I know you're okay. I know you can handle yourself," he said the words I'd been about to utter. He took a deep breath. "Your strength, the magic you exhibited…" he trailed off, shaking his head slightly. "You are the most powerful Sorceress I've ever seen—maybe the most powerful one in the world."

The words caused the magic within me to roll with glee, to swell in pride. My heart fluttered with it.

"You are one in a million," he whispered, hands clutching me tighter and I watched his eyes darken. "And you are mine," he said in a low voice.

Heat flushed through me at the words, but I nodded.

"Yes. I'm yours," I whispered, moving forward to brush my lips over his. "And you're mine."

He shuddered and nodded; I could feel the way his brows furrowed against my forehead.

"Always."

I smiled and slipped my hands past his shirt's collar to pull him against me. Our kiss was deep and I felt his urgency down the bond. I felt the way he needed me. As we kissed, and he grappled for my body, I marveled at how only minutes ago I'd been convinced I'd scared him away. That he'd hate me for what I was and what I could do.

He pulled away from me and began to kneel.

I tightened my grip on him.

"No," I whispered, and he looked up at me.

I knew what he'd been about to do, and I loved that, but now all I could focus on was how badly I needed to feel him inside of me and know that nothing could ever come between us. Not his fears, or mine.

"Not this time," I said softly, "I want you now."

His jaw hardened and his eyes melted into a deeper obsidian. He stood without a word as we began undressing each other. He unclasped my holsters as I did the same to his. The sounds of our weapons thumping onto the floor was the only noise besides our heavy breaths and frantic kisses.

He dipped as the last piece of cloth separating us hit the floor, his lips falling over my neck as his hands dropped to my thighs, lifting me as I wrapped them around him. I wrapped my arms around his neck and expected him to walk me to the bed, but instead I felt the chill of the wood door press into my back. I shivered.

"Not the bed?" I asked breathlessly.

"No time," he growled.

He was pushing inside of me by the end of his sentence, and a loud moan fell from my lips as my head fell back against the door.

His lips met my jaw, my neck, my shoulders.

"This is what I wanted to do that night of the wedding against the wall," he said, his voice gruff, between kisses.

I shivered. He was thrusting rhythmically, hard and deep and filling me completely.

"I hadn't known it at the time," I whispered back, "but this is what I wanted, too."

His hands tightened around me as he thrust harder, his breathing uneven as he moved.

"I don't know why the Goddess of Fate chose me for the blessing of receiving your love," he said, his thrusts accentuating his words. "But I will spend the rest of my existence praying to her in thanks."

I felt a single tear slip down my cheek for how wholly and completely in love he was with me, as I with him. I couldn't form a response, could only move forward and kiss him deeply and rock against him in time with the sway of the ship on the water, until we were both over the edge, and falling into it together.

Chapter Fifteen

Wyott

"I'm sorry again for all of the trouble," Evaline said to Saxon as she shook his hand goodbye.

He cocked a brow. "Why are you sorry? Pirates don't hit here often but it's not our first round with the bunch of low lives," he said, giving her a warm smile.

She smiled back and I saw that the gesture didn't reach her eyes. I knew she was afraid, that Maddox was afraid, because that attack was another abduction attempt from Vasier. Even so, I couldn't find it in myself to quell my anticipation as we said our goodbyes.

Evaline was safe. Maddox was safe.

We'd all be even safer in one minute when we deboarded this ship and stepped over the threshold of the invisible ward that protected Rominia from Vasi.

All I wanted to do was fucking sprint home.

I felt for the bond. While we'd been in Brassillion it had been quiet, just the dim rustle that indicated I was too far away to feel Cora.

But now, Gods, now it had come to life.

I wasn't sure if she could sense it, or if I only could because I was searching for it, but I could feel the way the bond ebbed and flowed with each of her breaths. I didn't know where she was, but I'd bet anything she was at the marina on the other side of the island.

Maddox paid Saxon for the trip, way more than we normally did but it was necessary considering the damage his ship and crew suffered.

We said a final goodbye and walked down the gangway. I felt a familiar pang of pain in my chest as we walked down the dock and past the exact spot where Maddox and I had knelt and cried after my father died. The wood of the dock had been replaced a few times over through the centuries, but the location never changed.

"Holy shit," we heard as we neared the edge of the dock. "Did I just pull the luckiest shift, or is that Maddox Vicor and Wyott Whitlock I see walking up?" Fredrik asked from the sand below the dock.

Clearly, he'd been working this shift lately because his normally fair skin was slightly tanned. Maddox laughed, and I saw the worry melt away with each step he took closer to the ward.

"It is your lucky day," he called out.

Fredrik pulled the gate of the dock back for us and let us through as his gaze fell to Evaline.

This was it; we were close. It was time. Gods, it was finally time.

Maddox stepped off the dock, and into the protective ward, and held a hand out for Evaline to do the same. I stood behind her, heart thundering in my chest and anticipation driving me to bounce in place as I waited for my turn to exit.

I took a steadying breath and searched for the bond again, ready to call down it.

"I can't believe we're finally here," Evaline started as she descended the stairs. "It's—"

Her words died in her throat, and mine did down the bond, as her boot hung in the air. She'd been about to step off the wooden steps, but she stopped.

"What the…?" she trailed off and my eyes widened.

Oh, fuck.

I flicked my gaze to Maddox and when he met it, I saw the worry that he'd just shed re-pile on his chest.

"There's no reason the wards should be holding her back," I insisted, and he nodded.

Fredrik moved into her line of sight, likely to look at her eyes, and his brows furrowed.

"Is there something wrong with the wards?" he mused.

"Let me see if I can pass," I said and gently slipped past Evaline.

I did so with ease, the ward didn't affect me.

I stepped beside Maddox and could hear the way his heart thundered in his own chest, for a far different reason than mine had.

"Maddox what's going on?" she asked.

We could all hear the fear lacing her words. And I knew Maddox was afraid, too. There was no reason she shouldn't be able to pass through the wards.

In frustration she kicked toward the ward again, and her foot hit the invisible wall with a thud. Tears sparkled in her eyes. As she looked to her mate, my brother looked to me with wide eyes.

I swallowed my longing to see Cora and stepped toward her.

"Do you feel anything? Like you did on the boat?" I asked her. My question was an attempt to gauge if she felt her magic rising like she had before. Perhaps there was something wrong with the ward, and it was blocking her because her magic was confusing it.

That shouldn't happen, the ward was created by a Sorcerer so it definitely shouldn't block one from entering. It should only block the being whose blood was used to create it; our Sorcerer used Vasi blood to create this ward.

Evaline shook her head. "Yes, but not any more than before. It's just constant."

I heard Maddox hold his breath, saw the way his hand fisted at his side, and dodged Fredrik's confused look.

Maddox stepped toward her and reached for her again. I knew he was prepared to stay here with her until we found a solution, and I was preparing to run for Ankin when she reached for him, too, and her hand slipped past the ward and landed in his.

The two Kova and I exchanged looks.

"Step forward," I instructed.

She did, without issue.

When her boots hit the sand, I saw her look up at Maddox, and knew they were communicating down the bond. But Gods, I was already clapping a hand on Fredrik's back and bidding him goodbye.

They did the same and we lumbered up the slight hill of the beach before making it past the two pillars that stood high above the entrance to Rominia.

Evaline gasped as she saw the island for the first time. From here you could see businesses lining the street ahead until it wound out of view. Mt. Rominia stretched toward the clouds, and I could see some of the homes that led up it. And to the far right, up on a hill of its own, the First's Estate.

I knew Evaline was taking it all in, but all I could focus on was the direction of my home.

Now. Now it was time. After months and months away from home, away from *her*, I was here.

Cora, I called down the bond.

Her response was immediate. The bond shook to life as she reached for me, and I heard her tear-filled voice. *Wyott?*

My heart raced and my tears misted, and I nodded even though she wasn't here to see it.

Yes. Yes, darling, I'm home.

There was a tizzy down the bond, and I knew she was moving.

Where? she asked.

We just landed.

Maddox turned to me then.

I better not beat you home, she commanded and my lips pulled up into a grin.

"What the fuck are you still doing here?" Maddox asked.

I quirked a brow. I felt guilty running off after what had just happened, but Gods I wanted to be home with Cora more.

"For fuck's sake, Wyott. You don't need permission. Go," Maddox urged.

No sooner than the words left his mouth was I sprinting at absolute capacity down the street. I passed a group of friends as I ran and didn't miss their smart-ass comments when they saw me. They knew exactly where I was going.

"Steer clear of that house for a week," said Nash, with a laugh.

"Someone tell the neighbors, those poor bastards," Dean called.

"I'll get right on ordering a new bed for you!" Grant shouted after me.

I only laughed as I ran harder. I got to the house and tore up the stairs that led to our home to find that the door was already open.

I stepped inside and flung the door closed behind me and slid the lock into place.

"Cora?" I called. She had to have gotten here first.

She rushed from the bathroom. All I could see was the smile on her face as she launched herself into my arms.

She kissed me and wrapped her legs around my hips. I gripped her thighs, my heart flipping at the feel of her in my hands after so much time, and walked us toward our bedroom.

Gods, I've missed you, I croaked down the bond so that I wouldn't have to remove my lips from hers.

Her hands ripped at my clothes, at the holsters all over my chest. Her fingers that had spent so many hours tying and untying knots expertly ran over the fasteners as she undid them and pulled them from my torso. The leather clad weapons thudded onto the ground as we entered our room and Cora let out a gasp as I dropped her onto the bed.

Her chest heaved, and so did mine.

"Clothes," I said huskily as I tore the rest of my weapons off of me.

She moved quickly too and removed her shirt before her fingers moved to untie her pants. She shimmied them down her legs and I stepped to the edge of the bed and smiled down at her.

Gods, it had been too long.

When she was done, she laid on the bed, propped up onto her elbows, and waited for me.

"I beat you here," she said as she watched me pull my shirt over my head. "You lost."

"What's my punishment?" I asked, my voice deep with want.

She only leveled me with her sultry gaze and wide smile, and I knew exactly what she wanted.

I chuckled as I pulled the tie from my wrist and pulled the top of my hair up into a bun.

"Darling," I said, smoothing my hand down my beard. "I lost. Why am I the one getting the prize?"

Her bronze skin flushed, and her heart raced, as I got to my knees in front of the bed and pulled her hips to the edge of it.

CHAPTER SIXTEEN

Evaline

My heart thundered in my chest as we made our way toward what I assumed was Maddox's home. It sat atop an oceanside cliff, and while it wasn't as large as a castle, it was much bigger than a house. Its walls were made of pink and white granite and it loomed in the sky over us. There were columns holding up arched walkways all the way around the building, or at least as much as I could see from here. Even though it was smaller than Kembertus's castle, the intricacies carved into it put Kembertus to shame.

As we approached the steps that led to the main doors, I could hear the waves crashing over the rocks below.

I took a deep breath as we stepped onto the first stair. They were made to match the walls of the manor, and something swirling within their milky tone sparkled in the sunlight.

I made an effort to look up, to stand straight, instead of gawk. I didn't know when or where we'd first meet Maddox's parents, and I didn't want to look timid when I did.

I knew Maddox could sense my growing unease. He squeezed my hand tighter each time I took a deep breath and threw sidelong glances at me as if I couldn't see the movement.

It's going to be okay. They'll love you. There's nothing to fear.

His voice floated down the bond. I nodded back in return. It was all I could manage.

It was better that he thought I was simply nervous to meet his parents, or maybe fearful to be in a country full of Kova, than to know the truth.

That I knew who his father was and how he was created—how Maddox's entire species was created—that my mother had been the cause.

Yes. It was best he thought I was just a nervous new mate who was afraid to meet his Lord-like Kova father.

The large doors creaked in front of us and pulled me from my thoughts. Maddox greeted the guard as he opened the door for us.

"They don't know I'm here," Maddox said softly while shaking his hand. "Let's keep it that way."

The guard smiled, throwing a nod in my direction as well, even though we hadn't gotten a proper introduction.

Maddox guided me through the doors that stretched several feet above our heads. They closed behind us, and my mouth dropped open as I turned to look at the entryway. Two wings fanned out on my left and right with massive sitting rooms on each side. Even from here, I could see that each had multiple hallways attached to them.

Another granite staircase rose up before us, this one a spiral. It wasn't a traditional spiral staircase that wound at sharp angles but much larger, stretching several paces wide, and winding in thick curls above our heads before the ceiling above us cut off my vision.

Maddox kissed my temple.

I'll show you around later, but for now I want to surprise my parents before they find out we're here.

I nodded and followed him toward the right wing. We walked past the sitting room and into a maze of ornate hallways. I tried to look at the artwork that littered the walls, craning my neck to peer behind as we passed them, but Maddox was walking too quickly.

He was excited. He'd missed his family and I'm sure his home while he was gone. I tried to be excited for him, but a swell of sorrow sprouted in my chest. I knew what it felt like to be away from home. Though, the sense of home I'd known had been gone for over two years.

But Maddox's homecoming was special. Based on how highly both Maddox and Wyott regarded mating, I knew it was important to Kova. And now, I knew Maddox was most excited to show his parents that he finally found his mate. I could tell by the thrum of energy that ran down the bond from him. His heart was racing, I realized, and my lips tugged into a smile at that.

It was sweet to know that he was this excited for a familial reunion.

He led me down another hallway and we stopped in front of a large door, this one wooden and ornate, and Maddox's hand paused just before he reached the handle. He turned to me.

I'm going to walk in ahead of you, just so he isn't alarmed by seeing a stranger.

I just gave him a small smile and nodded. He dropped my hand and turned the knob on the door before cracking it open.

I heard a voice call on the other side.

"Lauden, is that you?" A shuffle of papers. "We may have to push our meeting back."

Maddox walked in ahead of me so I was out of sight behind him.

I heard a chuckle as the door clicked shut behind us.

"Maddox, you're home," a masculine voice said from across the room.

From the little bit of the room I could see I could tell this must be an office or a library. The walls on two sides were covered in floor to ceiling bookcases.

I could smell the salt of the sea and feel a slight breeze, and knew a window of some sort must be open straight ahead.

"I am," Maddox responded, moving to sidestep. He put out an arm in a gesture of reveal. "And I brought—"

I didn't have time to take in the room, or even really see past Maddox, because as soon as his body cleared mine I felt a whoosh of air, before my face was picked up in two gentle hands, thumbs swiping over my cheeks.

Time seemed to slow then as I looked up into the gray, sad eyes of a man who looked like he'd just seen a memory. Tears welled behind his lashes, and I knew what name would come out of his lips before it did.

"Alannah."

I felt the rush of confusion that struck down the bond before Maddox was between us, pushing his father away from me.

"What the fuck are you doing?" he shouted.

Kovarrin stood back a few feet and I watched his glazed eyes take me in. My hair, my eyes, down the rest of my body before Maddox cleared his throat.

"I'll ask again—what the fuck?"

His father squeezed his eyes shut and shook his head before looking back toward us.

"I'm sorry. You look a lot like someone I used to know," he muttered. "A very long time ago."

I nodded but the uneasy feeling didn't fade. I didn't know whether to laugh or cry. My stomach knotted as Maddox looked at me, an eyebrow raising.

Are you okay?

I smiled at him. *Yes. It's fine. Just a misunderstanding.*

He nodded and turned back to his father, whose gaze moved between Maddox and I, taking in the moment of silence that had just passed between us, before he breathed.

"You're mates." A glimmer of disbelief flashed in his eyes as he said the words.

Maddox's hand found the small of my back and the warm weight of it grounded me.

"Yes," he said sternly. "That's what I was trying to tell you."

In mere seconds, a lifetime of questions flashed through Kovarrin's eyes. The ones I'd watched close blue and open steel gray.

"This is Evaline," Maddox said. He dropped his hand down to clasp around mine. "My mate."

Kovarrin schooled his features into a mask of feigned cheer. "That's amazing," he said, smiling, and moved forward to hug Maddox. "I'm so happy you're home, and even happier you've finally found your mate."

I watched as Maddox visibly relaxed into his father's embrace and released the tension that had built there in these last few very awkward moments.

"Thank you," he said when they pulled apart.

Then his father turned to me. He looked just like I remembered from the memory my mother showed me.

There was no doubting that they were blood. They had the same strong jaws, the same narrow temples. Even the shape of their eyes was the same. The only marked differences were that Maddox was taller and wider than his father, Maddox's hair was black while his father's was light brown, and Maddox's skin was darker.

"I'm sincerely sorry for my outburst when you walked in," Kovarrin said, taking a small bow. "I'm Kovarrin Vicor. First Kova and Keeper of Rominia."

He was trying so hard to be casual, but I could sense the misery whirling inside of him. Maddox didn't seem to notice that anything was wrong anymore, but I could tell that his father was reeling inside. As if we had some sort of unspoken connection, linking us together, despite never having met.

We probably did.

I curtsied and when my eyes met his again I saw they'd been tracking every movement.

"It's a pleasure to meet you, my..." I realized too late I didn't know the formal way to address him.

He gave me a small smile and waved his hand.

"Just call me Kovarrin."

He turned to walk back toward his desk and Maddox and I moved to sit in the two stuffed chairs that sat before it.

I got my first good look at the room and noticed I'd been right about a window being open—except it wasn't a window, but a floor to ceiling opening in the room that led out to a balcony overlooking the whole of Rominia. The view was breathtaking.

Maddox took my hand in the space between the chairs and as his father spoke I watched Kovarrin's eyes glaze for a moment and knew he was communicating with Maddox's mother.

Maddox must've noticed too because he asked where she was.

"She was in the garden but I've just told her a surprise is waiting for her." He shrugged. "If we know anything about her predilection for gifts, she should be at the door any—"

He was cut off by the turning of the knob.

She strode in, her eyes first aimed for Kovarrin but quickly diverted to Maddox. A look of sheer happiness fell over her face and she let out a sob.

"My Maddox," she choked out as he stood and swooped her into a deep hug. Her eyes were squeezed shut as she rested her chin against his shoulder. She opened her mouth to speak but then her eyes popped open, as if she realized there was a fourth heartbeat in the room, and her eyes slid to mine.

She pulled away from Maddox and I smiled at her.

Her eyes were wide, hopeful I realized, as her hands outstretched toward me.

"Is this…?" she trailed off, a smile widening on her face.

I saw the shine of true pride in Maddox's eyes and the tears that glistened there as he smiled.

"Yes."

Another sob of joy dropped from her lips as she pulled me into a hug. I wrapped my arms around her torso and inhaled the smell of jasmine and lavender that her raven hair seemed to be infused with. I didn't realize that there were also tears in my eyes until I looked over her shoulder at Maddox.

She finally pulled away and squeezed my hands as she spoke. "We have been waiting a very long time for you."

Her light gray eyes gleamed and her features were soft, kind. She had Maddox's thick lips and a similar bump in the bridge of her nose. Her skin was brown, darker than Maddox's, and her cheeks flushed as she gave a small, amazed, laugh.

Maddox came forward then and stood beside me. He introduced me to her, as he did his father, and when he said the word mate her smile somehow widened even further.

She kept one hand still clutching mine and pulled the other to her chest. "I'm Alairasa Vicor. Wife of the First and Keeper of Rominia."

I smiled and squeezed her hand. "It's a pleasure to meet you, Alairasa."

She shook her head and her hair jostled at the movement. She waved a hand. "Please, call me Rasa."

She released a deep breath and let go of my hand before clapping hers in front of her.

"I need to know absolutely everything. How you met." Her eyes flicked to Maddox then back to me. "How you knew. When you knew. All of it."

Before either of us could respond, she looked around and raised a brow. "Where's Wyott?"

Kovarrin laughed behind us and all three of us jumped as if we'd forgotten he was there.

"He's been away from his mate for months, where do you think he is?"

Rasa nodded in understanding and started shepherding Maddox and I from the room.

"We need to go get some tea and discuss. Or maybe wine." She linked her arm with mine as we walked back into the hallway. "Do you like wine, Evaline?"

I nodded and she immediately launched into another question.

"Do you like being called Evaline, or is there a nickname you prefer? It's a beautiful name, very unique, and it suits you."

I smiled. "Evaline is fine, thank you."

She nodded. I noticed Maddox fall into step behind me silently, and noted his father wasn't behind us.

Rasa seemed to notice then too. She stopped and turned toward the open door we'd just come from.

"Kovarrin!"

"Yes, my love, I'm coming," we heard from the room, then a squeak of a chair against granite flooring.

I felt sorry for him, he'd just needed a moment to collect himself. A pit of worry filled my gut. I knew I needed to talk to him at some point, preferably alone. I needed to learn more about what happened between he and my mother, and find out more about that night, before I told Maddox.

But for now I let myself shove the worry away and followed Rasa's lead to a sitting room as she told me about Maddox as a child.

Chapter Seventeen

Maddox

We told my parents how we'd met. About how I'd caught Evaline trying to pickpocket me. How she threatened me. How she'd known what I was.

My mother would interject to comment every once in a while.

To the fact that women weren't allowed to own weapons in Kembertus; "I hate how the Kromean Kingdoms treat their women," she sneered.

To Evaline's attempted pickpocket; "Oh, she'll fit in perfectly with our family."

To the knowledge that Evaline knew what Kova were; shock, from both my mother and my father. My mother wondered where Evaline had learned the information, but my father paled.

I didn't know why. Perhaps because he didn't want humans knowing about Kova and what our weaknesses were but I watched as he threw a worried glance at Evaline and how she swallowed hard.

I cleared my throat at the odd interaction but realized something important we'd forgotten to mention.

"Evaline's full name is Evaline Manor." Both of my parent's eyes widened in surprise.

"Wallace's daughter?" My mother asked, leaning forward in her seat.

My father just watched Evaline intently as she nodded. "Yes."

My mother's face dropped as she reached a hand out to Evaline. I gave a quick shake of my head, too fast for Evaline to see. Evaline despised pity, and I knew my mother understood when she pursed her lips and patted Evaline's hand.

"We're so sorry for your loss, dear."

Evaline nodded and gave thanks.

My father continued watching her, and it was beginning to get to me, especially after that odd first meeting, but I tried to ignore it.

The rest of the conversation flowed effortlessly. We told them about the Spring Solstice Ball, about Bassel, about Gabriehl.

It was my father who diverted the conversation then, away from our travels and to Evaline alone.

"And where's your mother?" he asked quietly.

Evaline straightened, and I noted she wouldn't meet his eyes. She was looking down at her wine glass.

"Of course, you know my father died two years ago."

My mother nodded with a reassuring smile, her brown skin crinkling around her eyes.

Evaline's voice wavered slightly as she spoke. "He's the one who taught me to fight and told me about Kova and the Vasi. He wanted me to be able to protect myself, and knowing what non-human beings were in the world would keep me safe."

My mother nodded and gave Evaline a warm smile. "And it's a good thing he did. Your skills made sure you arrived here safely, but now you're with us, you're a part of our family and we will protect you. You'll never have to be concerned about your safety again."

I thanked the Gods for my mother, and not for the first time.

Evaline smiled at her and I saw a sheen in her eyes. "Thank you."

The words had barely left Evaline's mouth before my father was interjecting. "And your mother?" he asked again. His voice was tight, impatient.

My brows furrowed and I looked at Evaline again. I wasn't sure if my father was taken aback by my return with my mate, or angry with me for some reason, but I didn't want to ruin Evaline's welcome by confronting him about his behavior now.

Evaline set her jaw and turned to him. Her eyes were soft and her tone even, but her hands shook as they held her glass. Worry tightened in my chest. I didn't like seeing her in pain, or even uncomfortable. And right now, it appeared to be both. I couldn't tell if she didn't want to mention what happened to her mother, or if she was still reeling from her interaction with her mother last week after we'd saved her.

"She died giving birth to me."

My mother gasped before she reached for Evaline's hand again. But I watched my father, who sat still as stone and let the words sink in. Watched the pain that flashed in his eyes for my mate for only a moment.

Finally, he cleared his throat. "How?"

My mother and I snapped our heads toward him at the same time. "Kovarrin. She just told you, drop it."

Evaline and my father shared a look, and then she met my gaze.

Are you going to tell them? she asked down the bond.

I nodded, setting my jaw and scooting my seat closer to hers, sliding my hand over her knee.

"There is something else," I started, and my father's head cocked to look at me.

"What is it?" My mother asked.

I looked to Evaline one last time to make sure she wanted to share this so soon, and she nodded.

"Evaline is a Sorceress."

My father stiffened. "Is that so?"

"The most powerful one I've ever seen," I explained that she wielded Air, Terra, and Water; how I'd watched her bend a tree at her will and manipulate massive waves to suspend in air.

My mother's eyes widened. "How can you wield more than one element?" she asked, looking to Evaline.

"I don't know." My mate sighed. "I didn't know I possessed magic until recently. My father raised me as a normal human."

"Did he know?" my father asked.

She met his intense gaze. "Yes."

I stiffened beside her. She'd never shared that with me, and she must've noticed because she quickly clarified. "Or I have a feeling he did, at least. I'm not sure."

"If your father wasn't a Sorcerer, then it might've been your mother. It's passed down through families," my mother said.

"Yes, she was a Sorceress."

I leaned forward in my seat. "She needs training," I interjected. "Where's Ankin? We need to get her started with him right away."

My mother blanched but it was my father who spoke. "He passed a couple months ago."

Surprise had my eyes widening. "What?" I asked, looking between the two of them. "How?"

My father shrugged. "He was an old man. Your mother found him in his study, hunched over some books. Likely a heart attack of some sort."

I pursed my lips and nodded. It made sense, but I couldn't help the pang of loss I felt for my friend. Ankin had come to Rominia when he was a young man, and we'd watched him grow old. I supposed my father was right—Ankin was elderly and likely died of natural causes. But a part of me couldn't get past the surprise of his death.

"But soon after you left for Brassillion last year, Ankin's grandson, Lauden, came to Rominia. He's a Sorcerer, too," my father said. "I approached the other Sorcerers here to see if they wanted Ankin's position, but they all declined." He shrugged. "So Lauden took over for him."

My brow cocked. "I didn't even know Ankin had children."

My father chuckled. "Neither did he, until Lauden got here."

My brows shot upward.

My father sighed and explained. "Before he came to Rominia, he'd been in a relationship. It wasn't until after they'd broken up, and he settled here, that she discovered she was pregnant. She didn't know where to find him but once her grandchild was found to be a Sorcerer they knew it must've come from Ankin. Eventually Lauden sought him out."

My mother gave a sad smile. "It was all terribly tragic," she said, her voice soft. "For family to be united just before Mortitheos took Ankin."

"At least they got to spend time together beforehand," Evaline offered.

My mother nodded. "Definitely, they grew very close those months."

I took a deep breath as I sorted through all this new information, then turned to Evaline.

"Sometime this week we'll make an introduction so you can begin training."

She nodded but my mother squealed and stood.

"No! Not sometime this week, this weekend!" she exclaimed and turned to my father. "We have to throw a Ball to welcome Maddox and Wyott home, and to introduce Evaline." She took Eva's hand in hers, pulling her to stand and walking her out of the room. My father and I hurried after them as she led Evaline through the halls.

I could only chuckle at the thought of Evaline attending this Ball after the distaste she showed for them in Kembertus.

My mother glanced back at me. "What is so funny?"

I just gave a slight shake of my head as we followed them. "Evaline isn't one for Balls."

Evaline shot me a look as my mother turned to her. "Well, we don't have to! Instead we can—"

But Evaline interrupted her.

"No, I'd love to. In Kembertus I didn't like going to the parties because my guardians just tried to marry me off at each of them." Then she cast her eyes to mine. "But I'd love to meet the people of Rominia."

I couldn't help the smile that drew on my face as the appreciation I had for her—for her words—swelled in my chest.

My mother was quick to agree. "Perfect! We'll start first thing tomorrow! I will make the announcement to the kingdom, but in just a few short days we will host the Ball to welcome you all back. We can have it out here on the patio," she said before she led us all through the glass doors out into the mid-day light.

Tall pillars stood to frame the event area just off the patio, similar to what Evaline's aunt and uncle's castle had.

"The only major change since you left is that the Terra Sorcerers discovered that Mt. Rominia is nearing eruption," my father addressed me.

All the Sorcerers who lived here kept watch over any natural disasters that might befall our home and gave us ample warning if they could. The mountain hadn't budged in years, but we still preferred to have some time to prepare.

He continued to talk about various small things that had occurred, such as promotions in the guard and Lauden's assistance with the wards.

My mother was still prattling on about how she couldn't wait to tell Cora about the Ball, and for that matter that she couldn't wait until Evaline met Cora. When she started in on all the different types of flowers they'd need for the party, I noticed the fatigue in Evaline's eyes, and I had to interrupt and pull my mate away from my mother.

I knew she was excited to meet my mate, Gods she'd waited so long for this, too, but I needed to get Evaline some rest. After the travel, and using her magic to save us all on that pirate ship, I couldn't imagine how tired she must be.

"Do you want the tour now, or to go straight to our bedroom?" I asked softly in her ear as we turned the corner down the hall from where we'd left my parents at the patio.

"I just want to spend some time alone with you," she breathed, and my heart leaped in my chest. "We haven't gotten to spend much time together, just the two of us."

I smiled and nodded. "That sounds perfect."

We crossed back to the main hall and when Evaline went to cross to the left wing, I veered her toward the grand stairs that wound up through our home.

She looked up, her brows furrowed. "I thought they said you had your own wing?"

I smiled. "I do, but the bedroom is on the second floor of it."

I stopped on the first landing and pulled her down the hall to the double doors, where our suite stood.

My parents said they'd maintained it for me and when Evaline stepped in she gasped. It was far larger than her bedroom in her guardian's castle.

The doors opened to face a grand fireplace, where I had too much fun as a boy lighting things on fire. A set of sofas and a chaise stood in front of it, and beyond the hearth was a dining table with six chairs. On the wall behind were tall windows that stretched the height of the room.

Evaline snickered as she turned to the wall to her right and found my bookshelves, stretching floor to ceiling and just as wide.

She shook her head and turned to me. "How many of these are romance books?"

I laughed and swiped my hand through my hair. "The son of a ruler's answer should probably be that most of these books are on battle strategy and the histories of the world." He shrugged. "But an honest answer would be that over half of them are love stories."

She smiled up at me and stretched to kiss me, before turning to the doorless entry that parted the bookshelves and led to the bedroom. My large four poster bed stood there, propped up against the back wall. The duvet was a new one; white, with soft gray patterns running through it, and the usual delicate, white canopy that hung overhead. The tails of each side of it were looped around each post.

She looked to the left, where the wall was made up of multiple tall and narrow windows, that arched at the top, and stretched the height of the wall. She scanned the armoire and nightstands, then moved to the two doors on the right before she walked into the closet.

My clothes hung on the right and she ran her hand over the clothing. She smiled as she turned and saw that there was an empty rack, ready for her clothes to be added. She finally turned to me, where I stood with my shoulder propped against the doorway.

"What?" she asked with a chuckle.

I smiled and shook my head. "Nothing. I've just pictured being here with you a thousand times, I'm happy that it's finally happened."

She strode to me and ran her hands up my chest, looping them around my neck. I suppressed the shudder that always lit through me at her touch.

"Thank you for bringing me here," she said softly.

My arms circled her waist, and I pulled her closer. "Thank you for coming." Then my smile grew. "You haven't even seen the best part yet." I bent and swept her up into my arms, and she squealed as I walked us into the bathroom.

She giggled but as soon as she turned to see it, she gasped. "Gods."

On the wall where the doorway opened there were counters with two sinks, and mirrors that hung above them. Then, straight ahead and exactly where her eyes fell, was the large bathtub. It was large enough to easily hold Evaline and I, and angled toward the left wall where those same narrow windows stood displaying the view out over the Madierian. While she settled in, I prepared her a bath. I poked my head into the sitting room where she stood looking over all the book spines.

"It's all warmed up for you," I said.

She smiled and my heart did a flip. "You mean for us?"

I feigned a bow and straightened. "You know I only live to serve."

We soaked in the tub in silence for a while. I ran the lavender scented bar of soap over her skin and she tried to detangle her hair from the journey over the water.

She laid back against me, and we watched the waves that rippled toward the shore beyond the windows.

"What you did on the Strait was incredible," I whispered, and felt her shudder softly. "We'll get you setup with the new Sorcerer soon."

She nodded and tilted her head back against my chest to look up at me. "I liked your mother."

I smiled and kissed her forehead. "She liked you too. You've exceeded all of our expectations."

She smiled and straightened to look at the windows again. But the mention of my mother brought on the images of my father and his odd reaction to Evaline.

"I'm sorry my father had such a strange reaction to you," I said, my voice low.

She shook her head. "Don't be sorry, it was just a misunderstanding."

Sunlight filtered in through the linen curtains I'd pulled over the windows. Even if the sun wasn't shining directly into the room, the way the rays bounced off the ocean lit up the bedroom nearly as bright as being outside in the full stream of sun.

I smiled before I even opened my eyes, because I could feel Evaline snuggled up against me. A satisfied moan rumbled through my chest as I curled an arm around her to pull her closer to me and dropped my other hand to wrap around her thigh that was currently bare and hiked up to lay across my pelvis.

Though her eyes were still closed, I could hear her heart rate start to pick up, and I knew she would be exiting sleep soon. Evaline's hair was tossed behind her, falling partially on her own pillow that she'd left behind in favor for my chest, and partially down her back.

Laying here with her, with the sound of the tide hitting the sand outside and the stillness of morning lingering in the room, I was in utter bliss.

How many times had I laid in this exact spot, head buried in a romance novel, heart aching for my own? How many times had I begged

Rominiava to lead me to my mate? How many times had I worried that I'd never find her?

And now she was here, safe, and we'd never have to put her in harm's way again. We could travel the continent if she chose, with enough guards to withstand any more attacks orchestrated by Vasier or stay here and explore the island.

She stirred against me and flattened her hand on my chest, dragging it down a few inches, while she stretched her back and opened her eyes.

"Good morning," I said softly, watching her clear the sleep away with a few extra blinks.

She smiled up at me and leaned up onto one arm. "Good morning," she whispered.

I released her leg and moved my hand up to cup her cheek to drag my thumb across it. "I could get used to this."

Her smile grew as she leaned her head into my hand. "Me too."

My eyes dropped to her lips and I felt the ache for her deep in my abdomen. It had been there since the moment we met, and only intensified each time we touched, each time we fucked.

At that thought alone my cock pulsed and I flicked my eyes back up to hers to try to distract myself. But I could see the want churning in her eyes too, felt the way she pressed herself to me and watched her tongue dart out across her lip.

"Be careful, Goddess," I said quietly, running my hand down her shoulder, to her hip and back up her thigh. She was naked, we both were, so it didn't take much to get my thoughts running wild.

Her lips pulled up into a smirk as she leaned closer so that her face hovered just above mine. "Or what?" she asked, her voice laced in lust.

My hand tightened on her thigh and I pulled her against me.

"Or we'll never leave this room." My voice was rough. I wanted her, always. But I didn't know if she had the same appetite, and never wanted her to feel pressured.

She hummed. "That's not a threat."

Before I could retort, she dropped her lips onto mine and slipped her tongue through. I groaned and kissed her back just as desperately as one of my hands tangled into her hair, grasped the back of her neck and pulled her closer.

She ran her hand across my chest and it felt as if fire ignited everywhere she touched. I'd never get used to it. And I never wanted to.

Agile as a cat she slid on top of me until she was straddling my hips. I growled in approval and clasped my hands around her hips, biting her lip until she gasped. She pulled her lips from mine and planted her hands against my pillow on either side of my head.

I ground my jaw at the sight of her. It took everything in me not to flip us over and fuck her until we were so exhausted we had to sleep another eight hours. But I knew she liked to be in charge, knew she felt powerful riding me, so instead I watched.

"I love you," she whispered above me, catching her breath from our kiss.

I turned my head to place a kiss against her wrist. "I love you."

She stayed that way for a moment, eyes falling to my lips as I assumed she contemplated her next move, when I felt her moisture slide over me.

I tried to suppress a groan as I tensed my muscles, the ones in my chest rippling at the effort, to prohibit myself from taking over.

"You better decide what you'd like from me soon, sweetheart," I said, my breathing ragged. "Because the feel of your arousal grinding against me is going to drive me wild."

Her cheeks flushed but a wicked gleam lit her eye and she made a move to crawl away from me.

"What are you doing?" I asked, sitting up on my elbows, as she settled between my legs. I'd already accepted that she was sliding off the bed and starting her day, understood that I'd need to relieve myself, when her hand curled around my cock.

The air stuck in my throat as I watched her smile widen at my reaction before she lowered her lips over the tip and took me into her mouth.

"Fuck, Evaline," I groaned as she took all of me in, felt the back of her throat.

She hummed and I knew she reveled in the praise. Evaline slid me out, then in again, and I had to fall back against the bed, dig my head into the pillow, and ball my fists to keep from climaxing. Every second her mouth was sucking on my cock drove me closer to the edge and while I did want to, I didn't want to before her.

Her tongue slid over me as she moved, giving the slightest graze of her teeth. Enough to shoot a chill up my spine but not enough to hurt.

She started to move faster and I slid my hand down until it was tangled in the back of her hair, pulling her toward me.

"Come," I croaked and she sprang up, crawling back up toward me until she straddled my hips once more. I sat up to meet her and while she lined us up together, I raised her slightly by the waist until I could lower her over me.

She gasped as she sank down but as soon as our hips met, a deep groan ripped from her lips.

I wrapped my arms around her, helping her to bounce above me, and my lips found her throat. I kissed my way down it as she bobbed, and after a few thrusts I heard her agitated gasp.

"Bite," she demanded between breaths and I smiled against the smooth skin of her neck, felt the pulse of her vein beat underneath it, meet the rhythm she set with her hips.

"It's too soon," I said, even though I let my fangs slide out, skim along her skin.

She shivered at the feel and I felt her pussy clench around me.

Fuck. I couldn't even say the word out loud, had to growl it down the bond, because my jaw had dropped from the feel.

I pulled away enough to run my fangs along her lip before I pulled away completely.

I kept her gaze as I raised my fingers to my mouth, licked the pads of a few of them, and lowered them back down to circle her clit.

A choked sound left her lips and I grinned. I moved my fingers in time with her hips until we were both climaxing together and gasping each other's names.

We had to bathe after, which I didn't mind at all. I could live every day of my life in the presence of her naked body and never be satisfied.

As we dressed I remembered my mother would arrive soon to take Evaline shopping and had to swallow a grumble. I knew I couldn't keep her in here with me forever and that I'd have to share her time, but that didn't mean I wanted to.

I turned to Evaline as she walked to the counter to brush her hair.

"My mother will be here shortly."

She smiled up at me and smoothed her fingers over the wrinkles in my brow.

"We'll have plenty of alone time."

I dipped my head to kiss her forehead. "I know." My mother's knock on the door sounded then and I sighed. "I'll go keep her company until you're ready."

I moved for the door.

"What are you going to do today?" She asked as she gathered her hair in her hands.

I shrugged. "I've been gone a while, there's a few friends I should see."

She nodded and said nothing as I continued on my way out of the door. What I really wanted to do was confront my father, but I didn't want to cause any more tension than there already was. My mother was excited for this Ball, and I was starting to think Evaline was too.

Chapter Eighteen

Evaline

I stood at the counter of the bathroom in mine and Maddox's suite of the castle running my comb through my already tangling hair. I bent to the side and let my hair fall toward the ground as I brushed the ends of it and as I did, I looked to my barbed wire that sat on the counter and contemplated whether I was going to wear it.

I'd spent the last two years wearing it nearly every day. The thought of going without it should've made me happy. I was in a safe place now and that was exactly what I'd been yearning for, for the last two years. It'd made me feel protected when I didn't have a weapon, and even when I did.

The brush ran through my hair easily and I straightened.

My fingers pinched around the small space between silver thorns and I lifted it before meeting my own eyes in the mirror.

Why did I feel guilty for wanting to wear it?

But, of course, I knew the answer.

Maddox and Wyott had made Rominia seem so safe, and so far, I had no reason to believe otherwise. But it was still a new place, with hundreds—maybe thousands—of people that I didn't know, and there was a sense of unease that crawled through me at the thought of not wearing it.

"You never have to apologize for your feelings."

It was something my father used to tell me when I was young. When my body started going through changes and my emotions felt like they weren't in my control anymore.

I took a deep breath. Maddox would understand.

My fingers moved quickly through my hair as I pulled it back into a braid and wove the wire in. When I threw it over my shoulder after hiding the thorns, a bit of the worry in my chest dissipated.

When I made my way into the sitting room, I saw Maddox and his mother at the dining table with small cups of tea clutched in their hands. They both stood when I entered, and I saw that Rasa carried with her a few empty bags.

She raised them and smiled at me. "Ready to go shopping?"

I could've stayed locked in this room with Maddox for days, but knew it was best to get out and spend time with his family and to get to know more of the citizens of Rominia. It didn't hurt that the island was beautiful, too, so I nodded my head eagerly, excited to see more of the kingdom.

Rasa's smile grew as she turned to Maddox. "You should go down and see everyone at the training center. The young ones have missed you and I'm sure they'd love to hear all about your adventures." Her eyes shot to me. "Especially since you came home with a mate."

He bent down to kiss her on the cheek. "That's exactly what I'm doing today."

She preened and patted his shoulder before turning to me.

"I'll be outside whenever you're ready."

I turned to Maddox after the door clicked behind her and gave him a small smile. *I'm excited to go shopping,* I started down the bond, knowing that his mother would be able to hear us outside of the door. *But I'd be lying if I said I wasn't hoping you'd be the one who showed me around Rominia.*

His smile grew as he walked forward and slid his hands around my waist until they rested on the small of my back and pulled me to his chest.

"You don't have to use the bond if we're alone in a room, all the homes in Rominia are built with a layer of Rominium in the walls. A Kova can't hear past the barriers." He shrugged. "It gives far more privacy on an island where, otherwise, everyone would hear *everyone's* business."

I smiled and took a breath. "Oh, thank the Gods."

Maddox laughed. "And I have a few trips around the island planned for us, don't worry." He dipped his head to kiss me and must've only noticed the braid then, because when he straightened his eyes were moving away from it.

"I'm sorry," I rushed out, shaking my head. "I just, I don't know. I'm new here. It's all so new and—"

Maddox's hands tightened around my waist, and he shook his head.

"Never apologize for doing anything that makes you feel better, or safer," he said fiercely, his eyes trained on mine. "I understand. Just know that I'm working each and every day to make this a safer world for you." He shook his head. "We'll figure out what Vasier wants, I'll talk to my father about it. I'm sorry I didn't bring it up to him yesterday, I just didn't want to spend all night theorizing with him, and I know that's what it would've turned into."

I raised onto my toes and wrapped my arms around his neck. "It's okay. We have time."

Maddox smiled at that, and I knew it was because he had endless time.

I tried to hide my worry about that. I'd gotten better at it lately. Now, I could manipulate the bond easier. After I'd thrown it open when Maddox nearly drained Cradley, I understood how to open and close it. So now, when I became worried about our future, I closed the bond off so that he couldn't sense any of my unease.

I didn't know what was going to happen between Maddox and I in the long run. I didn't know if I was ageless like my mother was, and even if I wasn't, I wasn't sure if I wanted to make the change to become a Kova.

Maddox kissed me one last time and I turned to join Rasa in the hall when I felt his fingers flick the braid.

"I'm glad you kept it. You look cute in a braid."

Rasa had a bounce in her step as we left. I wasn't sure if she was excited to go shopping, for the Ball itself, or just to have Maddox and Wyott home.

The granite thudded beneath my padded boots, but beneath her thin loafers the granite clacked, meeting each step of her foot with a clap as we descended the stairs that led away from the estate.

"How did you sleep?" she asked, and I tried to will the blush that crept up my cheeks away as I thought back to the memory of Maddox and I in bed this morning.

"Very well, thank you. It's a wonder what a night in a bed will do for someone who's become so accustomed to sleeping outside, or not at all."

Rasa cast me a smile as we stepped away from the grand staircase and walked toward town. I could see it from here, it wasn't far at all, and I could hear the bustling of the carriages and Kova chattering.

"I remember when I traveled here," she started as she looped her hand in my arm and led me from the road that led to the estate, toward the shops. "I'd been traveling so far on a ship that it seemed like ages had gone by before I saw the rise of the island from the water, and something inside of me changed. Before I ever saw Kovarrin or discovered we were mates, I knew the moment I stepped on these shores that this was the home I'd searched for my whole life. I hope you're able to feel the same way about Rominia someday."

I smiled and willed my tears not to fall. She was so kind, so welcoming, so unlike Therese.

"I hope so, too." I swallowed. "The last two years have been so hard. There've been so many changes, and now I've grown so much even since we left Kembertus. It's hard to keep up with all the emotional, magical, and societal changes, when they're all happening at once."

Her arm squeezed around me as she veered us down the main road. I heard the playful shriek of a child nearby before a young boy and girl, likely siblings, darted across our path.

"We aren't a species that were meant to stay stagnant," she said but seemed to immediately catch her mistake before qualifying. "Kova, Sorceresses, and mortals alike." I nodded. "We're meant to change, to evolve. Every page in the story of our lives shapes us into the person we were meant to become. And sometimes the person we were meant to become has just been hiding away inside of us, waiting to be released. It's okay to hesitate and to be afraid, but it's important to know that change is a natural part of life."

I smiled at her but didn't speak, couldn't, past the lump in my throat.

Her head turned to the bakery as we approached, and a moment later the scent hit me, too. The smell of sugar and butter coasted through the air until it overwhelmed my senses and my stomach growled.

"Oh, Gods. Please tell me you ate breakfast," she said and tugged me toward the bakery.

"I forgot to," I said as I recalled the breakfast tray that I left on the table in our suite.

"Then I guess it's the perfect time for you to meet Rominia's best baker."

The bell above the door chimed as we entered, and a short, stout man approached from the back. His face went alight when he saw Rasa.

"Good morning, Rasa," he started in a deep voice, but then his eyes drifted to me and flashed with understanding. "Is this who I think it is?"

Gods did everyone in Rominia know about me already?

Rasa slipped her arm from mine and placed her hand on my back.

"This is Evaline Manor, Maddox's mate." She turned to him. "She needs to eat breakfast, and I'd like to discuss some of the desserts I'd like at the celebration."

He shook my hand and introduced himself as Gavin, his gray eyes sparkling from the sunlight streaming in through the front windows.

"What can I get for you, Miss Manor?"

I smiled at him as my eyes moved over the many treats that resided on the shelves behind him before picking a blueberry muffin. I ate at one of the small tables in the establishment while he and Rasa debated how many dessert options should be available at the party.

She wanted them to be finger-sized and easy to eat. "I want people to mingle and not be tied to a table. It's been so long since we had a proper celebration."

After I finished eating, I stood aside while she ordered an assortment of pastries.

Gavin called his goodbyes from the counter as we left, but his hand was already scribbling over a piece of paper, for what I assumed was his new task list, to prepare for the Ball that was in only a few days.

When we left she ushered us to the florist where she picked out plenty of wisteria to hang around the ballroom and peonies to fill all of the vases. Then, finally, we landed in our last store of the day—the boutique.

"Feel free to look around, Evaline, I'm going to get fitted for my dress and then we can find yours." Her voice was so cheery it made me smile.

I looked at all of the racks that lined the walls of the room and the small stage for the client to have their dress hemmed in the center.

My hands fell over the fabrics that hung off the racks, and I noticed that I didn't feel the same dread I did when I was forced to shop with my aunt.

Therese wanted to shape me into the model of a daughter that she thought she wanted; Rasa simply showed me my options.

I started pulling clothes from the wall and was met with an immediate pang of sorrow. Being here, shopping anywhere else besides Aurora's, made me miss her so viscerally I felt the ache deep in my chest. I missed her and Jacqueline and realized that this would be the first Ball in a while that I wouldn't get to hide away with them.

I tried to shove away the thought, but it was difficult. I worried for them and couldn't wait until they arrived in Neomaeros. Once they were there, once they were safe, perhaps Maddox and I could go see them. Perhaps he could take away their compulsion, let them remember me.

"Evaline, have you found any that you like yet?" Rasa called from the back room, where she was trying on her dress.

"Not yet," I called back, but, in truth, I had barely even begun looking yet.

At a rack near the stage for hemming I grabbed a hanger that's garment was a stark black and when I pulled it out saw that it was not a dress at all but an outfit that included both a top and flowing pants. I'd never seen any woman wear pants to a formal event, but felt the warmth in my chest that here, it didn't matter. It didn't matter what you chose to wear, or how you did your hair, or if you looked appealing enough for a potential courtship. Here, I didn't have to listen to Therese or appease her.

"Pardon me," a woman said behind me. "I think that might be mine."

I turned toward the voice to see a beautiful woman and was surprised to see her sage green eyes. A human?

She looked down at the hanger in my hand expectantly.

Rasa and who I presumed to be the store's owner came out from her fitting room.

"Oh, I'm so sorry," the woman said as Rasa shopped the store. "I forgot to put those clothes in the back." She waved a hand toward the woman beside me now. "That is Sage's set, but if you like it, I could make you a similar one."

Sage straightened beside me, and I got the distinct feeling that she did *not* want me to wear the same outfit as her.

I just shook my head and smiled. "It's no problem, and that's okay. It is beautiful, but it'd be far too hot for me to wear to the Ball."

I turned to Sage and handed it off to her. "I'm sorry about the mix-up."

She waved a hand. "Don't worry about it," she said, but there was a tightness to her lips. Sage shuffled the items in her arms over to her left side and extended her right hand to shake. "I'm Sage, it's nice to meet you."

I shook her hand and smiled. "I was just thinking that your eyes are sage colored."

A minor look of annoyance flashed across her face, but she hid it away just as quickly. "Yes, that's why my father chose the name."

I nodded, and she continued to look at me expectantly.

"Oh, I'm sorry," I said, jolting at the realization. "I'm Evaline. It's nice to meet you, too."

She nodded politely and the movement jostled some of her hairs into her face. She had fair skin, and it appeared only paler against her hair. It was so raven black that when the sunlight streaming through the windows caught it just right it had an emerald sheen.

Rasa joined us then with an armful of clothes.

"Evaline, Sage is the partner of Lauden, the Arch Sorcerer we were telling you about yesterday."

My brows raised as I looked back to Sage.

"Oh, I'm sorry for yours and Lauden's loss," I said, referring to Ankin.

Sage's eyes narrowed slightly but she waved a hand in dismissal. "Thank you, but truly not necessary. Ankin had a long, happy life." Then she looked between Rasa and me. "And Lauden got to have a great few months with him before he passed." Then she raised the clothes in her arms. "I'm going to get going, but it was a pleasure meeting you, Evaline."

Rasa bid her goodbye and started showing me different outfits as Sage purchased her garments and headed out the door.

I couldn't take my eyes off her, though. There was something about her, something darker, that I couldn't place my finger on.

The bell above the door chimed as Sage left, and as she walked past the windows at the front of the store, I watched as her shoulders sagged and her face fell before she walked out of view.

My heart sank at the move, because I knew it well. I'd worn a mask of my own once.

"And don't forget that we're here to shop for an entirely new wardrobe, too." My attention drew back to Rasa as I tried to catch up with what she'd been saying while I watched Sage off. "While the pants might be too warm for the Ball, this is the warmest time of year, in the winter it'll cool a bit." She ran her hands over a few of the dresses she'd pulled. They were far shorter than any of the floor length gowns I'd ever seen and been used to wearing. "In the summer the shorter dresses are far more popular, if only for the heat."

My eyes widened at them. "I've never seen anyone wear a dress this length."

She laughed beside me. "The kingdoms in Brassillion have more modest fashion." She shrugged. "Even the Madierian Kingdoms."

We spent another hour in the boutique, and eventually Rasa and I couldn't carry all the clothes she insisted I buy. If my gaze lingered a fraction of a second too long on an item, she grabbed it from the rack, convinced I secretly wanted it.

I did.

Even though I found several outfits I loved, many trousers and skirts and tops, I still hadn't found a dress I wanted for the Ball.

At least, until Rasa pulled a hanger from the rack simply because it was a soft pink that she said would suit my skin tone.

As soon as I saw it, I fell in love.

Shortly after, we hauled all of the bags we could carry back to the estate and Rasa assured me she'd send Maddox to get the rest.

As we trudged up the steps to the mansion, I turned to her.

"Rasa, and I don't mean this to sound disrespectful at all, I'm just curious—couldn't you have carried the rest of the bags? You're Kova, right?" I asked.

She turned to me with a wide smile. Her eyes were gray like the others, but perhaps she wasn't as strong, or was far older than the rest and had lost some strength?

She laughed and shook her head. "Of course I could carry them, my dear." She shrugged. "But my arms are short and I only have room for so many bags to loop around them. Why make myself uncomfortable when we can send Maddox?" She finished, bumping her shoulder with mine.

When we got back to the mansion Rasa excused herself and walked toward hers and Kovarrin's wing of the house. I went to mine and Maddox's suite and dropped the bags onto the chaise.

"Maddox?" I called, even though I was sure he wasn't here.

The bond sung when he was near, and when he wasn't, there was a tug on my chest that urged me to find him.

When he didn't answer I turned toward the door. I wanted to speak with Kovarrin, and I wasn't sure how many opportunities we'd have to do so without Maddox around. I desperately wanted Maddox to know the truth, and that would only happen if Kovarrin told him.

I'm sure the First wanted to gauge how much I knew, but I had to do the same. Did he know how he, and Vasier, were created? That it wasn't some gift from the Gods but that their immortality—their abilities—were born from desperation, from grief?

I made for the door, but my steps faltered just before I reached it, and I felt the muscles within them quiver. I tried to swallow to dampen my dry throat, but it was no use, and I wiped my clammy hands over my trouser covered thighs and stepped forward with a huff.

"You have to get it over with eventually," I murmured to myself.

I reached for the knob and made my way to Kovarrin's study. My heart stuttered in my chest, and I knew the cause. I was nervous to talk to Kovarrin, mostly because I was afraid that he'd have a hostile reaction. But more than that, I knew he'd have information about my mother, and I didn't know what to anticipate.

I'd spent so much of my life only hearing about how kind and beautiful she was, how much she loved me before I was born, before she died. My father loved her, and it made sense that he only had sweet things to say about her. But Kovarrin knew her centuries before my father did. What did he know about my mother? Who was she before she created two entire species?

And considering that I was a Sorceress too, that I was the daughter of a Sorceress powerful enough to create a new type of being, I was afraid of what that meant for me. For my abilities, and for my future.

My boots thudded softly against the ground as I made my way down the stairs and to the other side of the mansion, I continued through the same sitting room that Maddox had taken me through when we first arrived until I was standing in front of the large wood door of Kovarrin's study. I squeezed my eyes shut for a breath and then rapped my knuckles on the wood.

Before I could take another full breath, he opened the door. His eyes widened in surprise, but he locked down his expression in the next breath and nodded for me to enter. The door clicked shut softly behind me and the stuffing of the leather chair sighed as I sat down in front of his desk.

He shuffled some of the papers in front of him without meeting my eyes. The open wall behind him allowed the sun to stream in and the ocean air tussled his hair as he finally raised his eyes to meet mine.

"Maddox didn't know who I mistook you for yesterday," he stated, voice soft but so deep it still filled the quiet room.

I only nodded.

"But you knew." His gaze leveled on me.

"Yes," I said softly.

He took a slow breath. "He doesn't know who Alannah is."

I shook my head. "No."

He flattened his hands over the desk. "I'm sure you have a lot of questions."

I nodded, jaw clenched. "I do."

A flicker of worry flashed across his face as he looked down but then he waved his hand, indicating for me to begin.

"You loved her," I said. There was no use in dancing around the discussion. I didn't know when Maddox would come home, and I wanted to have adequate time to talk.

He let out a dry laugh as he met my eyes. "That's not a question." He lowered his eyes back down to his hands. "I thought I did, once. Centuries ago. But now my heart only beats for Rasa."

A wave of relief swept over my chest. I'm not sure if it was because I loved Rasa so much already that I didn't like the idea of her husband, her mate, pining over a lost love, or if it was because it made me feel better to know that Kovarrin wasn't mourning my mother like my father had for so many years.

"You're surprised by that," Kovarrin said, breaking me out of my thoughts.

I tilted my head down. "It's just that your reaction to seeing me, when you thought that I was her, it seemed like..." I trailed off before shrugging. "You can't even look at me without looking miserable."

His eyes snapped up to mine and he pursed his lips. "It's that obvious?"

I nodded.

He sighed and stood up, walking to the balcony to look out at the Madierian before leaning against a pillar.

"I'm not in pain because I love her." He paused. "I loved her when I was a far younger man. When I had no experience of the world, when she was my best friend and we were planning to run away together." He looked to his feet. "Not romantically. I'd already tried several times to tell her how I felt about her, but each time she voiced that she didn't feel the same. That I was a friend to her, a brother, and nothing more. The pain you see in my eyes is guilt."

My brows furrowed. "For Rasa?"

He shook his head. "No, of course not. Rasa is my mate, and after meeting her I understood what true love felt like." He looked to the bookshelves that lined the walls, but I saw that his eyes looked past them, into a memory. "I was never truly in love with Alannah, only the idea of her; the idea of being in love." He sighed. "I feel guilty because everything she did, everything that happened, was because of me. The consequences she had to bear were my fault."

"I—" I began, but he cut me off, coming forward and easing back into his chair.

"I'm sorry, Evaline. I thought I was ready to talk about this, I really did. But I can't." He ran a hand down his face. "Maybe another time I can tell you about that night, about what happened and what your mother did but—"

"I know," I interjected. There was no use in hiding it from him, especially if he was going to try to get out of having this conversation.

His face blanched. "How much?"

I swallowed. "I know what she did." He pushed back in his chair, away from me. "And I know that you've lied to everyone about it."

CHAPTER NINETEEN

Maddox

After Evaline left with my mother, I headed to the training center. It had been months since I'd seen most of my friends and I was excited to catch up.

I made my way down the hill and sighed as I thought about Evaline walking around Rominia with that barbed wire in her hair.

There'd been so many times I'd hoped to bring her here because I knew she'd be safe, and that she'd be able to wear her hair down and without the wire.

A mix of guilt and rage seethed low in my gut. Vasier had caused this. He wanted her for reasons I was unaware and it had not only put her in danger while we were traveling through Brassillion but made her feel unsafe even within the wards that protected Rominia. Vasier wanted Evaline for her magic, I just had to figure out why she was the key.

I bit back my anger as I approached the training center.

The large entrance was open, swung up on its metal rig, as it always was during the hottest time of year.

Before I even made it to the threshold, a few bodies flashed out and I was slammed back by my friend's embrace.

All my worries fell away as I felt arms around me and we all steadied each other to stand upright just outside the building's door.

"Gods, took you long enough to come home," Grant said as he squeezed my shoulder. His smile widened and crinkled the tawny skin around his eyes. "But I guess we can forgive you since you pulled yourself away from your mate to come see us."

Fredrik laughed and placed his hands on his hips.

"I saw the way he looked at her," he started. "No way he's ever choosing us over her."

Nash rolled his eyes and slung an arm over Fredrik's shoulders. "You say that as if you're any different."

Fredrik waved one hand in mock dismissal, but I didn't miss the way he looked up at his mate with bright eyes as he slipped his other arm around Nash's waist.

My eyes finally landed on Dean, who'd been the quietest, and I felt a pang of guilt. He hadn't found his mate yet, either. We weren't the only two Kova on the island who hadn't, and truthfully, he was far younger than me, but I knew the pain of seeing your friends find their mates while you waited for your own.

He smiled as he widened his stance and crossed his arms over his thick chest. "I'm happy for you, Mads," he said, tilting his head to the side. The movement caused the dark brown curls that fell to his chin to bounce along with it.

"Thanks, guys. I'm just glad to be home. You wouldn't believe the bullshit that we faced on this trip."

That grabbed their attention.

I told them about all of it. Killing the Vasi outside of Kembertus, how Evaline and I met, how Wyott and I got her out of there. About Gabriehl, and her abduction. Then about the sail here. I kept out any mention of her magic. While my friends wouldn't think anything of it, and in truth only find it fascinating, she was still shy about her abilities, and I didn't want to share that information without her consent.

"Who taught her to fight?" Nash asked, cocking his head and causing a few curls to land on his fair forehead.

"Her father, Wallace Manor." Of course, they were surprised by that. Most Kova knew exactly who Wallace was. We didn't know many humans by name, but we knew all the leaders and heirs to the different kingdoms in Brassillion. And when one denounces the alliance with Vasier, Kova are bound to take notice.

"No shit," Grant breathed and widened his light gray eyes. "What an odd—" he started, but stopped and nodded his head to the woman that walked up behind me. She turned past the group of us toward Ankin's loft, which was nestled between the training center and the beach.

The rest of us turned to see who he was looking at and from here all I saw was that she had long black-almost-green-hair and was a little shorter than Evaline. The door to the loft opened and my attention drew there immediately as I recalled that it wouldn't be Ankin that walked down the few steps from the door, but his grandson.

My spine straightened, as did Dean's, and I felt both the sorrow for the loss of a friend and the suspicion at this new Arch Sorcerer.

I barely saw him; he didn't come fully out of the loft. Only stretched his long arm to hold the door open for the woman and poked his head out to smile at her.

Once the door was closed, I turned back to my friends.

"Am I the only one who finds it suspicious that this new Sorcerer comes to Rominia, and only a few months later Ankin dies?" I asked, voicing the concern that I'd felt since the moment my parents told me of Ankin's passing.

The four of them looked between each other before turning back to me.

Nash shrugged. "I can see how it could seem odd, but it didn't at the time. Ankin and Lauden spent a lot of time together, they seemed happy. And Lauden was crushed when his grandfather died."

Grant nodded. "Ankin was elderly, it didn't seem a shock when he passed of natural causes."

I pursed my lips. "It was, then? Natural causes, I mean."

Fredrik's brows shot to his forehead. "Maddox," he warned.

I sighed. "Maybe I shouldn't be this wary, but I just find it alarming that when I left Rominia, Ankin was fine and Arch Sorcerer. Now I come back, not even a year later, and he's dead, and some brand-new Sorcerer has been given his title."

Grant slung an arm over my shoulder. "I understand, Maddox. I do. But we were here. Kovarrin did his due diligence. He went to all the other Sorcerers on the island, they declined. They wanted the flexibility to travel, or just didn't want the responsibility. Lauden was the natural choice after that."

I tried to loosen my jaw. Perhaps they were right, but I still needed to talk to my father about it.

"But if I were you, I'd be far more worried about getting your ass kicked," he said, his voice light. He led me through the door of the training center. At the far end, several of the Kova children I'd helped train before I left sparred over the protective mats on the floor. "They're a lot stronger than the last time you were here."

I spent the rest of the day in the training center, catching up with my friends and sparring with the children. Grant was right, they'd improved bounds since the last time I'd seen them.

When I got back home, I was barely through the door before my mother sent me back down the hill to get the rest of hers and Evaline's purchases from the boutique. I nearly laughed at the thought of Evaline shopping all day, but hoped she liked doing so with my mother, even if she'd hated it with Therese.

When I returned to our suite, the scent of soap hit me and I ran to poke my head in the bathroom.

"Did I miss the bath?"

She laughed at the counter where she brushed her hair. "You did."

I sighed. "And you're dressed? That's not fair." I placed the bags down and walked over to pull her into my chest. "Did you have a good day?" I asked as she wrapped her arms around my neck.

Her heart rate sped as she opened her mouth to answer, but just then I felt the land beneath us start the slightest of tremors. I tightened my arms around her, and her eyes widened as she looked up at me. She didn't breathe until the vibrations beneath our feet stalled.

Her breath burst past her lips. "What was that?" she asked, her brows pulled together in worry.

I pressed my lips against them. "A quake. We get them every once in a while. That was the first I've felt in years." I answered, keeping my voice soft in an attempt to calm her. "That one was minor, nothing to be scared of."

She nodded.

"I did have a good day," she said, but there was a slither of worry that slipped through the bond. I knew she'd had a block on it at times. I didn't blame her; the bond was new, and it was natural for her to want to keep some of her emotions private. "Rominia is a lot different from Neomaeros and Kembertus."

I chuckled. "Now you see why we don't like spending long bouts of time away."

She lifted onto her toes to kiss me. "I want to see more, though. We only went to a few shops."

"We're going to see everything. I already have a hike planned so you can explore the island, and finally get to meet Cora."

Her smile grew. "Tomorrow?"

I snorted. "Definitely not. The day after," I started. "Wyott's been away from Cora for almost a year. You couldn't pay me to go within a few hundred yards of that house before they've been alone at least forty-eight hours." I cocked my head. "Come to think of it, that quake might've originated from their bedroom."

She cringed and pushed away from me. "Oh, you're disgusting."

I caught her hand and pulled her back toward me.

"What? I know my brother." I dipped my head and kissed her neck. "And I know what it's like being away from you for a few days, I can't imagine months."

CHAPTER TWENTY

Evaline

I fell asleep to the soft sound of Maddox breathing as he fell asleep beside me.

And woke up to the sound of someone choking.

This was another memory my mother showed me, that I watched from behind her eyes. The woods looked the same, except that Kovarrin and Vasier weren't lying in the clearing covered in blood.

Alannah stood in front of the trunk of a tree and Vasier had his hand wrapped around her throat.

He looked different than the last time I'd seen him, when he was only just waking up, reborn as the First Vasi. Then, his hair had been disheveled, his face splattered with blood. It'd been dark, and he'd been a few paces away. Then, I could only make out the most basic shapes of his face, everything else was overshadowed by the red eyes that had pierced through me.

It wasn't until this moment, with his hands locked around her throat, angry tears flooding his blue eyes, that I realized I never actually knew what he looked like before. I only knew the eyes, but not the features.

But now… Now I saw him. I saw every detail of his face, the strong jaw and the floppy brown hair, and a shock washed through my body as a new understanding bloomed in my mind.

My mother fought against him while I watched from behind her eyes. She tried to scream, as much as she could with a blocked airway, and scratched at his face.

He wailed when her nails drug down his cheeks, drawing blood that oozed out of the cuts. She continued to scratch, slap, do what she could until her hands were covered in his blood.

The night seemed so loud. The blood raged in her ears, choked sounds gasped from her lips, he grunted and hissed. But in reality, if someone walked by, they might not have heard her at all unless they knew where to find her. Unless they'd been planning to meet her here all along.

"Vasier!" Kovarrin screamed from somewhere behind him.

A moment later he ripped Vasier away and in a heartbeat, they were on the ground in a heap of fists and shouts.

She reached out behind her for the tree trunk, catching herself against the rough bark while her other hand palpated her throat, checked the damages as she gasped for air.

I could feel the pain she felt, feel the anguish inside of her as she stared at the two men fighting.

This is wrong, she thought as she struggled to breathe.

Realization after realization dawned in her mind, the most potent of which was that she'd never seen them even bicker before. To see them now, drawing their blades as they wrestled on the ground, her heart jumped into her throat as she screamed and jolted forward.

Because Vasier wasn't just a random attacker, and Kovarrin wasn't just a happenstance savior.

I understood this before my mother showed me the memories of the three friends. I understood this the moment I saw Vasier's face in plain view.

"They're brothers," I breathed as the brawling men dissipated into nothing, as the world grew dizzy for a moment, and I was pulled back into my own body. My mother appeared before me.

She gave a small nod. "Twins."

I swallowed, stroking my throat at the phantom feel of Vasier's hands, and let this information sink in.

She grabbed my hand, pulled us to those same two boulders as last time, and we sat.

"Kovarrin hasn't told anyone that, at least not that Maddox has told me." It seemed like something my mate would've mentioned by now.

My mother pulled my hand into her lap and clasped both of hers around it.

"He's ashamed," she whispered.

Of course he was, otherwise he would've mentioned it earlier when I confronted him about his creation.

I clenched my eyes shut and shook my head. I tried to remember everything I wanted to ask my mother. Ever since our first encounter I'd had questions stowed away, ready for this very moment. Until I saw her again.

"Have you been reaching out since our last meeting?" I asked.

Her brows furrowed as she shook her head. "I haven't been able to. This takes so much concentration and focus on my part, I had to rest after our last encounter."

"I have so many questions," I confessed.

She squeezed my hand. "Ask them. As fast as you can, I don't know how much time we have."

"Did father know you were a Sorceress, that you were immortal?"

A pained look flashed across her face. "Yes. But you must understand that I wasn't immortal because I was a Sorceress, they aren't immortal unless they use blood magic to become so. The Gods granted me extra time in this world so that I could raise you. So that I could train you to use your magic."

"What element did you wield?"

The wind around us picked up as she answered. "Air."

"How did you create the Kova and the Vasi?"

She cringed. "I used a forbidden magic; one we are not supposed to tap into. We're gifted the ability to manipulate whatever element the

Gods choose for us but aren't supposed to utilize any more. But that night." she turned her head to stare at the ground where she'd kneeled before Kovarrin. "That night I used blood magic."

"Why is it forbidden?"

She turned back to face me. "It's dark and can't be easily controlled. Our magic lives in our blood, it's why it's inherited. But the Gods didn't foresee the harmful uses it could have until it was too late." She shook her head. "Some Sorcerers used it to change their fate or to rise to power falsely. It angered the Gods to intervene in their plans this way, so there are consequences."

I gritted my teeth. "How did they punish them?"

Her face paled and she took a moment to answer. "The Gods don't like Sorcerers intervening in their plans, and they curse those who do. But I didn't just intervene." She wrung her hands and I noticed there were tears in her eyes. "I created."

"What did they do to you?" I whispered.

Her hands shook as she gripped mine. "The worst possible punishment they could've given to a mother."

My brows furrowed. "But you weren't a mother when you created them," I said, but then reconsidered. "Were you?"

She shook her head. "No." She took a deep breath and looked to the heavens to blink away a few tears.

I shook my head. "I don't understand, what—"

She leaned closer to me, until we were only inches apart as she spoke.

"Evaline, you have to forgive me. I didn't know what I was doing at the time, I didn't understand the full extent of the consequences." A few tears escaped her eyes. "I loved Kovarrin like a brother, and he died for me. I knew I had to do everything I could to bring him back." Her hands shook with each word, causing the tremors to slide over mine until I was shaking with her. "And maybe the Gods would've been okay with that, because he was good, and he was kind." She took a shuddering breath as she continued to rush out her words. "But I accidentally brought back

Vasier too, and the Gods couldn't forgive." A sob worked its way out of her throat. "I'm so sorry, Evaline."

I shook my head. "Why are you apologizing to me?"

She took a deep breath. "The Gods traditionally curse those who disobey, but they punished me by subverting my curse."

My face fell and I pulled back. "What are you saying?"

Her chin trembled. "The Gods didn't curse me," she said softly and the world around us shifted, shadows trembled around us. I was starting to wake up. "They cursed you."

My mouth dried and a chill swept through my body until every hair stood on end and every nerve was lit like a fuse.

"What does that mean?" My voice was low.

She raised her hands to cup my face and she brushed away a tear.

"I created an evil entity, and my consequence was that my child would be cursed to end it." Her eyes darted between mine. "Your fate was forged hundreds of years before you were born. *You* are meant to end the Vasi's reign of terror on the world. *You* are meant to kill Vasier."

I shook my head as the tears came faster, as the world shook, and the shadows flickered.

"I can't do that. I don't even understand my own magic." My body quaked at the implications of her words, of her actions, but my words reminded me of the most important question I had for her. "Why do I have more than one element?" I asked in a rush. "If you had Air, why don't I just have one?"

She smoothed my hair from my face.

"You only wield one element in the true manner of a Sorceress; Water."

I shook my head. "No, you saw it. I can use Air, like you. And Terra."

"No, listen," she said in a rush. "You are a Sorceress, like me, but you're also more. You're a Sorceress who can manipulate water, but the Gods knew that wasn't enough to end the Vasi."

My eyes widened as she spoke and I felt the world move around me, as if there was a weight shifting beside me.

"Each God gave you a different ability, a gift from each of them so that you may fulfill your prophecy. You can use Water because you were born with it, but far greater than any other Water Caster alive because Merwinna granted you the power to do so."

I jostled in her arms, and finally understood that the world wasn't shifting around me—the bed was. Maddox was moving next to me.

"You can use Air because the God of Gale gifted it to you."

I felt my body shake and was unsure if it was involuntary, or if it was my mate trying to wake me.

"You have the power of Terra because Arlomandric gave it to you." The world darkened around us, the shadows started to creep up her form as they had the last time we met. "And so much more," she rushed out as she looked down at the shadows then back at me. "You aren't an average Sorceress. Your magic isn't natural. You're unlike any other being in the entire world. Your assortment of power was crafted and meticulously chosen by the Gods." The shadows crept up her jaw. "It was made with one intention, and one intention alone. To fulfill the fate they cursed you—I cursed you—with. And if you don't, they'll shove the responsibility off onto someone else." She shook her head, tears in her eyes. "I don't know if they'd kill you, or just take your magic away, but the Gods will get what they want, one way or another."

The shadows stretched to her chin, wrapping around to envelop the rest of her form. I tried to hold tight to her hands but she was yanked back and her fingertips pulled into the mass of writhing darkness. I stared in horror as she began to fade from view again.

"I'm sorry," she choked out.

A moment later, the image of her and the clearing dissipated into a wall of black.

Chapter Twenty-One

Maddox

I spent most of the morning worried for Evaline. She had a nightmare and was screaming and thrashing in the bed but when I'd woken her up, she'd just brushed it off and we'd laid back down.

Neither of us had fallen back asleep. She just rolled to her side, and I wrapped my body around hers. But her heart thudded so hard that I could feel it against my own as I pressed my chest to her back. We stayed like that until the sun came up and we finally rose for breakfast at the dining table.

She watched out the window quietly as the ocean churned below. It wasn't until she tried to cover a yawn with the back of her hand that I finally reached forward to place a hand on her knee.

"Do you want to go back to sleep? You hardly got any last night."

She turned her tired eyes on me with a small smile and a slight cringe. "Would you hate me? I know it's our first day alone together in Rominia."

"Absolutely not." I smiled and leaned over to kiss her forehead. "We have plenty of time here. You rest."

Her heart rate spiked at that, but she nodded.

After she laid back down I left the suite so I wouldn't bother her and as soon as I closed the door behind me I took a deep breath.

"Fuck," I whispered.

I shouldn't have said that. I knew better. Every time I mentioned the time we had together, her heart rate jolted. I was so used to the notion of my immortality and that Kova had decades—centuries—to spend with their mates, that I'd forgotten that Evaline and I might not.

Panic tightened my chest as I moved to walk down the hall. Sorcerers weren't immortal, they aged like humans, and the idea of only getting a few more decades with Evaline terrified me more than I knew how to handle right now. I'd nearly lost her once; I couldn't do that again.

But I couldn't ask her to change. It wasn't fair, and Gods knew what would happen to her magic. I'd never known a Sorcerer who'd turned into a Kova.

With that thought, I turned my path to seek my father.

I found him in his study, one hand smoothing a map over his desk and the other running through his hair.

"What's wrong?" I asked as I sat in one of the chairs in front of his desk. My father never showed much more emotion than the calm demeanor of a leader.

He sighed and sat back in his seat. "I'm just trying to prepare evacuation plans for when Mt. Rominia erupts."

I sat back into my chair, too, and curled my hands over the edge of the arms on either side.

"It won't erupt soon, though. Right?"

"No, the Terra Sorcerers have been monitoring it for the last few weeks. They've estimated eruption in about a month." He shrugged. "They said it had been dormant and they didn't think it'd erupt for another few years, but we've been having a lot of small tremors lately."

My eyebrows rose. "Evaline and I felt one last night. Those have been happening a lot?"

He pursed his lips. "More than we've ever had before. Almost one per day."

"Do they know the cause?"

He crossed his arms over his chest. "Not yet, they've been investigating but they originate all over the island in different places."

I nodded. "Well, just let me know what you need me to help with. I'll get Wyott out of the house tomorrow, and I'm sure he'll be ready to help."

My father laughed. "It would be nice to see him if he manages to pull himself away from Cora for five minutes." He shook his head. "So many years together and they still act like newlyweds every time he comes home."

My smile faltered then as my worries flooded back.

"What's wrong?" he asked, leaning forward and placing his elbows on his desk.

I closed my eyes and took a breath. "I'm worried about Evaline, and our future. What it means that we're the first mated couple who aren't both Kova." I rubbed a thumb along the leather of the chair. "Have you ever known a Sorcerer to make the change to a Kova?"

He was quiet a moment and I looked up between my lashes. "I haven't. I've had friends over the years that considered it, but there's an uncertainty about what would happen to their magic, so none have made the change."

"That's what I was afraid of." I sighed and dragged a hand down my face. "I was hoping you'd say that some had decided to change later in life."

He pursed his lips. "I wish I could, but to all the Sorcerers I've talked to, their magic is as a part of them as any of their organs, as their blood. They can't imagine living without it, and the idea that they might have to." He shrugged. "None have wanted to chance it."

I leaned forward and rested my elbows on my knees, wrung my hands between them.

"But maybe it'll be different for Evaline." He offered. "She's only just discovered her abilities. The Sorcerers I know were children when their magic manifested. They lived with it longer than she has, maybe she'll decide the risk is worth it."

I gave a shake of my head. I knew I'd never ask that of her.

CHAPTER TWENTY-TWO

Evaline

After Maddox had insisted I sleep after breakfast yesterday, I'd spent most of the day in bed. If I wasn't sleeping, I was reading one of the books he had on his shelves. It was nice to forget about my own problems as I dove into the problems of fictional characters.

I did my best to ignore what my mother had said about the curse. The Gods were asking too much from me. I'd only known about my magic for a little over a week, to discover that I was cursed too was unacceptable. The Gods needed to give me a break, and if they wouldn't, I'd take one. Who cared if the Gods shoved the responsibility off onto someone else? Whoever they chose would probably know what to do.

I definitely didn't.

But my day of rest had come and gone, and now Maddox was waking me for our hike with Wyott and Cora. Even if it was an ungodly hour, I couldn't put my clothes on fast enough. Of course, I was excited to explore the island but I was far more interested in meeting Cora.

Maddox's hand was warm in mine as he led me through the mansion and out into the morning. The sky was still dark with night, but Maddox assured me that I would want to get to our destination early to watch the sun rise.

We made our way toward the quiet street that Rasa and I had walked down when we shopped. All the businesses were stacked on top of one another, and right against the next, with alleys staggered every few clusters. Instead of being made of wood the walls were made of slabs of stone. Since each building was several stories, they had staircases that wound back and forth across their front side as well as enclosed lifts operated by a pulley system. I supposed when there was a limited amount of land, you had to make the most use of the space.

The streets were cobblestone, but instead of the dull brown stones that made up Kembertus's streets, these were a light sandy color, close to that which coated the beaches with a sprinkling of black pebbles throughout them. Even though it was dark, and even though the firelight from the lantern Maddox held for my benefit didn't bounce off the stones, I could tell what it was.

"If Rominium is so valuable, then why are your streets made of it?" I asked and he smiled down at me.

"Back when my father and his friends discovered Rominia it was desolate. There was some wildlife here but no humans." He shrugged. "No other beings of any kind."

"Your father built Rominia into this?" I asked, nodding toward the shops we passed.

He nodded. "When he started exploring, he didn't realize what Rominium was and how valuable it could be, once he did, he switched to the other natural resources in Rominia. He and his friends started building the streets and their homes and as the centuries went on, more Kova turned or were born and came here to live with him, and the city grew."

As we made it past the strip of businesses, I saw where the houses began. They, too, were stacked on top of one another almost in an apartment style, but the individual outlines of each home were visible and they weren't always perfectly lined up. It was as if they built the homes as they needed them, and sometimes that meant that they weren't proportionate or cohesive. Regardless, they were beautiful, and they too had staircases that went up and down the front of the buildings.

My eyes drifted past the street of homes to the mountain that rose in the distance. Even in the dim light I could see smoke wafting from its top.

That's when I remembered that it wasn't a mountain at all but a—what did Maddox call it again?

"Gods is that the mountain with molten metal inside of it?" I asked, horrified.

He laughed and threw an arm around my shoulders, pulling me into his side. "Yes, that's the volcano," he said. "And it's where we're hiking this morning with Wyott and Cora."

I laughed but Maddox did not. My smile fell. "Maddox you can't be serious."

"Trust me, it's safe, I wouldn't take you somewhere that wasn't."

A slow smile crept across his face only a second before I heard Wyott's voice come up behind me.

"Miss me?"

I turned around to see Wyott standing there with the biggest smile I'd ever seen on his face. Immediately my eyes drifted to where his hand was tangled up in the hand of a beautiful woman who I could only assume was Cora.

Her eyes were a lighter gray than Wyott's and her hair was a deep maroon; a crimson color that I didn't know was possible to see in hair. It wound in tight curls that fell around her shoulders and down her back.

Wyott wrapped an arm around her before looking at me. "Evaline, this is Cora. My mate."

She rolled her eyes. "I'm also his wife, but he always leaves that bit out."

He dismissed the thought with a wave of his hand. "I'm bound to you by the Goddess of Fate, what does the legality of it matter?"

She smiled and shook her head, and I reached out a hand to shake.

"I've heard so much about you Cora."

She laughed and the sound was melodic. Instead of grabbing my hand she wrapped her arms around me.

"You're my sister now, there's no handshaking in this family." A warmth spread through my chest at her words. I hadn't realized until just now that I had been worried that perhaps she wouldn't like me, that maybe I wouldn't be as close to Wyott here as I was on our trip if that was the case.

She pulled back and grabbed both of my hands. "At some point we're going to have to discuss everything that happened on your travels, but in the meantime, we should probably get going or else we'll miss the sunrise."

My eyes widened as I looked back at Maddox.

"We're going to the top of the volcano by sunrise?" I looked between the three of them. "How long until then?" I asked, then looked to the already lightening horizon. "That's not very long at all."

The three Kova laughed, and Maddox shrugged. "You'll make it, and if not, we could always run up."

We all turned and headed toward the path and Cora looped her arm through mine as we walked behind the two men who discussed something quietly. Cora asked about our travels, about my life, and how I'd grown up. She was easy to talk to, and the trek didn't seem so bad with her at my side.

The three Kova were graceful, but every once in a while I would start to trip over a root in the path and Cora would catch me through our linked arms. Maddox would look behind with concern, but each time he turned back around after seeing that Cora had already righted me. As if it was a habit, or an instinct, to help me when he thought I was in trouble.

"So Wyott told me that they trained you," Cora started at my side, casting her smile down at me; she was slightly taller than me, maybe by an inch or two.

"Yes," I started. "My father had already shown me quite a lot but by the time I met Maddox and Wyott I was really out of practice. I knew that I had to kill the man my guardians were attempting to marry me to," Cora squeezed my arm in reassurance. Clearly Wyott had already told her what had happened and why. And I was glad for it. I didn't want to keep having to justify what I'd done or explain it. So to know that Wyott understood that, and told her for me, spread a warmth in my chest. For the first time I considered that maybe Wyott was more than my friend, maybe he was starting to become my brother just as much as he was Maddox's. And with how kind and accepting Cora was, it wasn't hard to imagine her as a sister someday.

Cora's voice pulled me from my thoughts. "I must hear every single time you beat Wyott during training."

I laughed at the same time that Wyott turned and rolled his eyes at us. "It's not as many times as you'd think." His eyes flicked to Maddox. "And not more times than she beat him."

Maddox chuckled and shook his head. "At least I didn't get hustled by her."

Cora's eyes widened as she turned to me with a glimmer in her gray eyes and I launched into a retelling of our knife throwing incident.

Halfway through the hike the incline became sharper until I could only listen to the conversations of the three Kova because I was either so out of breath from the ascent that I couldn't spare any for words, or too focused on not tumbling all the way back down the mountain.

They all stayed at my pace, and never made me feel like I was slowing them down. Maddox and Cora talked a lot since they were close and hadn't seen each other in months, and all three teased each other often.

By the time the sun was getting ready to rise we stopped at an outlook a few dozen feet from the top of the volcano. There was absolutely no way that I would be going any higher if what Maddox said was true and there was a hole in the top of it.

No matter how much Maddox could assure me that this was safe, I drew the line at standing near the opening of the volcano.

"How are you feeling?" Maddox asked when we all made it to our destination.

I took a deep breath, finally catching it all, and nodded. "I feel great."

And it was true. I hadn't hiked in years, since long before my father passed away. And when I did, it was never up anything with an elevation like this. But it was still fun getting to be a part of this group of friends, of this family.

"Good," he whispered and bent to kiss my head. When he straightened his eyes moved to look at something behind me, and I could see the light shining in them. "Look."

When I turned, I swear to the Gods that I saw Kembertic himself pulling the sun from behind the sheet of the horizon. There was so much light I half-expected to see his sunburst crown glinting some of it back at me. But he wasn't there, he simply manipulated the sun from the heavens, and I watched as the sun rays bounced off the Madierian. Every ripple in the sea reflected the light and the glittering effect spread throughout the entire horizon.

But the higher the sun rose, the lower I looked away from it, toward the island. We were so high that I could see the entire village, all the shops, and the First's Estate. There was even a river that cut through Rominia, one that I hadn't even seen yet and only could now because of my vantage point.

I knew I was looking at a kingdom, a city that very few humans knew existed. The thought, the sight, caused emotion to swell in my chest. I was blessed to be here, to have found Maddox. I was lucky that I found this family; that they wanted me too.

The Gods had tested me, and maybe they still were. But where they tested, they blessed.

CHAPTER TWENTY-THREE

Evaline

"I sort of feel bad for my aunt now," I said to Cora as we fell onto mine and Maddox's bed.

Yesterday, after the hike, Maddox and I had spent most of the day with Cora and Wyott. We'd stopped to get lunch at a tavern in town and afterward Cora and I had gone to the boutique so she could shop for the Ball.

But this morning, all of us—Maddox, Wyott, Cora, the rulers, and several Kova that Rasa employed to help maintain the large estate—decorated and setup for the Ball.

Cora snorted beside me. "Why? From what Wyott told me she sounded like kind of a piece of shit," she said as she slid on her side and propped herself up on an elbow. "And by 'kind of' I mean that she was absolutely a piece of shit."

I laughed and looked to the ceiling, remembered when I laid just like this on my bed back in Kembertus, staring up and working through the panic attack I had at the idea of marrying Bassel. Gods, it felt like years had passed since I'd seen him at the Spring Solstice Ball.

"She was." I shrugged. "I think sometimes she meant well, but at her core, she didn't care for me. She only cared for her and the kingdom's reputation." I waved a hand in the air and turned to mimic Cora's perch. "I feel bad because she always asked me to help her with event planning and I either declined or manipulated my way out of it last minute."

Cora snickered. "And now that you've been up since dawn decorating for this Ball, you feel bad?"

I nodded and she reached forward to knock my shoulder so that I fell onto my back again.

"Don't waste time feeling sorry for those who never worried for you."

I nodded as I smoothed my hands over my face. Event planning really was exhausting.

"Fair."

She bounced up off the bed and I realized that she wasn't truly tired, not as much as I was. She reached forward to grab my hands and pulled me up until I stood in front of her.

"I know you're tired, but I've already sent Maddox to bring us up some coffee and lunch. We have a lot of preparing to do."

And instead of feeling the disdain I normally did for those words—when they came from my aunt—I smiled.

She went back to Wyott's old suite, the one he grew up in but that now was just available for guests since he'd moved out, and took a bath while I did the same in mine and Maddox's.

We were quick because we had to give our hair time to dry. By the time we were meeting again in my suite Maddox was coming back with food.

"Out!" Cora commanded as soon as he set the tray down.

He turned toward me. "What's it going to hurt if I stay?"

She scoffed as she went up behind him and pushed his back, shoving him toward the door.

"It's going to hurt *you* if you don't get out."

He threw a look back to me and an eye roll to her. "You know, whenever Wyott and I leave, it takes a few months before I start to miss you but every time I come back, I question why I ever missed you at all."

With one last shove he was out of the room and standing in the hallway, turned back to face us.

She cocked her head and gave him a sweet smile.

"Because you love me, brother," she insisted. "As I do you. But you're going to love me even more when you see your mate tonight after we are ready. Until then, go be somewhere else." She waved him away with her hand.

He gave her a deadpan look and then stepped forward to kiss my cheek before turning.

"Wait!" Cora shrieked.

He turned back at the same time she vanished into a blur, running to the closet at Kova speed before coming back to stand in front of him with a couple hangers in her hand. She shoved them into his chest.

"Get ready somewhere else, too."

His lids fell into an unamused glare as he took the garments. She'd shut the door on him before he fully turned away.

See you later, sweetheart. His words drifted down the bond.

Maybe be more chipper, then, I responded.

I felt his laugh down the bond and turned to Cora.

"What now?"

She clasped her hands against her chest. "Now we have fun."

The daylight passed quickly and we spent most of our time flitting between the bathroom and the bedroom. The windows showcased the beautiful colors of the sky as the sun neared its set and the waves below flickered the light.

First we used luxurious lotions while we waited for our hair to dry, and talked about anything and everything. Then we worked on our hair. Cora's hair dried in what I now realized were her natural curls. They fell down and around her shoulders in tight maroon ringlets. A more faded version of the color dotted her nose and cheeks in freckles until they faded away into her hairline.

We stayed in our robes while we worked. I helped her pin the top half of her hair up and away from her face, and she helped me curl mine. Cora pulled out a contraption I'd never seen before; it was made of metal—I wasn't sure what kind—and the handle was made of stone. She let the pipe-like metal heat near the fire and grabbed the stone with a quilted glove, then wrapped segments of my hair around it until my already wavy hair fell into perfect, thick curls down my back.

"Doesn't it burn your hand?" I asked as I felt the heat of the wand near my head while she worked.

She shook her head. "Nope, I have this glove on to protect my hand." Then she shrugged. "You could do it too. The glove is thick enough that even a human could use it and not feel any pain or bear any burns."

Finally we worked on our makeup. I wasn't very good at it because I'd never taken the time to learn, so she taught me as she did hers, and then mine.

When we were finished she insisted I go dress and when I came back her jaw dropped.

"Evaline, you look amazing."

In a second Maddox was in the room, standing beside Cora. "No, she looks divine."

Cora groaned and shoved him. "What are you doing here?"

His smile was bright when he turned it on me, his eyes skating down my form hungrily.

"Just came back in perfect timing, I guess."

She threw her hands up. "I tried." She came forward and hugged me. "You look beautiful, Evaline."

When she pulled back she fixed a curl that had fallen loose from my pin. My hair was fashioned so that one side was pinned back and the other half fell in curls over my shoulder.

"I have to go back to the suite to change, anyway." She cut a glare to Maddox. "But I'll see you down there later."

She gathered her belongings and left, and I heard the clack of the door shut behind her. I'd already turned away from Maddox to look at my reflection in the floor length mirror when I saw him come up behind me, his eyes black.

I stayed still as he approached, and it was only a moment before I felt the heat of him behind me. I met his eyes in the mirror as he dropped his lips to my bare neck.

"I'm not sure I can ever find the will to leave this room if you're going to keep looking like that," he said softly against my skin between kisses.

His hands slipped between where my arms rested at my sides and he clutched at my waist, pulling my body back against his.

My breath hitched and I smiled at our reflection. He was in his typical all black attire, albeit nicer than anything he'd ever worn in Kembertus. He wore a black leather tunic atop a black shirt with the sleeves rolled up to his elbows, black pants and a seemingly new pair of black boots. His hair was brushed back nicely, although a few of his curls were already falling forward like they always did, and he maintained his facial hair. For the first time since we'd been in Rominia I realized that he didn't have any weapons on. His swords that were typically strapped on his back, his daggers at his hips, even his hatchet, were all gone.

My thoughts were cut short as his fangs prodded against my neck and I sucked in a sharp breath. I pushed back into him, into his teeth, as I spoke.

"Feed."

His smile hid his fangs away as he straightened to look at me in the mirror, his hands on my waist tightening.

"Cora would gut me if we came down to the Ball with blood on your dress."

His words didn't match his demeanor, or his voice. His chest moved with heavy breaths and his eyes were dilated, voice deep. He wanted to more than anything. He raised one hand to cup my shoulder as he fingered the delicate straps that held my dress on.

"I like your dress," he whispered, and I watched him as his eyes followed his hand in the mirror, watched as it skimmed down my arm slowly. "I like the color," he said, referring to the soft dusty rose color of the dress. It matched the color of my cheeks as they flushed at his touch. "I like the silhouette."

Maddox's voice grew deeper and raspier the more he spoke. His eyes fell down my form and his hand at my waist tightened. The dress had a corseted top that cinched in the front, giving me the ability to get myself in and out of it without the need for help. The waist dipped in following my figure and then the skirt fell around my hips in only a couple layers of tulle so that it wasn't too puffy.

"And I *love,*" he said, placing emphasis on the word. "The length."

My skirt fell halfway between my hips and knees, far shorter than any dress I'd ever worn before. I was almost nervous to wear it, worried a rogue wind would flip it up and show everyone at the party *far* more of myself than I was willing to share. The nerves were eased slightly by the slip I wore beneath the skirt. It was skin tight so if the wind did jolt my dress, all they would see is the pink fabric around my bottom half. Cora assured me it would be fine, but I'd be lying if I said I wasn't concerned that Maddox would hate it, hate the idea of me wearing this in front of everyone. In front of the other men.

I straightened and turned my head so our faces were close.

"You aren't angry that it's too short?" I whispered.

He laughed and the breath caused my lashes to flutter.

"I would never be angry by something you wore, Eva. It is your body, what you put on it is your business." His lips caressed my shoulder in a kiss, and I knew it was because he could sense my unease.

I felt my heart shudder at his words and turned back to watch him in the mirror. His lips continued up my shoulder until his mouth met the back of my neck, up near my ear.

I wasn't sure if it was just that my thirst for him never seemed to fade, or if it was watching the way he touched me—kissed me—in the mirror, but my clit started to throb for him, and I knew there was absolutely no way I could go down to the Ball in this state.

I pushed myself back into him and immediately felt that he was hard behind me.

He groaned in my ear and pulled his lips away. "You have to stop if you want me to be able to leave this room and go down and socialize," he said, his voice raw.

He met my eyes in the mirror then, and his own darkened. I barely saw the smile on his face before his hand left my waist and moved up to cross my chest and grab my jaw, turning it back so his lips could connect with mine.

We both moaned into the kiss as our tongues slid together and I raised a hand behind me to grasp onto the back of his neck. He slipped his free hand under the hem of the tulle and tugged my slip up until it gathered around my hips.

I smiled into the kiss as his hand made quick work of diving straight for my clit and relieving the pressure I knew he could sense from me. I nearly screamed just by the touch of his fingers, my desperation for him had grown so intense.

His fingers swirled as I pushed myself back further into him and dropped my hands to the fastener of his pants behind me, desperately trying to undo them without turning to see.

A groan rumbled through his chest and he dropped his hands from me and unfastened them himself. I looked behind me, gasped for air after our kiss, and watched as he opened them and pushed them down until his cock sprang free. Without hesitating I turned to pull him toward the bed but he stood firm and turned me to face the mirror again. He lowered his head toward my ear, eyes locked on mine in our reflection.

"Oh, no, my Goddess. I'm not passing up the opportunity to fuck you against this mirror," he said and my pulse jumped at his words. "Besides, the bed would wrinkle your dress."

A wicked smile lit my lips as I nodded. "That's rock solid logic."

He only smiled and grabbed each of my hands in his before moving us until we were only a step in front of the mirror. He raised my hands above my head and planted them against the mirror. For a moment I was worried it might topple over on us, but then I looked to see that it was welded to the wall.

"Keep them here," he instructed.

I nodded and watched as he bit his lip and backed up until he was behind my hips. One hand fell onto my back and gently pushed until I arched it, pushing my ass even closer to him. I felt his boot tap the inside of my foot and I widened my stance. His chest rose and fell quickly in anticipation as his eyes hungrily took me in. I watched the reflection of his gaze rove over the bare sight of my back, my hips that I'm sure were exposed to him, and my widened legs.

"No foreplay," I said, and his eyes flicked up to mine in the mirror even though his head remained tilted down. "I need it now, and you're only teasing."

"Whatever you say, Eva," he said, his voice low. I felt his hands on my hips, gently gathering the tulle to rest on my back. I felt his hand sliding over me before he barely dipped two fingers in, and I gasped.

"I said no teasing."

I watched in the mirror as he met my eyes and slowly brought his fingers up and slid them in his mouth, a deep groan shuddering through his chest. "I'm not teasing," he said when he removed them. "I just needed a taste."

An involuntary moan slipped from my lips at the words and he smirked, lowering his hands over my hips now and lining me up.

I held my breath as I felt his tip and gasped as he thrust forward.

I let my head fall down between my arms and groaned. "Gods."

"No." One of his hands snaked around the back of my neck and around to grasp my jaw and tilt it up gently until I met his eyes in the mirror. "Eyes on me."

The command in his deep voice, the heat in his eyes and the feel of him inside of me sent a shudder of pleasure through me as I shivered at the words.

And I listened. My eyes stayed on him while he moved, and I'd never seen anything as beautiful as him. His eyes kept mine, a few of his curls fell on his forehead and swayed with his movements, and his hands held my hips tightly.

It didn't take long until the two of us were panting and shaking, so close to the edge. When he fell forward and locked his hands around mine against the mirror, we each looked into it as we rode the high together.

Chapter Twenty-Four

Maddox

My blood hadn't even cooled from fucking Evaline by the time we exited the room and saw my father coming up our hall.

My smile fell and my arm locked tighter around her. Something was wrong.

He looked up and pursed his lips. "I'm sorry to bother you two, but I need to talk to you all—the whole family. Your mother is getting Wyott and Cora, but I want to talk to you before the Ball begins."

We followed him as he aimed for the stairs and I felt the way Evaline straightened beside me. I wanted to tell her not to be nervous, but how could I when my own heart slammed against my chest?

He led us to the family dining room which was just as I remembered it. The room was large and bright. It had white walls with ribbed trim that reached up to waist height and extended around the perimeter. The table in the center of the room was carved out of a gargantuan block of granite. The only wood in the room was the chairs, which had still been painted in white with soft pink cushions to match the granite of the table.

My father sat in his usual seat at the head of the table and I was surprised to see he'd pulled my mother's chair to be directly next to his on the shorter end, sharing the head. Traditionally she'd sit at the opposite end of the table.

"Come, sit," Kovarrin instructed, gesturing to the first chair on one of the long ends of the table, placed adjacent to him. "Evaline."

Something was definitely wrong. The chairs were all sat too close to my father's end of the table. They were usually spread out down the length of it so that guests were evenly spaced between the First and his wife, but today all five chairs were clustered close to where his chair sat.

Evaline nodded and sat down into the chair and without instruction I sank into the chair beside her and reached out for her hand, holding it in her lap.

My mother entered and moved to sit by my father.

"They'll be right here," she said softly.

I opened my mouth to speak but heard Wyott through the open door. I closed my mouth and decided to wait until everyone was here to ask my question. But ever the loudmouth, as soon as he entered the room he froze in the doorway with a cocked brow.

"Who died?"

Rasa's eyebrows shot up as she chastised him. "Wyott!"

Cora rolled her eyes and shoved his shoulder with hers as she walked into the room and sat across from Evaline, while Wyott followed and sat across from me. He shot me a wary look and I only returned it.

"Seriously, what's going on?" I asked.

My mother only looked to my father, seeming just as bewildered. But he looked to Evaline.

Her cheeks reddened and she looked down at our joined hands.

What the fuck was going on?

"Someone needs to talk, now," I demanded. "This isn't funny. What's wrong?"

My mother squirmed in her seat. "It won't be long before the guests start arriving, love," she urged my father.

He took a long, slow breath and straightened in his seat. He lifted his head and set his jaw before he spoke.

"There's a lot that I have to tell you," he said before looking to Evaline. "That we have to tell you."

My brows furrowed. "Why are you acting as if you're conspiring with my mate?" I asked, my voice too sharp.

"Maddox," my mother said in a warning tone, but her eyes never left my father.

My father opened his mouth to speak, but didn't. No words came out as he sighed and dragged a hand over his face.

I watched as Evaline looked at him, concern pulling her features.

My heart raced and all the excitement for the night evaporated completely as I feared what they'd say.

Evaline, I whispered down the bond. She pursed her lips. *Look at me.*

She did and I shook my head. "What's going on?"

Her eyes scanned the rest of the table from mine to Wyott, then Cora and Rasa, finally landing on my father.

He shook his head. "I don't know where to start." His voice broke on the last word and I felt Evaline's seemingly involuntary squeeze of my hand before words began spilling from her mouth.

"The Gods didn't create the Kova and the Vasi."

The room was quiet for a moment and my father looked between the lot of us.

Wyott and I exchanged another look, but Evaline continued.

"Kovarrin and Vasier both knew a powerful Sorceress hundreds of years ago when they were still human."

Her words came fast, but that didn't stop Wyott from flinching at the name of the Vasi.

"One night, Kovarrin saved her life after Vasier attacked her, but in doing so Vasier and Kovarrin ended up killing each other. The Sorceress used blood magic to bring Kovarrin back to life and accidentally brought back Vasier too."

She took a deep breath, replenishing after the words had shot out of her, and looked to my father who was staring at her in relief.

"That Sorceress created the Kova and the Vasi," she said softly.

Cora's hand slid along the table until she placed it over Wyott's. My mother stared with wide eyes between my father and my mate.

I shook my head. "If that's true then why did you lie to everyone about how you were created?" I asked my father. "It's been *hundreds* of years."

"I didn't know how to tell the truth," he said quietly. "I was ashamed."

None of this made sense; this story, why Evaline was the one telling it, and for Gods' sake, why the fuck was he doing this minutes before the Ball?

"Ashamed of what? Saving a woman from harm?" I pulled my hand from Evaline and angled in the seat to face her and my father, draping an arm over the back of her chair. "Why were you and Vasier even there together? Who was she? Why was Vasier attacking her?"

Evaline put a hand on my knee. "One question at a time, Maddox."

I furrowed my brows at her. "How are you even involved in this?" I flicked my eyes up to my father. "Why did you involve her in this?"

She swallowed. "You know why."

I shook my head. How in the name of the Gods would I know?

But then images started to appear in my mind. Pieces of a mural that had once been shattered all pulling together until they started to form a whole picture again.

The painting of Evaline's mother in that locket.

My father's reaction to Evaline for the first time. Calling her the wrong name.

The conversation her mother had with her while she was unconscious after killing the man with the tree.

I twisted my head to look at her, brows pulling together.

"Alannah," I whispered.

My mother turned to me. "Who's Alannah?"

Evaline swallowed. "My mother."

Wyott shook his head. "What does your mother have to do with this?"

"She was the Sorceress who created them."

There was a long pause as all of us looked to Evaline. I didn't know what to focus on, so many thoughts ran through my mind at once. What this meant for my mate, what this meant for Kova as a whole, and how none of us had ever noticed that my father had been lying to us all.

My mother seemed to recover then. She reached forward, around my father, until she was grasping Evaline's hand.

"Blood magic is forbidden by the Gods, Evaline," she said hurriedly. "What did the Gods do to her?"

Evaline's eyes widened and I felt her terror wash down the bond which only ravaged my heart more.

I grasped her arm softly. "Did your mother tell you all of this when you saw her?" Then another realization hit me. "Was this what your nightmare was about the other night?"

She turned to me, and went silent. She opened her mouth but no words came out.

My father pushed his chair away from the table and a shrill sound filled the air at the contact with the ground. He didn't stand, but straightened.

"Enough." His eyes shot to Evaline. "Stop pressuring her. It's not her fault, or her responsibility, to explain any of this. It's mine." He swallowed.

"Hundreds of years ago, before there were Kova and Vasi, Alannah was my best friend. We lived in a small village on another continent not far from here, or from Brassillion. Sorcery was illegal there, not because of Vasier, like the Kromean Kingdoms, but because the humans couldn't understand it, and they killed what they didn't understand."

We all followed every word he said.

"Alannah had known she had magic for years before she was discovered, and it was only by accident. She'd been practicing in a shed I helped her build miles and miles from town, it was where she kept all the books she had on Sorcery. A boy from town had lost his dog, and was looking for him when he stumbled upon the shed and looked inside. He saw her creating a tiny vortex of wind."

He looked down at his hands as he spoke.

"I was there with her and I ran after the boy but he was too fast, and I couldn't stop him. We knew she'd be hanged, so we planned to run away that night." His voice wavered. "She stayed hidden out in the woods, and we planned to meet at a clearing at midnight."

My mother reached out and touched his knee.

"I went back into town to get supplies for our journey, and I ran into Vasier." He shook his head. "I didn't even think about what I was saying when I told him I was running away with her." He ran a thumb over his palm. "I thought he'd be happy for me, but hours later, when I found him strangling her in that clearing, I realized he hated her for taking me away from him."

Wyott and I straightened at that, but my father continued.

"We both ended up killing each other in the fight and when I woke I was washed up on the shores of Merwinan, long before it was ever called that. I woke up with knowledge placed in my head by the Gods. They showed me what happened to me, what I was, and how I could survive. But I never saw Alannah again."

He looked up to look between Wyott and I.

"When I told the two of you that scouts had reported back to me about some odd occurrences outside of Kembertus two years ago..." He trailed off and Wyott and I nodded. "That was a lie." He looked to Evaline. "That was the first night you'd ever used your magic. I felt it."

She pursed her lips and nodded. He looked back to Wyott and I.

"I sent you two out there because I thought it was Alannah. Evaline's magic is in her blood, and part of that blood was Alannah's. It created me, and when I felt it I thought it was her."

A million thoughts ran through my mind, too fast for me to pick out any one of them to focus on too long.

I shook my head. "Why didn't you just tell us?" I looked to Wyott before turning back to my father. "What is there to be ashamed of?"

My father swallowed. "I didn't want any of the Kova to think less of me once they found out. They looked up to me, and I tried to be as benevolent of a leader as I could." He raised his eyes and switched them between Wyott and I. "I was afraid of what they'd all think—of what *you all* would think—when you discovered the truth about Vasier and I."

Wyott's eyebrows furrowed. "Alannah creating the Kova and Vasi alters our history, of course, but it would never make us think less of you."

"That's not the only reason I'm ashamed," my father said. He continued before anyone else could speak. "Vasier attacked Alannah because he was angry with her for taking me away from him." He met my eyes before flicking them to Wyott's. "Vasier is my brother." Then his eyes fell to his wringing hands. "My twin brother."

CHAPTER TWENTY-FIVE

Wyott

Kovarrin's words hung in the air between the six of us. I wanted to react, to give any indication at all to how I was feeling. Mostly because every pair of eyes in the room, except for Evaline's, fell to me.

But there wasn't much I could do to convey how I felt, because I wasn't sure.

I wasn't sure if I should be angry, or devastated, or happy that Kovarrin was telling us the truth. I supposed I could at least be happy that the Gods didn't give Vasier the gift of his creation, because it meant he could be killed.

Mostly I thought about the only time I'd ever encountered Vasier in my life.

The day my father died.

I hadn't seen him; he'd had his back to the rock I hid behind. But after they'd killed my father, when I saw Vasier begin to turn around, I'd shrunk back behind the boulder to shield myself and prayed to the Gods he wouldn't kill me, too.

I sat there shaking as I heard his footsteps approach, until they stopped just on the other side of the boulder. I'd heard him plant his hands on the top of it, and saw his shadow fall over my shoes when he leaned over to speak to me.

"Tell Kovarrin I killed his brother," he'd said, his voice grim. Then he'd turned around and I heard his footsteps slowly move away. "Not the one he'd like," he'd said softly on his retreat, and I'd never known what he meant.

When I'd told Kovarrin what Vasier said, his face had gone pale. I assumed it was because my father was like a brother to him, but now I understood.

Rage slithered up my spine and I felt my body shiver with anger.

"Did my father know?"

Kovarrin's face fell at my reaction, but he nodded. "Yes, he was the only one who did."

I supposed that was a better answer than if he hadn't. Because if he hadn't, then he would have unknowingly been a target for Vasier, a point to tack onto his revenge for Kovarrin. But if he'd known, perhaps he just didn't think he'd ever run into Vasier on Brassillion. Regardless, Vasier killed my father for one reason alone.

"Vasier killed my father because he was hurt that you replaced him."

The First tried to reach forward for my hand on the table, but I pulled it away.

"You could've told me, I would've understood." I shook my head, pulled my clenched fists down onto my lap. "The only reason you're telling the truth now is because Evaline arrived here, and you were forced to reckon with what you've done."

He left his hand draped across the table, reaching for me. "You're right," he croaked. "And there's nothing I can say to take back the mistake. I can only do what is right now, and ask for your forgiveness. For all Kova to give me their forgiveness. That's why I'm telling you all now, because I have to tell the rest of them at the Ball."

The table fell silent for several long moments.

Cora's hand slid over to my lap where she placed it on my forearm and squeezed it comfortingly. Rasa covered her mouth and stared down in thought. Maddox stared down at the table and Evaline shot worried glances across the room.

As my eyes landed on her, I knew I could never hold any anger for her, or her mother. It was all a horrific accident, and if Alannah hadn't created them, none of us would be here today, and I never would've met Cora.

I sighed, and felt the tension from everyone in the room tighten as they looked to me. Kovarrin was a father, to more Kova than just Maddox and I. We all stemmed from him, as the Vasi did from Vasier, and Kovarrin had tried to be a good leader. He *was* a good leader.

I ran my hand through my hair and turned to Kovarrin.

"I accept your apology. I'm sorry I was angry, it just took me by surprise. But none of what has happened was your fault." Then I looked to Evaline. "Or your mother's."

The tension filling the room subsided as Maddox, Cora, and Rasa all agreed and gave their own forgiveness.

"Thank you all," he said when we'd finished, but then his eyes fell to Evaline. "But I also need to apologize to you, Evaline." She looked up at him, her brows pulled in confusion. "I'm so sorry that your mother performed blood magic to bring me back." He shook his head. "I've spent centuries ashamed of that, because the Gods would've cursed her because of it. I assumed they'd done something horrible to her when I never saw her again." He looked over to Rasa, met her eyes for the first time during this conversation. "It's a horrible thing to feel responsible for the destruction of your best friend."

Rasa reached forward and cupped his cheek in her hand. "She saved you because she loved you, and we do a lot for those we love."

He nodded. "I know that, but the thought of being the cause of a curse on her has haunted me." He looked to Evaline again. "Can you forgive me?"

She gave a nod as if she wasn't angry, but there was an uptick in her heartbeat. "There's nothing to forgive. She loved you like a brother, you were her best friend, and she felt so guilty that you died protecting her from your own blood that she started the enchantment before she could even think of the consequences. It was her choice. There's no reason for you to feel guilt."

He nodded and released a breath I'm not sure he was ready for, because it was so deep and shaky that it was evident he'd been waiting centuries to hear that.

When he calmed himself he looked at her. "Is it too much for me to ask what her curse was?"

Evaline pursed her lips at the question. Before she could respond, he interjected again, "It is, I'm sorry. Forget it."

She shook her head and looked down at the table.

"It's not that." She was uncomfortable and I saw Maddox squirm beside her. Her voice was tight when she spoke again. "You'll be glad to know that my mother wasn't the one who was cursed."

A smile broke out on Kovarrin's face. "Really?" He placed his hand on his chest and release another breath of relief. "Gods, I'd been so worried for so long that something horrible had happened to her."

He continued talking about how relieved he was, speculating that perhaps the Gods didn't punish her because her intentions were good, unlike most of the Sorcerers who wielded blood magic.

But I saw Maddox's mind working from across the table, knew he was cautious to celebrate because of the way she'd worded the statement.

He didn't say anything, even though I saw his mouth twitch to open. I knew my brother was afraid of asking the question, afraid of what the answer would be.

"Who was cursed, Evaline?" I asked softly, and Maddox threw me a look of gratitude, worry clouding his eyes as he looked back to her.

She raised watery eyes to Maddox, and my heart sank.

"That nightmare the other night was my mother. That's when she told me."

His jaw quivered for a moment before he asked, "Told you what?" His voice was so low, so afraid.

She looked down at her lap and I watched as a tear fell down into it. "The Gods chose to punish her by not cursing her, but her child."

Maddox's eyes clenched shut, Kovarrin's eyes widened, and Cora placed a hand over her mouth.

Rasa stood and walked around the table until she was kneeling on the ground beside Evaline, taking Evaline's hands in hers. "What is the curse?"

Maddox's heartbeat raised, but he opened his eyes and looked to Evaline.

"The Gods punished the Sorceress who created the Vasi by cursing her daughter to end them." She looked up at Maddox. "Since before I was born, before she was pregnant or even met my father, I've been fated to kill Vasier and end the Vasi's tyranny over the humans."

My ears perked up at the words, and I felt Cora turn toward me. Killing Vasier was all I'd ever wanted.

But as the thought formed in my mind, as the hope sprung in my chest, I realized too late that this news shouldn't excite me. Not when Evaline was looking up at Maddox in terror, when he was gritting his teeth and reaching for her with anger driving his heartbeat to soar.

Despite what I wanted, or what the world needed, how could the Gods put all of this pressure on one set of shoulders?

"That's why you're so powerful," Kovarrin said quietly.

Evaline nodded. "Yes. I was born as a normal Sorceress, the gift passed on from my mother. Where she used Air, I can manipulate Water. That is my natural gift." She took a deep breath. "But the Gods each gave me an aspect of their power too." She went on to describe how the God of Gale and Terra gave her their magic, how Merwinna enhanced her Water abilities. But then she stopped.

"There's eight Gods," Cora said softly. "What are your other five powers?"

Evaline shook her head. "I don't know. Maddox woke me up before my mother and I could discuss any more information." Maddox pursed his lips. "I only know that the Gods crafted my power to be unlike any other Sorcerer in the world."

Rasa's brows furrowed and she looked up at Kovarrin from her kneel. "If the Gods were so concerned with Vasier and the Vasi, why not just kill them all themselves?"

Kovarrin shook his head. "The Gods have never crossed into this plane from the heavens. When I awoke as a Kova and had the Gods-placed knowledge in my mind, they'd left behind the understanding that they refuse to intervene on the ground-level, otherwise they would've killed Vasier and I the moment Alannah changed us. It goes against the laws of being. The Gods cannot execute changes that they'd like to see in the world themselves, only work through those they bless." He looked at Evaline. "I'm sure the Gods don't consider your power a curse, but a blessing. They chose you to carry out their plan."

Evaline shook her head as more tears swelled. "I don't want it."

Rasa stood. "Stop. All of you stop. This is all too much." She waved her hands. "This was supposed to be a happy night, a welcome home," she said as she looked between all of us.

Kovarrin cringed. "I know, I'm sorry. But it wasn't fair to Evaline for me to hold onto this any longer. She'd been keeping it from all of you to give me the opportunity to explain myself."

Evaline looked down at the table.

"When I tell the kingdom tonight, is it okay if I mention your relation to your mother?" he asked her.

A beat passed as she seemed to think about it, but she only nodded. "I guess there's no reason to push it off, they'll all figure out who I am, about my magic, eventually."

Kovarrin nodded but Rasa covered her face for a moment and when she opened them her eyes were glassy. She pointed to Evaline and Maddox. "You two, go touch up Evaline's makeup." It had started to smear with her tears. She placed a hand over her chest. "I'm going to go start welcoming guests." Then looked to Cora and I. "And you two should gather yourselves too."

She moved to turn away, but then seemed to change her mind. She laid a hand on Evaline's shoulder and when the Sorceress looked up at Rasa, she swept a tear off Evaline's cheek.

"We're going to figure this out together. We're a family, and that means that your struggles are our struggles, too. But we don't have to execute a centuries old fate in one night." Evaline nodded slightly. "Try to have fun, and tomorrow we will start our work."

With that, she bent to kiss Evaline on the forehead before exiting the room. Maddox and Evaline followed, and Cora spoke down the bond.

Are you okay?

I pursed my lips. *Yes.*

She placed a kiss on my cheek. "I have to help Evaline with her makeup. I'll meet you outside."

I nodded and after she left, my eyes drifted from her retreating form over to Kovarrin, who sat completely still and looked at the vacant space where Evaline and Maddox had disappeared. The look on his face reminded me of the one he had after learning that my father had died. Worry and devastation all mixed up into one. But when his features settled I saw the true expression that sat there. Burden. The weight of the responsibility that he'd carried for centuries as the first of our kind and the leader of us all.

I followed his gaze to the door and understood Kovarrin's worry.

He'd been carrying that weight for centuries and knew the toll it took, the pain it caused. And now, he had to watch as the mate of his son bore the same responsibility.

Chapter Twenty-Six

Evaline

Maddox kneeled in front of where I sat on the edge of the bed. One hand was wrapped around the back of my knee and the other joined my hands in my lap.

Cora had just left from touching up my makeup, and I was so glad she'd come to help me with it. She finished it far faster than I could've.

Maddox didn't speak, but I could feel his eyes on me. I knew he was waiting to gauge how I was after the news, but I only felt guilty.

"Are you angry I didn't tell you right away?" I asked softly, tilting my head to meet his gaze.

His brows furrowed. "Of course not." He shook his head. "It's all a lot to take in, but I understand why you wanted to wait for my father to tell us." He raised a hand and stroked his thumb over my cheek. "You don't have to protect everyone all the time, you don't have to protect me. I can handle whatever the Gods throw at us. We will handle this, just like my mother said."

I took a deep breath and nodded. After my father passed I had to do things like this on my own. But I didn't have to do that anymore. Maddox was right. Rasa was right. I had a whole family here, waiting to help me in any way they could.

Maddox stood and helped me up before he took my face in both of his hands.

"I love you," he whispered.

My lips lifted softly. "I love you."

He dipped to kiss me then pulled away and grasped my hand in his. "Ready?"

I forced a smile and nodded. Rasa was right, we couldn't fix anything in one night. Despite that, I felt the anxiety in my chest coil as we headed for the Ball and I had to force myself to consider all of this logically. I could only deal with the stress by thinking through all the worst possibilities and how I would get through them.

The Gods gave me a power unlike anyone has ever had, with the sole purpose to enact their will through me.

It was a lot of pressure, but what was the worst that could possibly happen if I ignored my fate? They would find a new Sorcerer to give the burden to, to give my power to? Maybe that was what was best. The Gods *should* give it to someone who knew how to use this magic; who knew how to best utilize it to change the world for the better.

I took a long breath as I already felt my anxiety lessening. If my magic was taken, I'd survive. I'd go back to being the Evaline Manor I'd been before I ever discovered it, and Maddox and I could have a normal life here, together.

All I wanted was a break. I wanted to be done with the sorrow and hardship. I wanted to rest.

Fear slithered up my chest as I remembered my words to that pirate just before he died.

"There is no rest for those like you."

I looked up at Maddox, and he smiled down at me as he led me through the entrance to the Ball.

Everything would be okay, no matter what happened.

"Oh my Gods," I gasped when the full Ball came into view.

"It's one of my favorite spots in the entire kingdom, especially at night," Maddox said in my ear as he led me through the walkway with a steady hand on the small of my back.

I thought the space was beautiful when I saw it in the daylight, but the scene at night put all else to shame. The granite pillars still framed the perimeter, but somehow looked even larger than before with the dark night sky behind them. Wiring was strung from between them and crossed over the entire affair, holding lanterns and wisteria above the crowd.

The lanterns weren't lit and the moon was new and invisible, but the fire pits in each of the corners made up for it along with the sea of stars that hung over top of us all.

The floor was already bustling with bodies that either stood to chat or danced, and the music was rhythmic but wasn't so loud that the waves crashing at the base of the cliff we stood on could not be heard.

"Well," I breathed. "I think it's safe to say that this puts every other Ball I've ever been to, to shame."

Maddox chuckled behind me as he led us to the left, toward where his father and mother stood atop the landing watching the guests. There was a short staircase below them that ran the entire length of the mansion behind them. Rasa looked as if she tried her best to maintain a smile, and Kovarrin wrung his hands. I knew they were nervous for how the kingdom would take the news.

I felt dozens of eyes on me as we walked and knew it was because they saw Maddox's arm around me. I opened my mouth to speak, but then realized everyone around us could potentially hear, so instead I opted for the bond.

Is it normal for the entire kingdom to have this type of reaction when a Kova finds their mate? It seemed odd that everyone we'd encountered so far, and all the eyes on me now, seemed so genuinely happy and *invested* in Maddox's love life.

Maddox's dry laugh brushed against my hair. *Let's just say that I was outspoken on my distaste for being one of the only single men among my friends.*

I couldn't help the laugh that bubbled up from my lips. It was kind of charming that he'd pined for so long, but as the thought struck me another one came faster. My head cocked up toward him. *Were you constantly Wyott and Cora's tag along?*

His eye roll was quick. *Unfortunately.*

A smile broke out on my face as I tried to picture it. No wonder Wyott was always so understanding of Maddox and I having moments alone together on our trip. He'd gotten a taste of what Maddox had been struggling with for so long. And the thought of Maddox sitting down to dinners with the two, going out on adventures, made me laugh so hard that the rest of my worries over the evening's earlier events subsided completely.

I thought Maddox would take me to stand with his parents, but he only walked me over to stand a few steps below them, and off to the side. Cora and Wyott walked up too, and I felt Cora slide her hand into mine as she stood on my other side, Wyott standing as Maddox's reflection.

Kovarrin looked to see that the four of us had arrived and were, apparently, in position, so he stepped forward with Rasa at his side and cleared his throat.

Almost instantly, the music stopped and a thousand eyes turned to look at him. At their leader.

"Thank you all for coming," he said, a small smile forming on his lips. He placed a hand on his chest. "I'm grateful that you all have taken time out of your night to spend time with us," he said before waving his arm toward the four of us. "And to welcome my sons and our guest home."

A short round of clapping sounded from the crowd and Kovarrin waited until it quieted to resume.

He took a shaky breath. "I'm sorry to say that before we can make those introductions, I have something to tell you all." His eyes darted over all the people below him. "I'm afraid I haven't been completely honest." A small chatter formed among the crowd as Kovarrin started to tell them all the truth; that he'd saved a Sorceress from Vasier's attack; that the two of them killed each other in the fight; that the Sorceress had been kind enough to make a sacrifice of her own, and bring him back; that she accidentally brought Vasier back too.

His voice shook as he spoke, and I knew it was from the guilt of keeping it a secret for so many centuries.

When he confessed that Vasier was his twin brother, the crowd voiced an audible gasp.

"I cannot begin to express how terrible it has felt to keep this from you all." He shook his head. "Back when I came here, when we started building Rominia, I never imagined what it would turn into."

He paused and looked over the crowd, and even from here I could see his misted eyes.

"What the Kova population would turn into. So you can see how it was an easy lie to tell in the beginning, because I never imagined we'd be standing here all these years later." He took a deep breath. "I can only ask that you try to forgive me for keeping these secrets to hide my shame, and to please direct any questions to me." He turned to Rasa, then flicked his eyes to us. "I think my family has begun to forgive me, but they aren't the ones who need to answer to this, I am." He nodded to us, and we walked higher on the stairs to stand beside them.

"But if you'd be so kind, I'd like for you all to still have fun tonight, and to celebrate my family as we welcome back my sons, and Evaline," he said, waving a hand toward me. Maddox's arm around my waist grew tighter.

Kovarrin gave a small laugh. "I'm not sure who has been more excited for Maddox to find his mate—him," he said, then turned back to the crowd. "Or everyone who had to listen to him complain about how he had not yet found her."

The crowd laughed softly and I felt Maddox blush and the jolt in his shoulders when Wyott reached over and shoved him.

"We are so thankful to the Gods for uniting Maddox with Evaline." He paused. "Evaline Manor is the daughter of both Wallace Manor and Alannah Manor." A stirring began in the crowd. "You may recall that Wallace was the true heir to Kembertus, before he ended the Vasi alliance and left the kingdom."

I saw some heads nod in the crowd, saw some pitiful eyes land on me as I assumed they knew of his death, and I swallowed the tears that started to rise from them.

"What you wouldn't know, is that Alannah Manor is the very Sorceress who created myself and Vasier." He turned to me. "Evaline is a Sorceress like her mother, but with more than one element." A wave of gasps shook down the crowd, but Kovarrin continued. "Rasa and I are honored to welcome her into our family." He turned back to the crowd. "Please join me in welcoming into our kingdom, Evaline Manor, daughter of the Creator."

The crowd erupted in applause, and Maddox and I stepped forward as his hand raised on my back to loosely cup around the back of my neck. Tears sprung in my eyes at the welcome while I felt pride shift down the bond from Maddox.

As the cheers started to die down, some shouts sprung to life.

"Warp the wind!" someone yelled, while another pointed toward the ocean. "Make a wave!"

But soon the entire crowd was raising their glasses to the unlit lanterns above them.

"Light the lanterns! Light the lanterns!"

Dread washed a cold wave down my body as I realized that they were asking to see a show of my magic.

A magic I didn't know yet. A magic I couldn't wield in any great manner at the drop of a hat.

Maddox opened his mouth to speak, holding an open-faced palm to the crowd. I knew he was about to tell them to stop, to tell them I was still learning my magic and that we didn't even know for sure if I could use fire. But before he could say anything, a man to my right stepped out from the crowd and skipped up the stairs to stand near us.

He turned his kind smile on the crowd and waved a hand through the air.

"Where are your manners?" he chastised with a twinkle in his hazel eyes. "She's only just arrived. Surely you can give her time before she shows you all her power." He looked down at me with a smile before stepping forward and addressing the crowd again. "I know the Kova are proud of strength, but many Sorcerers are raised in kingdoms where our magic is illegal. Forgive me if I think it's a bit rude to assume that Evaline wants to showcase such a private part of herself."

The crowd hushed and began to nod, and Gods this might be worse than their requests that I show them my magic, but the man continued talking and the attention directed back to him.

"Besides, it is my honor to light this party tonight."

The crowd was quiet as they all looked to the lanterns above them. The man cupped his hands, rubbed them against each other for a moment, and when he pulled them apart a blazing light of fire was born from the darkness. The flame lit his face and caused shadows to dance around his pale skin. His short brown hair fluttered in the wind as his smile grew at his creation.

My eyes widened as I stared at it, unable to look away. Deep inside a piece of me begged to step forward to touch it, to hold the fire in my hands, as if my magic recognized a missing piece, a trick I hadn't tried yet.

We all watched in wonder as he continued to pull his hands apart. The wider the gap, the larger the ball of flames grew, until he flipped his hands out and extended his arms. The ball of light fractured into several smaller flames until a hundred all flew out above the crowd and found their homes in the lanterns. After the burst of light, the night darkened again until the affair was only slightly more lit than it had been before.

The crowd burst into applause, and it was only then that I realized how uncomfortable Maddox was.

What's wrong? I asked him down the bond.

Nothing.

I would've rolled my eyes if the whole of the kingdom weren't staring at me.

Maddox, I said in a warning tone.

Nothing is wrong, I just haven't met this Sorcerer yet, and I'm not sure I trust him.

Kovarrin stepped forward to shake the man's hand before the Sorcerer gave a quick bow and when he straightened, Kovarrin turned to face the crowd again.

"Please, enjoy the evening."

I gave a smile toward the crowd and was thankful when they began to disperse. Maddox and I tried to step away but before we could the Sorcerer stepped in front of us.

"Evaline, what an honor it is to meet you," he said with a bow. "I'm Lauden, the Arch Sorcerer."

"It's nice to meet you," I said, extending my hand to shake his.

Lauden slid his hand into mine but instead of shaking it he flipped them and placed a kiss on my knuckles.

When he dropped my hand, he turned to Maddox and in one move my mate swept around to stand beside me, an arm anchored around my waist, extending his hand out to Lauden.

"A shake will do," he said, his voice tight.

Easy, I said down the bond.

But Lauden didn't skip a beat, only straightened with a laugh on his lips.

"Of course," he said shaking hands with Maddox. "I meant no disrespect. Where I come from it is custom to greet high born women this way." His eyes flicked to mine. "Considering we didn't get to meet many of them."

"And where was that?" Maddox asked and I could tell he was at least making the attempt to soften his voice.

"A small village outside of Vestaria," Lauden said, clasping his hands in front of him. "A lovely place to grow up if you like frequent marauders, a high murder rate, and for your very existence to be illegal."

Maddox nodded and I felt a wash of guilt sweep down the bond.

Good. He hadn't even given this man a chance, and here I was having to embrace an entire kingdom.

I can feel your judgement, my Goddess, he said down the bond, his hand tightening on my waist. *I didn't mean to pre-judge, but he did come under odd circumstances, and Ankin was my friend. I'm only trying to be cautious.*

I just leaned back into him a bit in response as I looked to Lauden.

"It's nice to meet you too," I started. "What exactly is an Arch Sorcerer?" I asked.

Lauden smiled. "Kovarrin employed me to help maintain the wards around this island as well as those in the Madierian Kingdoms, run our mailing system, and anything else he may find useful." He waved a hand to the flickering lanterns. "And sometimes that includes making a show."

"You're a Fire Caster, then," Maddox said.

Lauden nodded. "I am, please don't hold it against me."

I cocked a brow and both men saw it. They both started to speak at the same time, but Maddox nodded to Lauden to continue.

"There is a certain fear society has with Fire Casters because of how dangerous fire can be and because we are the only Sorcerers who can conjure their magic out of nothing," he said with a shrug. "There have been Fire Casters in the past who've given us a bad name and used their power for evil." His eyes shined as he spoke. "But I was taught by a skilled mentor who ensured I learned to use my magic for good."

He turned toward the crowd then, searching. He seemed to find who he was looking for, and I watched as Sage, the woman from the boutique, came forward.

"This is my partner, Sage," he said.

I nodded politely to her. "Yes, we met in town a few days ago."

Maddox seemed surprised by that, and I realized I'd never told him about our interaction.

She nodded and Maddox reached to shake her hand as he introduced himself.

Lauden wrapped his arm around her waist and tugged her into his side. "Sage is a Sorceress as well, a Terra Caster."

My eyes widened. When I'd seen her at the shop I thought she was human instead of Kova and wondered if perhaps that was the something I hadn't been able to place.

Lauden turned to me again. "Kovarrin has told me you're interested in learning more about your magic. If it's alright with you, Sage and I would be honored to teach you."

A flutter broke through my chest, that same buzz I felt every time I used my magic, and I nodded. "Yes, that would be great. If you wouldn't mind."

Sage smiled, but it didn't extend to her eyes. "Of course not, it'll take a bit of time to master each of them. At first it might just be a few parlor tricks, but the rest will come."

She hasn't seen what you can do, Maddox said down the bond.

Those were just survival instincts. Gods know if I can do it on purpose.

CHAPTER TWENTY-SEVEN

Evaline

Shortly after Lauden and Sage excused themselves, I dragged Maddox to one of the tables on the perimeter of the dance floor.

"If you were hungry, you could've told me sooner," he said as we made it to one of the tables littered with small sandwiches and desserts.

"I'm not hungry," I said as I reached for one of the pre-poured wine glasses sitting at the edge of the table. His eyebrows raised as he watched me take the cup to my mouth and take a few deep gulps.

"Planning to repeat the night you showed up to the inn after a couple bottles of wine?" he asked, amusement playing in his eyes as he reached for my hip.

My brows rose. "I drank it to avoid thinking about something awful then," I said and tipped my glass toward him. "So yes, I guess this will be a repeat."

He only smiled and dipped to kiss me before I heard Cora behind us.

"Evaline, are you okay?" she asked, as she and Wyott came to stand with us. Her hand landed on my elbow. "Today has been a lot."

I pursed my lips. "I've survived worse."

A sad look flashed over her eyes but she waved a hand up and down my form. "Well, on the plus side, you look stunning." Her eyes flicked to Maddox. "You look okay."

He blinked half-lidded eyes and swirled his wine in his cup. "I'm so glad we rushed home for heartfelt moments like this."

I shook my head at them both and looked at Cora's attire. I'd seen her in the dining room, but I'd been far too worried to notice what she was wearing then; the flowing pants that matched her hair and a tight top of the same color were stunning. Her sleeves were capped and off the shoulder, and the hem of the shirt didn't quite make it down to her pants which exposed a bit of bronzed skin at her waist.

"You look extraordinary Cora."

She winked. "I try."

Wyott wrapped an arm around her and even in the dim light the lust in his eyes was evident.

I turned to the table and grabbed another glass of wine and downed it before taking Maddox's arm. "Let's dance."

"If you run away every time they get like that, you'll always be on the move," Maddox said low in my ear while I led us through to the dance floor.

I turned in his arms when I found a suitable spot and he tugged me closer by the waist and lifted our clasped hands.

"I'm just not used to it yet," I said blushing up at him.

He cocked his head as his eyes drifted down over my lips. "I suppose it won't be so bad, as long as when you flee it's with me." He pulled me flush against his chest as we danced, his voice dropping lower. "Into a private room." He dipped his head to run his lips over mine softly. "For hours."

I let out a breathy laugh and shook my head. "Are all Kova men this lustful, or just those who grew up in this mansion?"

He pulled back with a large grin on his face.

"Couldn't say."

But I couldn't respond, couldn't even form words, the way the lantern light flickered over his face; the sight of the stars and dark night behind him; and the shifting dark of his eyes that nearly matched the sky—I don't think I'd ever seen anything so beautiful.

"Keep looking at me like that and you'll find out just how lustful I am," he said with a gruff voice.

The music lilted just above the sound of a thousand voices around us and I cocked my head. "Who says I don't want to be enlightened?"

"Mmm," he grumbled as his hand on my waist traveled lower, until it was resting on my ass.

Keep teasing me, Eva, he warned down the bond, *but trust me, I'm a better gambler than Wyott. I will call that bluff. I'll call it all the way into that mansion until I'm fucking you in our bedroom again.*

My cheeks heated the more he spoke, but every word caused that want deep in my belly to grow.

And we might not make it that far. Might have to duck into a closet. His eyes flashed. *Or the kitchen. I could put you on the table just like I did at the wedding and this time, I could hide more than just my hands under your dress.*

I pursed my lips to hide my smile because I could already feel my clit pulse with every swipe of his eyes down my body.

You're as bad as Wyott, I teased.

He bent to kiss me. *Wyott was making up for a handful of months. I have to make up for decades.*

I laughed and shook my head. "I—" But I was cut off by a hand clasping on Maddox's shoulder. Annoyance flashed across his eyes, and I knew he had to restrain himself from snapping at Lauden as the Arch Sorcerer moved to stand beside us.

"May I cut in?"

Maddox's hold on me tightened.

Be nice, I cooed down the bond.

Do I have to? he responded.

I smiled at Lauden. "Of course you can."

Maddox nodded to Lauden, begrudgingly, I knew, and bent to kiss my head before turning and walking away but before he took a couple steps I heard his voice down the bond.

Of course, I could just take up your thoughts, so he doesn't get the honor of conversing with you. It's what he gets for interrupting us when we were so clearly enthralled.

I could've laughed, almost did, but instead let Lauden put his hand in mine and his other replaced Maddox's at my waist as we fell into step.

I felt Maddox's gaze sweep across me and was so taken aback by how similar this felt to the night he'd watched me dance with Bassel.

"I'm sorry for interrupting," Lauden said, pulling me from my thoughts.

I smiled. "It's no problem at all."

He nodded. "Good. I talked to Kovarrin," he said nodding toward the steps where Kovarrin had introduced me earlier in the night. "He said we should start training whenever you feel ready."

I pursed my lips. "The sooner the better, if it's not too much trouble." I shrugged. "I only just learned that I had magical abilities, and I don't understand them at all."

"Of course it wouldn't be too much trouble. Sage and I were each taught by her father to use our magic. He knew more about Sorcerers than anyone I've ever met. I learned a lot from him, and I'm happy to pass that on to you."

"Thank you."

"There's no need to thank me, it's part of my job here, and Sage will help too. She's very knowledgeable and since you have more than one element, she can help with Terra, while I help with Fire."

There was something strange about her, and the thought of spending any more time with Sage was mildly unpleasant, but I had to do what was needed to learn more about my magic.

I forced a smile. "That'd be great."

Lauden smiled and spun me out. I landed back in his arms and his hand was a little lower on my waist. I felt Maddox's gaze settle on it in an instant. "I don't know that I have Fire, though," I said quickly, and I wasn't sure if it was to distract me, or Maddox.

Lauden nodded. "Kovarrin told me you've only experienced three elements so far." He cocked his head in thought. "We will work on all of them, but Fire is far different from the others. Pulling from the elements around you is different than conjuring, but I'm sure you'll master it, too, in time."

Before I could respond, the world shook. Quaked. Rocked in a way unlike the smaller rumble Maddox and I had felt in our bathroom.

Maddox was at my side in an instant. Shouts rang out above the crowd, the music stopped.

"What's happening?" I shrieked over the noise.

Maddox looked to me with wide eyes and my heart stopped in my chest. He was afraid.

"The largest quake I've ever felt," he said, and his eyes swung around us until he watched as the pillars that surrounded us started to totter. "Gods. Stay here," he breathed before he took off running.

He aimed for the pillar that stood as a corner on the dance floor, the closest one to the edge of the cliff. It had begun falling, and I watched as several Kova moved to stabilize it as best they could.

The Ball was a whirl of bodies, all taking cover from the quake as the world still shook. Some ran for their homes, I assumed. Some held onto each other, and some only balanced themselves and watched as the Kova tried to right the pillar. From where I stood, I could see Wyott and Cora under it too.

Lauden was gone from my side, and I wasn't sure when that had happened. I turned and watched as more people fled. The Kova who ran home with their children were easy enough to spot, because they disappeared in a blur of speed. But the Sorcerers, the humans, were slower. Some ran to help with another pillar that started to fall, and I watched as they held up their hands and the wind whirred around them as Air Casters helped to right the pillars.

But humans only ran about and sought cover.

Maddox, Wyott, and Cora, among others, stabilized their pillar and ran after another further away from me as it started to fall. I could hardly see them anymore.

Evaline get inside, Maddox commanded down the bond.

Gods, what was I doing? I'd just been standing and watching, but Maddox was right, I needed to take cover.

I am, I said as I moved toward the mansion along with several humans. A few humans around me were swept away by Kova, and I realized they were helping to save the humans.

When I'd made it to the base of the staircase my foot was already lifted when I heard a cry ring out.

I turned for the noise; it was a baby's cry. I wasn't sure how I made it out above the crashing sounds of falling rock, the scream of the wind, and the shouts.

My heart stopped as I spun and saw a mother clutching her baby to her chest on the opposite side of the dance floor. She was close to the edge, and human, by her pace. Her eyes were wide with panic.

My legs were pumping before I even realized what I was doing. Between strides as I sprinted for her I kicked off the decorated slippers I wore, they only slowed me down, and when her eyes met mine, when she realized I was coming for her, they lit with gratitude.

The Kova must not have noticed her, or perhaps she'd been too lost in panic to call for help herself, but I wouldn't leave her behind.

My legs ached but I only pushed harder to get to her and thanked the Gods for the short dress. Anything longer would have hindered my stride.

"Clear the floor!" someone shouted. "They're going to fall!"

Be careful, I heard Maddox down the bond, and knew he'd spotted me. *Grab them and get inside.*

The baby wailed again, the pillar directly behind them shifted, and I flung myself forward.

Chapter Twenty-Eight

Maddox

The only indication I had that Evaline was in trouble was the panic that shot down the bond. I grunted against the pillar that Dean, Wyott, Cora, and I were trying to stop from falling and turned to place my back against it so I could search for her. My neck craned to look past the Sorcerer in front of me who tried to use his powers of wind to right the pillar, to no avail.

My eyes landed on Evaline in an instant. Across the expanse, sprinting toward the edge of a cliff where a human woman ran with a baby in her arms.

I wanted to run for her, but I couldn't. If I moved, the pillar would fall on my friends and there were too many other pillars unstable from the quake. Kova were flitting about in flashes to control them all.

Be careful, I urged down the bond. *Grab them and get inside.*

She didn't respond and I watched as the pillar behind the woman rocked before falling straight for the three of them.

Before I could think, before I could try to find a way to them without crushing the Kova around me, she jumped.

Evaline leaped forward, flinging her body over the mother and child, and threw her hand straight above them just as the pillar plummeted down.

The quake stopped, the pillar behind me stabilized, and the world went silent, save for some sighs of relief and a lone baby's wail.

My eyes were already locked on my mate as everyone around me turned to face Evaline. She stood over the humans, shielding them with her body, the pillar suspended in the air an arm's length above the tip of her fingers.

The mother seemed to notice that they were safe and jumped up to flee.

The movement pulled me from my daze, and must have for Wyott and Cora too, because the three of us were by her side in a breath.

"What do I do with it now?" Evaline asked, her breathing labored from the effort.

I looked up at it, trying to gauge how we could lower it safely to the ground, or stand it back up. But just as I opened my mouth to speak, shouts came from the mansion where several Kova, humans, and Sorcerers had taken cover.

"The volcano!" one yelled.

"Mt. Rominia!" another screeched.

It seemed as if every head in the area angled up to look at the volcano as a burst of light shot from its top.

I turned to Evaline as the kingdom's emergency bells started to ring, and watched as she stood up from where she'd been squatting, and put both hands up toward the pillar, and shoved it back.

The pillar fell back with a force I've never seen and toppled over the side of the cliff into the churning waters below.

I pulled her into my arms and ran to the doors of the mansion, Cora and Wyott on my heels.

"You need to stay here," I instructed. "We have to start evacuating everyone below the mountain."

My parents met us at the doors with Lauden and Sage.

"The strength of that quake must have triggered the eruption. We need to go," my father said.

I bent to kiss Evaline after standing her upright, but she shook her head. "Why wouldn't the different Sorcerers just stop the eruption?" she asked, looking between my father and me.

"What do you mean?" my father asked.

"The Terra, the Water, the Fire Sorcerers...Why don't you have them stop the eruption?"

Lauden's brows rose and he looked to Kovarrin. "I'm the only Fire Caster here, but we could try."

Kovarrin seemed to be thinking it over when Sage stepped forward. "The other Sorcerers won't be happy," she said. "Sorcerers are taught not to intervene with nature in that way. The Gods have created a balance, and some Sorcerers don't believe in disturbing it. Some view it just as forbidden as blood magic."

Evaline put a hand on my arm. "Blood magic doesn't scare me," she said. "I can try. I don't know about stopping the quake or helping manipulate the fire, but I can try to douse it with water."

Lauden nodded. "Sage and I are in."

I ignored the way he didn't allow Sage to make up her own mind, but we didn't have time to continue talking it over. We all leaped into action. Some Kova stayed behind in case of another quake, some shot up the mountain to start evacuating, just in case, and my family and I ran straight for the top of the volcano.

I ran with Evaline, Kovarrin with Lauden, and my mother with Sage.

By the time we got up the mountain, the lava had already begun seeping down and we had to be careful to stay out of its path.

"How much experience do you have with volcanos?" I asked Lauden and Sage.

They looked to each other before Lauden turned to me and shook his head. "None," Lauden said.

An ember hissed as it shot past me.

"The lava isn't fire," I said, nodding toward the puddle of light that crawled past us. "It only looks like it. It's molten rock and metal. I'm just not sure what that means for a Fire Caster."

A look of annoyance flashed over Lauden's face before he turned to Evaline and Sage. "Sage, you try to stop the eruption from the inside." Now that we stood atop it, it was clear that the mountain was still shaking, even if further down on the island was calm. "Evaline, begin siphoning water to stop the lava in its tracks." He shot a look to me. "Water will still help, right?"

I nodded. "Yes, it can slow it down, or stop it, depending on how much is used."

He turned to the Sorceresses. "I'll try to take the heat away and put out the fires that the lava is igniting."

The next several hours were spent trying to not only maintain the damage the volcano had already caused, but to stop the eruption all together. Several other Kova and I ran up and down the mountain, bringing water to douse the lava and flames. Evaline siphoned what she could from the air, but the heat from the volcano actively worked against her. It wasn't long until she moved to manipulating a stream from the river that cut through Rominia.

Lauden put out the fires that stray lava started, running around patches of clear land as fast as he could. Sage knelt with her hands on the side of the mountain, trying to quell it from the inside.

All we'd really managed to do was halt the damage in its tracks, but new lava spewed from the mouth of Mt. Rominia too fast for us to slow down our pace.

Well into the night we were all exhausted when I looked to Sage. Her eyes darted to the Kova flitting around her, to Evaline, to Lauden, and it was clear even from several paces away that there were tears running down her face.

I ran over to kneel beside her. "Are you okay?"

She shook her head but said nothing, forcing her hands deeper into the dirt. I could see the tension in her shoulders as she gritted her teeth.

"It's okay," I said, placing a hand over hers. "You can't expect to control an entire mountain all by yourself. We'll maintain the damage as long as we can. Everyone else is evacuating, if we have to stop, we can always repair whatever damage there is afterward."

She turned to me with furrowed brows. "You don't understand," she said softly, her black-green hair blowing in the wind. "Being weak is a luxury that only the great are afforded."

I started to shake my head, to disagree, when Lauden saw us.

"Sage, what's going on?" he asked and moved to stand over her on her other side. "What's the problem?" He looked up at the mouth of the volcano where more lava slipped out.

She tried to stand but her knees buckled beneath her, the result of wielding her magic for hours without rest. I caught her elbow and helped to lower her back down, but she was still looking up at Lauden, craning her neck at what must be an uncomfortable angle to meet the glare that bore down on her.

"I'm sorry, I'm trying," she bargained, shaking her head.

He started to speak, a look of annoyance on his face, when I stood. "She's doing her best, Lauden," I said, and moved around Sage until I stood over him. "Give her a break. None of this is her responsibility."

He looked up, and I heard Wyott move behind me, knew he could sense that my patience was wearing out.

But it was Evaline who spoke over the rest of us.

"We can try together," she said, and I turned to see her running over and dropping to her knees beside Sage. I backed myself and Lauden away to give them space.

Sage turned to her, and Evaline slipped her hand over Sage's that was currently closed in a fist into the dirt. "You can show me what to do, and I'll try."

Sage's pinched shoulders flexed tighter. "There's no use. It can't be done."

Evaline shook her head. "There's no harm in trying. You're meant to teach me, remember? Consider this my first lesson."

Sage went silent and Lauden opened his mouth, but before he could speak, I snapped my hand up to his chest and pushed him back. He locked his jaw and we all watched as Sage gave a slow nod of her head.

She coached Evaline through what she was trying to do. To quiet the shake of the mountain, to ease the eruption, something that she struggled to put into words because it was such a complicated act.

But they sat there together and placed all four hands against the land. They clenched their eyes shut, gritted their jaws, and very slowly, the mountain below bent to their will.

The rumbles quieted before the lava slowed. The change was hard to see at first, as waves of molten rock still flowed past. After a while, I noticed that what flowed from the mountain top was cooling faster than it could escape, turning to hard rock next to us. Soon, the smoke wafting around us dissipated.

Cheers rang out and I looked around to see all my friends with soot smeared across their faces and fatigue in their eyes. Finally, I looked to the two women who pulled off the feat.

Evaline turned to Sage with a smile that quickly dropped into a slacken jaw. Her eyes glistened with disbelief. "Holy shit, I can't believe we actually did it."

I stepped up to congratulate them but stopped as Sage's nostrils flared at Evaline, and her upper lip pulled back into a look of disgust, her breaths fast. Evaline's face fell at the reaction, but Sage only showed her disdain for a moment before she cringed the look away.

She stood and whirled and this time when she started to fall, she shoved Wyott's hands away as he tried to right her.

"Don't touch me," she barked before we all watched her fumble her way down the mountain.

Lauden followed behind in slow, casual steps.

Chapter Twenty-Nine

Evaline

In the week that passed since the Ball and Mt. Rominia's eruption, we'd spent the time cleaning up the damage the quake had left behind. The damage to the mansion and the patio outside of it wasn't too severe. Several buildings throughout the kingdom took more of our attention.

In actuality, the volcano caused the least amount of damage. Sure, some vegetation in the upper areas of the mountain would need time to grow back, but no homes were destroyed because of it.

There were several homes, however, that sustained severe damage from the prolonged quake. None that toppled, thank the Gods, but many bore cracks up their sides or had collapsed staircases and lifts.

The entire island had come together, though, and I'd never seen a kingdom work so completely as one.

We'd spent so much time in the cleanup, that the family hadn't sat down to figure out what we would do about my curse, like Rasa planned.

In the time since the eruption, something inside of me had changed.

My magic had transformed from something that I would call forward if I needed it, to something that seemed to buzz just under my skin at all times. It ebbed and it flowed, but always remained within reach for me to use if needed.

It didn't feel odd anymore, like something that was completely apart from the rest of my body.

I recalled that each time I'd used it previously, it felt a little stronger; a little easier to use. So much so that I was beginning to wonder if my magic was akin to a muscle, strengthening with each use. It definitely felt stronger after Sage and I had stopped the eruption.

But I knew that I had changed, too. After stopping that pillar, and the eruption, something foundational inside of me had shifted.

My power was crafted by the Gods for me to use, and after what I did to help the people of Rominia that night, I realized that perhaps the Gods were right in choosing me. Maybe I did need this power, maybe I did deserve it. Maybe my magic was meant for more than just killing—Lonix, the man killed by the tree, the pirates—maybe it was meant for saving, too. Just like I'd saved the mother and her baby at the Ball. Maybe my magic could be used to save countless humans from the Vasi if I defeated their First.

And much like my thoughts when it came to deciding to kill Lonix and Bassel during my attack, my mind changed about the curse. Back during my attack I'd vowed to kill them because I knew I was potentially the only one who could. My father taught me combat, and I hadn't wanted to waste his gift by not ending the lives of the men who attacked women in the night. In a moment, killing them had become my responsibility. After seeing the good my power could do, to help an entire island of people, I decided that perhaps the Gods had a reason for choosing me to give this curse to. Maybe it wasn't a curse at all, maybe it was just another one of their blessings.

I didn't have the faintest clue on how I would kill Vasier, how I would end his and the Vasi's tyranny over the humans. But I'd have to at least try.

Fate had led me to Maddox. Fate had led me to this new family. It seemed selfish to only accept the gifts fate granted me, and not the responsibility, too.

So, after the week had passed and the damage in Rominia was mended as best as it could be, it was finally time for me to meet with Lauden and Sage for my first lesson in controlling my magic.

Maddox tried to walk with me, but I forbade him. It was just down the hill from the mansion, a clear path that would have been impossible to miss. Besides, I knew he was only offering because he wanted to try and stay to watch my lesson. He still didn't trust Lauden but I refused to be monitored. I had a lot to learn, and this was one area where he couldn't help me.

When I got to the door of the office I wasn't sure whether I should knock or just enter but considering that Maddox had told me there were living quarters inside for the Arch Sorcerer, I opted to knock.

I was greeted at the door by Sage.

"You don't need to knock," she said in welcome before spinning on her heels to walk into the office. I hurried after her and shut the door behind me.

The building was lofted. A kitchen sat to the right with a dining area and when I peered up, I could see a bedroom in the loft above. Straight ahead the room opened into a greenhouse. Even from where I stood, I could see how the plants thrived and wondered if Sage had something to do with that.

When I heard a rustling, I craned my neck and saw the edge of a cage through the greenery and I realized that it was where Lauden kept the ravens.

Sage led me to the left to an open study with large wooden desks, a centralized fireplace, and books lining the walls.

She perched on the arm of the leather couch on the right side of the office, the bun on top of her head bouncing with the movement, and looked to Lauden who straightened from his position bent over some open facing texts on the table.

He came around the desk with a smile on his face and extended his hand for me to shake.

"Welcome, Evaline. I hope you don't mind coming here to train instead of staying at the estate."

I shook my head. "Of course not." I waved at the space around us. "This is a beautiful home."

Lauden smiled. "Thank you, but truthfully, I can take no credit. Rasa designed it and I only inherited it from Ankin." He nodded toward the ground. "May my grandfather rest in the Night."

I murmured the line as well, mostly because it felt awkward not to, but as I did, I recalled what Sage had said at the boutique. I looked up to her now, and saw that she stared back, her green eyes pinning me in place.

I clenched my jaw and ignored her, turning to Lauden.

"So," Lauden started, clapping his hands together. "Are you ready to begin?"

I nodded. "I'm not completely sure what I'm doing."

He smiled. "That's what I'm here for." He held my eyes for a moment longer than necessary before guiding me to an empty desk. It was tall so when we stood beside it the top rested at perfect height for working on.

"How much do you know about Sorcerers?"

"Only that the gifts are passed through bloodlines, they have one element that they can utilize, and that it's illegal in the Kromean Kingdoms."

Lauden walked around to stand on the opposite side of the table as I spoke.

"That's all correct. We aren't sure who the first Sorcerer was," he said, nodding his head in the direction of the First's Estate. "Not like the Kova, who know that their First was Kovarrin. But all the history books tell us that our kind has been around for thousands of years. Even longer than the Vasi and the Kova." He tilted his head with a smile then. "But, of course, after hearing of your mother and how she created them, that's pretty obvious now." There was a pause. "How did you know your mother created them?" he asked, and I cursed myself at the audible swallow his question emitted from me.

"Kovarrin told me," I lied.

After sharing so much information about myself with the family, and Kovarrin sharing most of it with the kingdom, I wasn't sure why I didn't want to tell Lauden that my mother came to me in dreams. But I didn't.

Lauden seemed to sense my discomfort and dropped it.

"Since it's a gift that is often passed down through each generation, most families know their children might develop a gift. Not all do, but some." He shrugged. "Parents will usually test their children to see if they've gained the gift, and if so, what element. But sometimes it manifests accidentally, before the parents have had a chance to figure out which element their child has."

"How did you discover yours?" I asked. "Did your parents test for it?"

A smirk crossed his face. "They did. Unfortunately, nothing happened. I was too young, I guess. It was a few years later, when I was seventeen, that I accidentally used Fire when I was fighting with another boy in town. The village would have hanged me, so my parents and I fled in the night and traveled in hopes of finding somewhere that I could learn to understand my powers without living in fear." He nodded to Sage. "They met her father along the way, and he mentored me."

I nodded, and tried to pretend I wasn't doing mental math to decipher how old that would've made Sage when they met; how old she was when they started their relationship, considering she looked to be about my age, and Lauden seemed a bit older.

"Sage's powers also manifested by accident," he said, turning to face her and nodding his head to summon her to the table.

She stood, her movements fluid as she strode toward me and spoke. "When I was five, I climbed too high into a tree and couldn't get down. While I was up there, I disturbed a beehive and they started to swarm me. I knew I was going to die, and all I could think about was wanting to be held in my mother's arms one last time." She stood beside Lauden before dropping her elbows onto the table and leaning over it. "And as soon as I thought about how my mother would hold me, how she'd spin me and place me gently back onto the ground, the branch I was holding onto lengthened and lowered until it sat me down onto the ground." She swallowed. "Like my mother would."

A cold chill swept up my spine until goosebumps coated my skin.

I cleared my throat. "That's amazing."

She clenched her jaw, gave a tight nod, and straightened. "We don't have all day; we best get at it." Then she turned toward the door.

I followed Sage out the doors and to the left until we were standing beside a few bushes that separated the home from the sand on the beach.

"How many times have you used Terra?" she asked, crossing her arms.

"Only twice, to protect myself by manipulating a tree and during the eruption with you."

Her lips downturned for a moment before she straightened and raised her chin.

"The hardest part of using your magic is understanding how to call for it. It's something that gets easier each time, but in the beginning might feel impossible." She plucked a stem from the bush and raised it into my eyesight. Four small, rounded leaves hung from the stem she held, and before my eyes, three more sprouted. "When you're using your magic, for any element, focus on how your magic feels inside of you. Until you know where it is at all times. Until you can flex it like a muscle."

I straightened. "Is that what it's like? Because that's already how it feels. It seems like it gets stronger every time I use it, like a muscle would."

Her lips lifted and I couldn't tell if it was into a smile, or a grimace. "Yes," she said, clipped. "That's what it's like." She flicked her eyes to Lauden, who stood at my side, watching, then she straightened her arm to hand me the stem. "You try."

I plucked the stem from her hand, but it slipped from my fingers almost as quickly. Sage's other hand shot out to catch it, and she did. It laid across her open palm, right beside a long, white scar.

"Thanks," I said, and took the stem. I did not miss the way she straightened and pulled her hand behind her back.

I looked down to the greenery and tried to focus on creating a new leaf.

Nothing happened for a moment.

My magic still felt as if it hummed beneath the surface, and I could feel it within my grasp, I just didn't know how to ask it to do what I wanted it to.

Another moment passed with no progress.

"You have to imagine what you want to happen, and ask your magic to give it to you," Lauden said softly beside me. "Like Sage said earlier, she pictured her mother setting her down, and the tree did. Be explicit. Tell your magic what you want."

I took a deep breath and focused again. Closing my eyes and imagining the leaf growing from the very tip of the stem. I imagined what the sprout would look like and how it would bloom open.

When I opened my eyes, there was nothing.

Sage turned to walk up the steps to the loft. "It's okay if it doesn't happen right away. Almost no Sorcerer can do it that quickly. Take it home, work on it and maybe when you come back next, it'll come quicker."

I followed after her. "What do you mean, take it home? I only just got here," I said walking into the loft behind her, the stem still pinched between my fingers at my side.

She moved to the kitchen and grabbed an apple, then leaned over the high-top dining table.

"What do you want me to do, sit there and watch you stare at a leaf?" A ghost of a smile passed her lips.

I straightened and heard Lauden enter the building behind me.

"Well, yes. I assumed that's what a teacher would do," I snapped.

Sage glowered at me. "I can't teach you until you know how to call your magic," she scoffed. "You think just because that fluke on the mountain that you—"

Lauden shut the door to the loft behind me with a hard thud that cut Sage off. She looked at him over my shoulder and pursed her lips.

"It wasn't a fluke, and you know that," he snapped. He moved to stand beside her, towering over her. "Evaline is the only reason that eruption stopped. We are here to mentor her. So, mentor," he barked his command, and she didn't even flinch, only hardened her eyes and stared past me.

"It's okay," I offered, uncomfortable with the way he was talking to her. "I understand, she's right. It is hard to teach if all I can do is stare at it." I sidestepped back. "I'll just be out here trying, if you get bored and want to join me." I looked at Sage, then turned and walked outside.

My boots slipped over the sand as I walked closer to the water and sat. Whatever happened back there wasn't out of the ordinary. Maddox had already sensed it. It must've been why he distrusted Lauden, and I saw it on the mountain the night of the eruption. Lauden talked to Sage like she was only meant to do his bidding, like she wasn't a partner.

My legs were crossed beneath me on the sand, and I slid the stem until it flattened over both my hands.

It was only a few minutes before Sage came outside, too. She didn't say anything as she sat beside me and watched me try.

CHAPTER THIRTY

Wyott

"We should run my errand first," I said as Maddox, Rasa, and I walked down the main street of Rominia.

Maddox glowered at me over Rasa's head. "I'm the one who asked you both to come with me today, why wouldn't we do mine first?"

I huffed and looked to the road again. "I've been waiting to do mine all week." Then lolled my head back to look at Maddox. "And you'll like it, too."

Maddox shook his head. "Why? Because it's the Blacksmith's?" he joked.

When I didn't say anything, he pinched the bridge of his nose. "Wyott, is your errand the Blacksmith's?"

I raised my chin. "And so what if it was?"

Maddox scoffed. "We literally—"

"Good, Gods!" Rasa shrieked between us. "Have you two always bickered this much?"

Maddox and I looked at each other, then back down at Rasa.

"This isn't even bickering," Maddox said, at the same time I voiced that we were just being silly.

We had been bickering, but there was something about having a parent call out sibling spats that unified the siblings no matter the circumstances.

She sighed and waved a hand. "It doesn't even matter, because we're going to get breakfast first, anyway."

"Where's Evaline?" I asked Maddox as I opened the door for the three of us to enter Rasa's favorite restaurant.

"First training. Cora?" he returned as he passed me.

"Marina."

Rasa huffed as she sat. "What? You can't be happy spending a morning with your mother?"

Maddox and I both reached for one of her hands at the same time as she sat between us.

"Of course," we said in unison.

She straightened with a content smile and squeezed my hand. "I've missed you both so much." She shook her head. "And I'm just happy to finally have some alone time with my boys."

Maddox smiled. "We missed you too, Mama." He shook his head. "It was a wild time."

"I want to hear all about it," she said, looking between the two of us.

We took turns telling her about our trek to Kembertus. I told her about the father and daughter we'd saved, and Maddox told her about the wedding and how he watched the ceremony. My heart ached for my brother when he talked about it. I'd always felt guilty that he'd gone alone, that I wasn't there with him when he saw Evaline in her wedding dress and thought he'd lost his chance with her.

We told Rasa about the abduction and about the pirate ship.

By the end, we'd finished eating breakfast and she patted both of our knees.

"It sounds like you both had fun." She turned to me. "Thank you for being there for your brother." Then turned to Maddox. "It sounds like you and Evaline were made for each other, just like Rominiava intended."

I nearly choked on the tea I drank, mostly because immediately a joke about how Evaline was *clearly* made for Maddox came to mind, because her blood was the only blood he could drink.

Maddox's glare pinned on me and Rasa looked over with concern.

"What?" she asked. Then turned back to Maddox. "What am I missing?"

Maddox told her about the blood, about how impossible it was to drink it from anyone besides Evaline, and Rasa's face only showed horror as he talked.

By the end of it, she was wringing her hands. "That is troublesome, Maddox."

He shrugged. "It's not ideal, but we'll manage. At least there's no problems feeding from her."

I cringed, knowing Rasa's next words.

"But what if she's not available?" she asked, her voice tight. "What, are you going to take her on every trip you take onto the mainland? You'll never be able to have an extended stay away from each other."

I knew what she'd say, because I'd already worried over all of it. The moment he told me back in Kembertus.

Maddox was my brother and my best friend. We may fight from time to time, but there's no one more important to me besides Cora. And the thought of this obstacle he'd have to work around for the rest of his life, it worried the fuck out of me.

He sighed. "I know, but everything's okay for now. We'll figure it out."

She nodded but looked away in thought. "We'll have to discuss with Lauden and your father, to see if they've ever heard of this. Maybe with some of the other Elders, too."

Maddox cringed and I knew he worried that this conversation was devolving. He'd asked Rasa and I out for a surprise errand, and I felt guilty for starting this conversation in the first place.

I stood. "Are we ready to go?" I asked, looking to Maddox.

He threw a look of gratitude my way as the two of them stood and made for the door.

We let Maddox lead the way as we exited the restaurant, and she looked up at him. "Where are we going?"

He smiled. "Trust me, you'll enjoy it."

We only passed a few more buildings before Maddox stopped and swept an arm toward the front door of one of the shops that stood on the first story. My brows rose and Rasa squealed.

"Really?" she asked, nearly singing in excitement.

Maddox smiled and nodded and opened the door for us to enter. I clapped his shoulder as I walked past him into the building. "I'm happy for you, Mads."

And when I turned inside, the brilliance of the sunlight filtered in through the windows and reflected through the many gemstones in glass cases, drawing my eye. I couldn't help the grin that spread across my face at the array of colors and dazzling reflections we faced.

Rasa went home after the jeweler, as she hated the smell of the liquid metal and avoided it whenever she had the chance.

Maddox and I continued alone, and when I swung my smile to him, he groaned.

"Do you at least have an idea of what you want? Or are you going to wander around the store for hours like normal?"

I laughed and slung my arm around Maddox's shoulder. "Don't act like you haven't missed spending time with me."

He pushed me off but there was a smile on his face.

Maddox and I had grown up spending long days together, even before my father was killed. But after, we only became closer. I did enjoy the time we spent together, which was why I always volunteered to go with him when Kovarrin asked him to check out the Madierian Kingdoms.

Kovarrin always requested Maddox take those trips, and hardly ever directed the question to me. I think it was his way of protecting me, he never wanted me to go to Brassillion if I didn't feel up for it, and I knew it was because of my father. He always assumed I wouldn't want to go back, but I always did, with Maddox.

One of the only instances where Kovarrin did ask me directly, was for this last trip, and it had been because he trusted the two of us more than anyone else, when he had thought it was Alannah using her magic in Kembertus.

"Fine," Maddox conceded. "I have missed you, but only because I finally have the chance to talk *your* ear off about *my* mate and repay you for all those decades I spent listening to you drone on about Cora."

I shook my head and held the door open for the Blacksmith. "That's not the reason."

He didn't argue when he walked inside.

Otto heard the door open and poked his head out from his workroom in the back, a smile already radiating across his face.

"My two favorite customers." He laughed, meeting us halfway through the store and grabbing us both in hugs. He was a lot shorter than Maddox and I, but just as strong, and I was reminded by the way he squeezed me.

"How have you been?" Maddox asked.

Otto shrugged and crossed his arms. "A little offended that it took you two so long to come see me, but other than that I'm doing well." He tilted his head, looking to Maddox. "Although I hear you have a pretty good excuse," he said, referring to Evaline. Then Otto swung his gaze to mine. "You don't."

I pulled the paper out of my back pocket. "If I told you I had a custom order, would that make up for it?" I asked, waving the folded paper toward him.

He straightened and his eyes grew. "You know me well."

Otto turned and rounded to stand on the opposite side of the counter and cleared a space on top of it.

I opened the paper and smoothed it until my full sketch was visible. Maddox walked up beside me, arms crossed, and looked down at it.

"Throwing knives?" he asked.

I nodded and tapped a finger against it. "Yes, and a bandolier."

Otto was too busy bending to look over the sketch to notice the minor eye roll Maddox gave.

"Gods, Wyott. You need another one?"

With my head cocked and a smug smile, I turned to him. "It's not for me. It's for Evaline."

Maddox's expression changed from one of mock annoyance, to one of disbelief.

"Really?" he asked, bending down to look at the sketch over Otto.

I gave an exaggerated sigh of superiority and placed my hands on my hips. "Yes, I know. I'm an amazing brother." I shrugged. "It's from Cora and I, a welcome home present."

Otto whistled lowly. "Gods, I've missed you, Wyott," he confessed before he turned to grab a notepad and something to write with. "Your sketches are always the easiest to follow."

Maddox nodded, using his index finger to slide the paper to the side so he could see the entire piece.

"Wyott's always been a gifted artist." He knelt closer, eyes narrowing over the handles of the several throwing knives I'd drawn. "Roses?"

"Yes." I spoke as the two of them still looked over the sketch and I had to hide my blush of pride. "It's meant to be etched into the blade." I explained. The drawing could've been interpreted as a few variations, and I wanted to make sure Otto saw my complete vision.

He scribbled down onto his pad. "Rominium, obviously?" he asked, cocking his head. "What did you have in mind to fill the etches? Or did you just want to leave them bare?"

"I'd actually like silver-plated Rominium, if it's not too much hassle."

Maddox straightened beside me and Otto nodded, running his fingers over the roses I'd drawn.

"Yes, I can do that. Then black to fill in the etches, to make them more pronounced."

I smiled. "Yes, exactly."

Maddox turned to me now, brows furrowed. "Why silver?" he asked, in a tone that confessed he already guessed at my reasoning.

I tilted my head to meet his gaze. "For the myth."

The tears filled his eyes in an instant and I knew I'd made the right decision.

Otto was still making notes to himself when he spoke up. "The Silver Rose myth?" His voice grew excited. "This will be very fun to work on."

Maddox shook his head, and I knew he understood why I'd picked it. If Evaline's fate was to kill Vasier, then she deserved to sport a weapon that represented the lore that there was a third way to kill the Kova and Vasi.

Maddox laughed and raised a hand to clear his tears using his thumb and index finger.

"That's amazing, Wyott. Very thoughtful," he said and then took a deep breath. He met my eyes. "Thank you."

We hadn't had much time to discuss the curse, or what it meant for Evaline, since the Ball. But I knew it was weighing heavily on his mind, because if it had been Cora, it would've weighed on mine. Cora and I had already planned on commissioning a one of a kind set of throwing knives for Evaline, but after the Ball, when we'd gotten back to the house after the volcano, I'd stayed up a few more hours to draw up these plans.

Otto took down the rest of my requests for the knives, and the bandolier, and then Maddox and I aimed for the First's Estate.

There was a moment of silence before he turned to me.

"Are you okay? After hearing about all of it? The curse, and about Kovarrin and Vasier?"

I took a deep breath as we walked down the street and smoothed my hand over my beard.

"At first, I wasn't," I confessed. "But the look on Evaline's face, watching her carry that burden." I shook my head. "It's not about me, even if everything related to Vasier feels that way sometimes."

Maddox nodded, looking to the ground as we walked. He knew as well as everyone in our family how much I hated Vasier, how much

I longed—even plotted—for his death. I wanted to be the one to execute it.

I shrugged. "I don't mind giving that to Evaline if it'll take this curse off of her." My jaw set. "But Gods, I'd love to be there to see it."

Maddox smiled. "Of course you will be, we'll need all the help we can fucking get." We met eyes for a moment before his sobered. "I'm sorry for what I said back in Brassillion," he started, and I knew exactly what he was referring to; when I'd forced him to rest that night, to stop pursuing Evaline's abductors. When he'd accused me of not wanting to kill Vasier, if it was to save Evaline.

I shook my head. "Don't apologize. I knew you didn't mean it."

"I didn't," he confirmed. "But it was still a shitty thing to say when you were only trying to do what was best. So, I'm sorry."

I only nodded and another beat of silence passed for a few steps.

"I hate Vasier," Maddox said, and I didn't flinch anymore when I heard the name.

Not like I used to. Maybe it was hearing about the curse, maybe it was knowing that the Gods acknowledged his evil, I didn't know.

"I hate what he did to your father," Maddox said, stopping to face me.

He didn't mention my mother, and what Vasier had done to her, but I knew why. No one thought Vasier had anything to do with her death, and I didn't let anyone besides my mate know that I disagreed.

"I hate that he's trying to take Evaline." He placed a hand on my shoulder and squeezed. "But at least he did our family one kindness; he spared you."

Chapter Thirty-One

Maddox

Evaline had spent the last few days practicing Terra, both at home and with Sage. It seemed to be all she could think about, and I didn't want her to overwhelm herself with the responsibility of it all.

So I planned a date for us.

"Why would we go to the beach now, it's dark out." She laughed as she looped her arm around my waist.

I tossed my arm over her shoulders as we descended the stairs outside of the mansion. "You've clearly never been to the beach at night before."

We went to a beach far from the main streets, so we wouldn't be overheard. I laid out the blanket I'd packed, and the food.

"How romantic," she said playfully as she sat down onto the blanket. Then she turned to face the water, and her eyes drifted up to the stars too, and she breathed in a gasp.

"Exactly," I said, chuckling and sitting down beside her. "It is romantic."

She only nodded and I bent to kiss her on the cheek.

We ate the small dinner I'd packed, and drank the wine, and it wasn't long before Evaline was laughing at everything I said.

"See, this is how you should laugh at all my jokes," I said and her gasps of laughter only increased as she fell into my chest. "It would shut Wyott down. He thinks he's the funny one."

Her hands grasped at the shirt on my chest as she laughed, and she only nodded.

"He," she gasped out, "is the funny one."

I could only chuckle and shake my head. "Half the time the only reason you think he's funny is because he's making fun of me."

She shifted to straddle me, mid laugh, and I smiled up at her, wrapping my hands around her waist.

"That's when he's funniest," she teased.

"If you're going to make fun of me, you can at least soothe the sting with a kiss," I said softly, inching my face toward hers.

Her laughter subsided and she blinked those big, ocean eyes at me, before lowering her face to mine.

The kiss deepened quickly, and she slipped her tongue against mine. I groaned, and curled one arm to meld her to my chest and raised the other hand to tangle in her free falling hair.

"I love you," she whispered against my lips and my heart flipped at the words.

At the reminder that she chose me, that this was all real, and that I finally got the girl of my dreams and she wanted me right back.

"I love you," I whispered back.

I wrapped an arm around her back and lifted her to flip us so that she was pinned on the blanket beneath me.

She wore a short linen dress that blew in the wind, and when she landed on the blanket its hem fluttered up until it hardly covered anything.

I growled at the sight of her and lowered my face to hers to envelop her lips in another kiss.

She wrapped her legs around my hips, wound her fingers through my hair, and pulled me closer. When my groin met the warmth of her hips, I pulled back with a groan.

"Eva" I rasped. "We're out in public, anyone could stumble upon us. I might not notice until it's too late."

She shook her head. "I don't care. We'll be quiet," she whispered, and that got a chuckle out of me. If there was one thing Evaline wasn't, it was quiet.

She pulled me back down to kiss me, but I pulled back. "Are you sure?" I asked. "We can go back."

Evaline lifted her head off the blanket and caught my lips in hers again. "I want you now."

Those words were all it took for a growl to rip through my chest, and I lowered back down.

I propped one arm beside her head to hold myself up and lowered the other hand down between her thighs. She widened them to let me in, and her soft gasp met the wind as she felt my fingers slide along her.

I shivered at how wet she was already, and my cock twitched at the thought of tasting her, before I slid one finger in.

Her whole body shuddered and she let out a soft moan. "Gods, Maddox."

I captured her words in a kiss and slid my finger out before moving down her body. I didn't care that half of my body laid in the sand, the only thing that mattered in this moment was the sight of her beneath the Rominian stars.

I shoved her dress the rest of the way over her hips and I heard her breath increase in anticipation. I opened her knees more and groaned at the sight of her arousal dripping down to the blanket before I flicked out my tongue to catch it.

"Fuck," she moaned as she slammed her head down into the ground below her.

I kissed, and licked, and my tongue slipped inside. I didn't know what was better: the way she felt against my tongue, the way she tasted, or the way she writhed beneath me as I moved up to capture her clit between my teeth, and sank my finger back in.

It didn't take long before her hands were wound through my hair with her thighs tightening over my head and her relentless moans filling the air.

I swirled my tongue around her clit, moved my finger faster, curling it up. And as she hit that peak, I flicked my eyes up to watch as her chest heaved, and her mouth dropped open.

It was my favorite sight.

I'd barely pulled my lips away from her before she was grasping at my shoulders and pulling me up toward her.

"Now," she whispered, hand fumbling down to my pants. "I need it now."

I smiled and stood up, and pulled her with me.

"I want to swim," I said, and pulled my shirt over my head.

Her brows furrowed for a moment, but when she saw my intention, her eyes lit up. She pulled her dress over her head, and we both ran for the water.

CHAPTER THIRTY-TWO

Evaline

My strides were quick as I made my way to Lauden and Sage's loft. I was late.

Braiding my hair had taken far longer than normal, mostly because I could still feel the crunch of seawater and sand clinging to all the strands from the night before. I thought my bath last night would've solved it, but it hadn't even come close.

"You're late," Lauden said in a clipped tone when I entered the loft.

"I know," I said, out of breath. "I'm sorry."

Sage sat on the leather couch and Lauden stood with his hip propped against the work table.

"What are the plans for today?" I asked.

I'd practiced using Terra for the last few days and had made a lot of progress. I'd finally been able to sprout leaves on several different types of plants and to grow some of the vines that crept up the walls of the First's Estate until they stretched to nearly the roof.

Sage stood. "We're going to do one last test for Terra today and if you pass it, you can move on to Air."

My ears perked up at that. "What's the test? Something with the volcano again? Or with the quakes?"

Sage's eyes widened and she shook her head. "No," she snapped. "We can't do anything involving quakes, that's what caused the eruption in the first place." Her face blanched. "All the smaller quakes we'd been experiencing."

I nodded, I understood her reasoning but couldn't help the small part of me that was disappointed.

The more I'd used my Terra magic, the more I *wanted* to use it. The more I could feel all the plants living, growing, around me. And the more I felt all of that, the more I wanted to test my ability on something more colossal and important than growing Gods-damned leaves.

"We're going to go into the forest, and you're going to work with a tree," Sage explained, and I smiled. It was better than a bush or a vine.

The three of us moved to leave as Lauden spoke. "If you can do this, then I'd say your Terra magic is pretty well developed. We'll work on Air next, and—"

He stopped speaking at the sound of the raven in the greenhouse. I'd never seen any fly in while I'd been here, but that was probably because Sage and I spent most of our time outside looking at the plants in the ground. Now, I could see that there was a small open window in the side of the greenhouse, and a white raven perched on the sill of it.

Lauden turned back to Sage and I. "You go ahead, I'll deliver this to whomever it's for, and be right behind you."

I couldn't help but feel relieved to be free of him. The more interactions I had with Lauden, the more I disliked him. What was the most frustrating, though, was that I needed him. He was my mentor, but more, he was the only Fire Caster on the island and if I was going to learn to use that, I needed him.

That fact did not make me despise him any less for the way he treated Sage.

I looked sidelong at her as we trekked toward the woods and couldn't help but wonder why she stayed with him.

"We won't go too far in, I just want to find a good sized tree," Sage said, pulling me from my thoughts.

I nodded.

"I know you used a tree once to save yourself, but the point of this test is to see if you can utilize your magic even when you aren't in danger."

"That makes sense."

An awkward silence fell over us before she eyed the Rominium dagger at my thigh. Not all the Kova here carried their weapons around, Maddox and Wyott certainly didn't carry their full arsenal like they did in Kembertus, but I liked to have my dagger with me if I left the mansion, especially without Maddox. Like the wire in my hair, it was more of a comfort to have it than a necessity.

"You can fight?" she asked as she stepped over a root.

"Yes, my father taught me."

She straightened at that but stayed silent.

"Do you know how?" I asked, cocking my head to look at her.

She clenched her jaw. "No. My father said that my time was better spent honing my magic than learning any combat skills."

"Did he know how to fight?" I asked, but then continued. "Because it's very normal for fathers not to teach their daughters, especially in the Kromean Kingdoms. My father was a soldier so he—"

"Yes," she interjected. "But he knew I had other skills, I didn't need to waste time with combat when I had my magic."

The set of her jaw indicated that the conversation was over, but it bothered me for the rest of our hike.

I wasn't sure if it was because I was raised with such a loving father, or because I thought all women should be trained to protect themselves, but the idea that a father would know how to fight, and refuse to teach his daughter, haunted me. As it always had.

"This one's good," she said, stopping and looking up at a chestnut tree.

It was old, by the size of the trunk. It had to have been spared during the last few volcanic eruptions, because it looked at least a century old. The trunk was a few feet across and the canopy hung high and wide overtop of us.

"What do you want me to do?" I asked, tilting my head back as far as it would go to look up into the leaves.

She shrugged. "Make it grow, bend it, do something that will prove that you have adequate control over Terra."

I sighed, unhappy with the vague instruction, and stepped back. I wanted to try to see the full view of it, which still wasn't possible after retreating several paces.

Sage followed, and stood behind me.

There was a minute of contemplation, but the moment I'd decided what to do, and raised my hands toward the tree, it jolted into action.

In front of our eyes, the tree grew. The bark sang as it broke apart, and reformed anew when the trunk grew a few yards higher than it had been before. The branches elongated and reached farther out into the sky. New leaves sprouted and some grew so quickly, they fell from the tree altogether and fluttered noiselessly down to where the roots deep underground curled and stretched until some of their new knots crested out of the grass.

When I was finished, I half-turned toward her with a smile on my face.

"That was good, right?" I asked.

Sage rolled her eyes with a scoff and threw her hands up in the air. "Gods, do you always need to be celebrated?" she snapped. "Obviously it was adequate."

Her words stung, but I did my best not to take them personally.

Sage was damaged. Broken, like I'd been. Like I still was, even if I was being mended. She said hurtful things because she was hurt. I didn't want to be the cause for any more, so I ignored them.

"I'm sorry," I said, my voice low. "I only meant, was that adequate to pass your test? So I can move onto Air," I elaborated.

She dragged a hand down her face. "You don't always have to be perfect, Evaline." Her words were sharp. "Even now, being meek in response. You're so kind," she said with a tilt of her head. "So sweet," she said, then set her jaw. "So perfect. *Always* perfect."

I opened my mouth, to tell her that she was as far from correct as she could possibly be. Gods, if my aunt was here she'd have the time of her life in explaining each and every way I was the *furthest* thing from perfect. What had I done to Sage to ever make her think that?

But before I could say anything, Lauden's voice was behind us.

"Sage, what the fuck is wrong with you?" At the sound of his voice, his words, Sage straightened and I swore to the Gods I saw her hold her breath.

I turned to Lauden. "Nothing is wrong, it's fine." I met his angry gaze. "I'm ready for Air."

He only looked past me and narrowed his eyes on Sage.

"It's not fine." He gave a tight shake of his head. "And she's going to jeopardize our place here by acting that way."

"I would never ask Kovarrin to take away your position," I said, then raised my chin. "Please, let's move onto Air."

I watched as the scowl on Lauden's face flipped into a charming smile as he waved a hand and shook his head. "You're right." He shrugged. "Sage is just competitive, and it took her years to manipulate a tree."

Sage straightened and even from the corner of my eye I could see the flush up the back of her neck.

"You were a child, though." I asked, turning to her. "Right?"

She nodded. "Yet everyone seems to forget that," she muttered.

Lauden wrapped an arm around her shoulders. "She knows I'm only giving her a hard time." He looked at me. "Sage performs best when she's trying to prove herself."

She didn't speak, only set her jaw, and Lauden launched into explaining what my next task would be. He wanted me to practice Air in a similar way that we'd been practicing Terra. Focus on the power and what it felt like, then ask it to do what I bid by imagining it.

"Start out small," he said. "Run a wind through the leaves." He nodded toward the chestnut tree.

We spent the next hour waiting for me to get the hang of it. I managed to flutter a couple of leaves, but nothing more than that.

I could feel the way the natural wind moved around me, how it swept up the coastline and all the way back at the loft, but I couldn't pull it to where I stood.

And I knew why.

I was distracted, again uncomfortable around Lauden and the way he talked to and about Sage. And as we started our walk back to the loft, Lauden with a hand entangled with hers, I decided I wouldn't stand by silently anymore. Whether he was my mentor or not, I wouldn't let him talk to her like that. I wanted her to know that this wasn't normal, and that she shouldn't allow him to treat her that way.

"I'm going to start combat training again," I said when the training center came into view. I missed it, and Maddox was right; I needed to get better at fighting the immortal beings at full speed if I ever stood a chance against Vasier. "Sage, do you want to come, too? I could teach you some basics."

Sage turned, brows furrowed. "Maybe. I'll think about it," she said.

For the rest of the day, until night fell and I laid in bed beside Maddox, I couldn't help but think about what Lauden had said.

"Sage performs best when she's trying to prove herself."

I'd only known them a short time, but already I could see that perhaps she didn't perform best when she was trying to prove herself, maybe she just constantly felt like she had to.

CHAPTER THIRTY-THREE

Wyott

"Did you remember to light the candles?" Cora called from the kitchen.

I laughed, shaking my head. "Yes," I called back. "The first time you asked…" I paused for emphasis. "An hour ago."

Annoyance bristled down the bond before I heard her shout back. "Don't be a prick, I was just making sure."

I stood from the chaise in our sitting room and tossed another log on the fire. The embers sparked and swept up the chimney in a flurry before I heard Cora curse in the kitchen. I closed the fireplace cage and ran in to see if she was okay. I was met by the image of my mate with an apron tied loosely around her waist and a pan of baked goods on the counter.

"What's wrong?" I asked as I moved to see if she was okay.

Cora turned to me with flour marks on her cheek and forehead, her eyes wide. "They didn't rise the way they were supposed to."

The pastries were flat, but the chocolate could be seen melting from the insides.

I walked toward her and wrapped my arms around her, pulling her to my chest.

"They're perfect."

She narrowed her eyes up at me, resting her hands on my shoulders. "They are so clearly not perfect, Wyott," she huffed. "They're a disaster."

"But I'm sure they'll still be delicious, darling. And that's all that counts."

She scoffed. "That is not all that counts! This is Evaline's first time here, I want to make sure everything is perfect."

I dropped my eyelids at her. "Evaline quite literally ate rabbit over a campfire on our trip. She'll love everything you've made tonight."

Cora sighed. "Fine, you're probably right."

I smirked at her and opened my mouth to speak, but before I could a rumble shook the land below us. We locked eyes but the quake was minor, so we waited for it to pass like we always did.

Gods, what was causing these?

After the world stilled again, I turned to her. "I'm almost always right. Besides, you're perfect enough as it is. No reason to stress over making things *around* you perfect, too."

She lightly smacked my chest. "That was Gods awful."

I shrugged. "You'll have that after going months away from home." I dipped my head to kiss her.

"You've been home for weeks now. Surely you're sick of me," she said as she looked up at me through her lashes. The sight of her in my arms, flour sprinkled across her face and her flirty eyes looking up at me sent blood straight to my cock.

"I could spend eternity by your side and never tire of you," I said as I fanned my hands over her back and pulled her against my chest.

Cora grinned. "Even if my pastries are flat?"

I nodded seriously before the corners of my mouth tugged up. "Even if your pastries are flat."

A hard knock sounded at the door.

"Horrible timing," I grumbled as I pulled away from her. Cora snickered behind me as she ran around me and pulled the apron off. We stopped at the door and I turned to her before pulling it open to wipe the flour from her face.

When I opened the door, Evaline stood there smiling, her hand in Maddox's.

"As always brother, you have impeccable timing," I said to him, rolling my eyes.

Maddox's brows furrowed as he looked between Cora and I before realization flashed in his eyes. He scoffed.

"You've got a lot of nerve saying that to me considering how many times you had *impeccable* timing with Evaline and I."

Evaline's eyes widened and she shoved Maddox in the side. "What in the Gods are you talking about?"

Cora laughed and pulled Evaline into the house and toward the sitting room.

"To be fair," I said to Maddox as he strode in behind Evaline and I closed the door. "You've been doing that to Cora and I for decades."

He pursed his lips and continued into the living room where Cora sat with Evaline. Something was off about him, he seemed on edge. I didn't want to bring it up in front of our mates, but knew I'd have to ask him about it later.

Just as I sat down, a knock sounded again. And again, and again, until everyone had arrived.

Maddox introduced Evaline to our friends; Grant and his mate, Chrissa. Fredrik and Nash, also mates. And Dean. She must not have had a chance to be formally introduced at the Ball, or during the eruption.

After everyone arrived, we all went up to the roof where the table was set beneath the stars. It was my favorite place in the kingdom.

The rest of the evening passed without issue. The food Cora prepared was divine—even her flat pastries, and everyone made sure to tell her so.

"But they're flat!" Cora exclaimed, waving her hand at the tray.

"Who cares what they look like when they taste like this?" Evaline mused after taking a bite. The chocolate fell onto her chin and Maddox leaned over to swipe it off with his thumb. Their eyes met and I knew they shared an exchange down the bond, especially considering the blush that filled Evaline's cheeks a second later.

Grant and Fredrik cooed at Maddox mockingly, and my brother shot a glare at them.

I ignored them and turned to Cora. "See, I told you."

She smiled and shrugged. "They're just easy to please."

Evaline laughed and nodded. "It's much better than the rabbit Wyott prepared for me when we camped."

I pointed at Evaline as I turned to Cora with wide eyes. "That's exactly what I said!"

Cora rolled her eyes and turned to Evaline. "I truly need you to stop validating him. It's making him insufferable."

Grant, Dean, Fredrik, Nash, and Maddox all nodded vehemently and I rolled my eyes.

"Oh shut the fuck up."

After dinner Evaline, Cora and Chrissa stayed up on the roof. We lived on top of a column of homes and the best part was the roof with a gorgeous view.

Maddox, Dean, Grant, Fredrik, Nash, and I brought the rest of the food in and started doing dishes. As soon as the six of us walked in, Maddox turned to us.

"I haven't told Evaline yet because I didn't want to worry her. But there have been several Vasi attacks outside Merwinan."

My brows raised, Fredrik stopped his stride toward the kitchen, and Nash swore.

The Vasi rarely made it far enough into Brassillion to make it past River Brawn, let alone Merwinan.

"Are you sure?" Grant asked, putting the dishes he carried onto the dining table.

Maddox nodded, concern evident in his eyes.

"Yes. Lauden delivered the raven to my father today. Lord Leo said there've been three bodies found near the docks in the early mornings." He shook his head. "Saxon found one of them and reported it. The rest were found by guards patrolling, and they have questions about the bloodless bodies with wounds on their necks."

"What did Kovarrin say about it?" I asked, tightening my grip on the dishes I held.

He clenched his jaw. "He's afraid that Vasier is trying to start another war. But it has to be about Evaline."

Maddox explained that it wasn't the first time that Vasier had come after her to the other Kova in the room, and they all mirrored the same, grim look.

My brother shook his head, and clenched his eyes shut. "It wasn't supposed to be this hard."

After everyone left, Cora came back inside where I was finishing the last of the dishes.

"I hope everyone had fun," she said as she came into the kitchen.

I smiled and nodded. "Of course they did darling, you always make sure of that."

I heard the cork pop on another bottle of wine as I placed the last plate back in the cabinet, and turned to see her pouring two more glasses for us.

"Thank you, Mrs. Whitlock," I said, accepting the drink and leaning against the counter.

"You're welcome, Mr. Whitlock," she hummed and moved to stand between my legs.

"Did Evaline and Chrissa get along?" I asked, dropping a hand on her hip.

She nodded. "I don't think either of them could ever not get along with somebody."

My brows raised. "You didn't see Evaline in Kembertus."

She laughed and shoved my chest. "Be nice."

I dipped my head to kiss her. "What did you three talk about all that time?"

A flash of pain passed her eyes. "Just the future."

Realization had my features falling before I could help it. Future. That meant children, and Cora knew the pain that caused me every time she brought it up.

I sighed. "Cor, so much is uncertain right now." I shook my head and waved toward the door. "Gods, just earlier Maddox told us there were Vasi killings near Merwinan. Can we at least wait until everything settles before we start this again?"

Her anger simmered down the bond before she slid it shut. She didn't speak, but I knew what she wanted to say.

She wanted to say that we'd had this conversation countless times over the last several decades. She'd say that she was ready, that she *had* been ready for a family for so long and that the longer we waited the more it hurt her.

I wasn't sure how many times I'd explained it to her, how many different ways I'd need to find to tell her before she understood.

She knew I wanted a family too, that it was what I wanted most in this world right alongside her. But when would she hear me when *I* spoke, when *I* expressed that *I* wasn't ready yet?

And it wasn't because I didn't want children, or because I didn't think we'd make good parents. It wasn't because I hadn't traveled enough or accomplished enough.

It was because Vasier still walked this world, and his reach was only getting closer. It was because he'd already taken my mother and my father, and I feared that he'd somehow find a way to take someone else I loved from me.

It was because the fear kept me up at night that Vasier would harm Cora, or take Maddox, or Rasa, or Kovarrin, or now Evaline. It was because I already had too many people I loved that he'd taken from me, and too many people left to protect from him, to add a child. He'd taken my blood twice over, what was to stop him from taking a third?

Chapter Thirty-Four

Evaline

The wine I'd had at dinner, and then on the roof after with Cora and Chrissa while we talked and enjoyed the view had caught up to me. Maddox's arm was looped around me as he guided me to our suite. I wasn't drunk, but I was on the brink based on the tingle that buzzed through my body and the slight fog I could feel over my mind.

Maddox had seemed tense most of the night, and I didn't understand why.

But I wanted him to relax, so when we entered our suite and the door closed behind us, I kicked off my shoes and turned around to wrap my arms around his neck.

"I love you," I said.

Maddox smiled down at me and wrapped his arms around my back. "I love you, too."

I stood up on my tiptoes. "Want to take a bath?"

His smile grew and amusement flickered through his eyes. "I think you know the answer to that."

After we'd heated the water and filled the tub, Maddox stood behind me in the bathroom and helped me start to remove my clothes.

His hand paused on my back as the sound of a bell chime sounded through the kingdom.

He pulled away from me, his eyes wide. "Something is wrong."

In a second he was crossing into the other room and strapping his weapons on.

I ran after him, the fog of wine evaporating with the race of my heart. "Another eruption?" I asked, anxiety seeping into my voice.

Maddox spoke as he strapped on his last sword. "I don't know."

His voice was grim as he grabbed my Rominium dagger and my father's sword and crossed the room in a blur. He dropped to one knee, strapping the former to my bare thigh and the latter to my hip. The light dress I wore swayed around me as he did. When he finished, we raced down the hall until we met Kovarrin and Rasa at the mansion's front door.

"Do you have any word?" Maddox asked as Kovarrin reached for the door and the four of us ran out of it.

Kovarrin shook his head. "None, but it sounds like the eastern gate's bells."

When we all made it out of the door, Kovarrin and Rasa took off in two bursts of speed as they sprinted to the sound, and Maddox pulled me into his arms and took off, too.

I tucked my head into his body since it was hard to breathe with the strength of wind that wrapped around us.

When we get to the beach, stay on land. The wards only reach to the water. You'll be protected if you stay on the sand, he urged down the bond.

I nodded my understanding against his shoulder and tightened my grip around him. Gods, would we ever know peace?

Maddox cursed and set me down, and I finally saw what had raised the alarm.

Only a few paces from the lapping of the water in front of us, a large ship was half beached, half in the water. It had lolled onto its side with a mound of sand piled up underneath its hull, like it had been sailing haphazardly and crashed onto the beach.

It was an eerie sight, made only more ominous by the sound of the bells overhead. It was dark, the only sources of light were a few lanterns lit around the beach and the crescent moon that hung over the ship.

Wyott and Cora appeared on the beach beside us, as did several dozen other Kova.

"What happened?" Rasa asked, looking up at her mate. "It just crashed here?"

Kovarrin turned to Cora, and I was reminded that she was the head of their naval forces. "Was anyone crossing the Strait home tonight? Were any ships scheduled to be out?"

Cora shook her head, adamant. "I don't know if anyone crossed from Merwinan, but none of our ships have been checked out of the marina. They would've cleared it with me first."

"What's going on?" Lauden asked as he rounded the edge of the crowd and ran toward us, Sage on his heels.

Kovarrin turned to him. "This ship just crashed here." The wind blew past the ship, ruffling its sails, and floating over us before every Kova around me straightened.

"What?" I asked Maddox.

"We can smell that someone's on it."

We all walked closer to the far side of ship. Maddox shouted, asking whoever it was to reveal themselves, and all of us paused to listen. Over the chime of the bells, I heard Oscar's shrieking bark.

Everyone lit into action and ran, them faster than I, into the shallows of the water. Maddox turned when he realized I was behind him.

"No, you need to get back—" But I was already summoning the water around me to rise below my feet as if I stood on a pedestal, until it reached up and dropped me over the edge of the ship.

"Oscar!" I screamed. "Saxon!"

Maddox cursed and I heard his boots hit the deck behind me. But it was too late, and I'd already seen all of it.

Several of the men who'd been on this ship nearly three weeks prior lay lifeless on deck, their limbs tossed at different angles and bodies fallen over each other, likely from the crash.

Maddox called for Lauden, and in another moment Kovarrin was aboard, followed by Wyott with Lauden in tow.

"Light," Maddox said grimly, striding forward to stand in front of me in a protective stance.

The Sorcerer's hands lit with flame and he strode forward to reveal the rest of the scene, displaying all the details that I couldn't see in the dark.

The light showed that the men had died long before the crash. Their bodies were pale, completely devoid of color, and they each had fang wounds on their necks.

I looked up at Maddox. "You didn't smell blood, because they don't have any. Do they?" I asked softly.

He clenched his jaw and shook his head. "No, they don't."

Oscar's bark sounded again and we all turned to hear his scratching at the door inside the captain's office.

Wyott yanked it open, and Lauden followed with his light.

I pushed into the room behind Maddox, and saw that Saxon sat in a chair behind his desk, rope tied to keep him there with a cloth around his mouth.

We all audibly sighed with relief at seeing him alive.

By the time they'd untied him and gotten him and Oscar back to the First's Estate and sat in front of a fire, he was explaining what had happened.

Vasi.

They'd stormed his ship, just two of them. They'd killed his crew but had spared him. They steered his boat, but must've abandoned the ship just before they hit the wards for Rominia.

He shook his head, tears in his eyes. "My entire crew is gone." He looked to Oscar who'd fallen asleep in front of the fireplace. "I couldn't save them."

Maddox stepped forward then. "I'm so sorry, Saxon. But we will figure out why this happened. We will avenge them."

Saxon looked up then. "That's just it," he said, his voice low. "They didn't want there to be any confusion as to why they did what they did. They left a message with me."

Kovarrin strode forward then. "What was the message?"

Saxon's eyes drifted to mine as he pulled a tattered piece of paper from his pocket. "It was for you. They said it came straight from Vasier."

Maddox straightened as I walked forward and took the paper from Saxon.

My hands shook as I opened it and my eyes filled with tears with each word I read aloud.

"Come to Mortithev. I've tried twice now, and you're wearing my patience thin. Don't make me ask again, or I just might have to pay a visit to my favorite boutique in Kembertus."

Chapter Thirty-Five

Maddox

My father's study buzzed with a tense energy. It reverberated the anxiety and the anger we all felt. It didn't help that the room was too small for the amount of people inside of it.

Saxon and Oscar were resting in a guest room in the mansion, but the rest of us were here. My father sat at his desk, my mother on the edge of it at his side. Evaline and Cora sat in the two seats facing them, and I stood behind Evaline with my arms crossed. I didn't dare touch her, she was vibrating with anger. But I wanted her to know I was here for her. Wyott stood by the fireplace with Dean, Nash, Fredrik, and Grant alongside him.

No one spoke, and all that could be heard were the various rapid heartbeats and the bouncing of Evaline's leg.

The worry I'd been feeling for Evaline for so Gods-damned long now completely shifted into downright rage. I couldn't fucking believe this was happening.

The ship was bad enough—to see so many innocents dead, and to know that their deaths were far from peaceful—but to know what Saxon went through and the message they sent with him. To know that the others died because Vasier wanted my mate and that Vasier was now sending a threat for Aurora and Jacqueline. It was too much.

I clenched my eyes shut for a moment.

Gods. The Gods had done so much for me, given me so much, but since the moment I met Evaline it'd felt as if the Gods had done nothing but take. Or at least, interfere.

It was hard to have faith that Evaline and I could have a good, happy life together when the world felt as if it was crumbling down around us every other week.

My heart did a painful lurch. Gods, how I missed the days when our only concern was getting her out of Kembertus.

I thought back to the despair I'd felt back then. When I saw her ring, and then again when I saw her walk down the aisle. Each time, I'd sworn there was no worse pain than that moment. And each time, the Gods had proved me wrong.

Fuck.

The door creaked then and I turned to see the two Sorcerers walk in. They strode into the office and stood tucked against the bookshelves. My father nodded to Lauden, and Dean straightened beside Wyott.

My eyes narrowed at Lauden before I snapped my head to my father. "I thought we said only those we trust."

My mother hissed my name, thinking me rude, but I didn't particularly give a fuck. It was my mate whose life was not only at risk, but actively being pursued. I had the right to dictate who was in this room when we made our plans. I got to decide who was privy to our secrets if Evaline's life was the one that hung in the balance.

My father looked at me with furrowed brows. "He's the Arch Sorcerer. They've always been involved in affairs like these throughout our history."

I shrugged. "In the past. When we'd had years to get to know each other before they needed to be invited." I looked to Lauden. "When there'd been time to build trust."

Lauden just gave me what I think must have been a charming smile, but it only agitated me further.

"I understand, Maddox. We haven't had much time to connect, but I assure you, I have the kingdom's best interest at heart."

I gave a curt nod. "Well I have *Evaline's* best interest at heart," I said walking toward him. "And you hardly know her, and until *I* can trust you," I said, placing a hand on my chest. "You can get the fuck out."

"Maddox!" It was Evaline who hissed my name this time.

I clenched my jaw and turned to her, she was standing out of her chair.

"Maddox." The boom of my father's voice filled the room, and I turned toward him. "I understand that you don't trust Lauden, but we've known him for months. He helped this kingdom even before you came home, and he's been actively teaching Evaline how to use her powers. If you don't trust him, that's an issue for you to resolve on your own time. I am the First. This is *my* study, and you will obey *my* commands."

I didn't dare speak, I knew that if I did he'd throw me from the room entirely. I only clenched my jaw as Evaline sat again and turned back to face my father.

"You know Vasier better than any of us, you must know why he wants me."

My father's brows furrowed as he looked down at his desk. "I think it's safe to say that it has something to do with your mother."

I dragged a hand down my face. "For fuck's sake."

My father snapped his eyes to mine, and I knew he was about to scream at me again, but I didn't care. We didn't have time to keep dawdling on the obvious.

"It's obviously her magic," Wyott said.

I gave him a look to communicate that he shouldn't reveal to the two Sorcerers in the room that her abilities were Gods-gifted, the less they had to know the better. But of course he already knew, because he gave me the slightest nod.

"We just need to understand what he wants to do with it."

My mother looked at Evaline. "Perhaps he intends to use her as a weapon." She looked down to my father. "He hasn't come close to the Madierian in decades because he knew it'd start another war. He's lost every single time he's made a move against us without the numbers. What if he plans to use her magic to even the field?"

I felt the anger that now mixed with worry as it shifted down the bond, and heard her heart rate quicken. The floor creaked below me as I strode back toward her.

"I will never let that happen." Her shoulders eased a bit at that. "But we can't sit here, caged up on this island, while Vasier finds more innocent people to harm," I said, my voice grim.

Evaline flinched at that, and I knew it was because of the threat to her friends.

She raised her chin. "I'm going."

"No, you're absolutely not," I said, along with my mother, Cora, and Wyott in different variations. "And you won't have to." I turned to look at the four Kova beside Wyott. "You boys willing to go on a hunt?"

Fredrik's lips lifted into a smirk before I even had to finish the sentence. "Fuck yes."

Wyott tensed out of the corner of my eye. I knew he was upset I hadn't invited him. But I ignored it. I'd have to talk to him later.

Evaline turned and narrowed her eyes. "Why would you all go when I'm the one they want?"

"It's the only way to understand what he wants with you. We can't protect you or prepare you for a fight if we don't know that."

Lauden and Sage straightened at that, and I wondered if they didn't believe in using magic as a weapon.

"You can stay here. We'll send a raven to Neomaeros and ask them to summon Aurora and Jacqueline, and then we can send a few Kova as an escort to get them from Kembertus and safely within Neomaeros' walls," I said.

Her worry seemed to ease at that.

Wyott spoke then. "This hunt is a bad idea. You have no idea how many are out there."

"Saxon said there were only two Vasi on the ship. Even if there are a couple more, the five of us could handle it," I said, nodding to the men beside Wyott. "Vasier isn't stupid. He wouldn't send too many Vasi right here near our shores. If we felt threatened, we could prepare our forces far before he could on the opposite side of Brassillion." I turned back to my father. "We'll go hunt one, and be done with it."

My father leaned back in his chair. "Even if you do manage to capture and question a Vasi, how do you know Vasier doesn't keep his intentions hidden from them?"

I leveled my gaze with my father. "I don't. But if they don't know anything, then we kill them." I shrugged. "No downside."

My mother's voice was small as she spoke. "What if it's a trap?"

Evaline looked up at me. "She's right, what if he's only doing this to draw us out?"

I looked to the four Kova who would accompany me, then back to Evaline and my mother.

"It is a trap. Which is why we'll let them think that we're walking right into it. He gave a specific threat to people you love, they'll expect us to go get Aurora and Jacqueline. We'll go to Merwinan, and the Vasi will assume we're going to move on to Kembertus after." I shrugged. "But instead we'll lay a trap of our own."

The room fell quiet for a moment before Cora spoke. "If they've already gone through all of this trouble to get Evaline, she'd be the only one they're looking for—the only one they'd make a move and expose themselves for."

She was right, and annoyance had just started to plague my mind when I saw Sage shift uncomfortably on her feet in my peripheral.

My eyes flicked from her, to Evaline.

Every Vasi that was involved in an abduction attempt on Evaline had been killed. None that would be waiting for us near Merwinan would have seen her.

The only obvious marker they would know to identify Evaline was the color of her hair.

I looked back to Sage and her brows furrowed as she noticed my gaze.

Wyott saw it too, and cocked his head as he looked at her. "It could work," he said, his arms crossed. "But you'd need a good wig."

"What is wrong with you two? We're not putting a guest on our island up as bait for the Vasi," my father hissed when he realized what Wyott and I were thinking.

Evaline's brows shot to her forehead. "That is ridiculous, you can't ask that of her."

"She'll do it," Lauden's voice rose above the rest and we all turned to him. Sage snapped her head toward him, her eyes flashing with surprise. But Lauden only looked at her with a smile. "We do everything we can for the First. We are in his service, no matter what is asked of us."

We watched as she took a slow swallow and clenched her jaw. "Fine."

But I was uncomfortable with the entire situation now, and immediately felt guilty for even thinking it.

"I'm sorry, I shouldn't have even thought it," I said and turned back to my father to further discuss, but Sage's voice pulled me back.

"No, he's right. I'll do it."

Evaline shook her head. "You really don't have to Sage, we'll find another way."

Sage shook her head and crossed her arms. "No, it's fine. It's the least we can do, you've all been so kind to us."

Evaline stood. "Are you sure?"

Sage nodded, meeting Evaline's evaluating gaze. "Yes," she said before shrugging. "Besides, it is a good plan. My magic is strong enough to protect me if needed."

She turned to look at the men beside Wyott. I heard Dean hold his breath and swore his already ivory skin paled even further as her eyes swept over the four of them.

"I agree with Evaline. This isn't a good idea." Dean spoke up for the first time, his voice hoarse.

I turned to look at Sage to see her face break out in a deep blush, her wide eyes still aimed at Dean. She swallowed slowly, and shook her head.

"No, it's fine. I want to go." She said, nodding to me.

I turned to my father. "Do you think it'll work?"

He wagged his head back and forth for a moment in thought. "It could. You five are fast and strong, if they have five or less Vasi then you could take them, but you all need to feed before you leave."

We all murmured our agreement.

My father turned to my mother. "Will you go to Theo's house and see if he'd mind opening the shop tonight so you and Sage can find a suitable wig?"

My mother nodded and the two of them left. Lauden stayed, and while I would've preferred to keep him out of the rest of the plans, it was his right to be here now that his partner was involved.

We'd leave the next morning, after we prepared our supplies and made our plans. We spent the rest of the evening discussing our strategy.

The four Kova left, along with Lauden who confirmed he'd relay all of the information to Sage when she got back home with her wig. My father retired for the night and I sent Evaline and Cora up to the suite while Wyott and I discussed.

As soon as he heard their footsteps fade away, he turned to me with crossed arms.

"You know you can't come," I said before he had a chance to speak.

He clenched his jaw. "No, I don't know that. Why don't you enlighten me as to why."

I took a deep breath and leaned on the front of my father's desk. "You just spent nearly a year traveling with me on the mainland. Did you already forget how much you missed Cora? How agonizing it was? You haven't been home long, Wyott. I'm not taking you away again so soon. Even if it is only for a week."

He rolled his eyes. "Maybe you should consider what I want when making decisions for me."

I sighed. "You know the best place for you is to be here with Cora." I shrugged. "Evaline needs you too. While I'm gone, she's going to need even more training than before. If Vasier is this adamant about getting to her, we need to make sure she's as prepared as possible. So she needs to be training at full speed, with more than one opponent."

His gaze didn't falter, but he didn't speak.

I stood and took a few steps closer to him. "Of course I want you to come. But I need you to stay here. For yourself, and for me."

Wyott sighed, likely because he knew I was right, and dropped his crossed arms.

"I can stay here and watch over her, but you can't be gone long." His gaze fell to the floor. "Neither of us have been on the mainland without each other since my father's death."

A wave of guilt crashed through me as I understood where his concern stemmed from. I raised a hand and clapped it over his shoulder.

"Everything will be okay, you know that. If a week passes and we still haven't caught one of them, we'll come home so I can feed and so we can regroup, then head back out."

Wyott digested my words then nodded.

Chapter Thirty-Six

Evaline

It was only a few minutes after Maddox sent Cora and I up here that he was coming through the door. Cora shot me a reassuring smile before she left to head home with Wyott.

Maddox closed the door behind her, his movements slow, before he turned to me. He had a worried expression on his face, likely because he knew I was angry, and walked toward where I sat on the chaise in front of the small fire with my arms crossed.

He didn't speak as he got down on his knees in front of me. Even though I was angry with him, I opened my legs so he could move between them, and he wrapped his hands around my hips to slide me along the chaise until I was close to him.

"I'm sorry," he said, his voice low.

I pursed my lips. "I don't like this. I don't like any of it, at all."

He sighed. "I know, but you don't need to be scared. Between Nash, Grant, Fredrik, Dean, and I we can keep Sage safe and trap a Vasi easily. It won't be long before we're home."

I leveled my jaw to meet his eyes. "And if you don't catch one, you'll come home in a week to feed? So you can stay strong?" It was one thing to let him go out of the protection of the ward, but to let him go without me, without my blood—I was having a hard time not locking him in our suite. If he could only feed from me, what would happen if we couldn't make it to each other in time?

He smiled and nodded. "Yes. I promise."

I let out a sigh. Of course I knew I wouldn't be able to talk him out of it. I couldn't control what he did, even if I wanted to make him stay back to keep him safe, too. The other Kova shouldn't have to go, either. All because of me. But they'd seemed excited to go—other than Dean; he seemed preoccupied.

I unraveled my arms and reached forward to hook my hands around the back of his neck, placing my palms on each side. My thumbs spread up closer to his jaw, and I felt the way his pulse thumped against them.

"I just don't want anything bad to happen to you. To any of you."

He smiled and squeezed my sides. "It won't. We'll be back before you know it."

The world shook then, another quake. It was just as quick as the others we'd been having, and I'd grown accustomed to them even if each left me with a pit of worry in my gut.

When it passed, I nodded. "You better."

The night was late, and I knew they were leaving at dawn. I didn't want to waste time talking, especially because he needed to feed.

I lowered my lips to his then and our kiss was soft. It was slow, but the fire between us roared nonetheless. It always did, no matter how we touched each other. Whether it was fierce and desperate, or gentle and slow.

I'd already removed my holsters before he'd come back to the room, so I moved to undo his now. They thudded to the floor, and in the next moment he tightened his grip on my hips until he was pulling me flush against his chest and rising to stand. I knew he was taking us to our bed before I felt the soft cushion of it below my back. He removed my shoes and his own before climbing on top of me, but we didn't tear each other's clothes off like we normally did. This was delicate and slow, as if each of us cherished the moment as much as we could.

By the time our clothes were off and he was inside of me, I wasn't sure if hours had passed, or only minutes. Time didn't make sense when his lips were on mine and his hands moved over me in the gentle but firm way they always did.

He lifted his lips off mine as he moved and looked down at me, his strokes deep but slow.

"What?" I whispered, even though we were alone.

He swiped a thumb over my cheek. "I love you," he said, dipping to kiss me softly before pulling back again. "More than I could've ever imagined."

I moved my hands on his shoulders up, until one tangled in his hair and the other flattened against his broad cheek. "I love you too. More than I thought I could ever love anyone."

He smiled and lowered himself until his lips were on my neck and I held my breath, turning my head away so he had clear access to feed.

But he didn't scrape his fangs along the skin, only kissed trails all around it, down my neck, to my collar bone, over to my shoulder. Up again, to my jaw. Behind my ear. With his thrusts inside of me and the flutter of his lips over my skin I was barely holding myself together, unable to stop the string of moans from my lips at his touch.

"I want to do this for the rest of my existence," he groaned.

"Me too," I whispered back, without even having to think about it.

We hadn't discussed my mortality yet, of course because we didn't really understand it. But I'd thought about it, and I'd had concerns over whether I'd turn. What it would mean not only for my lifespan but also for my magic. But in that moment, I didn't care about the risks. All I wanted was this. This moment, this love, this man. Every day, until the end of time.

I felt his smile against my skin before I felt his fangs. I gasped when they sank through in time with a thrust.

He fed until he was nourished, and then I made him take just a little more to be safe. We both rode the bliss that came with it, with all of it, and when we finally settled into bed, he pulled me close to him. Our heads rested on our pillows, but our legs entwined as we wrapped our arms around each other, our chests flush together and our faces only separated by our breaths. It reminded me of our first night together, and when I fell asleep I'd never been so thoroughly in love.

The next morning passed too quickly. I stood on the beach and watched as Cora threw orders around the ship that the Kova would take across the Strait. She was meeting with all the men who would run the ship. They picked a human crew instead of a Kova. Maddox was afraid if they had more Kova on the ship that the Vasi wouldn't go for the trap, because they would be severely outnumbered. I didn't like the idea of the humans going, especially after Saxon's crew was killed, but they were told of the risks and still agreed.

Maddox and his friends loaded their supplies onto the ship. They'd packed a few bags, but mostly they hauled in the Rominium chains they were taking.

Chrissa looped her arm through mine then. "It'll all be okay," she said quietly beside me.

I took a deep breath and nodded, tilting my head to face her. "I guess I'm just not used to saying goodbye to him yet."

Her gray eyes softened at that as the coastal breeze blew some strands of her short blond hair across her ivory cheeks. "That's understandable. Through time, it'll get easier."

She cast a glance up to Grant who walked up the gangway of the ship with several feet of chain draped over his shoulder.

She gave a breathy laugh. "Especially with how often they like to put themselves in danger."

I tried to smile at that, too, as she walked me toward a couple that stood in the sand, waiting to say their goodbyes.

Chrissa extended her hand toward the man and woman, their brown hair rustling in the wind. "This is Williem and Emily, they're Dean's parents." They smiled at me, his father shook my hand and his mother gave me a hug.

"It's nice to meet you," I said when I pulled back. "I'm really sorry about all of this. I'm sorry that they're making this trip all because of me."

The guilt had not stopped wrenching through me since the moment I awoke this morning.

They all shook their heads and Chrissa spoke. "It's not your fault, Evaline. Vasier shouldn't have done this. He's lucky Kovarrin isn't waging a war because of it."

Williem nodded. "They're all some of the most highly trained Kova that Rominia has to offer." He shook his head and laughed. "And I'm sure they'll all enjoy some time away."

I smiled at him but then saw a streak of white hair flutter in the corner of my eye. I turned, almost expected to see my mother, but it was Sage who made her way down the beach and toward the dock.

I excused myself from the Kova and ran over to meet her.

"Sage," I called, and she turned toward me with a blank expression on her face. "How are you?" I asked, stopping in front of her.

She blinked. "Fine."

I pursed my lips. "I just wanted to say that I'm sorry you were volunteered for this." Her eyes hardened. "There's still time to decline," I said, throwing a look to the ship. "You don't have to go for me, it's not a fair thing to ask."

Sage straightened and clasped her hands in front of her.

"You are not my mother, Evaline. I'm perfectly capable of making decisions on my own."

My words came out before I had a chance to consider them.

"You didn't, though. Lauden did." Her eyes flashed, but it was too late to take any of it back now, so I pushed forward. "He seems to do that a lot. I just want you to know that no one will be angry if you decide against it." I reached for her hand and my words rushed out. "This isn't where you grew up. This isn't a Kromean Kingdom, here we have a say over what happens to us. Women can choose who to be with, and how to live, and if you decide that isn't with Lauden, there's plenty of space in the mansion for you to stay with us."

She stepped back as if I'd hit her, and ripped her hand from mine. "You don't know me, Evaline. Don't pretend to care."

My lips pressed together as I gave a fervent nod of my head. "I do, though," I said. "I care, but I also know you, even if we only met a few weeks ago." My eyes flicked between hers, willing her to understand. "I see you."

Her brows pinched. "You may think you do, but you don't."

"I do," I said, clasping my hands together on my chest. "Pain sees pain, and I sensed yours the moment we met."

Something I couldn't place flashed over her face then, and she opened her mouth to speak.

"Pardon us, Evaline," Lauden said as he sauntered up to us, cutting off whatever she'd been about to say. "I want a chance to say goodbye to Sage."

I stood still, giving her a chance to speak up if she wanted to change her mind, but she just closed her mouth, and schooled her features. He took her elbow and guided her away from me.

I tried to swallow back the anger that seared up my throat. I couldn't help but be grateful for the fact that she was going to be getting a few days away from him.

"We're ready," Maddox said behind me, and I nearly jumped from surprise. In an instant, all the despise I held for Lauden, and the worry for Sage, dissipated as I looked up at my mate.

He pulled me closer to the boat and wrapped his arms around me.

"Be safe while I'm gone," he said. "Train with Wyott and Cora." Then, a bit begrudgingly. "Work on your magic with Lauden. The more you understand it, the safer you'll be." I nodded along, until he pulled back. "I will be back in a week, if not less. Try not to let Wyott and Cora get to you. They can be quite annoying to hang out with alone. Trust me I know," he said jokingly.

"I heard that," Wyott called from a few paces away.

I snorted and Maddox smiled down at me.

"You be safe," I said softly. "Take care of each other, and take care of Sage." I pushed my hands against his chest. "And come home."

He nodded before he pulled his arms from my waist and held my face in his hands. "I love you. Until the end of my days," he said.

"And in the Night that follows," I whispered back.

He kissed me then, not for nearly as long as I would've liked.

Then they all loaded into the ship, leaving the rest of us on the beach, waving as they sailed away.

Chapter Thirty-Seven

Evaline

The rest of the day passed slowly, and I found myself checking the bond every few minutes to see if Maddox was already on his way back, already within range of our tether.

But I knew he wouldn't be, not so soon. Gods, a full day hadn't even passed and I was already checking, even though I knew that it took more than a day to cross the Strait.

I wasn't alone, and I was thankful for that. After we'd seen him off, Rasa and I came back to the mansion to have tea on the patio that overlooked the ballroom floor, and past it, to the endless ocean.

I knew Rasa was trying to spend as much time with me as possible because I didn't have any training scheduled today for combat or magic, and she knew I was worried. By mid-day we'd already had breakfast and lunch together and were touring the parts of the mansion I hadn't seen yet when Cora arrived. She popped her head into the armory, where I was admiring the selection of weapons that were on display.

I smiled when I saw her. "Where's Wyott?"

She shrugged and came closer. "Don't know, he's been in town all day I think. That, or training." She strode closer until she was peering down at the arrows I was looking at. "He's not happy that he didn't get to go with them."

I pursed my lips and straightened. I could understand that, but Maddox was only trying to be fair to his friend.

Cora bounced up before I could speak.

"Do you want to go swimming?" she asked.

It wasn't long before we were hiking to the other side of Rominia, to a part of the island I hadn't seen yet.

"Can't we just go to the beaches around the mansion?" I asked as we hiked around the base of the volcano.

She shrugged. "If you want to go to just a plain old beach."

I cocked my head. "What makes them different?"

She shot me a wicked grin. "This one has an underwater cave."

When we finally made it to the water, I saw a large rock formation that jutted out of the water and saw the cave she was referring to.

"On the other side of it is the marina. It's where we store the ships that are not in use, or that just need to be repaired. There's a few that are in storage on the island to protect them, they're not in use anymore, but they're historical so we keep them. We can go sometime if you want," she said, turning to me.

"That reminds me," I said, placing my hands on my hips. "I've been wanting to know how you came to be the head of Rominia's Navy."

She sat the basket that held the food she packed for us on the sand. "I grew up on various ships," she said, looking up at me from where she knelt. "My parents were Kova too, and they were travelers. They sailed all around the world, I was born on a ship in the middle of a storm."

My eyes widened. "That must've been terrifying for your mother."

She smiled and shrugged. "Honestly, once you meet her you'll understand that almost nothing phases her."

She set our towels down on top of the basket and shielded her eyes from the sun, smiling as she spoke.

"But I grew up on the ship with the rest of the crew and my parents. My father captained it. When we arrived here I was about twenty. Twenty in Kova years, but still like a child in human years."

I nodded. "Maddox told me that Kova age at a slower rate."

"Exactly," she said. "My parents hadn't been back to Rominia in a few decades, but they wanted me to experience growing up with other Kova children. So we came here, and that's when I met Wyott and Maddox. When my parents left on expeditions, I'd miss them, and I always found comfort in the marina working on the ships that smelled like childhood. After I started spending time with Wyott and Maddox, and became more well acquainted with Kovarrin, he realized that I was an asset on the water." She pulled her hair back into a tie as she talked. "When the previous head of the Navy decided to leave Rominia to travel the world, Kovarrin offered the position to me."

Pride beamed in her eyes and I felt my chest flutter for my friend. I was thankful to be in a place like Rominia, and not Kembertus.

"Where are your parents now?" I asked, assuming they also helped with ship maintenance and the Navy.

"They're on a trip with my little brother." She laughed and shook her head. "He's young to me, but he's just over a century old."

My smile fell slightly at that, as it was only another reminder that I wasn't sure what would happen with Maddox and I as I aged.

Cora stood, noticing my change in demeanor.

"Speaking of the incredibly long life spans of Kova," I started, crossing my arms. "I've been wanting to ask you about the change."

Her brows furrowed and she reached a hand to touch my arm.

"You don't need to be worried about the future right now, Evaline. You have enough on your plate."

I sighed. "I know, it's just that I don't know what's expected of me."

She shook her head. "Absolutely nothing is. You know Maddox would never force anything onto you, least of all this massive change in not only your life, but your future."

My eyes moved to the water that lapped softly beside us.

"I guess I just feel conflicted. It would make me stronger, faster. I would feel safer knowing that any human I came across would be the one who needed to fear me, and not the other way around." My heart did a painful lurch at that. "But if I'm meant to kill Vasier, and no Sorcerer has ever turned, then what if I lose my magic and the Gods punish me for that?"

Cora stepped around the basket sitting at our feet and pulled me into her arms.

"It seems the Gods have spent your lifetime placing burdens on your shoulders that you do not deserve to carry," she said in my ear as I wrapped my arms around her. "If you decide to turn, and you lose your magic, we will find another way to kill Vasier if that is what will free you from this curse." She pulled back but kept her hands on my shoulders. "But if your magic is too important for you to risk, then Maddox will understand. We all will."

My eyes closed briefly with my sigh, and I shook my head. "I just don't want to make the wrong move. I don't want to anger the Gods, and I don't want to disappoint Maddox."

Cora's head cocked. "Tell me Evaline, do you always put the needs of others before your own?"

I didn't have anything to respond with, and she seemed to sense that.

She nodded and straightened, looking over the rock that protruded out from the water. "Depending on the tide, it's either half full or completely underwater. The tide is going out right now so it's safe to swim."

It didn't take long for us to strip into our swimming garments and run into the water. Just like the last time I swam in the Madierian, I felt the current's tug and the ripple of bubbles up my body that stirred with each movement I made. The smile on my face was impossibly large, and I felt my magic soar to the surface inside of me.

When we made it into the cave, I lost my breath.

The dark black rock that surrounded us made the cave far darker than the open water we'd just left, but the sunlight that streamed in through a large hole in the ceiling lit the cave up and subtle strokes of blue and green swirled through the water around us.

I treaded just below the opening and gazed up to see the sun shining above us with a few clouds breaking up the sky in light whisps.

"Gods," I mused.

I heard Cora swim closer. "See? Better than a plain old beach."

I laughed and nodded. "Much better."

We explored the back of the cave and as deep into the water as I could manage before I needed a breath.

I played with my magic while we were there, making small waves in the cave and even a column of water that could raise myself or Cora up and out of the opening in the ceiling, just wide enough for one of us to go at a time. We swam and explored for what felt like hours and very well might have been, because the sun was no longer directly above us when I looked back up through the hole in the cave.

When I grew tired, we floated our way back to the beach and laid on the sheet Cora had brought.

A rare silence fell over us as we laid back and I closed my eyes. I allowed myself to reach for the bond, feeling slightly guilty that I'd been so preoccupied for the last few hours that I hadn't done so since we'd been here, but there was nothing. Only the distant hum that told me he was too far.

I listened to the soft waves that kissed the shore, the gulls that squawked overhead, and the whisper of wind that wound through the trees behind us. I don't think I'd ever experienced a moment where the entire world felt at peace. As if there were no wrongs to undo. As if there weren't innocent people dying because of me, as if my mate wasn't out there hunting a Vasi, as if my best friends hadn't been threatened by Vasier. But instead, as if the Gods had placed the little piece of bliss that was this moment right here for me to experience, right now.

"You falling asleep over there?" Cora asked quietly.

I snorted. "No, but I definitely could. This is so relaxing."

I opened my eyes and turned my head to look at her. She was smiling toward the sky.

"Mmm," she hummed. "This is my favorite place to come when I'm feeling anxious. I knew you'd like it."

My brows furrowed as I looked at her. "Then I hope you don't come here often."

She turned her head to meet my gaze and gave me a small smile. "From time to time. A lot while Wyott was gone, but even when he's here I find myself needing the space to think."

I reached my hand across the gap that separated us and took hers in mine.

"You don't have to tell me but I want you to know that you can if you want to."

Pain flashed across her eyes almost as fast as the guilt pulled at her brows.

"I'm not going to vent to you, you're the one who should be comforted right now."

I shook my head. "There's no rule that says that two troubled friends can't comfort each other."

She snorted at that and nodded, looking back to the sky but squeezing my hand.

"Wyott and I have discussed starting a family for years, but he always pushes it off."

My heart pounded painfully in my chest for her and I recalled the conversation Cora, Chrissa, and I had last night on the roof together after dinner. We'd talked about the possibility of starting families in the future. It was only an option for me right now, and not a plan, but the two Kova seemed ready.

Wyott and Cora would make wonderful parents, and I'd pay good money to see Wyott navigate fatherhood, but clearly there were more complex matters at hand.

"He doesn't want to?" I asked softly, not wanting to overstep.

She let out a sigh. "He does want to. That's the issue. We've both wanted to for decades now. We have our life set up together, we have a support system, it should be a good time to at least begin making arrangements." She shrugged. "I'm ready, I've been ready, and he has too. But he's afraid."

My brows furrowed. "Afraid of losing time with you?"

She pursed her lips and turned away from me again.

"No, of something else." She took a deep breath and sat up. "Wyott should be the one to tell you the rest, and I know he will." I rose to sit beside her and she tilted her head. "You two have a lot in common."

A sinking feeling filled my stomach as I knew exactly what she meant—or rather, I feared I knew what she meant.

But neither of us said anything about that, and I only patted her knee. "I'm sorry, Cora."

It was all I could say.

She smiled softly. "Thank you. Are you okay?"

I pursed my lips and looked out over the water.

"I'm afraid, too," I started. "Of so many things that anymore, it's hard to keep track of which one is worse. I'm afraid of losing Maddox. I'm afraid of what part I have to play with Vasier." I shrugged. "I'm afraid of the curse." I looked down at my hands. "I'm mostly afraid that more people will die because of me."

CHAPTER THIRTY-EIGHT

Maddox

The sail through the Strait seemed quick, and I wasn't sure if it was because we had the wind on our side or if it was because my mind was completely occupied by my worried thoughts.

Dean, Fredrik, Nash, and Grant were bouncing with excitement and Sage had ducked below deck into a cabin as soon as we boarded.

"When was the last time you were off the island?" I asked the four Kova with me as we helped the boat's crew dock.

Grant shrugged. "Not too long, but it's been decades since we had a proper hunt."

As he spoke, Sage came up from below deck and stepped off the ship. She didn't bother looking down at us as we tied the ropes to secure the ship to the docks, just walked ahead toward the walls of Merwinan. I turned to Grant.

"I know you're excited," I mused. "But let's hope it ends quick."

The guards at the castle let us in, no doubt already having orders from the Lord and Lady to do so if we arrived, considering the turmoil that had been overtaking the city. Even if the citizens didn't wholly understand what was happening, there would still be concerns after finding dead bodies dropped outside the walls.

One of the servants had gone to fetch the rulers while the guards directed us to wait in the castle's war room. Not every kingdom had a formal war room, it had been so long since there'd been wars for them to plan for, but Merwinan dealt with pirates on occasion and still maintained theirs.

"Thank the Gods you're here," Lady Veronica said as she came through the door, her long brown hair fluttered over the bronze skin of her exposed shoulders as she wrapped her arms around me. "We were days away from calling in help."

I hugged her back and when we pulled away, I shook the Lord's hand.

"We're glad you're here," he said, his brows furrowed, and the movement crinkled the copper skin on his forehead.

The other Kova greeted the rulers, and I introduced the Lord and Lady to Sage, then turned back to them with crossed arms.

"Have there been any updates here since the last raven?"

Lord Leo nodded with worried eyes. "There have been a few more bodies found by the docks, and one of our ships and its crew are missing."

I told them about the shipwreck in Rominia and the men who'd died. We didn't tell them about Evaline's magic, or that Vasier was looking for her. Even though I trusted the Lord and Lady, I didn't want to risk telling others unless it was absolutely needed. But they did agree to let us hunt the area and offered to give us guards if needed to set the trap.

"Absolutely not," I said, shaking my head. "We can handle it. There's no reason to put more Merwinians at risk. We've prepared and brought along all the help we'll need. You two try to get some rest while we're here. We'll stay at the inn and each night will go out to hunt until we catch one." The Lord and Lady nodded while I spoke. "We'll try not to bother you both while we're here. If a week goes by and we've been unsuccessful, we'll let you know before we head back to the island to replenish. Then we'll be back. But if you don't hear from us, it's likely because we caught one and had to head back immediately. Once we're on the island, we'll send a raven to update you."

Lady Veronica stretched her reach and I shook her hand. "We can't thank you all enough for helping with this. I never thought he'd stoop this low and come this close." She nodded to the others with me. "Please, be careful." Her wide brown eyes fell to me. "Especially you, I'm sure Vasier would take every opportunity to get back at your father by harming you if he could."

With that, we left and headed for the inn to reserve our rooms. We'd spend the rest of the day scouting just outside the city's gates.

It was unclear whether Vasier would know that I was also Evaline's mate. Every Vasi who'd interacted with her was dead, and unable to report back to him. He likely only discovered all the failed attempts at abducting her by the scouts he would've sent out when she wasn't delivered to him. And each time they would've had to report back that the Vasi were dead, and she was nowhere to be found. Until there was only one place she could be—safe in Rominia.

I knew he was likely growing angrier by the day; it would be the only reason he would've risked coming to Merwinan and causing chaos, or dumping dead bodies at Kovarrin's door.

But if they were twins, then Vasier knew my father better than anyone. And he likely knew that my father was not quick to anger, or to make decisions without proper thought put in first. Vasier was gambling with these moves, willing to call my father's bluff about whether these acts of war would actually *lead* to a war.

And so far, he was right.

After we left the castle the six of us had spent the majority of the day scouting around the outskirts of Merwinan. We hoped that while we were out and about in daylight that the Vasi might make an attempt at Sage but they hadn't, so we continued to search potential areas for our own trap.

We split up, concerned that having too large of a group would hinder an attempt from the Vasi. Dean, Nash, and Fredrik were on the eastern side, just outside the kingdom. Sage, Grant, and I navigated the western side, closer to the beach.

Sage had worn the white wig since the moment she stepped on the ship, and it really did look convincing. Theo was very skilled at his job.

We didn't talk much and I'd instructed the other three Kova not to discuss the trap or anything of the like, either. If the Vasi were spying on us from afar, they'd only think we were looking for clues as to where they were hiding out. We didn't stay in one area too long, and never made it look as if we were hunting for a good place to set a trap.

When I thought up a plan, I kept it to myself.

When Sage, Grant, and I finally got back to the inn, I could sense her rising tension.

"Are you okay?" I asked as I opened the door for her to walk into the tavern. Where furrowed brows and worry had lingered before, Sage dropped her face into a blank expression.

Her already tight jaw clenched. "I'm fine," she said as she walked through the door past me.

She started to head toward the stairs and back to her room and Grant walked in behind me.

"Don't you want to eat first?" I asked her.

She turned back toward me and cocked her brow. "I can on my own."

I shrugged. "I'm just trying to be nice. I really appreciate what you're doing to help the kingdom and Evaline." I shook my head. "I'm not your enemy. I know you and Evaline haven't always gotten along, but that doesn't mean that you don't belong or that you aren't an asset to our island."

Grant nodded his agreement beside me, and the mask she wore flickered for one moment before she snagged it back into place and gave one slight nod of her head. "Fine, but only because it takes longer for them to deliver it to your room."

I hid my smile at how similar she was to Evaline, when we first met, and grabbed us a table. I got one large enough for the rest of the Kova in case they came back in time. Grant and I ordered an ale, and I turned to her.

"Do you want anything?"

She shook her head. "Water will do." When the waitress walked away, Sage looked between Grant and I and shrugged. "I don't like drinking before something like this. It dulls my ability to control my magic."

"That's smart," Grant said, nodding.

There was an awkward bit of silence as I tried to think of what conversation I could start that wouldn't have her regretting her decision to stay and eat with us. My eyes flicked to Grant and knew he was doing the same.

"Have you gotten to see a lot of the world?" he asked, leaning back in his chair.

Sage pursed her lips and looked down at the table. "I have not," she said. "Only the small town I grew up in and the farm my father raised me on. And then once Lauden and I grew up and took our trip west, we just stopped in small towns along the way on our route to Rominia."

I nodded, leaning back in my chair.

"Well, there's much of the world Evaline still needs to see. Perhaps you and Lauden could come with us."

I didn't like the idea of Lauden being there, but Sage seemed kind enough. Even if it wasn't outwardly shown, I could tell that she didn't have an evil heart, only that she tried to pretend that she did.

Grant nodded. "Chrissa and I are planning to go to Correnti next year. You should all come with us," he said, looking between Sage and I.

She gave a soft laugh at the idea, I guessed, and I chuckled, too. "What?" I asked, but she waited to answer until after the waitress dropped off our drinks.

She watched the waitress's back as she walked away and then shook her head.

"Lauden isn't much for travel."

I shrugged. "You never know what you'll find when you travel." My hand dragged down the back of my neck. "When we were going to Kembertus, I was dreading it every step we took. But that's where I met Evaline." I smiled to Grant. "You should have seen the look on her face when I caught her pickpocketing me." I took a swig of ale. "Before she promptly ran in the other direction."

Grant's deep laugh rumbled beside me, but Sage furrowed her brows as she pulled her hands into her lap.

"What do you mean? You're mates, why would she run away?"

I slung an arm over the back of my chair as I leaned into it. "She didn't know we were mates, all she saw were the gray eyes, and she was afraid." I made sure to keep my voice low so none of the humans around could hear. "She's the first non-Kova who's ever been mated to one, that we know of. So when she first met me, she didn't know."

Sage shifted in her seat at that. "But you knew?"

Grant snorted. "He waited for decades. Trust me, he knew."

I rolled my eyes at him but met Sage's gaze. "For us, we know immediately. As if the Goddess of Fate reaches down and places the knowledge in our heads."

Sage's jaw was tight as I spoke, and she looked everywhere but Grant or I. "All Kova know, even if their mate doesn't?" she asked, her voice tight.

I nodded. "Every Kova I've ever met knew the moment their eyes locked."

She pursed her lips and nodded. "And Evaline—" But she stopped talking and looked to the door.

I heard my friends a moment before they entered and when they burst through the door and made for us, I wondered if Sage had extra abilities like Evaline did.

After the lot of us finished eating, we headed upstairs. I gathered everyone in my room and we sat around the table and chaise by the fire. I wanted to be able to talk freely and discuss, and I didn't want to do that with hushed voices downstairs by all the humans.

The wall groaned as I leaned against it. Dean, Nash, Fredrik and Grant sat at the table facing me, and Sage sat on the chaise with her legs crossed, staring at the fire, facing away from all of us.

"Did you guys end up finding any good spots?" I asked Nash, Fredrik, and Dean.

"We searched for a long time, but couldn't find anywhere that was suitable," Fredrik said.

"That's okay, I have an idea." The four Kova leaned forward and Sage continued to look toward the fire. "We've already tried to lure them out by having Sage with us outside of Merwinan's wards, and it hasn't worked." The Kova all nodded. "What if we, and I mean just Sage and I and one of you, go to the docks tomorrow night and talk to the ship's crew as if we're preparing to leave and head back to Rominia?"

Fredrik laughed. "So, if the Vasi are within hearing range, they'd fear they'll lose their chance at grabbing her, and have to make a move."

"Yes, exactly. If the other three of you stay just within the city's gates, you'll hear my shout when they close in on us, and you can come with the chains. We'll load the Vasi onto the ship and leave."

The four Kova looked to each other, then nodded. Sage only sat with her spine looking uncomfortably straight as she stared at the fire. I turned to Dean.

"Do you have the Rominium chains?" I asked.

Vasi likely didn't even know that the metal existed, or that it was strong enough to withhold a Kova, and thus a Vasi. We brought enough to wrap up a few if needed, and extra to leave in Merwinan if we had to come back for another hunt.

When Dean didn't respond, I tried again. "Dean, is the Rominium ready?" I repeated.

He jumped when I said his name and turned from where he'd been watching Sage. "Yes, I'm sorry," he said, dragging a hand down his face and over the short scruff of his beard. "It's ready. Whoever stays in Merwinan can carry enough to restrict a few Vasi when they come in as backup when the attack starts." His eyes darted back to Sage.

I nodded and made eye contact with the other three Kova. "Does that sound good to you?"

They each nodded.

"Sounds good to me," Fredrik said.

"We've had worse plans," Grant shrugged.

"I'm ready when you all are," Nash said, one of his legs bouncing beneath him.

I turned to Sage. "What about you? Are you okay with this plan?"

She stared at me for a moment, the mask falling from her face. Her brows furrowed and a flash of shock lit her eyes.

"What?"

I tilted my head toward her. "You're the most important person in this plan, and your opinion matters the most. If you aren't comfortable, we'll figure something else out."

Confusion passed over her face before our eyes met. Her mask slid back into place, and she looked back to the fire.

"Yes," she said. "It's fine."

Guilt twinged inside as I realized that she might not be used to the idea of having a say.

CHAPTER THIRTY-NINE

Evaline

Lauden was far more relaxed than I was today.

I hadn't talked to him since they'd left, only knew that he sent a raven for the Lord and Lady of Neomaeros just after the hunting group had set sail. Two full days had passed, which meant that they would've landed in Merwinan by now.

When I walked into the loft, Lauden was sitting on the leather couch of the study with one ankle propped on the other knee, reading a book, with a cup of tea on the table beside him. He greeted me with a smile before standing and setting his book on the couch where he'd just been sitting.

"Good morning, Evaline," he said as he strode to lean against the large wooden table.

I cocked my head at him. "Hi, Lauden. How are you today?"

He shrugged and nodded his head back to the couch. "I'm good, I've just been catching up on some reading."

I furrowed my brows at him. "Aren't you worried for Sage?" I shook my head. "I haven't been able to concentrate long enough to read, I just keep thinking about all of them out there."

Lauden smiled and shook his head. "I'm only worried that Sage will not do what needs to be done."

I narrowed my eyes at him. "What is that supposed to mean?"

Gods, I hated him.

He waved a hand through the air. "That she won't use her magic to harm," he elaborated. "She's never had to, and I just hope she does if she needs to protect herself, or the Kova."

Dread flooded through me at that. I'd never considered that not every Sorcerer in the world had to use their magic to protect themselves as many times as I did. My guilt swelled again, then, because I was reminded that I shouldn't have let her go in the first place.

Lauden clapped his hands. "Are you ready to practice Air again?"

We spent a few hours working on it. When we'd been at the tree, I'd been able to flutter a small breeze through its leaves, but nothing more impressive. Today, using Air came much quicker.

I wasn't sure if it was because I'd spent yesterday practicing in mine and Maddox's suite, or just because I was getting better at calling my magic.

After I successfully flew a feather around the room, Lauden and I went outside and he watched as I created a small cyclone of air on the beach. It was half my height and picked the sand up off the beach as it moved.

When I flattened my hands in the air, halting my magic, the sand hung for a second before it fell to the ground with a sigh.

Lauden turned to me. "You've shown that you're competent with Terra and Air." He paused. "You've already told me that Water comes easily. Do you want to show me?"

I simply swung a hand toward the water beside me and a wave lifted at its beckon. Lauden swallowed, and nodded.

When the wave fell back to join the water, the tide lulled up at the change in volume and crept toward our feet.

He clapped his hands between us. "Then that just leaves one more element."

Goosebumps rose along my skin. I don't know why I had the reaction; I knew we'd likely start Fire today. But there was a violence associated with the magic, and the thought of wielding fire—holding the flame in my hands—terrified me.

But I followed Lauden back into the house. He stopped at the work table, reached into the drawer, and pulled out a small piece of tissue paper.

He pinched it between his fingers and held it out until it flopped forward, bowing to me.

"Fire is going to be more difficult than all the rest," he started, looking at the piece of paper. "With the others, they're natural. Those are elements that are constantly all around you, and all you have to do is manipulate them. But fire… you have to conjure. It's an entirely new type of magic to you. It'll feel different in your veins, you'll have to ask for *exactly* what you want from your magic. You'll have to be explicit, and concentrate every single second in order to do it successfully."

He raised his other hand to me, palm up, as if he were asking for me to take his hand. Instead, a small flame appeared. Lauden rolled it about his hand, between his fingers, held it on his fingertips.

"Your own fire can't burn you, but all other fire can. That means natural fires *and* other Sorcerer's."

I nodded, trying to ignore the fear that crept up my neck.

"You had an upper hand when learning all of your other elements, because you'd already wielded them before. You knew what they felt like. But you've never used fire, and it's the hardest," Lauden raised his eyes to mine until I lifted them to meet his. "Don't be frustrated if you don't catch on right away, it might take some time."

He handed me the sheet and I stared down at it for a few moments, calling my magic just like I always did. But where I could usually connect my magic to something around me—the air, the water, the dirt—I couldn't link it to anything. I tried until I got tired and bent to lean over the table, my elbows propped on its top.

I'd envision what I wanted, reached for my magic… and nothing. Gods, I could almost hear the sizzle of the magic expanding, growing inside of me, just to dissipate at the threshold. Like steam hissing into cold air.

After a while, Lauden suggested I sit so I could be more comfortable, so I sat on one end of the leather couch while he picked up his book and continued reading.

Every once in a while he'd call out new cues to help me.

"Imagine the feel of fire, the pure power of it."

"Think of how it sounds when it consumes its fuel."

"Imagine the entire world engulfed in the flames, what that would smell like, what it would look like."

But no matter how many words of encouragement or instruction he uttered, I couldn't get it. After a few hours, a migraine started to pierce the front of my skull.

I let the hand holding the tissue paper fall and rest on my leg while my other hand came up to massage my forehead. I clenched my eyes shut against the pain, frustrated.

"It's okay, Evaline," Lauden said beside me. "You can't expect to master everything on your first attempt."

He leaned over the cushion that sat between us and plucked the paper from my hand. It disintegrated into a burst of fire in his before he threw the ball of flame into the fireplace.

I nodded while I continued to massage my scalp. "I know. I just thought there'd be something after so many hours. Especially now that I'm competent in all of the other elements."

The couch squeaked as he stood up and I heard his footsteps across the room. "I know, but like I said, Fire is unlike all of the others. It'll take some time. You may never master it, and that's okay."

I sighed and dropped my hand until it thudded against the leather wrapped arm of the couch. I tilted my head against the back of it and looked over at him.

"What are you doing?"

He pulled a tea kettle out of the cupboard and filled it with the water pitcher before placing his hand below the kettle. The pot was whistling in a minute, and the tea was ready, heated only by the fire emanating from his hand.

I scoffed. "You make it look so effortless." I wasn't sure what was more infuriating. How much I disliked him, or the fact that I was envious of him.

He laughed. "That's because it is for me. I've been doing this for years now."

I straightened, realizing I'd never asked how old he was. I voiced the question now.

"Thirty," he answered. "And Sage is twenty-five." I nodded, I knew she was close to my age. He came back and handed me the teacup. "Here, it'll help with your headache."

"Thank you," I said before softly blowing on the tea and then taking a sip. I let the hot liquid slide past my tongue and forced myself not to ask the question I so desperately wanted to know.

Lauden made me uncomfortable most of the time, and if he was five years older than Sage, and they met when he was seventeen, I feared what age she was when they started dating.

But it felt like an invasion of her privacy to ask it, so I opted for a different question.

"Do you think I'll ever get fire?" I asked as he leaned his back against the tall table.

He shrugged and crossed his arms. "It's hard to say, I've never worked with someone who had all of the elements before, and we don't really understand your magic yet, anyway. We don't know why you have all of the elements."

He cocked his head and I kept my features schooled as his gaze flitted over my face. On the best of days I disliked Lauden. On the worst of them I hated him. I wasn't going to tell him about my Gods-gifted abilities.

He continued, "Water is clearly stronger than the rest, but Air and Terra seem to be pretty even. And even then, at times they still seem stronger than any Air or Terra Caster I've ever seen. So if you're weaker elements are still that strong, then perhaps Fire will be the same."

I raised my brows, looking down to examine the tea leaves floating in the bottom of my cup. "Based on how I feel right now, that's hard to imagine."

The fatigue was already starting to settle in me, and I knew that even though it was only the start of the afternoon, I'd need to go to sleep as soon as I got back to my room.

Mine and Maddox's room.

It felt so empty without him there, and the thought had me looking back to Lauden.

"You really aren't worried about them? About Sage being bait?" I asked, hoping he'd show even the slightest bit of worry—any care at all—for Sage.

He gave me a warm smile. "I'm not. I'm confident that everything will go according to plan."

Chapter Forty

Maddox

We spent most of the day before the trap preparing for every possible deviation, every possible surprise. Sage rested in her room while we planned and once early evening hit, I sent everyone else to their rooms to rest as much as they could before the fight. We didn't know how bad it would be, and I wanted all of us to be as alert as possible.

Of course, I didn't have much luck. Sleep eluded me, and when I finally started to drift away the ground below rumbled just as it had been in Rominia these last few weeks.

I shot up in bed, and listened. This quake felt far stronger than the small rumbles we had in Rominia, but nowhere near as severe as the violent quake at the Ball. Not big enough to cause a tidal wave, or trigger Mt. Rominia, just enough to be unsettling.

Shortly after I laid back down and made a mental note to ask the Lord and Lady about it, a second round rattled the paintings hanging on the wall of the room. I sat up again, perplexed, but after several minutes of nothing, I decided not to worry about it. I had to rest for the night and I was running out of time to do so.

"Are you still up for this?" I asked, turning my head toward Sage.

I was giving her my last words of advice as we left the inn for the Merwinan gates. We'd be just out of earshot of any Vasi lurking about, and I wanted to make sure she still felt comfortable.

She cut her eyes up to me, and I could hear how her heart raced in worry.

"What, you don't think I can handle it?" she snapped.

I raised my brows and shook my head. "Of course I think you can, I was just making sure you were still okay." I slowed my pace. "No one will be angry if you change your mind. Not Evaline or I, and not my father."

Her lips twitched to purse but she turned to stare forward. "I'm fine. I'm ready. I've trained my magic my entire life for this. I will do my part."

I only nodded and continued forward. When we reached the gates, I nodded to the four Kova standing there, who bounced on the balls of their feet, ready to run.

Dean stepped forward, he'd been the one who volunteered to go to the dock with Sage and I.

Grant nodded to us, he was the closest to the gate, as we passed them. "We'll run at the first hint of a scream."

"Good," I said softly, then turned to the gate and took a deep breath.

The gates creaked behind us as they closed and Dean and I flanked Sage on each side as we stepped out of the protection of Merwinan's walls.

We walked toward the beach in the darkness. The moon was bright against the water, even if it wasn't full, and the stars glinted above us. The water was rhythmic as we neared it and the gentle coastal breeze fluttered through my hair.

We were silent as we hit the sand. Out of my peripheral I could tell that Sage was anxious. Her heart was still racing, but her brows were pinched in worry and her hands were fisted at her sides, so tight that her knuckles were white. Dean glanced at her, too.

I wanted to tell her that everything would be okay, that she could relax, but I knew I couldn't do so in case there were any Vasi nearby. I strained to listen for any sound of them, but there was only the patter of crabs, the sigh of our feet sinking into the sand, and our heartbeats.

I ran through the plan again in my head, over and over, until I imagined every move I'd make and how I'd ensure Sage's safety while the other Kova locked up a Vasi, or two.

Finally, we hit the docks and Sage and I continued down them as Dean kept watch at the entrance.

The thud of our boots on the dock sounded as we looked for our ship and once we found it, I called up onto it. The captain came down, and I asked him if we could leave soon. He sighed and wiped a tired look from his face, but nodded.

"Give us a couple hours to get everything ready, and then we'll set sail."

I nodded and shook his hand. "Thank you. We'll go gather our belongings and be back in a bit."

Sage's shoulders were tight as we made our way back to Dean. He held out a hand to help her down the steps of the dock, but she walked past him. I couldn't tell if he was annoyed or embarrassed when his eyes flicked up to mine, but he turned to follow her.

One moment we were descending the stairs behind her, and the night was calm around us. In the next, a Vasi shot through my peripheral. Dean and I lunged toward her, but we were too slow. When we both landed in the sand where she'd been standing, she was gone. A Vasi had plucked her from right in front of us, and the only sound had been her muffled shout.

Dean and I scrambled to our feet and screamed for her. We turned around and around, nearly falling as the ground shook viciously with another quake. It settled after a minute and we screamed her name, darting around the beach looking for them.

How could she have been grabbed like that without either one of us hearing the Vasi sprinting for her?

We screamed her name, darted around the beach looking for them, but they were gone. There was no one in sight.

I ran both hands through my hair as I paced around the beach and listened to my own heartbeat in my ears, and Dean's heart hammering too hard against his chest.

"No. No, no, no," he murmured to himself.

It was only a moment before Nash, Fredrik, and Grant met us.

They looked around as they arrived, and Fredrik spoke.

"What happened?"

I shook my head so hard my neck ached, my eyes wide as I met his. Dean was screaming beside me, and I didn't know if he was calling her name or cursing the Gods.

"I have no fucking idea. We'd just stepped off the dock, I was listening for them, but they snuck up without a sound." I continued to shake my head as I looked around. "How can they not make a sound?" I rasped, turning again.

Guilt ripped through me at the thought of what they'd do to Sage. I thought they wanted Evaline because of her relation to her mother, but maybe I was wrong. Maybe Vasier just wanted a Sorceress, and I'd just offered one up to him on a silver platter.

"Fuck!" I screamed.

Grant came up to me, gripped my shoulders, and shook me.

"Calm down, and walk us through what happened," he said in my face. I turned to him. "Where were you when she was taken?"

I shook my head as I spoke, replaying the entire scene for them. Dean didn't contribute, he sprinted around the beach, calling for her. His voice so loud, so spent, that his words were hardly discernible.

I took them back to where she'd been taken, and as I did the rain began. A downpour so vicious I was convinced it was Correntan himself and that he was disgusted that I botched this plan so completely. Dean appeared at my side again, rain streaming down his face.

Nash looked between all of us, from my shaking hands and Dean's furrowed brows, and turned to Grant and Fredrik.

"We need to split up," he turned to Dean and I. "All of us need to search the beach for any sight of where they could've taken her. There has to be footprints left if the rain, or the speed of their sprint didn't hide them by now. But even so we have her scent, we can track them." He grasped mine and Dean's shoulders. "Can you handle that?" he asked, dipping his head to catch our eyes until we nodded our confirmation.

He turned to Grant and Fredrik. "Are we all good? This is the hunt now."

We all nodded and he released us to search. We searched up and down the beach. All of our backs were to each other to search more ground, but we were still able to turn around and see each other if needed. If we couldn't hear the Vasi approach, we couldn't be alone.

I bent down in the sand, convinced I saw a print but rubbed my temples when I saw it was only a hoof print from a horse that must've been here before. I squeezed my eyes shut in annoyance, but they shot open when I heard a grunt as the ground rumbled.

The sand spit out around me as I spun to look for the others. They'd turned, too, at the noise, but I could only see Dean, Grant, and Nash.

"Where's Fredrik?" Nash screamed, eyes wide as he snapped his head around to look for his mate.

Guilt wracked my gut as we all started screaming for him. Surely he got a lead and took off after it. Even if the Vasi did sneak up again, Fredrik would've been able to hold his own and we would've heard him fighting back.

I turned my head to the right, to the string of woods that lined the edge of the beach. I was stepping to run to investigate, and hopefully find Fredrik, when the land shuddered below us, and Nash cursed.

As I turned, Grant shouted from somewhere behind me, and he was gone, too.

I spun, and only found Dean staring with wild eyes at me from across the beach. The sand around us shook violently. It was a horrific time for a quake that didn't seem to be going away as the others had after a few minutes, and we sprinted toward each other.

"What the fuck is happening?" Dean asked.

I shook my head. "How could they sneak up on us, without warning?" I asked.

Dean looked toward the water. "Could they be knocking them out?"

I pursed my lips, it was possible, but it still seemed off that we wouldn't hear any of that. The ground continued to shake as we ran to where each of them had disappeared, and looked at the sand, looked for any prints.

Dean stood beside me as I bent to look at the sand, he was barely out of my line of sight when I felt him jolt forward and grasp for my back. When I turned around, he was gone.

Fuck.

Fuck.

What was happening?

My heart raced in my chest. I hadn't only caused Sage harm, but now my friends, too. I turned around wildly, looking for any of them. I screamed out in frustration, in guilt, and in annoyance because the way that the ground shook was beginning to become worrisome.

But I didn't scream for long, because just as they'd come for Sage and the others, they came for me, too.

I heard someone behind me, out of nowhere, felt a blow to the back of my head, and before darkness had completely enveloped me, arms closed around my chest.

CHAPTER FORTY-ONE

Evaline

Before I took a step, I knew I was in a nightmare. But this wasn't in the forest during my father's death or even the clearing where my mother usually met me.

I took a step off of a gangway from a ship and onto the dock below. The wood planks creaked under my weight and I looked back to see that the boat was the same one that Maddox, Wyott, Saxon and I'd crossed the Mad Strait to Rominia on.

The night was still; there wasn't even a midnight wind blowing down the beach. The stars were bright, the moon was full. A reminder that this was a dream, because in reality the moon wasn't whole right now.

It wasn't until my feet hit the rough dock that I realized I wasn't wearing shoes. I looked down to see that I was wearing exactly what I'd gone to bed in, my silk button-down night shirt and matching shorts that fluttered around me as I walked.

This was unlike any dream I'd ever had before, because I didn't understand the purpose. Usually my dreams existed only to terrorize me with reminders of what I'd survived, or what I'd lost. But here, it was as if I was meant to just enjoy this time on the beach.

For a moment I wondered if my mother was going to appear in this one, but the more I walked the more I realized that I was utterly alone. I could be the only person in the entire world with how quiet it was. Even the waves lapping at the shore didn't make a sound. A chill ran up my spine and I stepped into the sand.

I took a deep breath and tried to ignore my unease. There wasn't any clear objective for this nightmare, and instead of trying to decipher it, I opted to walk down the beach toward the moon. Hopefully, I'd wake soon.

Merwinan loomed in the distance, but I could only see its outline against the moonlight. Shadows moved around me, and I noticed the way they hummed, just like my other dreams.

I walked so far that I couldn't see the docked ship anymore.

Another chill scattered goosebumps across my skin, and I considered trying to wake up. I'd never been any good at that. If I had been, I would've forced myself to wake every time I realized I was in a nightmare. I pinched myself, shook myself, even stepped into the water a few feet until it almost touched the hem of my shorts. I hoped the cold would wake me, but nothing happened.

I sighed and ventured back onto the beach. My legs dried as I continued walking.

"Gods, why am I here?" I huffed to myself.

I stopped when I felt a warm air sweep over me. It was familiar, and smelled like leather and amber; like my mate.

I spun in every direction to look for him.

"Maddox?" I called out and when he didn't answer I shoved it down the bond.

Maddox?

But I couldn't feel him nearby, only that same hum of static I felt in Rominia. Similar to the shadows around me, actually.

Perhaps this wasn't a nightmare at all. Perhaps this was just a product of my longing.

I heard a scuffle and a grunt and swung around again, but I was still alone on the beach. I stepped forward and found that same heat from my mate.

"Maddox," I whispered.

I felt the air shift, like he turned around. I heard him shout in alarm, and then the warmth was gone.

I didn't realize that I'd screamed until I was sitting straight up in my bed, the sound climbing up my throat.

My chest shook as I sucked in a deep breath, and it was all it took for the memories of what I'd just experienced to come hurtling back.

That was nearly as vivid of a nightmare as all the dreams that my mother visited me in, and it didn't do anything to quell the worries I'd had over Maddox and the others out on their trip.

I took a deep breath and tried to calm my raging heart, reaching my hands out and fisting them into the blankets.

"It was just a nightmare," I whispered to myself, but my eyes had already filled with tears. When I shook my head, my hair fell into my face. "Just a nightmare."

I eased back down and curled onto my side, reached out a hand, and laid it over Maddox's spot.

CHAPTER FORTY-TWO

Wyott

I hadn't been able to shake the worry from my gut in the three days since Maddox and the others stepped foot on that ship.

I knew it was silly to be superstitious, but I couldn't help the part deep inside of me that agonized over what might happen to them while they were gone. I knew Maddox had felt bad once he realized why I was concerned, but it was true; we hadn't been outside of this island without the other since the trip my father died, and I didn't care to ever do it again. Before that trip with my father, I'd spent all my time on the island, and the few times I had been on the mainland had been with Maddox.

But even if I knew it was illogical, that didn't shake the anxiety.

Cora left the house for the marina so I headed to the Blacksmith's to pick up the throwing knives for Evaline.

I was in and out of the Blacksmith's within minutes and heading toward the estate. Otto had been just as excited as I was to show me the final product and I couldn't wait until Maddox came home so I could show him, too.

But thinking about his absence only caused worry to wind through my gut, and instead of going to Evaline and Maddox's suite, I found myself walking to Rasa's study.

When I was young and feeling anxious, or when I was deep in grief after losing my father, I'd go to her study while she worked. Rasa believed in maintaining our histories and would often spend her days duplicating old texts that had begun to wither away into nothing.

But when she saw me at her door, she'd drop everything she was doing, gather me into her arms and sit with me on the chaise in front of the fireplace. We'd read together, and sometimes to help me work through my feelings, she'd have me invent characters and tell her their story.

Back then I just thought it was fun, but as I grew I understood her intentions. When I built these worlds in my head, the many adventures of the two young boys who always starred in my stories, I was able to process my emotions through them. If I was anxious, they fought beasts as tall as the sky and as wide as a castle. The beasts would breathe fire and the two had to work together to slay them.

If I was sad, the friends would save innocents from the enemy, hunt for treasure, or discover new worlds together.

Today, when she saw me in her doorway, Rasa smiled and closed the book she was working on before standing and moving to sit on the chaise without objection.

When I sat down beside her and placed the package I carried on the table in front of us, she turned to face me.

"How are you?"

I smiled softly at her, but knew it didn't reach my eyes.

"I'm just worried." I shook my head. "All the time. If it's not Maddox being on the mainland without me, then it's concern that Cora will grow to hate me for not being ready for children, or it's what it's always been, which is Vasier."

Rasa reached out and covered my hand with hers. "That's a lot to carry all by yourself, Wyott."

I cringed. "I know. I try to talk to Cora, but sometimes that doesn't help anymore. She's grown frustrated with my excuses for wanting to wait for children."

Rasa squeezed my hand. "It's not an excuse if it's how you feel, it's a boundary. It's okay to have them, and I know it seems like she's frustrated, but she's not, dear. She's hurting. She wants children, and so it hurts to wait. Especially when she sees other people getting pregnant, or giving birth. It's nothing personal to you, and she isn't angry. She's hurting, and just as she needs to work to understand where you're coming from, you need to understand her, too."

I pursed my lips and looked down at our hands. The tears misting my eyes stung and I wasn't sure if the thought that I'd been causing my mate pain caused me pain, or if it was because the tears themselves stung.

"I guess I've never considered that before," I said, my voice low.

"Instead of working against each other, you two need to work together to decide what it will take to move forward and how long you think it'll be."

I swallowed past the unmoving lump in my throat. "That's just it, Rasa. I can't do it, not while he's still alive." I turned to look at her, having to do it past the tears. "He's come for us before, he could do it again."

"My dear," Rasa cooed, lifting a hand to swipe over my cheek. "Vasier doesn't have any personal vendetta against you, or your family. He didn't kill your mother, one of his men did."

"At his order," I growled.

Rasa shook her head softly. "He ordered them to kill everyone they'd captured. Not just your mother."

I looked down at the rug beneath my boots.

"And your father," she said softly. "He did that because he was cruel, and jealous. Your father replaced him as Kovarrin's brother, and even if he didn't want to admit it, he was hurt by that. But he won't come after your children, or Cora. He won't come after your family at all."

I looked over at her and shook my head. "He's doing it right now."

My knuckles rapped against the wood of Evaline and Maddox's door, and after a minute she swung it open with a confused look on her face.

"Did we have a training session planned?" she asked as she moved back so I could step into the room.

I shook my head and shut the door behind me. "No, I just have a gift for you," I said, and tried to hide the excitement that slipped in through my voice but of course, I was unsuccessful.

She straightened. "Really?" she asked and joined me as I strode across the room to their dining table.

The leather bundle made a thud as I dropped it on the table and turned to her.

"You're a part of our family now, and Cora and I wanted to get you a welcome home present." I shrugged. "She let me pick it out since I'd known you longer, and I think you'll like it," I said, patting the bundle. "I'm sorry it took so long, I only just picked it up from the Blacksmith."

Several emotions passed behind her eyes, and I could tell she was touched by what I'd said. She smiled then and cocked her head.

"You said Blacksmith?" She leaned to look around me at the bundle.

I shrugged. "I knew that was the way to go. Cora wanted to get you matching holsters for your weapons but I knew you'd prefer more weapons to that." I playfully rolled my eyes. "Especially considering how many times you've begged for mine."

She shook her head. "You both really didn't have to get me anything."

"We knew we didn't have to, we wanted to." I waved my hand. "Besides, going to the Blacksmith is, like, my favorite pastime so it isn't as if it was some tedious task. And I think these rival the beauty of Maddox's Rominium dagger."

Her curiosity seemed to pique at that. "These?" she asked. "Plural?"

A wicked grin lit my face as I finally bent to unravel the leather until it lay flat on the table and showed off her gift. There, sitting in a perfect row amidst their black chest bandolier, were six glistening silver throwing knives.

"My Gods," she whispered as she bent to look at them.

"I figured since you're so skilled at throwing them, and have wanted my bandolier for the *entire* time we've known each other," I feigned annoyance. "That you should have your own set."

She didn't speak as she looked down at them, and I looked over her shoulder to see them myself. Earlier when I'd picked them up from the Blacksmith I couldn't believe how well they'd turned out. For a moment, I'd considered keeping them for myself.

They were glistening silver throwing knives, but had dark black etchings all across the handles. I looked down at them now. At the way the black engravings curled around the silver. How in some places they pointed, and in some they swirled.

Otto had perfectly brought my illustrations to life.

She turned her head to look at me. "How did you know roses were my favorite flowers?"

My brows raised and I shook my head. "I didn't know." I shrugged and felt a wry smile on my lips. "But even better. I just got the roses because of that old myth."

She straightened to her full height again and shook her head. "What old myth?"

My eyes widened. "So you know about Kova and Vasi, how to kill them, and compelling, but don't know about the myth of the Silver Rose?"

I heard her braid thump against her back as she shook her head. "My father never told me anything about that." She rubbed her thumb over the butt of one of the blades. "Maybe he didn't know either."

I thought back to Maddox and I's time with Wallace, and what we'd discussed with him after discovering he knew what we were.

"It's possible he never knew." I shrugged. "It makes sense though, it is an old myth. It's just floated around Kova communities for centuries."

"What's the myth?"

I waved a hand. "That essentially there's a third way to kill a Kova and Vasi, and it's the Silver Rose." I thought back to hearing the myth as a child, reciting it hundreds of times. Kova kids usually sang it when jumping rope. Each time you'd finish the verse, you'd spin, or add another rope, or add another kid into the mix. I'd said it so many times as a child, it came to me just as quickly as if I'd recalled it last week:

"From despair borne centuries toil,
Duty called for ways to foil.
A beating heart plucked from a chest,
Rids the world of the pest.
A gnashing head ripped from the shoulders,
Ends the march of death's soldiers.
A silver rose's lethal cleft,
Restores the balance of all that's left."

Her brows were raised by the time I finished. "I didn't take you for a poet, Wyott."

I rolled my eyes with a snort. "I'm not, that's the old myth. Someone found it in a text centuries ago and it's made its rounds since."

She cocked her head. "I've never seen a silver rose."

I shook my head. "They don't exist, or at least I've never seen or heard of one. Most people think it refers to some old sword. Some Kova, even humans, name their weapons. Specifically, their swords. Blood Bringer, Silencer, Sentence Passer," I said, rattling off a few.

She nodded. "So the Silver Rose is a sword."

I shook my head and laughed. "No, it's just a silly myth that some poet created and kids recited when they played. It's a running joke that beings as powerful as the Kova and Vasi could be taken down by a fake flower, or a single sword." I nodded down to the knives, my demeanor softening. "But we got these for you because of the curse." My voice lowered as I spoke. "I know you're afraid of it. That your fate is to kill him. I figured it might make you feel better if you owned your own mini versions of the Silver Rose." I raised my eyes to meet hers, and felt mine turn glassy. "Myth or not."

I watched as her chin quivered before she flung her arms around me.

"Thank you," she whispered in my ear as I wrapped her in a hug. "I don't know what I did to deserve friends—family—like all of you. But I'm so grateful."

I pursed my lips at that, and rubbed a hand down her back to comfort her. "You didn't have to do anything to deserve a family who loves you, you're one of us. You always will be."

"I'm sorry Maddox made you stay here with me."

I sighed and we pulled away from each other. "I'm not angry that I have to stay here with you, or Cora. I'm scared."

She shook her head, her brows furrowed. "You can't be scared, I'm already scared enough for them. I need someone to remind me that everything is going to be okay."

That brought a smile to my lips. "I know. And I am confident everything will be okay, I'm just…" I sighed, realizing that it was time I told her about my father. I reached for one of the chairs at the dining table. "Can we sit?"

Her brows furrowed but she nodded. "Of course."

She sat in a chair right next to her daggers, so I took the one at the head of the table. I wrung my hands in my lap.

"Evaline, the reason I hate Vasier so much, the reason I cringe every time someone says his name—or why everyone looked to me when Kovarrin told us the truth—and why I'm so nervous about Maddox being out there without me, is because Vasier killed both of my parents."

Evaline gave a soft gasp, but continued listening.

"You and I have a lot in common," I started. "I never knew my mother, either," I said, and her spine straightened. "She was killed when I was so young, I didn't know anything about her. At the time, we lived here, but she had gone to see her friends in a small town south of Neomaeros. I was young, only one or two, and she'd gotten a raven that one of her friends wanted to move to Rominia, and had a few human friends that wanted to make the change. Back then, before…"

I struggled to find a way to describe the situation we were in now, with Vasier so actively hunting Evaline down.

"Before Vasier was like this," I said, and her jaw tightened. "Kova traveled all the time, as long as they were west of River Brawn, they were fine. A week or so had gone by after she'd left, and my father hadn't heard from her. He mailed the friend, and no response came. Eventually he was forced to send some scouts to see what had happened, and by the time they got there they saw that the small town had been burned to the ground." I regurgitated the story I'd heard from my father's mouth before, and looked at my hands while I spoke. "Apparently living on River Brawn wasn't far enough. Some Vasi had come through and torn the village up. Since it wasn't technically part of one of the Madierian Kingdoms, it didn't warrant a war from the Kova."

I shook my head and met her gaze, her eyes were full of tears.

"The Vasi didn't know there were any Kova staying there. It had only been my mother's friend and her mate, and of course my mother. There was a fight, a lot of humans saw, and Vasier had ordered the entire village to be wiped out. Including the Kova that the Vasi had found there and beaten down."

A moment of silence passed between us.

"How did they discover it was Vasier who gave the order?" she asked softly.

"We didn't. Not for years. Decades. It made perfect sense that the Vasi would've just killed them all and left it there to burn." I sighed. "But I heard Vasier admit it himself."

Evaline straightened. "What?"

I told her about my father. How I'd watched him die, how Vasier made the comment about telling Kovarrin about his brother, and that I'd run back on my own, scared out of my mind. Her hand reached out to cover mine while I spoke.

"Right before he killed my father, he made sure to tell him that he'd given the order that day." I looked down at the tabletop. "Kovarrin and some of the others don't think that he really gave the order, only that he wanted to hurt my father by making it the last thing he heard before he died."

I looked up at her. "I wanted to tell you all of that so that you understood that we're the same. We're the orphans who found themselves embraced by their mates, by families that would open their arms to them. I wanted you to know that I watched my father die too, and I—" My voice cracked and I had to stop talking to clear my throat. "I wanted to explain why I wanted to go with Maddox and the rest. We haven't been on the mainland apart since then, and a part of me is superstitious about that."

"I understand," she started. "I'm so sorry for all the pain you've had to go through, and I'm so sorry that Vasier coming after me must be bringing all of these memories back."

I waved off her response. "Don't be sorry, it's not your fault that your mother angered the Gods."

She nodded, and a moment of silence passed between us before she spoke softly.

"So what do you believe?"

I looked up and tilted my head in question.

She waved her hand toward the window. "About your mother and the village. Do you think Vasier gave the order?"

My jaw clenched. "I think that I wasn't there, and have no real reason to believe anything at all. Especially because I never knew her." I took a shaky breath. "But I think that Vasier ordered the death of my mother, and I know that he killed my father. I think that either he, or the Gods, must hate me because he won't stop coming after my blood." I swallowed the lump in my throat. "And I fear he never will."

Chapter Forty-Three

Maddox

I came to when I was thrown forward, knees hitting the stone floor beneath me. I was unsteady, my balance off. I had no idea how long it'd taken to get here, or how many times they'd had to knock me out, considering the quick speed with which I healed. But when I opened my eyes, I saw the blood covered stone that stretched all around me.

No, not covered in blood; the color of blood.

The stone looked like granite, but instead of the normal hues of pinks or whites or grays, this was dark red, nearly maroon.

It took me a moment to rid myself of my daze and realize that my wrists were bound behind me. The bones in them ached as I pulled against my restraints, but they did not budge.

No.

I tried again, harder this time, but there was still no give.

Please, Gods. No.

I heard a chuckle in front of me. "I must say, bringing the Kova and Vasi-proof shackles was quite generous of you." The voice was deep and gritty as he laughed. "Sure, we would've found another way to restrain you, but you made it so easy."

A chill shook my frame as I looked up and away from the floor for the first time. The figure wore all black, his attire was some of the finest

I'd ever seen; his boots were so shined I could almost see my reflection; his dress pants gave way to a black silk shirt. My eyes continued to raise until they met his, and my stomach twisted.

"Hello, Nephew." His red eyes sparkled with amusement and the smile that played on his lips was the same as my father's. If I'd only spared a glance I would've thought I knelt before my father. But even though they were twins, there were subtle differences. Namely, Vasier's crimson eyes and the few fine wrinkles between his brows. He was an angry man. "I must say, I'm surprised by the resemblance," he said as he strode forward, placed a finger below my chin and raised it up. "Not as much as your father and I share, but close enough that it's clear we're blood."

I used the opportunity to push off my knees and launch forward, my fangs were out and ready to rip into his throat. But when I jolted toward him, my movement was stopped by a pain spiking up my wrists and I was hauled back. I looked behind me to see two Vasi standing a few paces away, their hands gripping two sets of chains to control me.

I growled and turned around to face Vasier, but he only cocked his head.

"Did you expect we'd be alone?"

He shook his head, and turned around to walk away from me.

I looked up to see a throne, made up of the same stone as the floor, that rose up from the ground, almost as if it was molded out of it. I watched with disgust as Vasier stepped up the few steps to it, turned, and sat.

He waved a hand to the room around us.

"Welcome to my home." He shrugged. "Or my castle, whichever you prefer." He looked to the windows that lined the wall on his right, and my eyes fell there, too. The ocean was a deeper blue color than I was used to, the waves wild and appearing just feet from the protection of the windows. My stomach sank as I realized where I was, that this wasn't just some stronghold he had in Brassillion, or Arlomandrah or Vestaria. This was Mortithev.

Gods, how long had I been asleep?

I looked around frantically, straining my head as best I could behind me to look for my friends, to look for Sage.

When I only saw more Vasi, I whipped back around to face Vasier despite the pain that shot up my knees at the movement.

"Where are they?" I rasped.

Vasier shrugged. "Maybe they're dead. Maybe they're in their cells. Maybe they gave me all the information I asked for, and I sent them on their way safely back to Rominia." He sat forward and placed his elbows on his knees. "Doesn't much matter to you, because nothing will ever matter to you again if you don't cooperate."

I ground my teeth. "The *only* thing that matters to me is getting them home safely, and keeping *her* away from you," I hissed.

His smile widened. "Good," he said, then clapped his hands. "This is marvelous." He waved toward me. "You already know exactly who I want, this saves us time." He sat back and crossed one leg over the other. "Why don't you go ahead and continue making this easier on all of us, and tell me about her magic."

"If you already know she's a Sorceress, then there isn't much more I can tell you." I clipped back.

He shrugged. "You and I both know that's not true, Nephew. So why don't we stop pretending? You tell me why she has more than one element, and I don't have to torture you."

I tried to school my expression into stone. I didn't want to give him any information. My mouth didn't twitch, my eyes remained steady on him, and my breathing was even.

But it was my heart that gave me away.

Vasier cocked his head with a smirk at the way my heartbeat stuttered at his words, at the knowledge that he knew far more about Evaline than I thought he did.

"Tell me, Nephew, what has your father told you of me?"

I jerked against the restraints. "Stop calling me that!" I barked.

His smirk widened. "It's only the truth. You're my nephew," he started, ticking his statements on fingers as if he were counting. "Your father is my twin. And your mate will be kneeling where you are someday."

Without thought, I lit into action. The threat against Evaline forced my body to move as I ripped my arms forward. When there was give, I realized it was because my wrists weren't bound to each other behind my back, but only that they were each bound to a chain in the hands of each Vasi behind me.

I pulled again despite the pain that pulsed in my chest, ripped at them so hard the Vasi stumbled forward. I got to my feet and in the portions of a second that I had to act before they regained their footing, I sprinted at him with everything I had.

By the time they stopped me, I was up the stairs and his smug smile was only an arm's length away from my gnashing fangs. I wanted to rip that smile off his face. I wanted to tear his beating heart out of his chest. I'd do it with my teeth, if I had to. I wanted him to suffer a thousand deaths each time he spoke of her. I wanted to take him to the edge of death, and give him time to heal, only to do it all over again for every thought he'd ever spent considering what he would do to her, how he would get her, and how he could use her.

But all I could do was try to pull against the chains that the Vasi had full control of now, try to catch my breath, and stare into those crimson eyes and plot all of the ways that I would pay this back tenfold.

"Your father has likely told you much about me. About our upbringing, about our creation, and Evaline's mother," he said, and his eyes flashed with something I couldn't pinpoint. "You've been raised your entire life to believe that I'm his lesser twin brother. That I don't have the numbers, or the skill to rule. To create an army. To get to him. He feels safe in his cage, doesn't he?" His smile widened as he shook his head. "My brother is never safe from me, and if he keeps withholding my Sorceress, he'll discover that sooner than later."

"You're wrong," I growled, voice strained by my still active attempt to reach him.

His eyebrows rose. "Oh?"

"We've heard stories about you. About your diminishing control over Brassillion. You're weakening relations with Vestaria. And how each time you've tried to wage war against the Kova, you never bother to show up and lead your forces yourself."

Vasier's jaw tightened, but he only tilted his head toward me. "Well then, as I said."

I wasn't sure if it was my rage at his threat to my mate, or to my family, but the words that left my mouth dripped with venom and vitriol and as hateful of a chuckle as I could muster.

"No. You're wrong about what he's said about the two of you."

His brow furrowed.

"Before a few weeks ago, he'd never told any of us that you were his twin. Not that you were his brother. He'd never mentioned that he ever knew you personally at all."

A flash lit his eyes again, but this time I knew what it was.

Pain.

He nodded to some Vasi behind me, I heard something swing through the air, felt the blow against my head, and the world went black.

CHAPTER FORTY-FOUR

Evaline

"Can we practice throwing knives today?" I asked Wyott as we lumbered down the hill that the mansion rested upon.

He scoffed. "Do you really think I'd buy you throwing knives and not try them out for myself?" he asked, looking down at me with a brow cocked. "Of course we're practicing."

I smiled and couldn't help the bounce in my step. My heart still ached for Maddox, and the worry still wound through me, but Wyott knew exactly what to do to help get my mind off of it.

My hand smoothed over my bandolier, and my smile grew. It was black and stretched from my left shoulder down to my right hip, where I could tie the fastener and secure it to my frame.

I had six tiny versions of the Silver Rose.

The sentiment behind the gift meant a lot to me, and I knew Wyott could tell. But after everything he shared—about the loss of both parents—I knew he understood me in a way most never would. We were orphans, but together—all of us—we were a family.

My smile promptly fell from my face when I saw Lauden standing outside of the training facility, arms crossed, and staring at me.

"We didn't have a lesson today," I said as Wyott and I got closer.

Lauden shrugged. "If you really wanted to understand how to cast Fire, you'd spend every minute of every day trying to figure it out."

Wyott and I stopped in front of him and both crossed our arms over our chests.

"That's not fair, you know I want to learn, but I have other skills I need to hone, too."

Lauden rolled his eyes. "And it's a waste of time. Why would you rather learn a useless skill when you could be getting closer to understanding the greatest power the Gods have blessed this land with?"

Wyott laughed at that, and when Lauden shot him a scowl, his smile dropped.

"Oh, I thought you were kidding."

"Of course I'm not kidding," Lauden snapped. "Evaline will be far more useful if she can wield her magic than if she can throw a punch."

Wyott took a step forward toward Lauden just as my jaw fell at the latter's words.

"Luckily for us, we're more concerned with Evaline's ability to protect herself, not how *useful* she may be to us," Wyott shook his head. "But I can understand the confusion, considering that you treat Sage like she's a tool you have at your disposal rather than the woman you love," Wyott growled out the last part and I saw a flash of fear over Lauden's face.

The Kova inside the training center heard the interaction, and must've heard Wyott's anger, because several of them came out to stand in the wide opening at the side of the building.

After Lauden recovered, he narrowed his eyes as he looked up at Wyott.

"Keep out of mine and Sage's business."

"Gladly," Wyott barked. "When you stop involving yourself in hers."

A few of us, the Kova and me, winced at that. Wyott, Maddox, and I had seen the way Lauden had volunteered Sage for something without consulting her twice. I hadn't realized it angered Wyott so much, but I knew that with all the pent up worry he had over his friends in Merwinan, he had a short fuse, and Lauden was better than most at stoking it.

"You have no right to tell me how to live my life," Lauden said, taking a step toward Wyott.

"And you have no right to tell Evaline how to live hers," Wyott said, closing the distance between them.

"Let's all calm down." I heard Saxon's voice from my side, and turned to see him walk out of the throng of Kova standing there, Oscar prancing near his feet. "Lauden, you go back to your office, Wyott, you come train."

Saxon flicked his worried gaze to mine, and the air was sucked out of my lungs as I saw that his once green eyes were a dark and stony gray. For a moment I wondered when he turned, but was pulled from the thoughts as Lauden spoke again.

"No," he said loudly. "I won't go inside, because I am Evaline's mentor, and I do have a right to tell her how to live her life, because I'm the one who has to prepare her magic. If it isn't ready, it's my ass on the line, not yours," he hissed at Wyott.

I flew into action then, running forward the few steps that separated us and wedging myself between them. I placed one hand on Wyott's chest and one on Lauden's.

"Back off," I said as I pushed. Lauden stumbled back a few steps from the force, and Wyott politely took one back. I descended on Lauden.

"You have no right to tell me how to live my life," I said, walking toward him. He backed away from me until he was in the sand of the beach behind him. "You may be Arch Sorcerer, and Kovarrin may trust you, but I don't. I don't trust any fucking man who thinks he can tell a woman what to do." A few more steps into the beach. "And you've done it to Sage enough. You won't be starting with me."

"Oh?" he asked. "What will you do to stop me?" His fists at his side tightened, and so did mine.

I laughed. "Pick your fucking poison, Lauden. I've killed men with daggers *and* my magic." I cocked my head. "Which form would you like to fight today?"

Fuck him, and fuck the way he treated Sage. He'd been left unchecked on this island for far too long, and I was rooting my feet deeper into the sand to stop myself from marching back up to the mansion to demand that Kovarrin fire him. Sage could stay, she could live in the mansion. He, on the other hand, would not.

He shook his head, a smile bright on his face. "You think I'm afraid of anything you're capable of, Evaline?" He tilted his chin up. "I'm the only Fire Caster on this island, and I can do far more damage than you could."

I heard a few murmurs behind us, and saw Wyott out of my peripheral, knew he was moving into striking distance to protect me.

But I didn't need protection. I was Evaline fucking Manor and I'd survived far worse than an egotistical prick like Lauden.

"Whether you think I can use Fire or not, you've seen what I can do with the rest of the elements." My smile grew. "But you haven't seen what I can do with a knife." My hand flicked up to my chest, resting on one of the handles of my new throwing knives. "Care to find out?" I asked.

"Yes," Lauden said quickly. "But only one thing."

In a second he was manifesting a ball of fire in his hand and throwing it at me. I felt the air move as Wyott sprinted and stood in front of me, but my own instincts kicked in. I felt my magic writhe inside my blood, felt it swarm to the surface.

It was the gasps of the Kova behind us that forced me to realize that my eyes were clenched shut behind Wyott. When I opened them, the entire world was in flames. Wyott turned around to look at me, his eyes wide.

No, the entire world wasn't in flames, I realized as I looked around. Just a thin veil of fire that created a protective shield around Wyott and I. Lauden's ball of fire must've died once it hit mine.

I gasped and the shield dropped. The air around us felt cool as it infiltrated into the space that had just been occupied by flames and Wyott moved out from in front of me as we both turned to Lauden.

He had a smug smirk on his face, and I'd never wanted to slap the shit out of someone so much in my entire life.

"Sometimes, the only way to use Fire for the first time is through anger."

My jaw clenched as I stepped toward him. "You did all of that just so I'd use Fire for the first time?"

He shrugged. "Better than wasting time watching you fail at another lesson."

Wyott stepped up beside me. "So you embarrassed her in front of all these people, with no warning?"

Lauden met his eyes with a cocky glint in his. "I'll do whatever I need to do to ensure that she is fully powered, so that when the First needs to call upon her, she is ready." He lowered his eyes to me. "This time, anger didn't completely cut it. So I had to make you protect yourself. You could've used Water, it would've extinguished the flame. But you were angry, so you chose fire." He pulled something out of his back pocket. "You can take this, it came today," he said, handing me a raven's scroll before he moved a few steps toward his loft.

"You can go enjoy training."

He waved his hand toward the Kova who stood outside the training center before marching to the door of his loft. As he grabbed the handle, he looked at me one last time. "And you can thank me later."

I scoffed but he only went inside and closed the door. I swallowed my anger and looked down. There was a perfect circle in the sand around Wyott and I, and I could see how the sunlight shimmered over it.

It wasn't burned, or bare. It was glass.

When Lauden was gone, and all the Kova had gone back inside, Wyott turned to me.

"What does it say?" he asked, his voice hurried.

I fumbled my way through the scroll and immediately saw that it wasn't from Merwinan, but Neomaeros. My heart thundered as I read the letter from Lady Margot aloud for Wyott to hear.

"Evaline,

We received the letter from Kovarrin regarding our sending a summons to Kembertus for your friends. I wanted to let you know that after you left and your concern for them was clear, I sent them a raven that I thought it best for the next courting season, if they came to Neomaeros sooner, and gave themselves more time to prepare the boutique. As I write to you now, I'm happy to report that Aurora and Jacqueline are safe within Neomaeros' wards in their new home. They arrived today, and I've met them. They're both lovely. I will do everything I can to keep them safe. I know that you said they don't remember you, and thus can't write to you. I will do my best to always keep you updated on how they're doing.

May the Gods be kind,

Lady Margot"

Tears streamed down my face by the end of the letter and I pulled it against my heart, looking up at the sky above me.

"Thank the Gods," I gasped and Wyott placed a reassuring hand on my arm.

"That is great to hear, Evaline." I smiled up at him and he slung an arm around my shoulder and directed me to the training center. "Today you got to tell off a prick." He brought his hand up briefly to block his mouth toward me as if he was telling me a secret. "And scare him, frankly." I laughed as he continued counting. "Used Fire for the first time," he said, ticking the items off on his fingers, "And now you know your friends are safe."

We stopped outside of the training center and he pulled away. "That's a pretty fucking good day."

Chapter Forty-Five

Maddox

I woke up in a dark cell.

Everywhere I looked, I saw red.

The floors, the door, the walls, the ceiling. All of them were made of that same crimson granite I'd seen in the throne room. There were no lanterns or fireplaces to light the cell, but I did notice a small barred window in the upper corner of one of the walls that let in a bit of fading daylight.

It was a moment before I realized, again, that I was chained. My face was near the floor, and my wrists were bound behind me, together, I guessed, by my lack of range of motion. My ankles were shackled together, too.

My breath came fast as I took stock of everything that had happened, and all of my injuries.

My friends and Sage were gone, I had no idea where they were or if they were safe. Vasier held me captive and wanted to get more information out of me about Evaline's magic. It still wasn't clear why he wanted her.

I had no idea how much time had passed since I'd last seen her. I had no idea what she was doing, or if she was safe. I didn't even know if she knew I was missing yet.

I groaned and heaved myself over to lie on my back, ignoring the pain in my hands as they bent at an awkward angle behind me, and I stared up at the ceiling with tears in my eyes.

A painful ache lurched in my chest at the thought of her worrying about me; at the mate that Grant left behind wondering where he was; at Fredrik and Nash captured together, but likely kept apart; at Dean's family worrying for him.

I ached for my parents, who'd find out I was gone. And I hurt at the thought of Wyott and what he would think, once he found out. Vasier had taken so much from him, and I'd disregarded his concerns about our separation when I left. But here I was, exactly where he feared I'd be.

I supposed it was better than being dead. At least for now.

Mentally, I scanned down my body, searching for any injuries. My head didn't ache anymore, so I assumed enough time had passed that I would've healed from that. Perhaps a few hours. My wrists and ankles were irritated from the chafe of the shackles, but it was nothing I couldn't handle. Everything else seemed to be okay.

I sighed and tilted my head back against the ground, and listened.

My ears strained for anything—the sound of a heartbeat or a whimper or the smell of blood or charred skin. I'd heard of the ways Vasier liked to torture, and they were slow.

My chest started to heave with anxious breaths as I felt my worry begin to take over. Before it could, I forced a deep breath down my throat, just as I'd instructed Evaline to do each time she had a panic attack.

I focused on the logic of it all. Vasier may be fucked, but he wasn't stupid. He couldn't be stupid if he'd survived this long with loyal Vasi beneath him. Perhaps he didn't inspire love like my father did, perhaps only fear, but regardless, he was smart. And if he was smart, then he wouldn't kill me. If he killed the son of the First, he'd start a war. And considering he'd been making attempts to steal Evaline for a reason, he likely *needed* her for that war. So if he didn't have her yet, then he wasn't ready. So he wouldn't kill me.

It didn't mean my friends were safe. That Sage was safe. I squeezed my eyes shut to dispel the tears that had begun forming there.

Gods, I prayed. *Please keep them safe. Please get them home safe.*

The guilt tore at my chest, at my gut, and I couldn't believe I'd ever been so stupid. So *naive.* I'd spent so much of my life not *needing* to fight Vasi, or outright beating them, that I never considered failure might be an option. I'd hunted Vasi before, sure, but they usually weren't operating in a coordinated attack. Only in groups of ones or twos.

I shook my head as my mind unraveled again and I considered what the Vasi had done to capture us. I'd never seen Vasi move so soundlessly, so quickly. It seemed impossible that they could do so, and for a moment I wondered if this was all a dream, if perhaps I was still in that bed in that Merwinan inn.

But I knew it wasn't, and I didn't have any more time to ponder, because there were footsteps down the hall.

I wriggled until I sat up straight, squared my shoulders, and lifted my chin.

The door opened, letting in a bit of light from the lanterns in the hallway, and Vasier swept through it with two Vasi flanking him. He gave me a smile and crossed his arms.

"I don't suppose you're ready to tell me more about your mate's magic?" he asked.

My blank stare was enough of an answer for him.

His smile widened. "To be honest, Nephew, that's what I was hoping you'd say." He nodded to the two Vasi, and they came forward to grab my upper arms. "This will be far more fun," he said as he watched them drag me out of my cell.

We didn't travel far, and I tried to fight them as best I could, but there wasn't much to be done even if I did fall from their arms. We ended in a different cell. One that was much bigger and lit with several lanterns lining the walls that cast shadows around the crimson room.

I didn't need to see the drain on the floor to know what their intention was. Didn't need to smell the hundreds, maybe thousands, of different types of blood that had flowed down it and dried in the pipe to know what they planned.

"Last chance," Vasier said, dragging a wooden chair from the wall of the room and bringing it to sit right in front of me.

"Go fuck yourself," I hissed at him.

He cocked his head and crossed his legs, and waved to the Vasi to my left, closest to the drain.

The Vasi with brown hair pulled a dagger from his hip and flipped it in his hand before lowering it over my thigh. The slice of the blade hurt, but not enough to surrender a show of it to Vasier, and I watched as my blood dribbled out of the wound.

He didn't cut along any major arteries or veins, only horizontally across my thigh. He knew it'd heal quickly, so if their goal was to drain me in order to torture me, I wasn't sure why he'd opted for such a slow bleed.

But he didn't stop moving. He cut open my shirt, left a deep gash across my chest. He went to my shoulder and cut one there, too. And on and on until he'd littered my chest, shoulders, abdomen, and thighs with small, inconsequential cuts. They all spilled tiny amounts of blood, before they healed in front of our eyes only a minute later. And then he did it again.

And again.

And again.

And again.

And again.

In the same spots, over the same slices, until I knew I'd have scars. Until the pinch of the pierce was enough to drive me mad.

After what felt like hours, but based on how much oil had been burned in the lanterns around us had probably only been one, Vasier spoke.

"Stop."

He'd said it only when all the cuts had healed, and the Vasi had gone in for what felt like the thousandth round.

"Why does she have more than one element?" he asked, leaning forward in his chair.

I only stared at him blankly, focusing on the peace my skin felt at this moment of reprieve.

"There's never been a Sorcerer in existence that had more than one," he said, eyeing me.

I let my eyes glaze over as he stared. Thought of anything else in the world that I could to occupy my mind away from what he was saying. Hoped it would help my body not to react as it had last time.

"Did her mother grant her more power? Did she create her as she created us?"

A thought struck at his words. At the way he'd referred to Evaline's mother each time he spoke of her. A small smile lifted at the edges of my lips and he was quick to notice it, leaning forward in his chair.

"What? She did?" he asked, his eyes blazing.

That was his tell. Mine might have been my heart, but his was this desperation he had for more information about Evaline's mother.

"Alannah," I said, my voice hoarse.

He flinched at the word, but tried to hide it. He didn't pretend he didn't hear, didn't question what I said. Because he knew.

"You won't say her name. But you know what it is." I cocked my head. "Seems odd that you knew her all your human life, and when you refer to her you do so only by her relation to a woman you've never met."

Vasier sat back in his chair and gave a bored sigh. His desperation to make it sound real was almost amusing enough to distract me from the pain I knew I was about to face as Vasier waved to the Vasi behind me.

And so the Vasi started again. I expected this round to be longer. More rounds of cutting and bleeding and healing. But Vasier stopped him far before I thought he would.

He tilted his head. "I can't tell if you have an unreasonably high pain tolerance," he said. "Or if you just love her that much." He shook his head. "I couldn't imagine loving someone that much." But his voice hitched in a way that told me he was lying. He turned back to face me. "What elements does she have?" he asked again, and I only stared.

This time, instead of looking at his eyes, I opted for the small flame that flickered back and forth in an oil lamp. I concentrated on the way it danced and thought about all the times I'd seen similar firelight radiate off of Evaline's form. The way her figure cast shadows against the wall the night I told her she was my mate.

And even though he was still talking, still asking the questions, I was thinking about that fire, and how she should be able to wield it. I wondered if right now, at this very moment, she was back in Rominia mastering it for the first time.

But I stopped because the thoughts led me to wonder what Lauden was doing. If he realized that Sage was missing yet. If he would take out his hatred for me for putting her in harm's way, on Evaline.

Just then Vasier said something that caught my interest and while I didn't flick my eyes back to him, didn't want to be too obvious that I was interested, I did begin to listen again.

"Her mother had Air," he said. "So it makes sense that she would have one element, but not more than that." He leaned back in his chair and crossed his legs together, hands clasping and resting on his knee. "I'm sure you're dying to know how I knew that Evaline had more than one element." He started.

I was. But I didn't want to give him any way of knowing that.

"You and your father and the rest of the Kova probably sat in your war room laughing at what little information I had. Joking about how there's no way I could know as much as I do, because you've killed all the Vasi I've sent after you. And the humans, too." I saw his head cock out of the corner of my eye. "But that brother of mine did always have a way of underestimating me. Did you all really think I wouldn't send more? Did you think that I wouldn't send back up? I've been alive nearly a millennia," he said with a dry laugh. "And yet you think I won't have any insurance? You might not have seen them, might not have noticed them, but I've sent others. They've seen her magic. They've seen her kill. Just because you didn't see them lurking in the shadows, doesn't mean they weren't there.

"Sure, it hurt losing them. I didn't anticipate they would die, but they understood the sacrifice they were making before they ever left. They knew they were only soldiers in this way, and they would do anything for their father," he said. "The Kova see Kovarrin as their First. Their leader, but do they see him as their father?"

After he finished his rant, he sat back in his chair. He nodded to the Vasi.

"Continue."

And so it went. For hours. Until the consistent draining of blood, even if it was only a spoonful at a time, took a toll. Until it wasn't a minute before the cuts healed, but ten. Until it was clear that I was weakening. Until it was obvious that he would bleed me out before I ever saw Evaline again.

I awoke in my cell. The red walls, floor, ceiling, took up all of my vision. Surrounding me until I didn't know if I was bleeding or not, didn't know if any of my wounds had healed. I was too underfed, too weak to even lift my head.

I'd heard of Vasier's torture before from the few Kova who survived to come back and speak of it. They usually only survived because Vasier found it amusing. His entertainment was manipulating their minds. Not with compulsion, but with fear. He'd send them off, but they'd never know if he'd come after them again.

Those men said that they'd feed them before they died from their draining. They'd use one of the several human slaves that he kept on the island, and let the Kova feed—not enough to thrive, just enough to bring them away from the brink of death. Then they'd continue the torture.

I knew that wouldn't work for me, but there was truly no way that he could know that. No one had seen me feed from Evaline, no one had seen me attempt to feed from humans when it failed. Only my close family and friends knew about it.

I knew he'd try to feed me soon, and soon I'd be close enough to death to warrant it. And I knew that in this weak state, it would be hard to resist the pain that the molten blood would cause. It would be hard not to show it on my face.

I didn't know which was my better option. To refuse to feed, and raise more questions. Or to feed, and give him more reason to want her. It would only further his belief that her magic was special and give life to a new belief; that her blood was.

I didn't even remember falling asleep, but I was waking again.

I wasn't completely sure how much time had passed since I'd entered Mortithev, but when I woke up, my cell was still dark. And that could've been because it was only a few hours later and the night still lingered, or because three nights had passed. I had no way of knowing.

I thought I'd been malnourished just before I fed from Evaline in Neomaeros, but this was unlike anything I'd ever experienced. This felt as if my stomach was eating its way out of my body, begging and searching for an ounce of nutrition. I hadn't even had any water or human food to curb the hunger. It wasn't only my stomach that burned with a searing heat, but also every mark where the Vasi had cut me a million times over. Even lying here now, I could feel a thousand phantom cuts.

I knew they'd scar, which was a difficult feat for Kova. We had to be severely malnourished or get cut over and over in the same spot. There'd been hunts decades ago when I'd gone hungry and been sliced over the lip and the eyebrow, but those were so faint you could hardly see them.

I didn't mind the scars, never had, and I wouldn't mind these. But I had a feeling I wouldn't have the opportunity to mind them anyway. I knew I would die here. I accepted that even if Vasier didn't intend to kill me, if he planned to feed me to bring me back some health, he would still kill me.

And even though it would be an accident since he didn't know about my feeding issue, my father would start a war. I feared how many would die for me and the toll it would take on the ones I loved, and the burden Evaline would have to carry for the rest of her life. She'd already lost her mother and father and left behind all the friends she knew. And now, she'd lose me too.

Before I fell back asleep, I thought that perhaps I should've left her alone when I saw her for the first time. Maybe she would've been better off.

CHAPTER FORTY-SIX

Evaline

"Stop fucking cheating!" Wyott yelled from across the training center patio.

We were stationed outside behind the facility.

Wyott had swung the great back door open to mimic the front, and it was suspended in the air on its metal tracks. Considering how excited I'd been to practice with my new daggers, Wyott invented a game for all of us to play. Cora had arrived shortly after the ordeal with Lauden and after all his bullshit, we decided that instead of strictly training, we wanted to have some fun, so we called Saxon over and Wyott explained his idea.

There were several targets setup in the outdoor area. Some were for archery, others for throwing knives. There was weighted equipment to throw around, like balls filled with sand for the young Kova and anvils for the older.

This game involved two targets, stood to face each other but several yards apart, and two teams. Cora and I were on a team, and Saxon and Wyott were on the other.

The game was really just target practice but Wyott assigned points to each ring around the target. The closer to the center, the higher the points.

Two of us stood behind each target and threw to the opposite. But Wyott announced that the rules required one person from each team to stand on either side, so that we had to stand beside our opponent. Wyott and Cora stood behind the target opposite from Saxon and I, and Oscar slept near Saxon's feet.

We'd all questioned why two teammates wouldn't stand beside each other to strategize, but Wyott justified that it was more competitive to throw against your opponent, since we'd each take turns throwing at the target.

But it was far more likely that he made the rule just so he could stand beside Cora.

"I'm not cheating," I called back to him.

He pointed at me. "Yes, you are, Sorceress. Don't lie!"

Cora and Saxon laughed, but I only shook my head and tried to hide my smile.

"I have absolutely no idea what you're talking about."

Every time Wyott's dagger came close to my target, I'd flick a little bit of wind at the tip of his blade so it would land higher than he expected, on an outer ring.

Wyott and Cora finished their round, and Saxon and I pulled the daggers off the board to start our turn. It was the first time I'd gotten to use my new throwing knives, and I couldn't have been happier with them. The weight in my hand, the way they sliced through the air, the beauty of the roses on the handle, was perfect.

Saxon and I both ended our round rather evenly, and Cora and Wyott removed the daggers to start throwing.

I turned to Saxon. "Please forgive me, because I don't know the etiquette when someone changes," I started, and he gave me a knowing smile. "But when did you change?"

Saxon waved a hand and chuckled. "There's no etiquette, not that I've heard of anyway, but I am new to this. I changed a couple nights after the wreck."

"I'm sorry," I said softly. "For all of it. It's my fault that your crew was killed, that you were put in danger."

Saxon let out a long breath. "Vasier gave those commands, and Vasier is the one who needs to die for it," he said in a low voice. "Whatever reason he wants you, that's on him. You shouldn't feel guilt for my men's death. Only he should."

I nodded. We were quiet for a few moments, while Cora and Wyott finished their turn. We summed up the scores and grabbed the daggers.

"What made you decide to make the change?" I asked as I pulled one of my knives out.

He pursed his lips. "I'd been considering it for years. So many of the friends that I'd met throughout the years on the ships were Kova and after a while I started seeing more reasons to turn, rather than reasons not to. It felt right."

"If I'm being honest…" I flipped my eyes up to his to find him listening intently. "It's been on my mind—with a Kova mate, and all."

"You need to make whatever decision feels right for you."

I took a deep breath and threw one of my knives. "What were the reasons you found not to turn?"

He threw a knife, closer to the center than mine.

"There was really only one that caused me the most pause."

My dagger drove in, right next to the one I'd last thrown. "What was it, if you don't mind me asking?"

"Someday," he said, rearing his arm back. "Every mortal you love will be gone."

He threw his dagger, again closer to the center than mine.

When I raised my knife again, my heart pounded against my chest.

It wasn't because of what Saxon had said, that every mortal I knew would be gone someday, because the truth was that every mortal I'd ever loved was gone; gone from me.

My parents were gone forever, and my friends—Aurora, Jacqueline, Priscilla, and Megin—didn't remember me. Even if Maddox replaced their memories, Aurora and Jacqueline would never be safe, not until Vasier was dead.

Every mortal I loved was already gone from my life, and it wasn't the reason my heart raced harshly in my chest.

I loved Maddox, and I wanted to be with him until the end of my days. I wanted to feel safe and strong as a Kova, I wanted to never fear what someone may do to me again.

My only reason for pause was the status of my magic.

If I changed, I didn't know what would happen to it. I didn't know if it would prevent me from stopping Vasier, and what that would mean for the Gods and my curse.

If I didn't fulfill it, who knew what the Gods would do to those I loved, to me, or to whomever they shoved the curse off onto.

And unfortunately, that was a factor in my decision to change.

Because so far, I hadn't been able to think about life after Vasier. The thought of killing him and having the ability to do it seemed so far out of the realm of possibilities that I could only focus on the world of right now.

The one where he existed, where he lived, where it was my job to put a stop to that.

Chapter Forty-Seven

Maddox

I was vaguely aware that my body was being moved without any active effort on my end. I was jostled about by the shoulders, where two people, likely Vasi, carried me by my upper arms down the halls. My feet weren't shackled anymore, and they dragged out behind me. My heart raced the closer we got to the torture cell, and I think they slowed their pace once we were close just to fuck with me. But they didn't stop there, instead they turned down another hallway. Then another, and another. I tried to pay attention to the layout of the castle so if I ever had the energy to escape, I could.

But it was no use. I could barely keep my eyes open.

Before I knew it, they were dropping me to my knees just as they had when I arrived in Mortithev. And when I looked up between slitted eyes, I saw that I was again in the throne room.

Vasier smiled down at me from his throne with amusement sparkling in his eyes.

"Nephew. I'm so glad you were able to join us," he said.

The words had my eyes straining to open as wide as they could. I sat back on my heels and tried to control the way my head lolled back with the movement. When I finally summoned the strength, I tilted my face.

A wave of relief swept through me as I saw them. On my right, sitting in the space between Vasier and I, sat Fredrik, Nash, and Grant. They were in a similar position as I, and the two mates had huddled close together. They all looked weak, and I could tell they might've been tortured, but it didn't seem that they looked half as rough as I felt.

And that made me happy.

They were already staring back at me, and when my eyes drifted up to meet theirs, I could tell by the way their faces crumpled that they didn't like what they saw.

I looked worse than I thought, I guess.

Their mouths were gagged with some cloth wrapped around their face, so they couldn't talk. They tried, but it was muffled, and I couldn't understand.

My head flopped to the left and I saw Dean and Sage. He looked just as disheveled as the other Kova, but the worry in his eyes wasn't just for me, because they flicked between Sage and me.

They must've all arrived moments before I did because it looked as if he was checking over her injuries. I was happy to see they were all alive. I hoped that meant Vasier would let them go.

Sage looked the best out of all of us. Her hair was disheveled, and the white wig was nowhere in sight. She had some soot on her face but I didn't smell any blood on her, and I thanked the Gods for it.

I turned to Vasier. I opened my mouth to try and speak but words did not come out. Not because I was gagged, but because my throat was so parched that I had to stop and force my mouth to wet in order to speak. After a moment I threw my head back with my swallow and tried to begin again.

"Let them go," I croaked. "Let them go and keep me instead." All four Kova heads snapped to me, and I felt Sage's evaluating stare.

Vasier smiled and stood, hands flexing into a brief fist. "You don't mean that," he said as he waved his arms out wide to both parties. "You don't truly mean that. You wouldn't die for these people."

He descended the stairs and threw his head back with a groan as he did.

"I wish the Gods-damned Kova would get off their high horses and admit that every time they say they'll sacrifice for one another, the words are hollow. These vows, these oaths, are empty." He cleared the last step and continued walking toward me. "You say you have these mates that are tied to your soul..."

He waved a dismissive hand.

"It's all bullshit. You're no different than the Vasi. Maybe you don't kill to feed, but you're not half as holy as you say you are," he snarled his last few words.

He stopped halfway between the throne and I so that the other Kova and Sage were on either side of him. All six of them stared at me and I shook my head.

"You're wrong. The Kova aren't like you. Rominiava gifted only the Kova mates because she knew the Vasi would never deserve to know that love. It's greater than any you'll ever get to experience."

I raised my head so that I could lift my chin to look at him. I puffed out my chest and tried to appear as convincing as I aimed to be. To look like the leader I should've been before I put their lives in danger.

"I *would* die for them. These words aren't hollow and the vow isn't empty. When I say something, I mean it."

Vasier smirked, looked to his right, and stepped toward Sage. He grabbed the back of her hair with his right hand and pulled her to his chest. He grabbed her jaw with his other hand and turned her to face me. Dean shouted through his gag, but my eyes were on her. Anger and guilt warred inside me as I watched her look at Vasier with wide eyes, watched as they blinked rapidly and saw her jaw go slack against the gag.

"You would die for her?" Vasier asked, turning her head back to face me when she tried to meet his eyes.

"Yes," I said without hesitation. "Of course I would."

I met Sage's eyes as I said the words. I wanted her to know the truth in them, that she was important to me, to all of us. That she was a Rominian and I wouldn't rest until she got back home safely. Maybe Lauden didn't treat her how a partner should, but Gods-dammit, I'd treat her the way a friend would. She couldn't speak back to me, but her brows raised.

Vasier cackled. "Why?" he asked incredulously. "She's not your mate, and from what I've gathered, she hasn't even known you that long." Vasier shook his head. "She's nothing."

My stomach dropped as I realized that he had been torturing her to get her to talk. I wasn't angry with her, couldn't be. I was the one who put her in danger, she had every right to protect herself.

My lips parted, as I was about to pledge my life for hers again, but we all stopped when we heard her soft sob. She looked up at him, met his eyes with a crumpled face, and her tears came in faster bursts, soaking into the cloth tied around her jaw, as Vasier gave her a bemused look.

"I would die for her," I said after I'd gathered myself.

She took a ragged breath as the sobs continued and turned to face me again.

Vasier rolled his eyes and laughed. "No, you wouldn't. You will do anything you can to get back home to your mate, or your home, or your family. Whichever of them you hold in higher regard."

Out of my peripheral, I saw the way Dean's chest heaved. His spine was pin straight, each muscle in his body was coiled, and he stared at Vasier who still gripped Sage by the jaw.

That look in Dean's eye… I knew it well. I'd had it a few times myself.

An ache of guilt banged through my chest and a loud breath expelled from my lips as I realized that my friend had found his mate, and I had put her in danger.

"Let them go," I rushed out, turning back to Vasier. "Let them all go back to Rominia, unharmed, and keep me."

His smile widened as he threw Sage onto the ground, back near Dean. Her unshackled feet tried to keep up, but she couldn't gain her balance. She began to topple face forward, and we all watched in horror as she was about to slam her face onto the hard stone.

But Dean launched himself toward her. His hands were still bound behind his back, and his ankles chained close beneath him, but he raised onto his knees and folded forward so she landed against his back, instead of cracking her head on the ground.

Sage let out a gasp of surprise. He waited until she gathered some of her balance and slid off him. When he straightened and turned to make sure she was okay, the agony in his eyes was as vivid as I'm sure mine was on the night Evaline was nearly killed by Gabriehl's men.

But Sage wasn't looking back at Dean, or toward me. She had her pained stare leveled at Vasier, and the tears on her face were beginning to dry.

Vasier continued as if the whole ordeal hadn't just occurred.

"And what kind of uncle would I be if I didn't let *you* go home?" He shrugged. "Of course, with the way my brother has treated me these last centuries, he deserves it and more. But you need to know that I am merciful. I'm not half as awful as your father says, nor am I half as naive. Besides, it's clear that none of you were going to talk," he said.

"And while there are many, many, more ways I could find to pull information from you." He shrugged and waved around the room. "It's not worth my time. Or my people's. They're wasting their time here stuck with you. They're much more beneficial to me if I send them out on their tasks." He took another step toward me. "Because they will get Evaline," he said.

I launched myself toward him, but the Vasi behind me only tightened their grip on the chains.

I knew they didn't have to pull hard. I was too weak.

I could feel the stares that slid to me at the move, and I looked around at my friends. I saw the worry in their eyes but looked back to Vasier as he spoke.

"But first you'll have to feed," he said. "I can't send my nephew back to my brother in this sorry state." A bright smile lit his face then and he turned toward a Vasi somewhere behind me. "Bring in the guest of honor."

I couldn't see who was dragged in, I could only hear a garbled voice and the scuffling of steps as they dragged someone toward Vasier. They were human, whoever they were, and for some reason their scent was familiar but I couldn't pinpoint it.

Vasier's smile grew wide, and he clapped his hands. "Now, since this is your first time in my home, Nephew, I wanted to get you a proper welcome present to show you that I'm not as bad as your father must claim I am. And I would love to have a relationship with you, whether it's today, a year from now, or a hundred."

The scuffle behind us grew closer and I tried to crane my neck to see who it was.

"I will admit that at one point, he was useful to me," Vasier said, looking to whoever the prisoner was. "I couldn't very well sneak into Kembertus to get Evaline myself, and neither could any of my Vasi," he said as he tossed his head in annoyance. "The Gods did do us a disservice in that regard. Red eyes had the effect they were going for." He replaced his look of annoyance with a smile. "Not the best for being discreet, but we've managed."

My spine straightened at his mention of Kembertus and I was reminded again of the fear I'd had after I found out that she was sought after. How easily she could've been taken before I ever had a chance to meet her, to save her.

Vasier laughed and shook his head. "You should've seen how scared Bassel was when I summoned him to Mortithev. He stood right where you kneel," he said, pointing to me. "When I charged him with going to Kembertus to marry Evaline and bring her back to me. Of course, her guardian's willingness to turn her over worked out in my favor. I did not foresee her murdering him, though." He threw his hands in the air in defeat.

"But what can you do? I guess it's a lesson in research. I should've done mine better beforehand. I had no idea they'd known each other prior. Still didn't, until I got to talking to *him*."

Vasier cocked his head and looked past me. The Vasi handed the man off to Vasier, who turned him around to face me. The human's eyes widened when he saw me.

Gabriehl shook out of fear, and I shook out of anger. He was lucky we'd even let him go last time, and that was only to tie up loose ends. His compulsion should have taken him back to Kembertus to tell his family that Evaline had died in his attempt to bring her back for their bounty. The only reason he survived was because he was useful.

Vasier smiled before he clapped a hand on Gabriehl's shoulder. "I do love reunions," he said. "Especially when there's revenge to be had. Do you like your present, Nephew?" he asked, but I didn't even have a chance to speak before he continued. "I thought my plan was immaculate. I instructed Bassel to marry her and get her to me. He was in charge of the rest. It wasn't my fault he picked the wrong team to do the job." He turned to Gabriehl. "Though I must say, it was impressive you found her on your own even without Bassel handing her off. How did you manage that?" He reached forward and pulled the gag out of Gabriehl's mouth.

Gabriehl stuttered, "I didn't—I don't—I'm—"

Vasier shook his head. "Don't lie now, the damage is done. You already abducted her. If the plan was that Bassel would hand her off, and he died before he could, how did you find her?"

Gabriehl opened his mouth, apprehension falling over his face as I was sure he was considering whether he should lie again, but when he spoke, I knew it was the truth.

"As soon as we'd been informed of the wedding date, we planned to get there a few days ahead of time to be sure that we weren't late. We camped just outside of the castle's walls so that we would go unnoticed, and when I heard the alarm bells going off early the next morning, I knew something was wrong.

"I went into Kembertus and sought out my parents, pretended I was just late to attend the wedding. The kingdom needed to be secured, so their forces were more concerned with protecting my parents and searching for her inside the city, in case she was hiding away. When they sent me and my team out to hunt for her, the guards had already swept the streets and were moving on to mandatory house checks for everyone in Kembertus." He looked down. "We knew she'd be heading west, so we started on the trail. We rode hard and stopped for dinner in that town where we found her, and one of my men spotted her in that tavern." He shrugged. "Her white hair was hard to miss."

Rage ripped through me as I realized that we should've dyed her hair back then or hidden it with a cloak. We'd been convinced that we had traveled far enough away that they wouldn't have been able to find us, and that no one would recognize her as a fugitive yet.

Vasier nodded and turned to Gabriehl. His words were to the human, but his eyes cut me. "So, you stalked her, captured her to bring her here, without knowing what I would do with her. Without knowing whether I would kill her or hurt her."

Gabriehl shook his head, his eyes pleading with me. "I didn't even know non-human beings existed. Bassel only told me I was meeting a few men, and when and where."

Vasier stepped forward and pulled Gabriehl along with him. "You may think I'm the evil one, Nephew," he said. "But I only made the plans. I only gave the order. I didn't pull her from the woods. I didn't gag her mouth. Men chose to do that for me." Vasier murmured. "And it didn't take much convincing."

He stopped walking when they stood right in front of me. My breathing was so ragged with rage that my chest felt as if it would give out from the pressure.

Vasier pushed Gabriehl's shoulder down until he was kneeling in front of me, and I was eye to eye with a man who tried to kill my mate.

"I thought he would be the perfect person to let you feed from before you left. I hope you'll remember this gift when you go back to Rominia and are reminded of how much you all hate me, Son."

Gabriehl's eyes were afraid, and my heart ravaged in my chest ripe with rage. I hated him, and Vasier made sure to remind me just how much.

And I was so weak, so *hungry*.

So, when Vasier stepped away with a smirk on his face, I didn't even need that deep voice in my head to instruct me to do it.

I lunged forward.

And this time the Vasi holding my chains didn't stop me. They let me latch onto Gabriehl's throat.

The burning of his blood be damned. Just like the night with that human who'd hurt Evaline, that voice in my head coaxed me to drink past the pain.

Yes. Yes. This is your right. He hurt her, the voice said from behind its barrier, deep in my head.

I was hungry—starved—and hated Gabriehl with every ounce of my soul. So I drank.

Yes. Yes, the voice in my head seemed louder now.

The world moved around me, but I only cared about pulling another drag.

My friends shrieked through their gags, the floor thudded and I knew it was because they were falling over themselves, trying to get to me.

I could feel Vasier's concentrative stare, could hear the snicker of the Vasi behind me. But I didn't care. Gabriehl deserved to die.

And I didn't mind that I'd have to wretch his blood back up when I was done; the pain was worth the knowledge that he suffered.

I took another pull and felt a jolt through my body. Felt someone grip my neck, and yank me back.

The world went black and I knew they likely knocked me out. I was thankful that someone stopped me from draining Gabriehl – glad that someone stepped in, before I did something I knew I'd regret, but didn't have the power to stop.

The cell they put me in this time was far darker than the others had been. My senses were dulled and I was vaguely aware that my body was moving, but couldn't tell how so.

Maybe Vasier had told the truth. Maybe he was taking me home. Maybe I was on a ship, crossing the Srotian Sea right now.

I tried to look around but felt pinned. I was so weak and tired that I could only lie in place and let the sway around me rock me back to sleep. When I closed my eyes, I thought only of Evaline, and was thankful that I was finally getting to go home to her.

CHAPTER FORTY-EIGHT

Wyott

Cora and I stood on one side of a wall of water that Evaline had constructed between us and her. The afternoon sun glimmered through the wave as Cora struck a punch at it, and her hand popped out the other side, blurred in front of us.

I tried to sprint through the water and was halfway through when the wall shifted to wrap around me, suspending me in my leap. Evaline left my face clear of the pillar, and I grinned.

"Neat trick."

She smiled and dropped the water so that I landed on my feet.

Lauden walked to stand beside her. "That's good, you need to get used to anticipating their moves and shifting your magic to do whatever it takes to keep them away. Or in actual battle, to kill," Lauden created vortex of fire on the palm of his hand. "Someday, you'll be able to create one of these. But instead of a couple inches tall, it'll be a hundred feet. And you can destroy anything in its path."

He closed his hand and the fire went away. I turned to Evaline.

"Have you been able to get Fire again?" I asked.

She pursed her lips and shook her head, looking out at the ocean. "Not really, it's proving far more difficult than the rest."

She continued to stare at the water, and I called her name.

"Are you okay?" I asked.

She shook herself from her reverie and nodded. "I think so. I just can't shake this worry I have."

Cora stepped up next to her and placed a hand on her arm. "They'll come home soon."

"I know. I know they're capable, and I'm glad for all of the distractions with training."

I raised a brow. "Is there something else?"

She sighed heavily. "I don't know how to put it into words, aside from an odd pit of dread that settled in a few days ago."

Lauden rolled a flame lazily between his fingers a few feet away. "They'll be fine," he said.

I grimaced and shot him a look. "Could you act like you care? Your partner is there, too. Or, did you forget?"

He rolled his eyes and stepped away. "We're here to train. Go again."

I ran at Evaline before she had a chance to completely reset—she had to practice under surprise, too. Not just structured training sessions.

She turned and flung a hand out, sending a massive rock shooting up from beneath the sand to stand in my way. I nearly face planted into it.

"Very cool," Cora said, laughing at the look on my face when I caught myself against it.

Evaline must have moved, because the rock fell on itself back into the ground and sand covered where it had protruded a moment before.

"I can't wait until you can show Maddox how much you've improved," I said just as I heard a raven's cry.

My head snapped to the skies, where a white raven was descending from the clouds, with a message tied to its leg.

We collectively held our breaths. Today was the seventh day they'd been gone, and Maddox had promised to leave Merwinan in a week if they were unsuccessful.

All four of us looked between each other, then ran for the raven's cages. Evaline had a hopeful look on her face, and I knew why. She wanted for the letter to inform us that they were beginning their journey home, just like he'd promised.

By the time we reached the loft, the raven stood on its delivery perch, and when Lauden approached, it held out its leg.

He pulled the scroll and rolled it in his fingertips until he saw the recipient's name, and then turned to me.

"It's for you," he said, handing it to me.

Cora and Evaline both turned to face me while Lauden moved to put the raven back in its pen.

I tried to keep my fingers from shaking as I pulled Lady Veronica's seal off the scroll and opened it, my eyes roving over the words quickly.

I tried to school my expression but knew my stuttering heart wouldn't allow me to hide my anxiety from my wife. I felt her eyes on me, knew Evaline would burst at any moment if I didn't speak, but I had to brace myself.

Because it was not good.

"Wyott, you must come to Merwinan at once. Bring a ship and the Sorcerer," I read aloud.

Evaline's hands clasped in front of her as she turned to Cora. "That's not bad, right? It could just mean that they need more help than they thought."

I knew she didn't totally believe the words, but Cora and I nodded along anyway.

Lauden's face was grim when I turned to him. "Can you be ready to leave in the hour?"

He only nodded and moved to the staircase to gather his things.

I turned to Cora. "We need to get home and pack me a bag." Then to Evaline. "I won't be long. I'll go, and as soon as we land and I see that everything's alright, I'll send a raven."

I turned and headed toward the door, but Evaline ran to keep up with me.

"What do you mean you'll send a letter?" she asked.

I clenched my eyes shut for a moment. "Evaline, you can't go. You know that."

She scoffed. "No, I don't know that. You'll have to point out where in that scroll it said Evaline was prohibited from going."

I shook my head. "Don't make this harder than it has to be," I said as we marched around the hill that the mansion sat on.

"Wyott, I am going. Even if I have to swim there myself, I'm coming."

I spun toward her and she skidded to a halt. "You know you can't come, because it'll put us, and you, in more danger than if you stay here."

I turned and continued walking before she could respond and heard her footsteps behind me again.

"Wyott, that isn't fair. Maddox would let you go if it was Cora."

"This isn't a discussion, Evaline. The note said Lauden and I, and that's who will go."

"I'm a Sorcerer, too," she hissed.

I threw her a glare as I turned to walk down the street toward my house. "You know that's not what it meant."

Cora turned to Evaline. "You can stay with me while he's gone. They should all be back within a few days, and we'll greet them at the dock. Wyott will let me know through the bond as soon as he's close enough, and I'm sure Maddox will do the same for you."

Then Cora turned to me. "You don't think it's a trap?"

I shook my head. "If it was a trap, what good would having Lauden or me be when they already have Sage and the son of the First?"

Cora nodded, and I knew she understood.

"Besides, that was Lady Veronica's handwriting. I'm sure of it." I nodded my head firmly, reassuring myself as much as her.

We made it to the house and Evaline watched while Cora and I packed. She continued her efforts to argue her way into coming on the trip, but I had to shut her down. Maddox would not want her to come.

I picked the bag up off the bed, and kissed Cora goodbye, pulling away sooner than I'd like.

"I love you. I will be back soon," I said, hushed.

She smiled and lifted a hand to my cheek. "I love you. Go get our Mads."

I turned to Evaline. "I'm sorry you're angry with me, but this is what is best. We'll be back before you know it, and you'll see that Maddox is okay."

She nodded with a tight jaw. "Be safe," she said softly.

I nodded and moved to the door, thinking of something else as I walked away. I turned to Cora. "You'll let Kovarrin and Rasa know?"

"Of course," she said.

I looked over her once more, the love of my life, before I turned away to face Gods knew what.

The winds were calm tonight, which didn't help the ship to move any faster along the water, and for a moment I regretted leaving Evaline behind. At least she could help push air through the sails, which would've been a thousand times preferable over the other Sorcerer that I had, because he wouldn't stop flickering his flames on and off.

For the near day and a half since we'd been on this ship, he hadn't stopped.

The ship was manned with a few Kova, a couple of humans, and Lauden and me. While the others flitted around the ship to prepare for docking, we neared the coast. Only Lauden and I stood on the deck, staring out ahead of us as if we would be able to see whatever we were summoned for just by will alone.

But he wouldn't stop lighting his thumb.

Flick, on.

Flick, off.

Flick, on.

Flick, off.

I ground my teeth. Gods, he was annoying. If he'd chatted while he was nervous, that'd be preferable to this. At least some conversation would distract me.

But instead, there was only the flicking of his fingers and the flicker of light that would appear and disappear out of the corner of my eye.

Flick, on.

Flick, off.

Flick, on.

Flick, off.

"Lauden if you don't knock that shit off, I will tear that thumb from your fucking hand," I growled.

He jumped beside me and looked up at me in surprise before clearing his throat and lowering his hands back to his sides.

"Sorry, I do that when I'm nervous."

I nodded. "Yeah, well I get nervous too. Want to know what I do when I'm nervous?" I asked.

He swallowed. "I don't think I do."

I turned to him. "I stab shit," I said, before I walked away from him and moved to stand near the bow of the ship.

The rest of the time went by agonizingly slow, but *finally* the coast became more and more clear and the Merwinan beach came into view. It was night, and the sky was dark, but as the coast became visible from the ship, I saw Grant in the distance.

My heart sank when I saw that it wasn't Maddox there greeting me, and I clenched my jaw.

Gods, I prayed. *Please let him be okay.*

As soon as the ship slowed enough beside the dock I jumped from it, and heard Lauden do so, too, not so gracefully.

I stalked toward Grant who stood in the sand just off the dock.

"What's happened?" I asked, forcing a gruffness into my voice to keep it from shaking.

The bags beneath his eyes were evident and he was wearing fresh clothes but it was clear that they weren't his. He shook his head at me, swallowed, and tried to speak but nothing came out. He ran his hands over his short hair out of despair and looked back at me with tears in his eyes.

"Show me," I commanded.

Grant told me what happened on our way to Saxon's home. He was in Rominia, and they'd needed a place to go.

They'd set the trap, it should've worked. But Maddox and Dean said that Sage had been taken, and they'd never heard the Vasi approach. How the same happened for all of them within moments.

My brows furrowed at that. It must've been the sand that hid the sound.

Grant shook his head then, and looked up at me.

"How long have we been gone?"

"It's been eight days since you left Rominia," I said, meeting his eyes. I watched as they flashed with confusion. "Why?"

"When we woke up after the abduction, we were in Mortithev."

I stopped walking and turned to him, willing the pace of my heart to slow.

"What do you mean you were in Mortithev? That's impossible. It would take nearly two weeks to sail there from here." I shook my head. "And two weeks back."

Grant shook his head. "I don't know, it should be impossible."

My face fell then, as I remembered my thoughts from the ship. How I'd wished I'd brought Evaline, to add air to the sails.

"They have an Air Caster."

Grant nodded and Lauden paled.

We continued our way to Saxon's. We kept the quickest pace we could around the humans while Grant told us about the torture, and how Maddox had been in awful shape.

"How did you all get back here?" I asked. "He just let you go?"

"They knocked us out, and when we woke up, we were on Merwinan's beach. They'd taken the Rominium shackles to keep in Mortithev, so when we came to, we were only bound in ropes." He looked up at me.

"We came to Saxon's and sent someone to tell Lady Veronica to send a note to you."

We landed outside Saxon's door and I turned to Grant. "Why didn't you go into the safety of Merwinan's wards?"

My heart beat through my throat, my skin washed with dread, and I tried to calm my erratic breathing as I watched tears well in Grant's eyes.

I clenched my jaw and walked through the door. Sage was sitting at the dining table with a vacant look in her eyes, and tears streaming down her face. Dean stood near her. Nash and Fredrik were in the living room, their eyes wide and red rimmed, hair disheveled.

They parted, and I knew I'd see my brother there. But where I'd hoped he was sitting up, or standing, he was laid across the chaise.

Chapter Forty-Nine

Evaline

I'd done little more in the days since Wyott left than sit and worry. He'd promised he would write as soon as he got to Merwinan if everything was okay and he hadn't. I was reeling from the implications of his lack of correspondence but chose to hope that it only meant that he'd landed in Merwinan and loaded them all onto the ship right away to start the trip back home. That he'd never even stepped foot into the city's gates, and thus wouldn't have had a chance to mail anything back.

Cora chose to believe that, too.

I'd stayed at their home since Wyott left, which helped with the waiting, but this morning when we woke and still hadn't received a letter, Cora couldn't sit still.

"You don't have to stay here with me," I told her once mid-day hit and she was beginning to wear a line in the hardwood with her pacing.

Her eyes flicked up to mine. "I just need to get out of here. I need a distraction."

I stood and crossed the room to her. "Do you want to go train?"

She pursed her lips and clenched her eyes shut for a moment. "If I'm being honest, all I want to do right now is go work." She shook her head. "I'm sorry, I shouldn't be trying to get away. We're both worried."

I waved my hands between us as if I could bat away her apology. "No, it's okay. You go to the marina."

Her eyes flashed with relief. "Do you want to come too?"

I shook my head and sighed. "I'll only get in the way. Is it okay if I use your bath?"

"Of course." She nodded. "All the soaps and towels are in there. I'll just go for a couple hours. We can turn in early for the evening and hope to the Gods that when we wake up, they're home."

I nodded my agreement, and she rushed out of the house after a quick goodbye. I clenched my eyes shut to will the tears to stop, but I felt so Gods-damned guilty that she was in this position now, worried for her mate, because of me.

My lungs expanded as I forced a deep breath down into them. I refused to have a panic attack before I ever knew if there was anything to panic over. For now, I'd take a bath.

And I did. But I wasted a couple hours first, trying to heat the water with my own fire.

It did not work.

Eventually I used the fireplace to heat the bath the traditional way and laid in the tub for another hour, until long after it cooled. I didn't mind the chill of it as I played with my Water magic to distract myself.

Finally, though, I did have to get out. I dressed in gray summer pajamas, since Cora said we'd turn in early.

"Cora?" I called as I walked out of the bathroom and slipped on a floor-length silk robe. "Are you back yet?" I asked as I stepped into a pair of slippers and moved to the kitchen.

I turned the corner, but she wasn't there. Her room was empty, too, as was the guest bedroom.

She'd said she'd be back within a couple hours, but it had already been a few. I decided to kill some time by making myself a cup of tea, and then sit on the roof. Cora and Wyott had a remarkable view of the town below and out into the water, and I could keep an eye on Lauden's loft, to see if a raven flew in.

When I got to the roof, I dropped onto one of the wooden chairs they had, folding my legs beneath me, and sipped the tea. The chair already faced Lauden's and I only now looked for the sun. It hung near the tops of the trees on the western side of the island, preparing for its set.

I stayed that way until I finished my drink. There'd been no ravens, but maybe Cora would be home soon, and I could make us dinner. I stood and stretched, before turning to the other side of the roof where the staircase led down to the front door, and further to town.

I stopped on the top step to take in how the street bustled below me. Rominians flitted about between stores, and from where I stood, I could see the entire stretch of the road that led toward the water. I could see the horizon, where the sky and sea met. And along the coast, I could see the top of a ship's mast.

"What the fuck?" I gasped aloud as the cup fell from my hand and shattered against the stone roof.

I started running down the stairs. I didn't stop at Wyott and Cora's level, but kept running down the rest of the flights until I was on the busy streets of Rominia. Everyone stared and moved out of my way, but I didn't care, I was sprinting as fast as I could over the cobblestone, toward the estate. The stones bit at my feet through the thin slippers I wore, and my robe flapped open so wind hit my bare legs as my heart banged in my chest.

A pulsing began in my head, and I realized that it was the bond. It pushed me forward until I was sprinting at absolute capacity, and still that wasn't enough. The beat of it was so strong, I almost heard its commands.

Go. Go. Go. You're too slow.

Because the ship at the dock meant that Wyott was back. And Cora's lack of return meant that he reached out to her down the bond to tell her he was here. And the fact that neither of them bothered to summon me meant something was wrong and they were strategizing a way to tell me.

I sprinted through the streets until I was fumbling my way up the mansion's staircase and heading straight for the front door.

The two guards standing there turned to me with wide eyes, and I wasn't sure if it was because of what they knew or how I looked.

I stopped in front of them, my chest heaving for air.

"They're back," I said, and the two of them nodded, eyes wide with fear. "Where is he?" I asked, my voice lethally low.

"Wyott's old room," the one on the left said. The one on the right shot him a look, but I didn't stay to find out why.

I pushed open the doors and kicked off the slippers inside of it. They were only slowing me down, anyway. I ran up the winding staircase ahead. I'd done enough exploring of the First's Estate to know exactly where Wyott's suite was. My legs begged me to slow, but I didn't—couldn't—as I sprinted down the hall of the third floor.

Even if I didn't know which door led to Wyott's before, I did now, based off the guard that was stationed outside of it.

I didn't stop running until I was standing in front of him, and he sidestepped away from the door, refusing to look at me.

My heart ravaged in my chest. I reached for the bond, like I'd done a thousand times before, like I'd tried to do since I saw the ship's mast, but there was nothing. Just the same thrum as when he was too far for me to feel him. My hand hovered over the doorknob.

I couldn't move it.

My entire run here had been out of worry, but now that I stood here, unable to feel him, I hesitated. What if I wasn't ready to see what was inside? My mind plagued me with images of him lying on the bed, dead. Of his heartbeat gone. Of his gray eyes closed forever. Tears welled in my eyes as I pictured these things, these horrific things, and knew I couldn't handle that. Couldn't handle losing someone *again*. Not him.

I reached down the bond again and felt nothing.

I tried to remember what my mind felt like before I met him, and I couldn't. Had there always been that fuzzy feeling in the back of it, a warmth that I could reach down anytime I needed?

What would it feel like if he was gone from me forever?

I swallowed past the lump in my throat and lowered my shaking hand over the knob, turned, and swung the door open.

The suite was designed similarly to ours, just in reverse. The door opened to the sitting room on the right, and my eyes swung around the room until they landed on him. I was vaguely aware of the soft snap of the door behind me as a relieved sob fell from my lips.

He sat in a chair on the opposite side of the room, beside the fireplace. He faced the tall windows that stretched to the ceiling to show the ocean swaying outside.

"Maddox," I whispered as I ran forward.

His head was propped to the side, resting on his shoulder. There was a blanket draped over his lap and halfway up his abdomen. I realized he was asleep as I moved around the chair to stand in front of him.

I reached one hand forward and placed it on his chest, felt the rhythmic thud of his heart and nearly collapsed in relief.

"Oh, Gods," I choked out, my voice breaking.

I caught myself against him and moved to grasp his hand that laid along the arm of the chair.

I took a deep breath of relief as I stared at his eyes fluttering behind his lids against whatever dream he was having.

Thank you, I prayed. *Thank you, Gods.*

I reached down the bond again, but still couldn't feel him. But he was asleep, and that was why.

I could've slapped myself for getting so worked up with worry over it.

I smiled down at him and slid my hand down his chest, thankful to feel him near me again. To feel his warmth and know he was here with me, safe.

My fingers caught halfway down his torso. I shook my head with a smile.

"Couldn't bother to take your arsenal off before you fell asleep?" I whispered playfully.

I moved the blanket out of the way, and as I did, felt his hand turn and wrap around my other one.

My smile faltered as I dragged the blanket completely out of the way. A black bar was locked around my mate's ribcage.

"What?" I asked softly.

I scanned the rest of the chair. In my relief at his safety, I'd missed that he didn't sit on a leather chair, or an upholstered one. It was a sleek black, made of metal by the way the light outside bounced off of it.

Rominium.

My brows furrowed as I shook my head.

"What the fuck is wrong with them?" I whispered as I continued to look down the chair's arms. On the left, where his hand curled over the edge of it, another bar clasped over his wrist, holding it in place.

Dread shifted through me, and I didn't know why. Because I couldn't understand why they'd ever lock him up like this. I tilted my head toward the ground and moved the blanket out of the way with my foot.

Another bar curled over his ankle.

My heart raced in my chest, panic beat through my veins, as I heard an awful laugh rumble from his lips. It wasn't the lighthearted Maddox laugh I was used to. It was deep and wrong, and my eyes slowly moved up to meet his as I straightened to my full height.

His eyes were raking up my body, an awful smirk on his face that reminded me of Bassel's, as they slowly rose to meet mine.

Wrong.

Yes, his laugh was wrong.

Because it wasn't his.

Because those eyes weren't his.

Because they were red.

There'd been moments in my life where I felt as if I stood still and everything happened around me, without me, as if I was in a dream.

When I saw Bassel at the Ball. When he proposed. And when I married him.

But I'd never experienced it with Maddox, until now.

There was no noise, even though his lips were moving. The light in the room felt like it dimmed, even though I knew it hadn't. A cold wave of shock washed over my body until I felt goosebumps raise across my skin.

He still had that same nick in his eyebrow, a similar one over his lip. His black hair still fell in a light curl over his forehead, but those charcoal gray eyes that once gave me comfort, were gone.

I think I felt pain, but I wasn't sure where.

In my chest, yes.

Behind my skull, yes. I felt a migraine.

In my throat, definitely, but I didn't know why.

Mostly, I felt it in my right wrist. In the one that his fingers had curled around. I think he was breaking it, but I couldn't be sure. Because I couldn't look away from his eyes. And he didn't break our gaze. Not even to blink.

Did Vasi have to blink?

Vasi.

Maddox was a Vasi.

My Maddox was a Vasi.

The ache in my throat was a scream. I was screaming. I think I had been this entire time without knowing it. Sounds started to pierce through the haze that my mind had shifted over my senses, and everything else came slowly back into focus.

Wyott was in the doorway in my peripheral, shouting.

"Who the fuck let her in here?" he screamed, but the words still sounded kind of garbled. Slowed down.

I don't think I'd ever actually heard Wyott scream before. Not like this. He sounded scared, and worried. And sad.

Mostly sad.

I could hear my scream, too. I might've fallen to my knees from how hard I was yelling, if they weren't locked in shock. I'd screamed like this only once before, and it was over my father's lifeless body.

Realization hit me then, because up until now it had felt like a dream. Like maybe I'd fallen asleep in Cora and Wyott's tub and any moment Cora would wake me, and we'd make dinner.

But it wasn't a dream, I realized that now. It was real.

My mate, my life, my Maddox, was gone. Worse than gone.

And pain, white hot pain shot up my wrist.

The world around me started to pick back up in real time as Wyott appeared beside me.

"Let go!" he roared to Maddox.

Blood.

I smelled it as it pierced the air. You didn't need to be a Vasi or a Kova to smell it. Because it was rushing, and I felt the cool air hit my wrist.

Oh. I was bleeding.

I didn't look down, only stared into the eyes of my mate. Eyes the same shade as my blood would be if I bothered to gaze down at it.

Wyott shouted at him again. I felt his gentle hands on my arm, knew he was trying to figure out what to do to free me.

It was the opposite wrist that Bassel broke; the one that didn't twinge with pain for an oncoming storm.

But my throat still hurt, my ears still pierced with the sound of my screaming. Air hit my cheeks, and I realized I was sobbing, too.

The red eyes in front of me started to blur, and I was thankful for that, because I couldn't force myself to look away but I needed reprieve.

I felt Wyott lean closer to me, saw him cock his arm back. The tears cleared enough for me to watch as Wyott's elbow bashed into the front of Maddox's face. He gave me a sick smirk, and Wyott hit him again. This time he passed out, and his grip on my wrist loosened.

The world moved around me. I think Wyott picked me up.

"I'm sorry," he said, but his voice was garbled.

I realized he was crying, too.

CHAPTER FIFTY

Maddox

I woke up and for a brief moment the bright light hit me, and I wondered when I'd ever made it out of that cell in the ship. But then I saw Evaline's face come into view and knew everything was okay again. She was in her pajamas and looked as beautiful as I'd ever seen her.

"Did you miss me?" I tried to say, but when I spoke the words, no sound came out. Did my lips even move?

I tried to lift my hand up to my lips, to make sure I was okay, but my hand didn't respond.

My heart started to race in my chest. Had Vasier drugged me before he let me go?

My eyes were running up her body—I didn't remember telling them to do that, but finally I could see her eyes. Finally, I could see her.

Instead of smiling, happy to see me home, her eyes widened in fear. My heart dropped, searching for what I could've done that would ever make her scared of me. I knew I'd never do it again because I would work my entire life to make sure she never had to fear anything, anyone, ever again.

My hand wrapped around her wrist. I wanted to hold her, but I didn't mean to do that.

Her eyes held mine, and she didn't even flinch as my hand tightened.

What the fuck? No!

I didn't want to do that. I didn't *mean* to do that.

"I'm so sorry, Eva," I said, but I didn't hear my own words. I didn't feel my lips speak them.

My heart beat wildly against my chest and my hand only tightened.

"No!" I screamed.

Every ounce of my might worked to unbend my hand. To loosen the fingers from around her wrist. But they wouldn't listen, they wouldn't fucking listen, no matter how many times my brain begged them to.

Her lips fell open. She was screaming.

I'd never heard that sound from her. It was deep and guttural and my insides shredded at the sound of her anguish. It was the sound you made when you experienced the worst pain of your life. I remembered hearing it from Wyott's lips when I caught him off the ship after his father died. But I'd never heard it from hers. I never wanted to ever again, and I was sick inside that I was causing it.

What the fuck was happening?

Her scream didn't falter, and neither did my grip.

I jolted forward when I felt her wrist snap beneath my hand.

"No!" I screamed. "Gods," I begged, sobbing. "Gods please!" But the words only bounced around my own head. I wasn't speaking them. Was I saying them down the bond accidentally?

The bond.

I reached for it, but it wasn't there.

Panic gripped me as I reached out to her. But the tether that had once connected us was gone, as if it evaporated from my mind.

Was I dead? Was this a nightmare?

I felt her blood trickle down my hand and heard Wyott scream as he entered the room.

Thank Gods he was here.

"Wyott, what the fuck is happening?" I asked but the words, again, only bounced around my head.

"Let go!" he screamed at me.

He was scared. I was too. I was trying with all my might to do as he said, but my hand wouldn't listen.

Why was this happening?

A deep rumble shifted through my mind. My spine straightened as a voice entered my head, because I was certain it was going to be Evaline, certain she'd found the bond, and was speaking to me down it.

Not so fun being the one held back, is it?

The voice was deep. It was low. And it was mine.

Heat fled my body as the cool reach of dread took hold.

No. I shuddered. I knew that voice, he'd spoken to me before. When I drank from the man who stabbed Evaline. When I drank from Gabriehl.

Yes, the voice responded.

I tried to retrace my steps, certain I'd find somewhere along the way where I'd been drugged. Or that I was still asleep, and that this wasn't possibly happening.

But instead, the images played in my mind without having to hunt for them.

See? the voice said, and I realized it was playing a memory.

Gabriehl stood on his knees in front of me. In Vasier's throne room. I'd lunged for him and drank.

What have I done? I thought to myself as I remembered it.

I recalled the way I'd drank from him. Again and again, until I took that last pull, and no blood came out. Until that hand wrapped around my neck and yanked me into the darkness.

I was never knocked unconscious. I was never in a black cell. I was never stopped.

No.

I was sobbing, the tears and the grief and the panic ravaged through my chest until I couldn't breathe. I tried to place my head in my hands but couldn't reach anymore. The world tunneled around me and I was shoved back.

I couldn't see Evaline in the forefront of my vision as I was thrown further into darkness. When the room stopped moving, I was in a long hallway of midnight black walls, and she was all the way at the end of it. I tried to reach for her, but couldn't. When I looked to each side, there were chains that bound my wrists and anchored them to the wall.

I looked at Evaline again, saw the tears clouding her blue green eyes. Smelled her blood coating my hand. Felt her wrist continue to crack below my grip as if I was the one doing it.

But I wasn't.

He had control now.

CHAPTER FIFTY-ONE

Wyott

"I'm sorry," I said again, tears choking my words before they could fully leave my lips. "I'm sorry."

I was sprinting through the halls of the mansion. I had to get her away from him, away from *seeing* him. Guilt ripped me raw at the thought that she was alone when she saw him like that. I was supposed to be there with her. Cora and I both were supposed to be there.

We didn't think she'd notice the ship if she stayed in the house like they'd planned. And those *fucking* guards weren't supposed to tell her where he was.

I sprinted past the study, where our parents, Cora, Lauden, the hunting party, and myself had been discussing what to do. I saw them come to the door as I ran. I wasn't even sure where I was going. But she was still screaming in my arms.

I wasn't sure which pain caused it; the ache in her wrist that I tried to stabilize in my hold while I ran, or the one in her heart.

I felt Cora begin to run behind me, felt her place her hands over Evaline's wrist, too, to protect it.

She was dripping blood everywhere but, still, I wasn't sure where to take her. She started to shake then, quake in my arms, and hyperventilate.

"I'm sorry," I sobbed again, blinking the tears away so I could see where I was going. "I'm so sorry."

She gave a choked sound and I knew she couldn't breathe.

Outside. We needed to get outside. She needed to breathe.

Patio, I said to Cora through our bond, and she sprinted ahead, opening the patio doors. I raced out of them and didn't stop until I went past the outdoor furniture down the steps to the ballroom floor.

I eased Evaline to the ground and tried to sit her up, but she fell back. I caught her head before it cracked against the stone and helped her to lie back in the center of the very floor that we'd all danced around all those weeks ago.

The wind around us picked up until all of our hair was whipping back and forth around our heads.

She was screaming, and hyperventilating, and Cora moved behind her. She got on her knees and propped Evaline's upper body up onto her lap. Tried to help her elongate her torso and instructed her to take deep breaths.

But Evaline didn't listen. I don't know that she could hear us at all.

Her wrist was lying against the stone beside her. I knew what I had to do, and I knew she'd hate me for it.

"Evaline, breathe. You have to breathe. Please," Cora coaxed her, tears choking her voice, too.

She ran her hands down Evaline's cheeks, wiping the tears away, moving the soaked hair away from her face.

"Breathe for me. Please."

But Evaline only continued to scream, sob, whichever made its way out of her throat faster.

The waves crashed harder against the cliff below us, and I turned my head to see the ocean in the distance. Wave after wave lifted from the nearly flat water and charged forward until it hit the base of the cliff below.

"I'm sorry," Cora said this time. "I'm so sorry."

I looked back to them to see her shake her head as tears filled her own eyes, and the sight of them both tore a piece of me away.

Evaline's wrist had a puddle of blood gathered below it. The bone had punctured through, he'd broken it so badly.

I looked up at Cora. *You need to do it,* I told her through our bond. She was far better with injuries like this, her slender fingers gentler and more precise than mine ever could be, and I didn't want to give Evaline one ounce more of pain than I had to.

She nodded with a tight jaw and we traded places. I cradled Evaline's head on my lap while Cora went to her side and picked up her wrist. We'd have to set the break while she fed, otherwise we risked the break healing incorrectly.

Evaline was still crying, screaming, but she watched me as I raised my wrist to my mouth and bit it. Her eyes widened and she screamed louder.

"No!" she shrieked as I lowered my wrist to her mouth.

She continued to scream it, to chant it, until she was writhing in my arms and whipping her head back and forth.

"You're losing a lot of blood, you have to heal," I begged.

The break must've ruptured an artery.

"No!" she screamed again, new tears flooding down her face.

The ground rumbled below us, hard enough that I wondered if the cliff might crumble beneath us.

"Not from you!"

Her voice was so scratched I knew it had to hurt, too. But the blood would heal all of it.

Evaline's eyes flicked to Cora as she moved to bite her own wrist.

"No!" Evaline screamed and a crack fractured the stone below us, running right beneath her. "Only him." She writhed in our arms, and more fractures stemmed around us. "Only Maddox."

She screamed as the wind, the water, the ground below us ripped and crashed and quaked.

I looked to Cora, both of our eyes wide in worry. Evaline was losing control of her magic.

I'd never seen her use it like this. Without using her hands to guide it. This power didn't stem from her hands like it normally did. This came from her *being*. The wind and the waves and the rock shuddered around us in response to her pain.

I saw the others appear out of my peripheral. The four Kova who'd witnessed what happened crouched or leaned with their heads in their hands. Kovarrin's expression was locked down, and he stood stone still with his arms wrapped around Rasa, who stared at Evaline with nothing less than agony flickering across her face and tears streaming down her cheeks. I saw Lauden arrive, too, with an unreadable expression, eyes roving over all the signs of Evaline's magic as mine had. And Sage stood next to him, weeping openly.

I looked to Kovarrin, unsure of what to do. I hoped he'd have advice, but he didn't move, didn't speak.

Evaline's heartbeat was accelerating, I knew she was losing too much blood, wasting too much energy on her magic, and her thrashing and screaming only made it worse.

I looked down at her and gripped either side of her face, tilting her head back to meet my eyes.

"Evaline," I said, willing my voice to be strong. "I made a promise to Maddox that I would take care of you no matter what happened to him," I said, and pain beat through my chest at the memory of that evening in Kembertus. "Don't make me a liar. Don't make me watch you die because you won't let us heal you," I begged.

She looked up at me, the tears still falling down her face, but her screaming stopped and calmed to dry sobs. Heavy thunder rumbled above, louder than her cries had been, before the skies released a torrential downpour.

She shivered as the rain soaked down over all of us.

"Don't let Vasier win. Don't let him break our family apart anymore," I begged.

She finally sniffed and swallowed before looking to Cora, and I watched her clench her eyes shut as tight as she could and grab for my wrist.

I quickly reopened the wound—it had healed by the time she grabbed for it—and lowered it to her face.

She wrapped her hand around it and I looked to Cora.

She nodded, though I barely saw it through the sheet of rain that pelted between us. She moved down to Evaline's wrist, both hands steadying on each side.

Evaline took a drag.

"Now," I instructed, and Cora's fingers moved so quickly you would've missed it if you were human.

Evaline shrieked against my wrist.

"I'm sorry," I repeated for the thousandth time. "You have to keep going."

Her renewed cries were muffled against my skin as she drank, and I only brushed her hair away from her face, looked to my mate, and looked back down to Evaline and apologized.

"It's done," Cora said as she looked up, running her hands and fingers over Evaline's wrist to ensure the wound was closed and the fracture was healed.

Evaline ripped her mouth away from me and it immediately healed.

The ground rumbled below us again. The wind shook the rain, and the ocean rocked.

Evaline lay back against my lap and stared up. But she stared past me, past the droplets that pattered across her face, up into the clouds.

"Why?" she asked softly.

I didn't have to ask who she was talking to, to know. Her chest started to heave again as she worked herself back up. As rage overtook the pain that had been ravaging her body and she stared toward the Gods in the heavens and screamed.

"Why?" she shouted against the rain and wind, against the rumble of the stone below us.

Cora gasped and I turned to see one of the pillars that lined the ballroom totter until it fell over, and another shockwave was sent through the ground as the granite cracked open.

The waves rose, the wind howled.

"Why?" Evaline screamed again.

Suddenly I knew what was coming next. I knew it before I ever saw the light. Because I knew her pain, and that rage. I'd known it well once before. Knew it a little less, now. She'd officially lost too much. But I knew what happened when she felt that fury.

I looked up to Cora.

"Run," I instructed.

Her brows furrowed. "What?"

"Run!" I screamed, and she listened.

Gone in a flash. Just in time, before the real flash ignited. The world erupted into oranges and yellows. There was a flash of heat, then the rain was gone. The world was somehow quiet and loud at the same time. Gone was the sound of the ground rumbling and the waves crashing and the wind beating against the manor.

A roar took over, so loud it almost reminded me of the one Maddox had let loose when he found her Rominium dagger near that creek. This roar didn't stem from a pair of lips, but from a blaze.

The fire lit around us, engulfing the entire ballroom floor. Flames slithered up the pillars that still stood. It burned so hot it popped the glass lantern bulbs that had survived the previous quakes and they burst one after another, down the line. I leaned over Evaline to protect her eyes from any falling glass.

It was then I realized we weren't on fire. But that we sat in a small bubble in the blaze. The fire raged all around us, but we were safe.

I looked down at her. Her chest was still heaving, but she was trying to catch her breath. Tears fell from her eyes as she stared up at the sky, though there was a wall of fire between us and the clouds, now.

Her cries dwindled until they were only whimpers. She finally looked up at me and showed me her pain for the first time.

She shook her head.

"It hurts so bad," she said, her voice was soft beneath the booms and crackle of the fire around us.

"I know."

It was all I could say.

"It's too much." Her voice was thick.

"We can carry it with you," I said firmly. I dragged a hand over her face to wipe the tears away. "We're a family." My voice cracked this time, even though I tried to stop it. "You're not alone. Not this time."

Her eyes flashed with something at that.

"Not alone," she said softly, and then gave a slight nod. "Just not mated anymore."

Her face crumpled in one last twinge of pain as she cringed against the words. The fire died out around us, the ground stilled, the wind stalled, the ocean fell.

The world went silent, and when I looked back down at her, she was unconscious.

Chapter Fifty-Two

Evaline

I scrubbed a hand over my eyes to wipe the sleep from them and tilted my head to see the curtains blowing in the wind, and rain pattering through the open window on the sill just beyond.

My brows furrowed. Why was I on Maddox's side of the bed? I always fell asleep on my side. Why was I here at all? I'd been staying at Cora's.

I turned my head to look over and saw Cora lying on my side. Confusion clouded my thoughts as I sat up quickly, but I immediately threw my hands out to keep from falling and slowed my movements as a migraine pierced through my head.

Cora sat up just as fast and placed a hand on my back.

"Are you okay?" she asked, her voice raised with concern. "What hurts?"

Her other hand palpated against my cheek, as if she were checking for a fever.

I shook my head. "I have a migraine," I said quietly, clenching my eyes shut. Even without seeing her, I could feel her worried stare. "I always get them when I wake up at odd hours," I said, massaging my forehead with both hands.

"We can get you some tea to help with the pain," she said softly, rubbing patterns on my back.

Just then the thunder outside rolled so loudly I cringed against the stab of pain that shot through my skull. My right hand moved out of reflex to massage my left wrist, it always ached during the storms because of the break from Bassel.

"Who's 'we'?" I asked.

Wyott appeared in the doorway behind her then. My eyes widened and my heart pounded painfully against my chest.

"You're back?" I asked, dropping a leg off the bed to stand. I shook my head as the room spun, and a clap of thunder sounded outside.

"Evaline…" Wyott said softly, starting to walk toward me.

I looked down at my wrist as the thunder rolled again. It still ached, but it was my right wrist I looked at now, as if I recalled some pain that had once been there, too.

I looked down at it, my brows furrowed. Cora crawled toward me on the bed. "Evaline, sit down for a moment."

She reached for me, and I looked past my hands and saw that the ground was shifting below me.

Wyott walked forward, near the end of the bed.

My head snapped up at him. "Where's Maddox?" I asked.

I took a step away from him, as my vision focused and I saw agony in his eyes like I'd never seen before.

Cora's hand slipped over my wrist gently as she tried to pull me to the bed to sit, but I stood firm. My head snapped down to her hand over mine and I remembered seeing her hand on it before.

A phantom shock of pain lit my right wrist and I jumped, eyes wild as I stared down at it. Images started playing in my mind. Flashes of a memory so horrific that it felt like a nightmare.

"No," I said, trying to back away.

Wyott and Cora exchanged a look, and he shook his head once. She opened her mouth, but no words came out.

I remembered Cora's hands on my wrist, the shocking pain she caused when she moved the bones in it. The images shifted until it was Wyott holding my wrist. I'd been wrapped up in his arms, and the world around us blurred as he ran at full capacity.

They fluttered again until it was Maddox's hand I felt closing over my wrist, until I was looking at his eyes.

"No!" I screamed and felt my knees buckle.

Wyott rounded the bed in a flash and caught me before I could fall but lowered me to the ground until we both kneeled.

I shook my head as all of the memories flooded back. Until the pain in my wrist, in my head, in my heart, all reestablished themselves in my memory and I knew I'd never be rid of them. I'd never be free from what I'd seen, never escape the knowledge of what the Gods had allowed to happen.

"I'm sorry," Wyott said as he pulled me to his chest.

I felt Cora come to kneel by me, felt her wrap her arms around me on the other side.

"I'm sorry," she whispered.

I remembered the way I'd screamed and cried, the way I'd screamed at my friends, and the way I'd hated Wyott for having to drink his blood to heal. I remembered the way Maddox's laugh sounded and the hatred and amusement in his eyes when he'd looked at me.

My friends held me while I cried, while the memories assaulted me with their return. It felt like an hour before I caught my breath and my body stopped quivering with the sobs.

When a moment of silence passed between us, I noticed something for the first time. In the space between my deep breaths, I noticed that I felt different.

I reached for my magic and, Gods, it was everywhere. It was in every pore, in every nook in my bones. I'd once felt as if it hummed just below my skin, but now it seemed to crawl along it, as if it broke free of a cage and existed outside of my body. It filled my lungs with each breath and slid through my mind but also reached out into my surroundings.

Now, I couldn't just sense the elements around me, I *was* the elements around me. I could feel the way the rain fell just outside the window, and pattered against the roof. I felt the wind that swayed the clouds high above us as I breathed in. I could feel the relief in the land as it soaked up the rain.

I turned in the direction of the fireplace in the other room. I could feel the way the flames flickered and consumed their fuel as a log splintered and fell into the bed of embers.

A gasp left my lips. What had happened to me?

Cora mistook my sound for more pain.

"Tell us what you need," she whispered.

I checked for the bond, and it was still there, but quiet. I flicked my eyes between the both of them.

"I need to see him."

Wyott and Cora strode on either side of me as I walked down the hall.

"You can't, Evaline," Wyott said beside me. "Not yet. Give us time to figure out what happened, figure out what to do."

I shook my head as I went. "No."

"Evaline," Cora started on my other side. "You need time away. And to grieve, it'll only hurt to keep going to see him," she said, her voice concerned even though she was trying to be comforting.

I shook my head. "No. He's not gone. He's still here." I turned my head to her. "Maybe he isn't fully changed yet. Maybe there's still time to save him."

Her brows knit together and tears gathered in her eyes.

"No," she said softly. "He's fully transformed. The change only takes seconds."

"It can't be. You'll see. Maybe it's a trick," I said, shaking my head wildly and then looking up to Wyott. "Maybe Vasier has some kind of elixir or *something* that makes it appear like he's changed."

Wyott's voice grew somber. "No, Evaline. He's turned. You saw his eyes. You saw what he did to your wrist. Maddox—the *real* Maddox—would've never done that to you. Elixir, or no elixir."

We made it to the staircase and I started jogging up them.

"It's not over," I said. "It's not real. You'll see. We'll go in there and he'll be feeling more like himself." I shook my head. "This is all a terrible, *awful* deception on Vasier's part."

Wyott's gentle hand found my elbow and stopped me from walking. He turned me to face him.

"It really is over, Evaline. He changed."

I shook my head, an incredulous laugh flitting from my lips. "But how do you *know*?"

His jaw ticked before he spoke. "Because he killed someone. The other Kova, Sage, they all saw it."

Tears crept into my eyes as I shook my head. "No. They misunderstood." I took a deep breath to steady myself. "Maddox would never do that."

Wyott's eyes flickered with pain. "He did."

I scoffed and threw my arms up. "Fine! Please tell me. Tell me that my Maddox, *our* Maddox killed some poor, innocent human. Does that sound like him?"

Wyott's lips pressed into a frown, and he shook his head. "No, it doesn't."

I nodded. "Thank you."

"It wasn't an innocent human," Wyott said quickly. "It was Gabriehl."

The hope fractured in my heart.

I turned away from them to face the stair banister. I bent over it, hands bracing over the handrail, and looked down at the ground that was several yards below me. My breaths started to come fast, but I was able to stop the panic attack before it could start.

I reached for the bond. It was still there, beating faintly in the back of my mind. As if he were sleeping and he'd wake and I'd hear him again.

The bond was still here. *He* was still here.

I pivoted and started jogging down the stairs.

Wyott and Cora moved behind me. "Where are you going?" she asked.

"I need to speak to everyone," I said, my voice low. "Kovarrin and Rasa. The Sorcerers, the Kova who went with him. Everyone."

Wyott nodded and then was gone in a blur.

I turned to Cora. "Is he going to get them?"

She looked down at me as we walked. "Yes. They're all here. You've been unconscious for a few hours, but they haven't left. We were waiting to see how you felt when you woke up." Her lips twitched into a frown. "They knew you'd have questions."

Cora and I walked to the study and by the time we got there, Rasa sat in the chair behind Kovarrin's desk and he stood behind her, a calming hand running over her back. Rasa raised her eyes to meet mine, but I looked away. I could hardly handle my own grief, I couldn't carry hers too. Maybe that made me a bad person, or an awful daughter in law, but I could hardly pass each breath without feeling like I'd crumple from the pain. Or from the rage.

Cora moved to sit in one of the chairs in front of the desk, I'm sure she thought I'd join her there. But I couldn't. I didn't want to be sitting down. I'd done enough of that since Maddox had left. Sitting and waiting. And look what had happened.

I moved to the side of the room and leaned my back against a bookcase, crossing my arms over my torso and a wave of nausea crept up my throat as I was reminded of the last time we'd all gathered here, before they left. They'd all been so confident that the plan would work. And it had failed, in nearly the worst way possible.

Lauden and Sage entered first and stood directly across from me against the bookshelves on the opposite wall. Lauden's eyes flicked over my frame, and I knew he could tell I was different. I knew he could tell that I'd changed; he'd seen my display of magic.

Sage didn't meet my eyes. Something had changed in her, too. Her shoulders were more slumped than they usually were, and there were bags beneath her eyes.

Guilt dropped in my gut as I realized she'd been harmed by Vasier, and my heart quickened against my chest as I wondered how—if he'd treated her as awfully as the men in Vestaria treat women.

I opened my mouth, I wanted to apologize to her, but I shut it again. There was no reason to do so when we had an audience. I remembered how I wanted to be alone after Bassel and Lonix's attack.

The rest of the Kova walked in then, and Wyott shut the door behind them.

The five of them stood in front of the unlit fireplace and faced the front of the room, and they didn't meet my eyes either.

Silence hung over the room for a moment, and I realized that no one knew what to say. Or where to start.

I looked to the ground, wondered if it should be me. I looked to Cora, then to Wyott, and Wyott started to open his mouth, but Sage spoke first.

"I'm so sorry, Evaline," she said softly. I met her gaze. She seemed sincere, and it might've been the first time. She shook her head, tears in her eyes as Lauden looked down at her with furrowed brows. "I'm so sorry."

Before I could respond, the four Kova stepped closer to me.

"Evaline," Grant said. "There's no way we can ever express our condolences, and our regret for not being able to prevent this." His voice choked then, and he looked to the ground to gather himself, then back to me. "Maddox was our friend, and I'm so sorry we couldn't stop this."

Dean turned to me, his face grim and paler than normal. "I wish I'd done more," was all he said, softly.

My eyes slid to Fredrik as he spoke. "If there had been a way." He shook his head to give himself a moment to swallow the lump in his throat. His words were garbled, too.

Nash continued instead. "Every minute, every hour, we all plotted what we could do to escape. I'm so sorry we weren't good enough to stop this."

I shook my head then, and clenched my eyes shut.

"Stop it. You have nothing to apologize for." I ran a hand over my face to clear my mind. "None of you," I said, roving my eyes between the four Kova's eyes and then Sage's. "Have anything to apologize for. You didn't hurt him, you didn't do this. He was lucky to have you all by his side."

Rasa let out a soft sob on my other side and I cringed away from it. I couldn't imagine the hurt she was feeling.

"Thank you all," I said after I'd taken a deep breath. "Thank you all for going and risking your lives for me. Thank you for surviving whatever it is you survived," I said, making a point to look at Sage.

I turned to the Kova. I was about to tell them that I was sure all their respective mates were happy to have them safe. But I couldn't finish the sentence. The pain ripped through my chest too harshly to even be happy for them. Because my mate never came back. Not really.

Lauden cleared his throat and started to speak softly. "I know that this is a time of grieving, but we all want to give Maddox the celebration he deserves, and that will take some planning," he said, his voice low. "If you'd like to tell me what you'd like in terms of a service, I'd be honored to start working on it."

Rasa cried out again, and covered her face in her hands, Kovarrin's brow furrowed in pain and he nodded to Lauden.

"Thank you. Give us some time to decide, and to discuss with Evaline," he said, looking over at me. "And we will get back to you."

My mind whirled with confusion and anger at the absurdity of their words. I turned to Wyott, and he too had wide eyes. His face paled, as if he never expected this to be the way that this conversation was to go. He turned to me, an apology in his eyes. I knew he'd never have let me come here to talk with them if he'd known this was what would be discussed.

Because this was ludicrous. All of it was.

I shook my head as if it would put all my thoughts in order and then locked eyes with Lauden.

"Pardon me?"

He side eyed Kovarrin, and swallowed, before turning back to me.

"Maddox's funeral services," he said quietly. "Please let me know what you would like me to help with."

Laughter filled the room, and it took me a moment, and several appalled stares thrown my way, before I realized it was me.

My laugh was loud and dry and didn't contain an ounce of humor.

"What the fuck do you mean funeral service?" I shrieked, taking a step off the wall toward Lauden.

Wyott ran to my side in an instant and put a comforting hand on my shoulder. But even he looked to Lauden and Kovarrin in confusion.

Lauden looked to the First, so I swung my head there.

Kovarrin's eyes were pained, almost like the first time I saw him, when he thought that I was my mother. But this was a far deeper pain, and it showed in the bags beneath his eyes.

"Maddox is gone, Evaline," he said softly, and Rasa's hands tightened over her face.

I let out an incredulous scoff. "No, he's not. He's right upstairs," I said, my voice raising again, as I flung my hand up toward the ceiling.

Pain flashed through Kovarrin's eyes again, and Cora moved to my other side to slide her hand into mine and squeeze it.

Kovarrin shook his head slowly. "I know it's been centuries since we've lost a Kova like this, and no one any of you has known," he said, flitting his eyes about the room to meet everyone's. "But when a Kova turns, we hold a funeral service for them, because it is nearly the same as if they'd died."

I shook my head, my eyes feeling as if they'd pop from their sockets with how widely I was opening them in my disbelief. "And what do you do with them, considering they're still breathing?"

Kovarrin looked to the ground. "They don't come back here. This is a first."

Dean spoke up behind us. "We didn't know what else to do. He's the son of the First. We couldn't just leave him."

I turned to Kovarrin again, and this time my voice was low, deadly. "What were you planning on doing with him?"

Kovarrin didn't meet my eyes. "We hadn't figured that out yet."

My entire body started to shake as I pulled away from both Wyott and Cora and took a step toward the First.

"You considered killing him?" I asked.

Kovarrin opened his mouth and lifted his hands as if he didn't know what to do. Tears filled his eyes as he spoke. "I don't know, Evaline. This has never happened. We never *thought* this would happen."

I shook my head and stepped into the middle of the room, spinning about it to look at everyone. At the way Rasa cried, at Lauden's furrowed brows, at Sage's obvious pain, at the four Kova who looked absolutely devastated. Up to Wyott who pursed his lips, his eyes glassy. To Cora, who had tear tracks down her cheeks.

My hands fisted, and I raised them at my sides.

"Am I the only fucking person here who thinks he's still in there?" I asked in disgust. I spun slowly again, looking at all of them. "You've all, already given up hope?"

Maddox's friends looked at me with tears in their eyes, and I turned back to Kovarrin who only shook his head.

"Evaline, you aren't a Kova. You cannot possibly understand. But we all do. We all know the difference. We know about the change. We *fear* the change. And we know it's irreversible."

Rasa cried harder. Cora looked between Rasa and I, then to Wyott, and walked over to comfort the mother. She kneeled beside her and pulled her into her arms.

I looked back up to Kovarrin.

"Have you ever turned?" I asked Kovarrin, my voice mocking. I shrugged. "Except for when you were created, and then lied about it to everyone," I said, my words dripping with venom. "Have you ever changed into a Vasi?"

His eyes clouded with something I couldn't name, and he shook his head.

I whirled around to Dean who was looking at Sage. "Have you?" I asked.

"No," he said softly.

"Grant?" I asked. He shook his head.

"Nash?"

"No."

My eyes slid to Fredrik, but he was already shaking it.

I turned to Wyott, and thought I saw pride in his eyes for a moment. As if he was proud that I refused to give up on Maddox, because I knew he hadn't either. I knew that deep down, he had the same hope I had and that it lived and waited to be nourished. He'd never say the words to me first, because he'd fear I'd get my hopes up if he planted the seed. But if *I* expressed hope, he could too.

And Gods, maybe it wasn't hope at all. Maybe it was blinding denial. But I didn't much care what word was used to name it, only that I felt it.

"No," Wyott said before I even had to ask.

I swung back around to look at Kovarrin.

"Then none of you understand, either. I may be some Sorceress who thought she was a human her whole life," I said, my hands collapsing onto my chest. "But Maddox and I have been abnormal from the start. Nothing has been the way it's supposed to. Maybe this won't be, either. I feel the bond in my head," I said, my voice catching and felt the eyes of every Kova in the room lift to me. "And if I'm the only one who still has hope, then so be it. But I *will* figure out how to change him back."

I started to feel the pressure in my throat build again, knew I would come to tears soon if I didn't take a breath, but I pushed through it and continued.

"I don't care if he's the first to ever turn back," I said, pinning my eyes on Kovarrin. "As a First yourself, I'd think you of all of us would have the most faith. I don't care if it takes me a decade, or two, or three. And I don't care if you all think it's impossible. I know," I said, and my voice cracked. "I know he's still in there. I will get him back, whether you help or not. Whether you believe or not. He is *my* mate," I said through a gasp as my breaths came faster. "And *I* didn't have enough time with him." My face was twisted in anger, but the tears crumpled it in a second.

Wyott's hand rested on my back. "You know I'll do whatever I can, Evaline. He's my brother."

Cora nodded from the other side of the room. "Me too."

"I will do whatever it takes to bring him back and hope he doesn't murder me afterwards for not stopping it in the first place," Fredrik said.

Grant nodded as Nash spoke. "Me too."

"I'll do whatever I can to make sure you get your lifetime with him," Dean said, his eyes dropping to the ground. "A mate shouldn't be without their other half."

Sage swallowed loudly, and I looked up to her.

"Me too," she said softly, and Lauden nodded.

We all looked to the head of the room, to the First and his wife.

Kovarrin pursed his lips.

"Rasa and I will mourn our son," he said, looking over us, sad. "I appreciate your hope, but I cannot dangle it in front of her when I do not think it possible. The Gods have laws for a reason." He took a deep breath. "We will keep him in the room he's in now. He will be a prisoner."

CHAPTER FIFTY-THREE

Evaline

My mother hadn't visited me in a dream since she'd told me about my curse, but as soon as I saw the clearing, I knew she'd appear soon.

But for now, I was in her body. As I always was when I entered this dream. Except this time, it wasn't Kovarrin standing before us, it was Vasier again.

He didn't have his hands around her throat, but he was screaming at her. Pain twisted his face. He was shouting and waving his arms and his eyes were wild with rage and fear and pain. I couldn't tell what he was shouting. But he was enraged, and I watched as he reached for her and slid both hands around her throat.

As his hands made contact, he dissipated into nothing and the darkness crept in around me. The shadows murmured and while I knew I always heard them hum in my dreams with her, I recalled that the shadows behaved in a similar way when I dreamt about hearing Maddox on the beaches of Merwinan.

"Evaline," my mother's soft voice pulled me from my thoughts.

There was pity in it. I turned around to face her and shook my head.

"How did you know?" I asked as the tears came.

She pursed her lips and clasped her hands in front of her. "I'm linked to you. Sometimes I'm able to watch over you even if I'm not trying to actively reach out. Especially in times of great stress." Her eyes moved down to my hands. "Is your wrist okay?"

I nodded. "It's healed."

She raised her eyes to look at mine again. "I'm so sorry for your loss," she whispered.

I gave an exasperated groan and stomped my foot. "Gods, I wish everyone would stop acting like he was dead." I shook my head. "You of all people should have hope that I can bring him back. You *created* them for Gods' sake."

Her eyes widened and she stepped toward me, her hands wringing. "What do you mean?"

"He's still in there," I said incredulously. "I know he is. I can still feel the bond. He's not gone. He's just unable to reach back."

Her lips pursed and she took another step toward me. "Evaline, it's not the same."

A chilling cackle ripped from my throat. "You brought two men back from the *dead*, yet you tell me it's impossible to simply change one immortal being back into his original form?"

She took another step and nodded. "Yes, that is what I'm saying. The Gods were strict when it came to putting the laws on the Vasi. Once they are changed, they cannot be changed back. Their soul is never the same. They're marred for life."

I dragged a hand over my face and shook my head. "That makes no sense. If the Gods want me to destroy Vasier and the pain the Vasi have caused, why in the name of the Gods would they make it impossible to turn them back?"

Her mouth tipped into a frown. "It's the consequence for their abuse of their power."

My hands fisted at my sides. "I thought of all people you would understand what this felt like." Tears welled in my eyes and blurred the sympathetic expression on her face. "That someone I love has changed in a way that everyone else finds impossible to recover from. That the only thing I can focus on to keep the pain at bay is the knowledge that I will bring him back to me. That I will never let him go. I felt what you felt when Kovarrin died." I pointed my finger at her. "You felt the pain, the loss, the guilt. It's all the same for me. You did what you had to do to bring him back." I caught my breath. "I won't stop until I can do the same."

Her expression was thoughtful for a moment as she stayed silent, and then slowly, a smile spread across her face.

"You're right." She grabbed my hand. "You're absolutely right. I'm sorry that I doubted it, doubted you. But I used illegal magic to bring him back. And you cannot do that. You're already bearing one curse, you can't afford another."

I swallowed and she led us to sit.

"Luckily for us," she started. "You have more resources at your disposal." She cocked her head. "More resources allowed by the Gods, I should say."

I furrowed my brows. "My different gifts?"

She smiled and nodded. "I've only told you about three of the Gods gifts, and you need to know the rest." She met my eyes. "Are you ready for that?"

I took a deep breath. "You're right, I need everything in my arsenal to bring him back. So yes, I'm ready."

"The Gods each gave you a gift. I never mentioned Fire before from Kembertic, but I know you've used it, too. Outside of the elements, you have abilities that no other Sorcerer will ever have." I nodded. "Vestari, she gave you her abilities; strength, speed, and battle instincts. It's why you're faster and stronger than humans, and nearly as fast and strong as the Kova."

The pirate ship, the ability to know where everyone was—friend or foe—had been more than just the capabilities my father taught me. That was a reflex from Vestari.

"Neomaeries gave you the gift of her moonlight."

"Is that why whenever I use my magic, my eyes glow?"

She laughed. "No, they don't glow every time you use your magic, just when you need the light in the darkness. Rominiava—" She started but I cut her off.

"Gave me a mate even though normally only Kova have mates, right?" I guessed, but she shook her head.

"No, you're mates with Maddox because you were both fated to each other. That's outside of the gift she gave you. She granted you the ability to utilize the bond in a way that Kova cannot. You can use it just like they do, communicate with your mate, send him your feelings or things that you want him to see. But you can also send him strength through the bond. If you two are close enough, you can siphon energy to him."

I straightened at that. "Do you think that would help him now?"

She pursed her lips. "I don't know. You said you can still feel the bond?"

I nodded. "It's quiet, but it's there."

She looked down in thought for a moment, then looked back up. "If you think it's there, sending him strength might help. But if the Vasi senses that, and Maddox is still in there, he might lock Maddox away or reject him completely. You have to be careful."

I nodded and took a deep breath.

"That just leaves Mortitheos," I said, my voice quiet. I was afraid of what the God of Night might've gifted me. Afraid that he was the reason I didn't feel shame or guilt about killing evil men or Vasi. Afraid that he was the darkness that lurked inside of me. Afraid that no matter how loved or accepted or happy I felt in Rominia with my new family, that the light would never find its way back in again.

"Mortitheos gave you perhaps your most unique and important gift," she said, reaching forward and taking both of my hands in hers. "He gave you the ability to pass through the veil into the Night."

I felt the warmth leave my face. "What?"

She nodded. "You can allow others to pass through to you, into the world of the living. And you can pass through to the Night."

Chapter Fifty-Four

Maddox

It felt as if I'd been asleep for days, but it could've been only hours, or minutes. Time shifted strangely here, and for most of it I had no idea what was going on in the world around me.

It became quickly evident that I couldn't see out of my own eyes, of my own volition. The Vasi had control of that, and he only showed me what he wanted me to see. Only let me listen to what he wanted me to hear.

Otherwise, I was locked in the depths of my mind in a black cell, day in and day out.

But the world filtered in now, and I watched from within as he turned toward the door, and I saw her.

Every cell in my body—or at least the part of me that sat in my own mind—lit on fire at her presence. I didn't dare blink, I didn't want to miss a second of seeing her. Gods knew how long it had been since the Vasi had crushed her wrist, or if she had any hope for me at all.

Wyott was with her and I thanked the Gods for it. If I couldn't be with her, to comfort and protect her, he and Cora were the ones I'd want to be.

I tried to reach forward but, still, what felt like chains on my wrists held me in place. I settled back, not wanting to cause any kind of commotion for fear that the Vasi would lock me away again. I wanted to see every second of her that I could, to gain every piece of knowledge that I could.

The Vasi rolled our eyes. "Thank fuck. I've been wondering when you two would come back."

He kept our eyes on them as they walked closer, and I felt myself nodding in pride as Wyott took a protective step in front of her.

"I'm starving," the Vasi said, and then lowered our eyes to the vein that pulsed just below the soft skin of her neck.

It was only after he'd said it that I realized I could tell. I could feel every part of my body—my real body, not just this mental part of me in my head—as if I still controlled it. Maybe he allowed me to feel it, maybe he didn't have a choice in that matter, but I could. I could feel the fatigue pulling at our muscles and how slow our heart beat through our chest.

For a moment I considered whether that fatigue would weigh on his control over me, but I didn't dare give more than a second's thought to it. I still wasn't sure how much of my thoughts he had access to. I'd slowly been starting to build up walls to keep him out, but I had no idea if they worked or not.

We didn't exactly receive training on what to do if we turned. But I tried to use the skills I had at my disposal, so I treated this mental connection I had with the Vasi like I did the bond with Evaline. To block him from hearing my thoughts or feelings, I created walls similar to how I would to block thoughts from going down the bond to Evaline. Gods knew if it was working.

Evaline turned to Wyott, and we watched as confusion pulled at her brows.

Wyott turned to her, but kept his gaze on us.

"It appears that Maddox's inability to drink from anyone but you has remained through the transformation."

She shuddered at the information, and I knew why. She was imagining the Vasi feeding from her, in my body. It took every ounce of will I still wielded over my own mind not to rush forward toward her, as if I could protect her. But she still stood at the end of that internal tunnel as he kept me at a distance.

Wyott turned to her, likely hearing the uptick in her heart rate, and reached a hand out to her elbow.

"We're going to figure something out, it'll be okay."

She only nodded and settled her gaze on us. Her eyes flicked to the upgrades that had been made to the crafting of the chair the Vasi and I were imprisoned in.

Inside, I swallowed at the memory of Otto here, making the additions. The way his gray eyes saddened the longer he stayed, each time he looked into the red eyes.

Mine and the Vasi's hands were no longer visible. Two sphered shields of Rominium had been welded to arch over them. A new Rominium bar stretched across our chest, and another over our neck. All repercussions of the harm we'd done, to Evaline, and to a Kova guard who came too close.

The Vasi hadn't shown me all of that, only the aftermath. The blood.

She took a step closer and stood directly in front of us, and I had to bear down on my guilt at the sight of her.

She looked so sad. Her skin wasn't as bright as it normally was and there were dark bags beneath her eyes. Luckily, those seemed to be the only discrepancies in her physical state. But in her eyes, I could see the sadness that enveloped her every time she looked at me.

Evaline hadn't met our eyes yet, and I knew she must be scared to. But now they slowly rose until they met ours, and she cringed.

"Expecting someone else?" the Vasi asked with a smirk.

She didn't respond, only straightened her spine and clasped her hands in front of her. She opened her mouth, but no words came out.

A moment of silence passed, and Wyott spoke for her.

"What is your name?" he asked, and I watched as my brother locked down his expression.

The Vasi let out a cackle. "Are you serious?"

Dread sank through my gut but Evaline and Wyott only looked to each other before facing us again.

The Vasi rolled his eyes. "My name is Maddox Vicor. I am the son of the First Kova, and a son of the First Vasi," he hissed the last part.

Evaline's face paled, her heart skipped, and the Vasi swung our eyes to her.

"You expected different?" He sighed in annoyance. "Actually, no. I understand. You're so young, have only just been brought into this world of immortals. Or at least, more than you ever were before. You not understanding, that makes sense." His eyes switched to Wyott's. "You not understanding, that's the bullshit."

Wyott's brow twitched to furrow, but he recovered to his blank expression.

"You've been raised to understand what the change means. That it breaks our souls until we are changed forever." The Vasi looked between the both of them now. "I'm still Maddox. I'm the same motherfucker you both know." He smiled. "Only improved. That pesky conscience? Gone. Emotions? None left. Love?" His eyes settled on Evaline. "As dead as that bond of ours."

My will had waned until he said those words, that lie. That I was gone, that he was me.

I lunged forward against the shackles, my fangs lashing out and my bones screaming in protest against the chains.

Liar! I growled at him.

I didn't care if he hid me away again. I didn't care if he turned off my ability to see Evaline for the rest of the day. He was a liar and I wanted Evaline to see that. I wanted to scream and fight and push until she could see me. Whether she saw my gray eyes through his, or if he'd just give a glazed expression like Kova did when they talked to mates. I didn't care the mechanism, only that she saw. That she understood that this was a Gods-damned lie.

Maybe. His cool, low voice drifted in. *But they'll never know.*

I fought with everything I had, but could only watch as Evaline's jaw ticked with the effort of clenching it. The move was one I knew from her.

Anger. She didn't see me.

"But don't worry, Eva," the Vasi whispered. "I remember every moment."

I screamed inside, thrashed. I knew deep down that this was exactly what he wanted, to torture me. But I couldn't help it.

Wyott stepped in front of her so that she had to look around his shoulder to see us.

"You have all his memories?" he asked.

The Vasi let out an exasperated sigh. "Yes. I am him. He is me. What don't you understand about that?"

"Well fucking pardon me if I don't know the ins and outs of being a Vasi, I've never been one, you fuck," Wyott growled back.

That got a smile out of the Vasi. "Mmm. Your fuse is thin. Maybe you'll join me someday."

Wyott began to move as Evaline shot around him and pushed him away.

The Vasi reached forward as far as he could against the bars over our neck and chest. "Don't feel bad. It didn't take much for me to blow, either."

Wyott's chest heaved with fury and I shrieked inside. Begged them to hear me.

It was hard to watch Wyott react, to become enraged. After knowing everything he'd suffered, to know that losing me was added to that list, it was hard to ponder on too long without the guilt ravaging me.

I'd made the biggest mistake of my existence, and it'd hurt so many people.

"What did you expect?" the Vasi continued. "You thought you'd come in here and realize that he could still be saved?"

Yes! I screamed. *I'm here!*

The Vasi only continued as if I hadn't spoken in his head. "She might be naive enough to believe that, but you," Wyott's eyes blazed as he made eye contact with the Vasi, and I knew every moment he saw the red of our eyes, he boiled hotter. "You're smarter than that. We were raised—"

Wyott cut him off. "Stop saying 'we' like you know me or I know you."

My screams stopped as I listened to my brother speak. I hoped he understood the truth.

"You are not him. You are *not* my brother."

Yes! Wyott, yes! I yelled.

"You may wear his face, but you are not him."

Evaline pushed harder against Wyott's chest to force him back, but I only smiled against the tears that flooded down my face.

He knew. He understood. He had hope.

"Stop," Evaline said to him, her voice hard.

He looked down at her, and cringed at whatever expression he saw on her face. He took a deep breath and pulled back. Evaline moved so they both stood beside one another and stared at the Vasi. She crossed her arms, and leveled her gaze with ours.

"I'm hungry," he said. "I need to feed soon."

I shook my head violently. I knew what he wanted.

Evaline only shrugged. "We all have needs that aren't being met right now."

The Vasi's interest piqued at that and a smile spread across our face as he swept our gaze down her body. "I'm happy to help with that need." He paused, bringing our eyes up slowly until they met hers again. "My Goddess."

At the same moment that pain flashed across her features, I leaped so hard against the shackles that I wondered if my wrists would break.

The Vasi made sure to show me everything he wanted to do with her. Every part of her body that he pulled from my memories, that he planned to touch one day. The places he'd like to feed from, and none of them could be seen with any of her clothes on.

I screamed and growled and wept against the images that flashed past. I felt the way he enjoyed it. He loved every desperate sob I released and lunge I made.

"You know that's not what I meant," Evaline said, but her voice gave her away.

She was hurt by his words. The Vasi smirked and showed no sign of distraction as I raged inside.

"You'll change your mind soon enough," he said. "Soon, you'll realize that he's never coming back, and that I am better than nothing. And I'm happy to play that role for you."

"Snide remarks won't get you far if you're looking to eat," she snapped.

The Vasi cringed. "Yes, it does appear that I am at the behest of you all." He sighed heavily and his scowl fell. "What do you want to know?"

Her eyes widened for a moment, and I knew she was surprised by the change in his demeanor. When she didn't speak after another moment, he did.

"Evaline, you need to understand that you will never get him back. That version of him—of me—that you knew is gone."

No! I'm right here, Eva. Please, I yelled, but she only swallowed as he continued.

"Your only options are to free me, or kill me. If you free me, we can go back to Mortithev together. We can be together, more than you and the Maddox you knew ever will be again. We can help Vasier." I pulled against the shackles, screamed and cried, but he only continued. "Or you can kill me, but he will come and get you regardless, and thousands will die. So really," he said softly. "It sounds like you only have one option."

She clenched her jaw. "What does Vasier want with me?"

The Vasi narrowed our eyes at her. "Do you really think that he would send me into enemy territory, *bound,*" he barked, "with that information?" He rolled our eyes. "Of course the first thing you would do is try and torture it out of me. Why would he ever risk giving me that information?"

Wyott's brows raised. "You don't know?"

"I only know that he wants you," he said, eyes still on Evaline.

She gave us a long look. "Even if the two of us did leave," she started and Wyott snapped his head to look at her. "You couldn't be free. You'd kill me."

The Vasi rolled our head back in annoyance. "I'm not some beast who's unable to think critically. Or take orders, for that matter. If Vasier wants you, then I won't kill you. I don't have to know his motive in order to not kill you. I also don't need a reason other than I'm not supposed to kill you, to not kill you. We aren't feral animals. You've been taught a lie. We're beings just like you," he said, shifting our eyes to Wyott. "We just don't squander our ambitions with morality. We are more free than you will ever be."

Wyott looked down and let his eyes fall to every part of our body that bars held us back.

"You know what I fucking meant," the Vasi growled.

Wyott ignored him and took a step forward. "If you're in control of your urges, then why did you shatter her wrist when you saw her?"

The Vasi pulled our lips into a sick smile. "Like I said, I'm in control of my urges. If I break her wrist, it's because I want to. You have me locked up in a chair, unable to move, to change clothes, or to feed. Day in and day out. I'm starving on top of it, so yes, I might've had a little fun. After all," he said, swinging our eyes to Evaline. "She's the reason I'm even locked up here in the first place."

Wyott scoffed. "And you expect her to trust you after that confession?"

The Vasi looked up at Wyott, eyes half lidded. "She's healed, isn't she? No harm done. Maybe there was a little pain, but she's no stranger to that." He shrugged. "Besides, pain will build her into a better Sorceress, a better weapon, for when Vasier gets his hands on her."

Wyott cocked his head. "So you do know why Vasier wants her."

The Vasi sighed. "No, you idiot. It's just not a leap to deduce that he clearly plans to utilize her repertoire of magic in some fashion."

I'd grown tired of fighting, and slumped back against my restraints when Evaline stepped forward, past Wyott, and bent to look into our eyes.

The Vasi looked right back at her, but I knew what she was looking for.

I jumped forward, I lunged, I pulled.

I screamed, I shrieked, I roared.

Eva! Please Eva. I'm here. See me, hear me!

She stared back and after a few breaths, the Vasi spoke.

"What are you looking for, love?" he asked with a smirk.

She continued to search.

"You're only going to keep hurting yourself, coming in here and trying to discover what we both know you're not going to find."

He's lying! I screamed. I searched for the bond, wanted to yell down it, but it was gone. My tie to her was gone.

"He's gone," the Vasi whispered.

Her eyes hardened and she pulled away.

No. Please, no Eva.

She was giving up on me. Giving up hope.

Don't leave me here.

Chapter Fifty-Five

Wyott

"Are you okay?" I asked, turning toward Evaline as we walked out of the mansion.

She gave a slight nod. "I…" she started but then trailed off. "I don't know what I was expecting. I guess I hoped I would look into his eyes and deep down see that they were gray, to know that he's still in there." She shook her head. "But it's okay, because I can still feel the bond. He's still in there," she affirmed, then looked up at me as we walked down the front stairs of the mansion. "Are you okay?"

I gave a dry laugh. "Not really," I said. "But we're all in this together, so we're going to keep each other from going under."

She swallowed and nodded.

Kovarrin and Rasa hadn't tried to keep Maddox's change a secret, and after Evaline's display of magic it would've been impossible to do so anyway. News of the turn quickly disseminated through the kingdom, so when I reached out to some of the Elders this morning, the oldest Kova that were friends with Kovarrin and Rasa, and asked them to meet, they already knew what we'd be discussing.

Evaline and I approached the training center and walked through the training area toward the lofted meeting room.

I could hear Evaline's heartbeat race in her chest as we walked, and I saw a few heads turn to look at her. Nash stood near the entrance, and I gave him a look. He nodded in understanding, and started shuffling the few Kova that were there out of the building.

I didn't want an audience for the conversation we were about to have with the Elders. What was happening to Maddox was profoundly personal, and he deserved as much privacy as I could give him.

The facility was cleared out as Evaline and I ascended the stairs. When the table came into view I saw that all six available Elders that I'd summoned were here.

The group was spread out on the different benches and chairs, and Evaline and I sat in the last two chairs and closed the loop.

"I wanted to thank you all for coming," I started. "I know that none of you have likely met Evaline personally, but this is Evaline Manor, and as Kovarrin said at the Ball, her mother is the Sorceress who created the Kova."

Foster leaned forward. "And the Vasi."

I saw Evaline flinch.

"Don't be a prick, Foster," Marcus said, and then turned to Evaline. "Sorry about him. He's had one too many run-ins with the Vasi. He's not their biggest fan."

Evaline's brows rose. "Neither am I."

"What is it that you need from us?" Penny said, looking between Evaline and I. "We've heard that no service is set yet for Maddox, and that he's still locked up in the mansion."

Evaline cleared her throat. "We haven't given up hope yet." She ran her hands over her thighs. "I can still feel the bond. He's still in there."

Penny's expression fell into one of pity and I feared what she was going to say.

"Evaline, it will feel that way for quite some time." She tilted her head, brows furrowed. "I lost my mate centuries ago." She paused to take a deep breath and gather herself. "Not as a Vasi, but he passed. And for decades, I could still feel the bond as if he was sleeping right next to me." She clasped her hands in her lap. "So whatever it is you're feeling, it might just be the after effects of the bond. After it establishes between the two of you, it takes a lot to remove it. More than their death." Her lips pursed. "Or their change."

I knew Evaline didn't want to be disrespectful and argue, she only clenched her jaw and gave a slow nod.

"Thank you. I'm sorry for your loss."

Penny gave her a sad smile. "I'm sorry for yours."

Evaline swallowed at that and I heard the way her breath shook.

"While you may disagree with us, or with Kovarrin." Barry said from my right. "He's not wrong. You young ones haven't seen anyone turn before, or known anyone who has." He shrugged. "Until now. But a lot of us have. We've seen several of our friends fall to the temptation of the Vasi, or be forcibly changed by the Vasi. And even for them, who never made the decision themselves to drain a human, they never came back. I don't mean to be harsh," he said, his light gray eyes softening. "But it's best that you just grieve. Let him go. The Maddox you knew is gone."

"And get that Vasi out of our kingdom," Foster spat and Marcus rolled his eyes.

"There are no resources on anyone that's come back? You don't know of anyone who reversed it, ever?" I pressed and looked around the room.

They all had signs of sadness on their faces. Downturned lips, furrowed brows, or glassy eyes. All except Foster, who just looked bored.

There was a collective "No." from all of them.

"That can't be done," Penny said, sitting forward. "It is best just to mourn." She looked to Evaline. "I wish I could say that it gets easier, but grief isn't a straight path."

Evaline's gaze was on the floor as she spoke. "Yes, I'm familiar."

"Do any of you have any books, resources we could look through, just in case?"

Evaline already planned to go through all the books in the mansion, but it couldn't hurt to ask if they had any lying around at home, too.

They all denied and claimed they'd donated their collections to the library of the Arch Sorcerer decades ago, and I thanked them for their time, even if it had only been disheartening.

Evaline was quiet on our exit from the facility.

"What are you thinking?" I asked as we hiked up the hill to the First's Estate.

She looked up at me with watery eyes.

"What if it's nothing? I mean what if Penny is right and this is just some odd echo of the bond in my mind?" She stopped walking and turned to face me. "Wyott, I don't even remember what it felt like to be alone in my head, to not have the bond beating in it. What if I'm just misinterpreting? What if all it is, is an empty link? That I could call down for the rest of my life and never receive an answer?"

I paused, I didn't want to respond right away. I didn't know what to do. Everything in me wanted my brother to come back, but I didn't want Evaline to waste her life trying to do so. If she wanted to grieve, if she needed to in order to get through this, then I needed to let her. I couldn't stoke her hope if it was not what was best for her.

But the silence seemed to give Evaline the space to consider her words on her own, because she spoke before I could.

"No, it's fine," she said, waving her hands between us. "Maybe Penny's bond is gone, but mine's not. I am Evaline Manor, I am the daughter of the Creator." She huffed out a breath and squared her shoulders. "And Maddox is the son of the First. If anyone has the ability to change him back, it's me. And if any Kova has it in them to come back, it's him. He's still in there."

I wasn't sure who she was trying to convince. She turned and started walking back up the hill.

"The answer is hiding somewhere on this island, in one of these books. Or at least a clue for how we can find the answer. And I'm going to find it."

We spent the rest of the day going through texts in the mansion. We started in Kovarrin's study, but that proved inefficient. Neither of us could focus with him giving his disapproval every few minutes. Finally, I helped her carry several books up to hers and Maddox's suite. At least that way she could sprawl out at the dining table.

After night fell, I stood.

"You need to go to sleep."

She was squinting down at a page. I don't think she realized that it was completely dark outside, or that it was rather dark in the room. She'd only lowered her head toward the book to read in the dim light. She didn't even have a lantern, only the soft glow of the fire on the other side of the room.

"Take a break, Evaline. That can't be good for your eyes."

She jumped up at her name, not having realized that I was speaking to her.

"What?" she asked.

"It's dark." I waved my finger at how close she'd been sitting to the books. "That can't possibly be good for your eyes. You need to go to sleep and get some rest."

She nodded and walked from the room.

I moved to the door and opened it, then turned back. "I'll be back tomorrow to help." I called.

"Sounds good," she said, and while I hoped she'd start getting ready for bed, instead I watched as she returned to the table with a lit lantern in her hand.

Cora and I arrived home at the same time. She wanted to be there for Evaline as much as she could, but she couldn't neglect her role at the marina. Especially not now when it seemed that war was on the horizon. Vasier had taken direct action at Kovarrin, and there was nothing he could do in response but wage war for his son. He just had to give the order.

Cora and I ate dinner then prepared for bed, and when we slipped under the covers we both turned on our sides to look at each other.

I rested my hand on the crest of her hip, and she rested hers on my bare chest.

"How is she?" she asked.

I relayed what had happened with the Elders and the hope on her face fell.

"So Penny thinks that feeling the bond is just a fluke?" she asked.

I nodded.

"Gods-dammit," she whispered under her breath.

It had been the only hope that several of us were holding onto. Since the moment Evaline claimed she could feel the bond in Kovarrin's study, it seemed possible that he could be in the Vasi, tucked away somewhere.

Because if the bond wasn't still alive, if what Penny said was true, then all of this was hopeless, my brother really was gone forever, and Vasier had taken someone else I loved.

Chapter Fifty-Six

Evaline

It wasn't until I heard the birds chirping outside that I realized I'd read through the night.

My back was to the window, and my head was angled down to the page I was reading, so I never noticed the change in light around me.

I straightened and felt the immediate resistance up my spine, tight from too many hours spent bent over a book.

"Fuck," I groaned as I pulled myself away from the table.

It had been like this all week. After the Elders had essentially dashed all hope, I vowed to prove them all wrong. My family had done things no one deemed possible before, and there was no reason I couldn't do the same.

Wyott had helped me research that first day, and the second. In the last week I'd locked myself in this mansion to study and he, Cora, and Rasa had come through to help occasionally. But none of them saw how late I stayed up, or how many books I was getting through all on my own.

It hadn't taken long for Rasa to come around. After a couple days, her initial sorrow for Maddox changed and she disregarded Kovarrin. She became just as determined as the rest of our family to bring Maddox back.

"Until his eyes close, forever. Red or gray, he will be my son. And we will get him back." She'd told me the first day she'd come to help me read through the texts.

Now, I placed the heel of my hands against the edge of the tabletop and pressed deeper into the wooden chair I sat in. I stretched my upper body back over the top of the backrest and tried to elongate my spine as best I could. As I did, a symphony of pops sounded through it.

One particularly hard crack took my breath away for a moment and I sat there, mouth agape, eyes wide, trying to catch my breath.

"Okay," I gasped, pushing away from the table. "Okay, that was too much," I said, moving to the rug that spread on the ground in front of the fireplace. "That was scary." I continued to mumble as I lowered myself to press my back into the floor. I stretched my arms above me and pointed my toes.

My head rolled to the side to look at the fireplace. The embers still snapped but the flames had died out. I kept my eyes on it and instructed my magic to relight the logs. After a moment, there was nothing. I furrowed my brows, wondering why my magic wasn't listening today, but after another breath the fire slowly grew in size until the warmth of its heat hit my cheeks.

I sighed and turned back to lay flat and stare at the ceiling.

It only took a moment for the tears to start. I'd spent so much time this last week absorbing new information, that I hadn't given myself time to ache for my loss. Despite the hope that I so desperately tried to cling to, I still found myself in pain. Whether Maddox came back to me someday, and Gods knew I was doing everything I could to find an answer for him, right now I was experiencing his loss.

And the only way I could survive it, was to solve it. Instead of sitting with my pain, I redirected it. I repurposed it until it wasn't pain, but determination. Until it didn't hurt, but it fueled. Until an entire week had passed, and I'd nearly finished reading every book this castle had to offer. The Kova who helped read could do so at an outrageous speed, and between the four of us, we'd almost covered all the texts here. Especially because previously Rasa spent so much of her time restoring texts, and the ink was fresh and clear on the pages.

I lifted my head to look at Maddox's shelves that stretched high in front of me.

Fuck.

I kept forgetting about those, because he'd said they were mostly romance. But I knew I needed to check, just to cover every possible avenue.

My head fell again, and I blinked away my tears.

"Okay, Evaline," I whispered to myself. "Get up, and get at it."

Despite the fact that I was racing through these books as fast as I could, they were an absolute fucking bore. Half of them were island statistics throughout the centuries. Some of them were histories of the Kova, which were interesting, but others were information about the plants on the island, the farms, or the rocks.

It wasn't fun to read them, and I wasn't enjoying myself. But I had a problem to solve, and right now that meant suffering through every book I could possibly find here.

Sometimes late at night, if I bothered to pay attention to what time it was, I'd go upstairs to sit outside Wyott's old room, where the Vasi sat.

Whoever was guarding the door would give me some privacy for a bit, and I'd sit and read there. But as soon as the guard left, I'd clench my eyes shut and try to use the bond in the way Rominiava gave me the ability to. I tried to shove power down the bond, to send my magic and my strength and my Gods-damned will, but each time it was only met by a wall. A barrier that I could nearly feel my magic slam into, before it retreated back to me.

Each time, a piece of my hope faded at that. Because every time I hit that block, I feared that it was because Penny was right; that he was gone, and this bond was broken. That I'd just be the last to know for sure.

A knock at the door jolted me from my thoughts and I sat up.

"Coming!" I called, then cursed myself. This sound-proof suite had been my home for over a month now and I still hadn't grown used to it.

I lifted my knee to plant a foot on the ground as Rasa cracked the door open. "Eval—" she called, but immediately saw me in the crack of the door. "Oh," she said, opening it the rest of the way with a small smile on her face.

It wasn't the normal, bright and warm smile she used to have. It hadn't been since Maddox changed.

"Hi Rasa," I said, pushing off my foot to rise from the ground.

Darkness encroached from the edges of my vision at the same time that my head went light, and I started to topple sideways.

"Gods!" Rasa exclaimed just as I felt her arms around me. "Evaline, when was the last time you drank any water?"

She righted me and pulled me to the chaise. I felt the cushion below me as she sank both of us down onto it.

My vision finally cleared, and I saw her wide eyes scanning my face.

"When's the last time you ate?" she asked, then reached her hand up to drag a thumb below my eye. "Or slept?"

I opened my mouth to tell her, but then realized that I couldn't recall. Not any of them.

Her eyes narrowed as my mouth closed, and she shook her head in disapproval.

"Evaline you cannot run yourself into the ground like this," she said, raising her hand to smooth the hair from my face.

"Nothing else matters right now, except finding an answer," I said, though I was starting to feel the fatigue set in.

She clicked her tongue. "Maddox would disagree." She lowered her hands to my lap and took mine in hers. "You cannot help him if you are not taking care of yourself. You need to eat, and sleep. You need to change clothes, and go outside." I opened my mouth to argue, but she shot me a look and my teeth clashed as I snapped my jaw shut. She straightened and looked around the room then, and must've found what she was looking for because she stood. "You drink this." I heard water being poured. "And I'm going to get you a bath started, and some food. Then, you're going to sleep." She came back and handed me the glass.

"I'm fine, really," I said, pulling the glass from her hand.

"No, you're not," she said. "And don't think that just because you're an adult, that you're past being parented. Now drink."

CHAPTER FIFTY-SEVEN

Maddox

Every moment spent in the cell within the depths of my mind was spent seeking a way out. No matter how long I'd been stuck in here, whether it was days or weeks. I'd spent each moment searching for a way out.

I'd been testing out the walls I'd built against the Vasi. I put the wall up, and then asked him questions. Always things I knew he'd answer if he heard me.

Will I be stuck here forever?

If they let you out, would you kill her?

Does every Kova stay locked in the mind of the Vasi they're in?

He would answer the first two questions, if he'd heard them, because he'd taken every opportunity thus far to torture me with the way he treated Evaline. He'd play images for me of what he wanted to do to her. Images of him feeding, of him inside of her, of her loving it.

I knew he wouldn't answer the final question because he wouldn't know the answer, but he seemed annoyed enough that everyone kept treating him like he was some new being instead of just being me, and I knew he would correct me on it.

But he didn't answer any of my questions, so I felt confident that my barrier against him was working.

I spent some time doing the best I could to poke around and try to feel out his mind, just as I would if I was using my bond with Evaline. He and I had some connection, it was how I heard him and how he showed me all the vile things he wanted to.

I wanted to understand what made him tick, and whether he truly didn't have any emotions or anyone he cared about.

But I was pulled from my attempts when he opened the tunnel he kept me down and let me watch as my mother came into the room.

I swallowed.

I hadn't seen her since before I left for Merwinan, and didn't know what to expect when she walked in front of me. I feared what she may look like, whether she was eating, if she'd already given up hope.

Wyott and I had never known anyone that had changed, but my parents had. And each time they recounted the stories, they told us how the Kova treated the change as a death. They mourned their loss, and they had a funeral service with no body.

But all I felt was pride in my chest as she stopped in front of us, looking as healthy as ever. She crossed her arms across her chest and leveled her gaze with the Vasi. She cringed at the sight of the red eyes, but recovered just as quickly.

"Maddox," she started, and the Vasi grinned.

"Yes, Mother?" he asked.

She gave one shake of her head. "No, you're not the one I'm speaking to. Maddox," she repeated. "You need to know that Evaline will not stop until she has you back. Until she brings you home to us."

Her brows furrowed but her eye contact with us did not falter.

"We are all helping her in whatever capacity we can, but you have to do your part, too. You have to fight for your mind back, for her, for us. She won't stop. She's not really sleeping, or eating. She won't go train, she won't leave the house." Her eyes searched both of ours. "She will run herself into the ground to bring you back. I only hope that you are willing to do the same."

Thank the Gods my wall was already up and standing against the Vasi, because as my mother said the words, all I felt was determination. A will to survive, to get back to Evaline, to all of them. No matter how long it took, no matter how much I had to fight.

The Vasi rolled his head to the side. "Are you done?"

"I love you, Maddox. You'll always be my son. I will always love you." She took a shaky breath to steady herself.

I love you, Mama, I tried to say to her, but of course, there was nothing.

"And if you're not in there, if I'll never see you again, I will look for you in the Night." Her voice broke and eyes teared at that.

The Vasi took his opportunity.

"Then I hope you are prepared to wait for death."

She left after that and I could feel the way he came near me, through our tether. How he checked to see how I reacted to my mother's words.

So I opened the wall that held me back from him, and let my emotions run through.

Pain. Loss. Guilt at what I had done.

But the emotion that I shoved down the hardest—and that wasn't a complete lie, even if I was only using it to convince the Vasi that I'd given up and wouldn't make attempts to free myself was hopelessness.

The Vasi was asleep.

I had no way of knowing if it was day or night, but he was sleeping.

I could feel the rhythmic rise and fall of our chest, and only now realized that I hadn't noticed that before since he'd taken control.

He must've been attempting to stay awake as long as he could, because that was when he was weakest against blocking me off. Vasi didn't have to sleep often, neither did the Kova, but he must have been up for quite a while.

I could feel his fatigue, feel the ache in our stomach from hunger and the thirst that dried our mouth.

While he was asleep, I wanted to take as much advantage as I could. I moved through the connection between us to learn more about him. I wanted to see if he was dreaming, if any images flashed through his mind.

And there, I saw it. Vasier standing in front of us, the way he looked at us the moment the change occurred. When I'd been locked away and the Vasi sprang forward. I watched the smile that formed on Vasier's face when he saw that, the gleam of pride in his eyes.

And apparently the Vasi was capable of emotion. Of the very one that they always claimed they did not harbor. When he looked in Vasier's eyes, and saw the way he smiled down at his creation, the only emotion that the Vasi felt was love.

CHAPTER FIFTY-EIGHT

Evaline

The next morning I forced myself to finally go back to training. Rasa was right, it wasn't good for my mental or physical health to be hunched over books all day with no rest.

I opened the door to Lauden and Sage's loft. They stood in the kitchen, finishing breakfast, but my eyes immediately wandered to the bookcases lining the walls.

Perhaps I had more than one motivation for coming to train today.

"Good morning Evaline," Sage greeted me from the island countertop she ate at. "How have you been doing?"

My head swung to face her and when I met her eyes, I could see it. Pain.

With everything going on with Maddox, I'd completely forgotten that I wanted to talk to her. To discuss what may have happened in Mortithev. To apologize, for all of it. But I couldn't do it with Lauden around.

After my attack, I didn't want to discuss it with or around men, not until Maddox. Whether Lauden was her partner or not, I feared he wouldn't show the kind of care Maddox had, and I made a note to approach her when she was alone, to let her know that I was here for her if she needed to talk.

But for now, I only gave her a small smile, more for her benefit than my own, and nodded.

"I'm hopeful, Sage. How are you?" It wasn't completely honest. My confidence in our ability to bring Maddox back had started to waver with each book I opened that had nothing to do with the transformation, with every wall my magic hit when I tried to send him strength through the bond, and with each replay of the Vasi's words in my head that had been on a loop since I'd talked to him last week.

He's gone.

Sage pressed her lips into a tight smile and nodded back to me.

"I'm fine," she said, and I saw Lauden's spine straighten slightly. "I'm glad to be home."

Lauden interjected then. "Have you had breakfast yet, Evaline?" he asked, standing and waving to the food still in the pans they'd prepared it in.

"I have, thank you though." Again, I wasn't completely honest. I'd had a cup of tea and most of a pastry. It wasn't enough, and I knew that. But it was all I could manage without an appetite.

Lauden nodded and put his empty plate near the wash basin before guiding me to the worktable.

He turned to me as we stood on either side of the table. "I know it's been a while since you've practiced, or used your magic at all," he said, not meeting my eyes. "What would you like to do today?" He scraped his thumb along a piece of the wood that was poked out from the rest of the tabletop. "Would you like to discuss what happened that day?"

He didn't elaborate, and he didn't need to. He meant the day I found Maddox as a Vasi. The day I used all of my magic—the full strength of it—at the exact same time. It was something I'd never done before, or even come close to doing in training.

He looked up at me and I knew he was trying to gauge my reaction. It reminded me of the way Maddox and Wyott had treated me after we'd fled Kembertus, after I'd killed Bassel. They'd treated me like I was fragile, like I was going to break. I hadn't felt that way then, but I knew that's how everyone saw me right now. How could they not? I literally caused cracks in the ballroom floor that day. Clearly, I wasn't whole. Maddox had done his best, and I'd made my own progress, but our efforts to repair all that was broken in me shattered again the day I saw his red eyes.

But this was different than back then. With Maddox and Wyott it was obvious that they were doing it out of care for me. They were worried, and that was the manifestation of it.

But Lauden, he seemed to be studying me. As if he were making plans and calculations in his mind over what this new magic of mine meant.

I realized he was jealous.

In all our interactions, he'd always been the one in a position of power. He was the Arch Sorcerer. He was the knowledgeable one, he could cast fire.

But so had I.

I'd mastered four elements. In one eruption of anger. Without having to use my hands to manipulate the magic.

It just *existed* outside of my body. It did what I wanted it to, and when my mind didn't give clear instructions, it listened to my emotions.

Lauden's jealousy irritated me.

I thought back to every interaction I'd had with him since I'd seen Maddox's change.

There was only one. Technically, two. He was there when I used all my magic, but I wasn't very aware of him. That night, in Kovarrin's study. He'd studied me then, similar to how he did now, before he started discussing the funeral arrangements for Maddox.

A swathe of heat lit down my arms as I realized that not only had he seemed somewhat disingenuous that day, but that he'd never come back to check on me, or even Rasa and Kovarrin as far as I knew, since Maddox came home.

There could've been a million reasons for his demeanor. He might not know how to act around people experiencing grief, which was fair. He might be angry that Sage was in danger, which was understandable. But my dislike of him made it so Gods-damned hard to give him the benefit of the doubt.

But I'd try.

I took a deep breath and realized it had been a moment since he'd asked, and I still hadn't responded yet. I cleared my throat and gave a slight nod.

"I don't know what there is to talk about besides the fact that you clearly were right. You said that it was anger that would help me harness my fire, that it would help me master it." I shrugged. "That day, I was angry at the Gods and my magic listened."

His brows furrowed at that. "What do you mean it 'listened'?"

I placed my hands on the table, and felt the ridges of the wood under my palms. "I don't know how to explain it further than that. My magic did what I wanted it to, without me ever having to tell it."

He straightened and I heard Sage move behind me as she came to stand at the head of the table to my left, caught in the middle between Lauden and I.

"It's true, then," he murmured. "You used your magic without having to use your hands to guide it? I wondered, but from where we stood and with all the commotion, and Wyott and Cora surrounding you, it was hard to tell."

I hesitated. Just as we hadn't told anyone outside of our family about my Gods gifted magic, I felt like I shouldn't tell them this. But there wasn't much I could do to deny it, there were others there. The other Kova standing beside Sage and Lauden on that patio. They could've seen it.

"Yes," I said. "I didn't use my hands for any of it. That's what I mean about my magic listening. It anticipated my every thought, each emotion."

He stood straight off the table and crossed his arms. "Well, that is something we should watch out for. You should always be in control. *You* should tell your magic what to do, it shouldn't act on its own."

It was hard to describe to him that it wasn't acting on its own. Every move it'd made, I wanted. I'd just never had to give the command. I wanted to show the Gods how angry I was. I hoped they saw it, heard it, from the heavens. I wanted Maddox to feel the way the land shook and the way the wind screeched. If he was deep down in there, I wanted him to know how angry I was. And on some level, I think I assumed Vasier had eyes on me. Whether he could see me, or he had minions on the water, or in Merwinan, or anywhere close enough that they'd be able to feel the effects of what I'd done. I wanted him to know how angry I was, so that he'd be afraid when I came after him.

It was only now that I realized that may have been a mistake. If Vasier wanted me for my magic, then showing that extravagant display of the damage it could do seemed ill advised. But I hadn't been thinking all of my actions through, then. I was only reacting.

"You're right," I said to Lauden. "I need to focus on keeping control of it in those moments of rage."

I spoke the words as if the rage was past tense, but it wasn't. It lived inside of me, breathed with each pump of my lungs and only quieted when I focused on the hope I had for Maddox's return.

And since that was wavering, it meant that I spent more and more of each day living in that anger.

Fear crept up my throat as I realized that perhaps I didn't have as much control over my magic as I thought I did. Maybe my magic seemed as if it intuited my moves, because that day each move I made was based on emotion.

Lauden seemed to understand this realization, because he nodded at me then. "I think we should postpone further exercises of your fire. In the meantime I'll do my research on other Sorcerers who've been able to wield without using their hands," he said, nodding his head behind him toward his shelves of books. "And you can focus on some of the other less damaging elements."

"Of course." I nodded, that made sense. "But I would like to stay and utilize your library as well."

Sage straightened to my left and Lauden cocked his head. "For what?"

Of course he knew.

"For information on the transformation," I said.

He pressed his teeth into a smile. "Today's not a good day," he said, half turning toward the bookshelves behind him. "I think your time right now is better spent working on—"

"I understand where my time is spent best, better than you do." My words were blunt and I did not try to soften them. "So I would like to stay for a bit and use the resources here."

He half turned back to me and shook his head, a tense smile on his lips. "Now is not the time. I will be busy sorting through my books for more information on—"

"Rominia's books," I corrected, standing taller.

He cocked his head. "What?"

I waved to the shelves behind him. "These are not your books. They belong to the kingdom. They were here when you arrived, and they'll be here when you've left. I have just as much right to them as you do."

He scoffed and held onto the edge of the table. "Evaline, I am the Arch Sorcerer. These books belong to the acting Arch Sorcerer. Furthermore, I am your teacher. I will say when we train and I will say when you have access to me or my office."

I nodded. "Perfect, I'll select some books and take them back to my room," I said, and felt the tension in the room rise. "That way I won't be taking up any space in *your* office or requiring *your* time."

His smile twisted as it widened and for a split second it reminded me of the smile on Maddox's lips, the Vasi's lips, from the week before.

"You don't seem to under—"

"No," I said, slamming my hands onto the table in front of us. As I spoke, the ground below us trembled. "You don't seem to understand," I snapped. Both of their eyes widened as they grasped that the rumble was not a quake, but me. "I am not asking for your permission."

"Evaline," Lauden said, and his tone was a warning.

"Lauden," I said back, just as patronizing. The light flickered behind him, and he must've seen the rise in light against my features, because he turned back to see that the fireplace, previously unlit, was now a roaring fire.

"Evaline," Sage interjected, looking at me. I turned to face her. "I need to speak with you. Privately." She turned to Lauden. "Go take a walk."

He looked between the two of us, scoffed, and walked out of the loft, but not before slamming the door behind him.

As soon as he was gone, and I saw the look of concern on Sage's face, all the anger subsided enough that I could breathe again, and guilt took its place.

I took a step toward her. "Before you chastise me, please just let me say this first," I said, and she didn't stop me as I continued. "I don't know what happened to you in Mortithev, and you don't have to tell me. I just want to say that I'm so sorry for everything you went through, and I'm sorry I ever let you put yourself in danger for me in the first place."

She shook her head, eyes squeezed shut. When she opened them again, I saw they were misted.

"Evaline," she started, but then trailed off. Her eyes scanned over mine, and I'm not sure what she saw. "They didn't do anything to me. They didn't hurt me at all."

"Gods," I said, a rush of breath leaving my lips as the tears started falling. "Thank the Gods." Her confession removed a heavy weight from my chest.

Sage's brows furrowed as she stared at me.

"What?" I asked as I wiped the tears away.

She shook her head. "You don't know me. I've been so awful to you, and yet you were…" She trailed off, searching for the word. "You felt guilty."

I shook my head. "Of course I felt guilty. I've seen what the Vasi can do, what awful men can do, I'd never wish that on anyone else. Especially not someone who put her life at risk for me."

Sage's forehead wrinkled and for a moment her eyes searched mine, but then she seemed to snap out of it and look to the table. "Well, it's no problem. Nothing happened." She raised her eyes back to me. "I promise. You do not need to feel guilty, not on top of everything else."

I took a deep breath and nodded. "Well, still. You shouldn't have been there at all, and I'm sorry for all of it."

She stared at me before whispering. "Me too." She cleared her throat. "Are you okay?" she said, and I wondered if the tension in her voice was because she felt sorry for me.

I sighed. "No. I'm not," I said honestly.

She was quiet for a moment, evaluating me. "You really loved him, didn't you?" she whispered.

My brows furrowed. "Of course I do. We're mates."

She nodded and looked down at her hands on top of the table. "I know. But sometimes I wonder if mates only love each other because they think they're supposed to. Because they think some Goddess fated it to happen."

I pursed my lips as I thought about what she said.

"I think I might've thought that, too, once. Before I met Maddox and even knew Kova had mates. When I was alone with my aunt and uncle, when they—" I cut myself off before I could upset myself further. I took a deep breath. "Before I understood the love I have with Maddox, I was a sad, broken woman. I think I would've disregarded the bond, too. But even after accepting the bond itself, and understanding how powerful it is, I know that even without it, I'd love him." The tears started to waver my words, so I took another breath to clear it. "I love Maddox because of who he is. What he's done for me, for others, the bond only magnifies that."

When I looked back up at her she was quickly blinking away tears. She looked toward the door that Lauden had walked out of and turned back to me. She must've thought he was coming in. But when her eyes settled back on me, I saw a flurry of emotions in her eyes and her brows furrowed.

"Do you think it's possible to ignore the bond?"

I smiled and shook my head. "It's a powerful thing, and it isn't born of nothing. It's there for a reason, because Maddox and I were made to be together. But even if I could ignore it, even if the bond was gone, I know that I'd still love him."

Her chin quivered as I said that and she looked away, clearing her throat.

We were quiet for a few moments before I looked up at her. "What did you need to talk to me about?" I asked.

She cocked her head. "What?"

I waved to the door. "You told Lauden to leave because you needed to talk to me privately."

"Oh," she said, wiping a hand down her face. When it fell onto the table she had a small smile on her face. "He was just being a prick, and I wanted to give you time to look for whatever books you needed."

CHAPTER FIFTY-NINE

Wyott

"Do you want to fucking feed, or not?" I snapped at the Vasi, extending the glass of blood toward his mouth. I'd already tried to tip it back into his lips several times and each time he jerked away, and spilled more of it on himself.

"Yes," he hissed. "From her. Not whatever poison this is."

I clenched my eyes shut. "If you have all his memories, then you should've remembered what it tasted like before you asked to be fed."

I'd tried several times to feed him and each time he threw a fit. Grant stood beside me with his arms crossed over his chest as he looked at the Vasi. He had a slight cringe on his face, and I understood why. This was the first time he'd come with me to try to feed the Vasi.

"This is all you're getting," I started. "So get over it."

The Vasi's lids lowered and he shot me a glare. "Even if I wanted to drink it, it wouldn't stay down. You saw every time Maddox tried. He had to wretch it up."

A dark smile cast over my face. "But you're a Vasi, you don't have feelings. You can get past it."

He rolled his eyes. "Oh, shut the fuck up. I can feel pain, you prick." I tried to tip the glass back into his mouth again and he jerked away. "Bring her to me."

I sighed. "You know that's not going to happen."

An annoyed breath puffed from his lips. "Then bring it to me in a cup."

We could.

I refused to bring her down here and subject her to this, or his teeth. I was quite sure that having him feed from her was a death sentence. I could gather her blood in a cup, just like I'd done the human donor of this glass.

But I didn't, and I wouldn't. Because I hoped that by keeping the Vasi weak, by starving him out, that maybe Maddox would have the strength to take back over. If he was in there, and willing to fight. Maybe he'd have the ability to take his mind back over.

"Like I said. This is all you're getting."

I tipped it back into his mouth and he took a sip and promptly spat it at me, sending a spray of blood over my face and beard.

I scoffed and swiped a hand over my face to clear it.

"Oh, fuck you then," I barked. "You can starve."

Grant and I left the room shortly after and headed to check on Evaline.

I was worried about her. She hadn't slowed since that first night after we spoke to the Elders. She'd only gotten faster at reading, and spent more time with her head buried in a book.

I tried to get her out of the room, but nothing I did helped. We waited outside the door as I knocked, but she never came to get it. After a minute I cracked it open, and called for her. No answer.

My brows furrowed and I turned to Grant. "She must be in Kovarrin's study."

"I'm right here," she said behind us and both Grant and I jumped.

"What the fuck?" I gasped as Grant cursed, too.

She smiled wide. "You didn't hear me?"

I shook my head. "Not at all. Did you?" I asked Grant.

"Nothing. Not even a heartbeat."

Her smile grew and she nodded. "I've been trying something new," she said as she slid past us to go into the room. "I thought of it after I read one of the books that explained the mechanics of the soundproof walls here," she said as she walked to the chaise by the fire and dumped her books. "It talked about how there has to be minimal airflow beneath the doors, because that would allow the sound out. So I wondered if I could create my own soundproofing, everywhere I went." Then she turned to us with her arms crossed. "It worked, I guess."

"You just manipulate the air around you?" Grant asked.

She nodded. "Kind of, I use Terra and Air. I force the air to form almost a shield around me. Invisible, but the sound can't escape, so you can't hear my heartbeat."

I cocked my head. "But we should still be able to hear your steps, and feel them. You use Terra for that?"

"Yes, I just force the ground to be still every time my foot lands on it." She shrugged. "Kind of like how Sage and I stilled the volcano and stopped its eruption."

Grant and I nodded and admitted that it was a pretty neat trick, but I looked her up and down. Her skin was still pallid, and her eyes were not as bright as normal. The bags beneath them were evident and her cheeks seemed a little hollow.

She was doing better, but she still wasn't okay.

"You went somewhere today?" I asked.

She nodded. "Training with Lauden and Sage."

"That's great Evaline—" I started, but she cut me off.

"And to use Lauden's library."

My smile fell at that. "Have you already finished all the books here?" I asked, moving my head toward Maddox's shelves.

"Most of them. I still have some to go, but I'm going to start at Lauden's too."

I took a few steps toward her. "Evaline, you need to make sure you're taking care of yourself. Start training with us again," I said, waving back at Grant. "And make sure you're eating enough."

Her expression fell. "Rasa already covered it, Wyott," she snapped. "I know my limits. It'll be fine." Then her brows furrowed and she squinted to look over my beard.

"Is that blood?"

CHAPTER SIXTY

Evaline

It was astonishing how time could slip by so quickly, but feel as if it crawled by slowly at the same time.

I'd experienced it before because every moment I'd spent in Maddox's arms had felt that way. As if each breath we shared was long but each moment quick.

Our time had felt fleeting, and it was starting to feel as if our relationship was, too.

Two weeks had passed since I started searching Lauden's library, which meant that it'd been over a month since I'd seen Maddox as himself for the last time before he left on that ship to Merwinan.

Rasa finished the last few books in the mansion while Wyott and Cora helped me go through the books at Lauden's, and when they were busy, Sage joined me. She'd sit with me in the loft, books piled high on the table. Hours would pass, the stack that was to be gone through would dwindle, and the pile of books we'd read and that held no relevant information would grow.

The first week after Maddox changed, this research seemed overwhelming. After the second, it felt like a slog, and after we finished sorting through the last of the books during the third week; impossible.

My hope was waning, and only grew weaker with each time I went to see him.

Each morning my feet were slower to hit the floor and each night was more restless than the previous. I found it hard to care about much of anything the longer time went on, and my meals became even less frequent.

Now, as I trudged to the training center, I felt the strain on my muscles to climb the steps down from the mansion. Each step felt as if it took twice the energy as it normally did, and I clenched my jaw. I tried to find it in me to be concerned, but there was no care left for myself. It had all been taken up by the sorrow that throbbed in my chest. At the loss of so many people in my life now that I didn't think I'd ever come close to whole again.

This blow, this one did me in.

I sighed as I approached the training center and Wyott swung the large door up until it nestled to hang over us.

"You're late," he said, but when he saw me his brows furrowed. "Evaline," he said softly, reaching forward for my forearm. "Are you okay?"

I knew he saw the bags beneath my eyes and the way my skin was pale from my lack of nutrition and sunlight. He hadn't seen me in about a week. He and Cora were busy, and he hadn't come by to help with the search this week. But if he had this sort of reaction after only a few days, then I really must've begun looking awful.

"I'm fine," I said, shrugging off his touch and walking past him. "I'm just tired."

That was the truth, regardless if it had two meanings.

He nodded but didn't take his eyes off of me as we walked to an area in the back corner of the facility. There were cushioned mats on the floor in case someone fell or was taken down. We passed several Kova who were training, even the young ones who were still awkward with their movements and had just started learning to fight. I didn't bother looking at any of them, but could feel a dozen pairs of eyes on me as I walked.

Word had spread quickly after I destroyed the ballroom, and now every Kova I passed walked on eggshells around me. At first it was annoying, but now I didn't mind it. It took less energy to be ignored than it did to fake a smile and chat.

We passed Sage and Cora who were working on some mats in the middle of the center. Sage had waited until we were alone one day in the loft, reading, to tell me that she'd decided to take me up on the offer to train. She'd been coming here even when I wasn't, and I could see that she was still learning to feel comfortable throwing her entire weight behind a punch.

Wyott turned to face me as we stood in the center of our training area. "You're sure you're up for this?" he asked, angling his head down toward me.

I nodded and wished he'd just get on with it.

My feet widened and I bent to get down in my stance as Wyott pulled the top half of his hair up into a bun, loosing some strands that were still too short to reach.

My fists balled in front of me in a protective stance, and we circled each other. He shot out a hit toward my head and I stepped to duck it, but lost my footing and stumbled a few steps before righting myself.

Wyott's hands grasped my shoulders to steady me. "Are you okay?" he asked and I shot him a glare.

"Wyott," I said, my voice a warning. "I don't need to be coddled."

He only nodded, a flash of worry on his face, and backed away until we both started circling each other again.

I punched for his nose but he sidestepped it and moved behind me to wrap an arm around my throat.

"That's too slow," he said as he pulled away from me.

"Clearly," I retorted.

He only looked at me for a moment before we continued.

This time I dropped to swipe a leg to knock his out from underneath him, but instead I only tripped myself and fell onto the ground face first.

I ground my jaw as I moved to push myself up.

Gods-dammit.

I felt Wyott walk over to help me and I shot him a scowl. He backed up with his hands in the air. "Sorry."

We stood and continued. It was a few moments before either of us moved, and I knew he was giving me time to get my bearings after my fall. Finally, his fist shot out toward my stomach. I jumped back to dodge it, but wasn't fast enough. By the time he realized I wouldn't move away in time and pulled back on his blow, his knuckles were already jabbing into my stomach.

I fell back, mostly because I was already falling away when he made contact. It was minimal, not hard at all, but he was cursing and running toward me all the same.

"Fuck Evaline, I'm so sorry," he said as he reached down to pick me up, despite my protests. He looked down toward my stomach, and then back up to me. "Are you okay?"

"Evaline!" I heard Cora say behind me before I felt her hands on my arm. She stepped around to stand next to Wyott.

I waved my arms at them. "I'm fine," I snapped.

I crouched down into my stance and they both shook their heads.

"Absolutely not," Wyott said at the same time Cora shook her head.

Cora put a hand on my shoulder. "Why don't you come stay at the house tonight?" she asked, smiling even though her eyes only showed concern. "We can relax, and I'll make us all a big dinner." She waved her other hand. "Whatever you want."

I cringed as I realized that she understood I hadn't been eating. I looked down, wondering if I'd lost any weight, but I didn't think I had. Maybe she just knew me well enough to know.

But I shook my head.

"No. I want to sleep in my own bed," I said and she nodded.

"Okay, what if I sleep over—"

I took a step back so that her hand fell off my arm. "No thank you, I just want to be alone." I looked to Wyott. "Will that be all for training, then?"

He pursed his lips but nodded and I turned to head back toward the door. As I stepped down off of our mat I looked up to see a few young Kova training, and beyond them a few more looking at the weapon repertoire hanging on the wall, picking what they wanted to use to practice with the bigger, older, Kova.

A giggle rang through the air and I cocked my head to see where it came from. It was a young girl who stood with a young boy. She pointed up at a weapon as she giggled and spoke. "Why is that hanging up there? Who would fight with it? It's not even Rominium."

My eyes followed her finger up until I saw the weapon that she spoke of. It was hung high. Even from here I could see it had collected some dust, no one was picking it up to practice with.

And for good reason. Because it was a lumber axe.

I stopped walking mid-stride, staring up at the wall. Wyott and Cora came to stand on either side, and I didn't move my eyes from it as I spoke.

"Is that…?" I asked.

Wyott's eyes followed my gaze and he gave a small snort. "Yeah, that's it. We hung it there decades ago as a joke."

He looked down at me, and even from the corner of my eye I could see he was smiling.

I looked up at him. "Mad Axe," I said, and chuckled.

He nodded. "Exactly."

I started laughing and Cora joined in. "I didn't realize you had told her that story."

Wyott nodded. "I did, at our first training session back in Kembertus."

My eyes drifted to the young boys that sparred across the facility from us, and I couldn't help but think of Maddox when he was that young. Fumbling around with an axe that was too big for him.

I hadn't stopped laughing, because it was *funny*.

It was hilarious, really. Not only the image of him being unathletic when I only knew him to be the epitome of stealth, but that I was here, standing where he'd grown up training.

And while I was looking at the axe that he used to practice with because he was too weak to use the other weapons, he was up the hill, holed up in a room he hadn't left since the moment he'd arrived back home, locked into a chair.

For all intents and purposes; gone.

My laughter grew louder and I felt a few stares from around the room. I was growing hysterical, and my cheeks started to hurt from smiling.

Wyott and Cora's laughter died away, though, and I could feel their worry as if it slithered through the air between us.

It was funny that my life, and its timeline, had been curated by the Gods. By Rominiava. That my mother's guilt created entirely new types of immortals. That the Gods were punishing me for that. That my attack by Bassel and Lonix forced me to use magic that I didn't realize I had, which alerted both Firsts to my location. That Kovarrin had sent his two best Kova out to check on me. That all of that happened so that Maddox would find me. So that the Gods could get what they wanted, which was Vasier gone. And the only way to do that was to ensure that at some point, I came into contact with the Kova.

And that all of that happened at the time I needed it most. When I needed to be saved not only from my kingdom, but from my own pain. And that all of that love and joy and peace that I finally felt and cultivated because of Maddox, all of that evaporated into agony once again when I saw his red eyes.

It was *fucking* funny, my life. For the Gods, it must be the best drama they'd ever seen. Watching my life play out just as they'd planned.

It took the cool of the air hitting my cheeks for me to realize that I was sobbing now. I don't know when the laughs turned to cries, but I knew that Cora was catching me as my legs gave out, that Sage had run over to catch me on the other side, and that Wyott was instructing all of the Kova to leave the building. I didn't need to see the pitiful stares thrown my way as they all left in order to know they were there.

But I couldn't find it in me to care, at all. Because the pain hurt worse than any embarrassment. And who had time to feel ashamed when nothing seemed like it had purpose anymore?

Eventually I calmed enough for them to walk me back to the mansion, but I made them leave before they could try to stay the night. I still wanted to be alone.

I drew a bath, mostly to postpone another sleepless night and any nightmares that might find me. I brushed my hair, but decided I didn't care if I slept on it wet. Once I'd donned a pair of satin pajamas, all I could do was lie back in bed and stare at the empty space beside me.

And before I even realized I'd fallen asleep, the nightmares came.

CHAPTER SIXTY-ONE

Maddox

One moment I was staring into the blackness that was the inside of my own mind, considering all of the ways that I might take it back—what I would have to do, how weak he'd have to become, for me to do so.

And the next he showed me Evaline, bathed in darkness. It was night, and the dimmest light from the stars outside crept in. When she came closer I saw that she was in her pajamas, her wavy hair was a mess all around her head, and I knew she had been tossing in her sleep. She stopped in front of us and wrapped her arms around herself. The movement drew the Vasi's gaze.

My heart gave a painful lurch as I saw how slight her arms had become, and how the curve of her waist dipped in further than it used to.

Gods, no.

She wasn't eating. Or if she was, it wasn't enough. Or she was training too hard. Whatever variation of events didn't much matter, she was malnourished and fading away.

"I couldn't sleep," she whispered, and only then did I realize that the Vasi hadn't spoken yet. He must've noted all of the same changes in her appearance, in her behavior, and I knew he wanted me to notice it all too. I think he thought this would torture me, seeing her like this. And

Gods, it did, but it also gave me a purpose. Another reminder of why I had to fight for her.

The Vasi didn't speak, only nodded and looked up to meet her eyes.

Gods, they were so sunken in.

They scanned down our face, before coming back up to meet ours again. Every time she looked at them, I watched a piece of her break away.

"I had a nightmare," she said quietly. Of course I didn't know what it had been, but I hoped it wasn't too vile. Between her nightmares of her father's death, her attack, and her mother reaching out to her from the Night, I wasn't sure which would hurt the most now. "It was about you," she whispered, and then shrugged. "Maddox, I mean. My Maddox."

Yes. Your Maddox is still here.

I thought to myself, locked behind the walls I'd put up against the Vasi. I wanted to send it down the bond, to feel it beat in my head the way it used to. But there was only silence, and it was far more deafening than what had existed before I'd met her. For a moment I wondered what would happen if I was successful in changing back to be with her again. To be myself again. I wondered what would become of our bond. If it was gone, and could never be recovered, I wasn't sure what that meant for the two of us. I had every confidence that we'd still love each other just as strongly but we wouldn't be mates anymore without it and the idea of not being able to hear her soft voice in my head, or her laughter, or feel her love, was heartbreaking.

But I forced myself to take a breath. I needed to solve one problem at a time, and if I could be with her again even without the bond, I'd take it.

"I dreamt that you killed me," she said.

The Vasi's voice—my voice—startled me.

"I already told you I would never do that."

What startled me more was how gentle it was. Not just quiet because it was the middle of the night, but soft. Kind.

Her chin trembled at that and it was only a moment before her tears began.

An ache slammed through my chest, and I half expected to feel the bond urging me to reach for her. But of course, it didn't.

"It doesn't matter," she said, shaking her head and clutching her eyes closed.

Fear at what she meant shifted through me.

The Vasi tried to lean toward her as much as he could. His voice came out rushed, desperate.

"It does. Evaline, I won't hurt you again. I'm sorry about the wrist, but it's completely healed now, isn't it? Let me go. Let's go to Mortithev. Together." A shiver wracked my spine at the last word. "Everything will be okay, we'll make it there safely and you'll like it. It's a beautiful castle."

The throne room was elegant, but we hadn't seen much else to make that claim.

She opened her eyes and shook her head, staring right into our eyes. And I knew without a shadow of a doubt, that she was staring directly at *me*.

"It doesn't matter because I'm not here to talk to you. I'm here to talk to Maddox."

Yes, yes sweetheart. I'm here.

"Maddox," she whispered and her brows furrowed. "I need to know that you're there."

The Vasi stared blankly at her and her tears came faster. She lowered until she knelt with bare knees on the hard stone floor beneath her. The only indication that it hurt was a slight twitch in her brow, otherwise she remained focused as she leaned toward us. The Vasi lowered his head as much as he could with the neck restraint.

"Please," she cried. Her hands moved to lay on top of our knees, and balled in the fabric as she pulled. "Please. I can't do this without you. I need to know if there's a chance."

She blinked rapidly through the tears and continued to look into our eyes, at me.

I'm here, Eva! I tried to scream, tried to pull against my restraints. There was more give than I remembered there being, but they still held me back.

"I need you," she croaked. "I need to know that you aren't gone."

Evaline! I roared inside, begging her to hear me. To know that I loved her, that I was fighting for her in every way I knew how. That I wouldn't rot away in here, that I'd fight and claw and rip for every moment I could, to get to her.

The Vasi cocked his head slightly. "You know that he is."

She held her breath, I could hear it, and her chin trembled again. Her brows furrowed, her face crumpled, and she lowered her head until one of her hands covered it, and she sobbed. She cried so loud that her voice cracked through her wails. She sobbed so violently that her frame shook and she had to keep her grip on the fabric of our pants on one knee so that she didn't topple sideways.

I could only hear her for a few seconds before the agony ripping through my chest was too much. In one move I ripped at both chains with all my might, and felt a little more give.

I'm here! I tried to scream at her.

I yanked again, ignoring the way the pain bit at my wrists.

I'm here, Eva! I screamed louder. But my lips did not move, no words came out, and just as I heard the strain on the chains prepare to break away, they were reinforced. They were tighter this time, my arms suspended into the air now that there was less slack, and a horrid laughter filled my head.

Stupid, Kova.

Chapter Sixty-Two

Evaline

He was gone.

He was fucking gone.

It was the first time I'd thought it with such finality. It was the first time I'd understood—with such little hope that it was almost impossible to detect—that this really could be it. The rest of my existence would be without him, forever.

The rain pattered on the windows softly, just loud enough to know it was there. It was gentle, and if this had been any other time and I'd been anybody else, it might've lulled me into a sleep. But it didn't. I only stared out the window, past the rain, at the night sky.

My body hurt from the way I'd cried in front of him. My knees hurt from the granite floor. My throat hurt from my wails. And my heart ached with the knowledge that I had no way to help him, no way to save him, anymore. I'd run out of options and it'd been weeks with no indication that he was still inside.

Going to him tonight, I did it because I'd woken from a nightmare, and I was alone. And it reminded me of how I'd sought that comfort countless times before. It reminded me how my father would run into my room when I cried when I was young. It reminded me of how Maddox would hold me when he was beside me in bed and wake me up out of my nightmares.

And sitting in our room, upright and out of breath with the covers strewn about and my legs tangled in the sheets, the only place in this entire world that I wanted to be was with him.

So I searched for him, and he still wasn't there.

There was nothing else I could do, not for now at least. Not unless we stumbled across some information that could help us, and even if we did, Gods only knew if Maddox was still in there.

So instead of crying, or fighting, or reading a thousand books until my mind ached with a migraine, I stared out of the window as the rain slithered down it.

And I kept staring until morning broke. And then the sun was directly over the ocean, and then it was setting.

I would've thought it took longer than the better part of a day for anyone to realize I'd never left my bed, or maybe I'd hoped. I hardly saw Kovarrin, and Rasa had been busy with the last of her books, so I thought it would take them a couple days to realize. But just as the sun dipped behind Mt. Rominia and cast shadows over the rest of the island and the water below, there was a knock at my door.

It was Cora. She came in and saw me, and was even kind enough not to mention that it was clear I'd never left my bed. She only moved closer and sat on the edge behind me to ask if I wanted company.

"I want to be alone," I said, and my voice cracked. Whether it was from the overuse last night, or the underuse today, I wasn't sure.

She disappeared without saying goodbye, and that kind of surprised me. I felt guilty, maybe she wanted company and that's why she'd asked. But ten minutes later I heard her soft footfalls again before I heard the sound of porcelain scraping the wooden nightstand behind me.

"There's fresh water here and a few snacks," she said softly. "Please let us know if you need anything, we're always here for you, Evaline."

She stopped just before exiting and her voice was filled with sadness.

"I love you," she said.

"I love you, too," I said, and then the only sound was the latch on the door as it shut.

CHAPTER SIXTY-THREE

Wyott

When Cora had come home four days ago and told me about Evaline, I knew something had happened beyond the training center, and it wasn't too much of a leap to gather that she likely had gone to see him.

Cora made it clear Evaline wanted to be left alone, but we both knew she couldn't be left like that in the suite. So between the two of us and Rasa we'd made a few stops throughout the last few days. Each time I'd see that her food had hardly been touched, I swallowed back the lecture on my tongue and just take it away to replenish it and her water.

I didn't stay to speak to her when I went, just reminded her that whatever she needed that was in my power to give her, I would.

She never responded.

But today was the final straw, it'd been four days since Cora had found her that way. I knew she was hardly eating or drinking water, and she wasn't getting up out of bed, which meant that not only was her body starting to fade away, but so was she.

Cora came with me to the castle, but before we went to see her I wanted to go see him.

Cora went to the kitchens to prepare more food and water, and to check on Rasa, and I went up to my old room.

It was storming out, so even though it was nearing noon, it looked as if it was already past sunset. The heavy gray clouds hung over the sky, rain fell hard against the windows, lightning bolted across the sky and the thunder rolled.

For a moment I wondered if Evaline was causing it.

I'd seen her do it before, so it wouldn't have surprised me. But in her weakening state, I didn't know how strong her magic was.

The Vasi nodded his head as I walked forward to stand in front of him.

"It's about time you came," he said when I stopped in front of him and crossed my arms. He looked up at me and cocked his head. "She's not doing well, is she?"

My jaw clenched at that. "What did you do to her?" I asked, my voice low.

His eyebrows raised and he looked toward the windows behind me. "Nothing I haven't already done."

Aggravation drove me forward until I was leaning toward him, wrapping my hand around his chin, and pulling him to face me.

"Listen here, you fuck. She's been lying in bed for four days straight. She's not eating. Tell me what happened."

Something shifted behind his eyes before they went void again. He shrugged.

"She came here in the middle of the night, said she had a nightmare." I released his jaw so he could talk and straightened back to stand away from him. "She was a mess." He nodded, and his voice sounded amused.

But then he stopped talking.

I wagged my head. "And?"

His face went deadpan and he looked up at me with his half lidded eyes. "And what the fuck is in it for me if I tell you the rest? I'm starving, here. It's been over a month since I've fed. Even for you Kova, that's too long." He jerked toward me but was stopped by the bars holding him in place. "Give me some blood."

I shrugged. "We've been trying to give you blood. Every day," I reminded him. "You refuse to take it."

He scoffed. "That's not blood," he snapped. "Not for me. Not anymore. It's poison. You know what I mean—what I need."

I cocked my head and looked down at him. He was right. The bags beneath his eyes were horrendous and his normally olive skin was paling. The beat of his heart was so slow, I'm not sure how he was awake.

I'd been avoiding this because I hoped Maddox would have the strength to come back if the Vasi starved. But perhaps this had gone too far.

"Fine," I said, cutting him off from whatever he'd been about to say.

He closed his gaping mouth and his eyes pinned on me. "What?"

I shrugged. "Fine. We'll need her permission first, so don't get your hopes up. It's her decision. But if she agrees, we'll draw some blood from her and bring it down here for you."

His face fell a fraction. "That's not—"

My brows rose. "It's as close as you'll ever get to her blood," I snapped.

He gave a huff. "Fine."

I waved my hand. "Now, tell me the rest."

He shook his head. "You bring me the blood, and then I'll tell you."

I crossed my arms again. "No, tell me." He opened his mouth to object but I sighed and tipped my head back to look at the ceiling. "You're not exactly in a position of bargaining."

I heard a low growl from him, but then he spoke. "She was crying and begging him to come back. She said she needed to know he was still here and that he wasn't gone. I reminded her that he was, and she broke down."

My jaw clenched. "What the fuck is wrong with you?" I hissed and then headed to the door.

"Nothing is wrong with me," he called. "I just don't care, remember?"

A groan of annoyance rumbled through me as I slammed his door behind me and nodded to the guard standing outside of it.

I headed toward Evaline's room.

Where are you? I asked Cora through our bond.

Sitting at the dining table in their suite, I heard her respond. *It went that badly, huh?*

I knew she could feel my frustration through the bond.

Yes.

I caught her up on the rest of the conversation as I made my way downstairs to their suite, and when I opened the door to the suite the two of us walked into Evaline's room. Their room.

She was on her side, just like she'd been for days. Her back to the door, facing the windows and staring out of them.

Out of habit my eyes moved to the nightstand to see how much she'd eaten, but I saw that Cora had already replenished it all.

How much? I asked Cora through the bond.

I felt her worry. *Not enough.*

I took a deep breath and walked toward Evaline.

"Evaline," I said softly. "It's Wyott." I shook my head. Of course she could tell it was me.

"I'm aware," she rasped.

I sat on the edge of the bed behind her, and turned so that I faced her upper body.

"Evaline we need to get you out of bed."

Her head gave the slightest of shakes and the movement caused her hair to slip down the silk pillowcase behind her. "No thank you."

I gritted my teeth and felt Cora move to lean against the bed post that stood behind me.

"We only want what's best for you," she said softly.

Evaline gave a small sigh. "I know."

She didn't turn to face us, only continued to stare out of the windows.

"You need to at least eat," I said.

Her response came back quick. "I have been."

I pressed my lips together. "Not enough. You know that."

She shrugged. "It's enough for someone lying in bed."

I closed my eyes and shook my head. "It's not." I raised a hand and lowered it over her shoulder. "I know what happened."

She tensed at that. There was a moment of silence. "Good."

My brows furrowed. "What do you mean, 'good'?"

A long sigh passed through her lips before she spoke. "If you know what happened, then you understand that I'm grieving. I've lost hope. It's over, all of it. Let me mourn."

A sharp jolt of pain lit my chest, and I knew Cora could sense it down the bond because her hand landed on my back.

I ignored it for now, I could deal with my own issues later.

"Evaline—" I started but she cut me off by turning and facing me.

"Wyott," she said, but there were tears in her eyes and her voice caught on them. That caused another flash of pain. "I need time. There's nothing else I can do, right now. I've done everything I can. I've given everything I had to give. There's nothing left, especially not to get out of bed just to make you feel better."

"You know that's not why I want you to get up," I said, but a part of me understood that she was right. I felt guilty that we were all in this position, and it would make me feel better if I knew I did everything I could to help her. If she got up and continued fighting.

She shook her head, and a few tears fell. "Either way, nothing is being accomplished by all of you coming here over and over and trying to get me up. It only makes me feel worse, which will only make me stay here longer. I want to be alone."

With that she turned back toward the window and let herself fall onto the bed. The mattress sighed with the movement and Cora's hand on my back caressed.

Let's go. She's right, she said to me through the bond.

I sighed and stood. "I know you want to be alone, Evaline," I said softly. "But sometimes it's the last thing you need."

Then Cora and I left.

We started our walk home in silence, and Cora slipped her hand into mine. She gave it a reassuring squeeze, but didn't make any attempts to talk to me. She could sense my rising panic through the bond.

That pain I'd felt when Evaline had confessed defeat was so many things all tied up into one. It was grief and fear and loss, and the death of hope. Evaline was giving up on him, and it wasn't until she'd said the words that I realized I'd been holding onto my own hope through hers. I hadn't had any when I'd seen that he turned, but her hope forged mine. Her refusal to surrender to what had happened to him—to all of us—breathed new life into a hope that I didn't even know existed. And it had fueled all of my actions since then.

She was the reason I wanted to study the books, to train harder, to talk to all of the eldest Kova I could around the island and pester them to confirm they weren't harboring any more information.

And now that she admitted defeat, now that she was surrendering to fate, it seemed as if my own hope crawled up into a ball and died there in my heart, right when she'd said the words.

My breathing hitched, and I just wanted to be home. Cora knew my intention as soon as I made the decision, and we both took off in a sprint. It was only a minute before we were through the door and I slowed to stand in the entryway, a hand over my chest as I couldn't catch my breath.

Cora came around to face me, worry etched on her face, and placed her hands on my chest. "It's okay," she soothed. "It's okay, just breathe."

I shook my head as memories of Maddox and I as children flashed through my mind. The nights we'd stay up too late, when we sparred at training, and when we raced each other up Mt. Rominia.

"No." I shook my head. "It's not." I gasped between breaths.

Because my best friend, my brother, was gone. He was, and Evaline was right. And the more I thought about it, the more I wished that all of us would've just fucking listened to Kovarrin in the beginning. That we would've grieved from the start because, fuck, it might've been less painful.

I gasped and the tears fell, which made Cora start to cry too, until we lowered ourselves to the floor just inside the door of our home and held each other and cried.

When the tears subsided and we calmed, my thoughts drifted away from Maddox and to Vasier.

He'd done it again. He'd gotten to me. First my mother, then my father, and now my brother. The anger started to rise and I stood up with Cora, started to move to pace the room.

"Wyott," she said softly. "Don't let it go there."

I knew she meant my grief. She didn't want me to let it devolve into rage, because she knew what that meant. She knew that meant another few months where I refused to talk about children, because my fear of Vasier had been heightened.

"Please," she said and I heard her take a step toward me. "We were just starting to get to a good place."

I turned to face her and my brows rose. "Yes, exactly. That's the point," I said and she cringed, she knew what I'd say next. "This is what he does. He lets enough time pass where you feel free of him, where you feel safe. Then he takes."

Tears gathered in her eyes and I felt guilty for making her cry. I loved her so fucking much, more than anyone else and more than I could've ever imagined, and I never wanted to hurt her. When she hurt, I ached just as much. And that dichotomy warred in my mind. The pain of hurting her, and the fear of him.

Couldn't she see I was doing this for us?

She shook her head. "I can't keep having this conversation."

I shook my head and threw my arms out to my sides. "Neither can I. When we keep being faced with the same outcome, why do you always bring it back here?"

"Because I want to be a mother!" she cried out, her voice rising and her eyes wide.

I shook my head, tears blurring my vision. "Never having children is better than losing one to him."

She released an exasperated breath. "That's not fair. You can't take this from me out of fear. You can't keep this future from *yourself*, out of fear." She pointed a finger at me. "You want children. We both do. We always have. You can't forbid us from having that life out of a worry of something that might never happen."

I shook my head, my emotions ravaging inside of me. It was an overwhelming thing to feel your own pain, and someone else's, at the same time. To feel pain that you caused, because of the pain that you felt.

"I'm sorry, Cora. I can't." I shook my head as my words were cut off by the lump in my throat, and I had to wait a moment before I could speak again. "I can't."

She stilled and I felt her slide the bond shut, keeping her emotions from me. Her tears stopped and she pulled back until she was standing straight and looking through me.

"It doesn't matter," she said, and then gave an insincere laugh. "It doesn't matter because if you truly think that Vasier lives day in and day out plotting against you, if that is a reality in which we live, then he's already won." I straightened at that. "Because you are putting your life—*my life*—on hold because of your fear of him. And if that's how we make decisions now, based on fear, then Gods." She took a breath. "He has already won."

She didn't stop to see her words cut through me, she only turned and walked out of the door, letting it slam behind her.

CHAPTER SIXTY-FOUR

Wyott

The metal stairs that hung outside of my front door rattled as I slammed it shut behind me.

Everything was too much.

The tears were down my face before I even finished descending the flights and I pivoted and walked the desolate streets of Rominia in the dark. I had no idea where to go but knew I couldn't sit at home.

It was all too fucked, all too unfair, all too tangled.

My mother, my father, my brother. All of them had been taken by Vasier and now Evaline was heading down the same path.

I knew Maddox wouldn't want me to let her waste away in that bed, but I didn't know what I could do to get her up. I didn't want to force her. But I knew, I'd been there. I'd been in that space where everything felt useless and hopeless, when I'd ignored every offer of help, just like she was doing.

I knew she'd ignore my attempts, but I'd never stop making them.

But I understood why she ignored them. Because right now, she was numb. She was as unfeeling as she could make herself, and the only thing worse than that, was accepting help and coming back. Because that would mean feeling all of it.

Come to fucking think of it, I'd kind of like to be numb right now.

I turned and headed for the tavern, and when I entered, I was thankful to see Dean sitting in the corner with a bottle of rum at his table.

I walked over to him. He looked up, and I could see that his eyes were bloodshot and that bags hung beneath them.

I placed my hand on the back of the chair in front of him, but raised my brows at him, waiting for permission. He nodded and I sat down. He moved to raise his hand, I'm sure to call for another glass, but I just shook my head and grabbed the bottle and took a swig.

He pursed his lips. "It looks like you feel just as shitty as I do."

I whistled. "You have no fucking clue."

We sat there for another moment, trading off the bottle for a few rounds, before he looked up.

"What's your shit?" he asked.

I laughed. "Nothing I can say here."

My eyes wandered around to the different bodies in the bar. I knew some were humans, a few Sorcerers, but most were Kova. I didn't want our conversation to be overheard. I tilted my head down to the table.

"What about yours?" I asked, looking up at him through my lashes.

Dean swallowed, and I watched as his skin blanched, but then he immediately flushed again.

"Nothing I can say here."

I looked at the bottle to take another swig, trying to think of a topic I could bring up to my friend that didn't involve everything we were dealing with. Dean was never the kind of guy to talk about his feelings. Maybe it was because he was one of the few on the island who hadn't found their mate. He'd never been outspoken about it, surely not as much as Maddox had been. It was probably because he felt guilty complaining when he was so much younger than Maddox. For his age—what was he, like ninety?—it wasn't too abnormal not to have found your mate yet.

I raised my eyes to his now, bottle halfway to my lips and ready to ask some random question, when I saw that his gaze was on the windows beside us. His jaw was clenched, his eyes were teary.

I lowered the bottle down to the table.

I knew the look of a man who needed to get something off his chest.

"Let's go stab something," I offered.

His eyes cut to me, wide with surprise. "What?"

I shrugged. "I feel shitty," I said, pointing the mouth of the bottle from myself, and then toward him. "And you feel shitty. When I feel shitty, I stab things. Let's go stab things."

He nodded and pulled money out to pay. I stopped him and headed to the bar. The bottle he'd been drinking was nearly finished, so I took the last gulp and bought another one, paid, and we left.

We passed our drink back and forth as we hiked to the other side of the volcano. It was more private, and I wanted to make sure Dean felt comfortable getting whatever it was off his chest somewhere it wouldn't be overheard.

I still had my weapons strapped on from when I'd hoped Evaline would get up and train with me today, so I knew exactly what I wanted to do.

Once we made it to the beach, I handed him the bottle and went to a tree with a wide trunk on the edge of the sand, picked up one of its leaves and shoved it against the trunk. I pulled my smallest blade out and nailed the leaf into the tree with it. I felt a pang of grief for the last time I'd done this, with Evaline. Just before I told her that Maddox needed to feed—when I'd been so relieved that my brother was going to get the help he needed so he wouldn't accidentally drain someone.

Look how that turned out.

I walked back to Dean and we faced the target. We stood right on the edge of the beach, and the water lapped only a few paces to our right. I pulled out one of my throwing knives and handed it to him, then pulled one for myself. I took the bottle from him and he threw his.

Since he had never opened up to me before, I didn't know what he preferred. If he'd rather I talk first, or if I just needed to let him know that he could talk to me.

With one hand I tipped the bottle back into my mouth, and with the other lifted my hand to throw the knife. It drove in right next to his.

I pulled another knife to hand to him, but before I let go of it, I spoke.

"You know you can always talk to me, right? I'd never tell anyone. We're friends, you can trust me."

His lips pursed and he nodded. I pulled another dagger and threw it. When it drove home the shock of vibration hummed through to the handle.

Dean turned to me. "I found my mate."

My brows rose and I slowly turned to look at him. "Come again?"

He sighed, grabbed the bottle from my hand and took a few gulps. He cringed away from the taste, and shook his head.

"I found my mate."

I turned to him fully. We were at similar height and I watched as his dark brown curls fluttered in the wind around his head.

"Do you mind if I ask who it is?"

Dean took a slow breath, raised his pained eyes to mine. "Sage."

I did my best not to react even though in an instant I understood why he was in pain. Why he was hurt and struggling.

Not only was Sage not available, but she was in a terrible relationship.

I slowly nodded. "When did you find out? She's been here for months."

He took another drink. "I never really interacted with her until the ship wrecked." He turned and threw the knife he still held into the tree. "I'd felt weird ever since she got here, but that's all retrospective. I didn't realize it at the time. I've just felt this strange anxiety in my chest for months, and I couldn't place it."

I nodded, I knew the feeling. I'd had it when Cora had first arrived. When mates were close enough for the bond to initiate, but not close enough to have looked into each other's eyes and know for sure.

He shrugged. "The only times I ever really saw her were briefly walking to and from the training center when she'd be going to the loft. And even then it was usually just her back." He took a shuddery breath. "But when we were all in Kovarrin's study after the wreck, she looked at all of us, and we met eyes."

"Fuck," I said, dragging my hands through my hair and then resting them on my hips.

"You found your mate and we instantly put her in danger." I cringed. "I'm so fucking sorry, Dean."

He looked down at the bottle. "None of you could've known," he said. I couldn't see his eyes, but I knew he was starting to cry when he spoke, because his voice broke. "You should've seen the things she had to see. To bear." He shook his head.

I reached forward and put my hand on his shoulder. "I'm sorry," I said again, softly.

He looked up at me and there were tears in his eyes. "She was tortured."

"She told you?" I asked.

"No, but Vasier said so. Right before…" He didn't have to continue. I understood what he meant.

"She was tortured, and the entire time I was in that fucking castle I was begging the Gods to keep her safe. To keep them from touching her, but I had no way of knowing what was happening to her," he croaked. "They had us all in different cells. And I don't know if they had sound proofing walls like we do here, or if they just separate the cells far enough so we can't hear each other." He took a deep breath. "But I had no idea where she was, or if she was hurt. I couldn't hear her, I couldn't hear any of them." A dry laugh left his lips. "What's worse is that my own torture lasted less than an hour. It was nothing. Like Vasier knew that I had no information for him, and he didn't want to waste his time with me. I guess I just hoped that the same could be said for Sage, but when he had all of us in the throne room, he admitted to it. And the way she reacted to him, the pain on her face and the way she sobbed." He shook his head. "He hurt her. And the worst part is that I can't even ask her about it. I can't talk to her about any of it. I can't know anything because she is with another man." At the last few words, his voice broke, and I reached forward and pulled my friend into my arms.

"We're going to figure this out," I said, and felt him shake his head.

"I don't even care about that right now," he said. "I just want to know if she's okay. I don't know how the bond impacts non-Kova, so I don't know what she's going through right now. After the bond snapped into place, and after the torture."

We pulled away now, but I kept my hands on his shoulders.

"Luckily, we know a non-Kova who went through it." Hope filled his eyes. "Trust me when I say that Maddox couldn't shut the fuck up about it right after he told her about the bond."

He laughed, and that'd been my goal. I took the bottle from him and took a swig. "She'd said that she could tell something was different about him, that she was really drawn to him, but she didn't know why." I shrugged. "Sage might feel the same."

He sucked air through his teeth. "But she doesn't know why, and she's still with that…" He shook his head and I knew he was working himself up over how much he hated Lauden. We all fucking did now that we saw the way he treated Sage.

I don't know why it took Maddox, Evaline, and I coming home for him to show who he truly was, but based off of the way so many Kova's impression of him had changed since we arrived home, he hadn't outwardly shown how awful of a partner he was before.

"Do you want me to ask her?"

"What do you mean?"

I shrugged. "I could go talk to her, alone and away from Lauden. I wouldn't ask her outright, but I'd just get a feel for how much she knows."

I could see that Dean was chewing on the inside of his lip. "I don't know what to do. I don't want her to be worried about the bond, but I also don't want her to be confused about what's happening to her and feel like something's wrong."

"I could be vague. And if I get the slightest idea that she might know, if she tries asking me about it, I can confirm that's the bond. I won't tell her you told me."

He pulled the bottle from my hand and drank the rest of it before looking up at me and nodding. "Thank you."

"You can always count on me."

He smiled and went to retrieve our blades.

We stayed for a few more hours, talking and throwing knives.

After, I made sure he got home safely. He was stumbling which was quite the feat for a Kova, since it wasn't easy to become inebriated.

When I headed home, I had a few realizations.

First, that the entire time I was with Dean, I'd never confessed why I'd been upset.

Second, that I'd felt better after helping him. As if helping my friend made me feel better. Maybe that's who I was—someone that everyone else could count on, and when I helped them take care of their problems, I felt a sense of relief from dealing with my own.

Third, we now knew of a second Sorceress mated to a Kova. The first was Evaline. Part of me couldn't help but think that part of the reason that Maddox, the son of the First, and Evaline, the daughter of the Creator, were fated was because he had a part to play in this. Together, they had to fulfill her curse of killing Vasier.

And if that was the reason the Gods mated them, if that was part of the purpose for deviating from the traditional Kova-only mating's, then what the fuck did the Gods have planned for Sage?

Chapter Sixty-Five

Evaline

Rasa's visits made me feel the most guilt.

It wasn't her intention, of course, but the guilt that seeped through me when she came to visit was almost too much.

Almost.

Five days after Wyott and Cora had tried to get me up, she came.

I'd stayed put this last week. Before, when I was researching and reading through all the texts, it was easy to lose track of time. Days bled into each other until I didn't know which was which.

But now, all I did was understand time. I watched the sun arc across the sky every day through the window. Saw the tides come in and out. Saw the day fade to night.

I only moved to take small bites of the food that they'd all leave for me and take sips of the water, and even then I only did it to avoid a fainting spell. I didn't want to risk the nightmares if I could help it. Every so often I'd have to go to the bathing chamber, but then I'd be back in bed and on my side, staring out of the window. Occasionally I'd see one of those white ravens fly across the sky.

Rasa sat on the bed behind me, and I felt her light touch on my shoulder.

"Evaline, this isn't good. To lie here like this, it will only hurt worse if you isolate yourself." I almost snorted at that, because it was exactly what she had done the first couple days. "At least allow me or Cora to stay the night with you." She ran her hand over my shoulder and down my arm. "You know he—" she started, but her voice cracked and she had to take a deep breath to steady herself. "You know he wouldn't want to see you like this."

I nodded, because she was right. But that didn't mean I was going to get up, because he couldn't see me right now, and who knew if he could see out of his own eyes, anyway.

"Can I get you anything?" she asked, and I shook my head.

"No, thank you." I turned to look at her and saw that her eyes were puffed from tears. "I appreciate you coming to check on me, but I just need time."

Her lips pursed, and she gave a nod. She knew exactly what I meant.

She reminded me that there was fresh food and water on my nightstand, and then took the previous of each away.

I watched as she walked away, and then turned my head to face the window again as the door clicked behind her.

Chapter Sixty-Six

Wyott

My knuckles rapped on the door to Lauden and Sage's loft, and when she opened it and let me in, I pretended to look around.

"Is Lauden here?" I asked, hands in my pockets.

She strode to the counter in their kitchen and propped her hip against it.

"No, he's meeting with Kovarrin, I believe," she said.

I nodded as if I hadn't been scouting his whereabouts for days trying to catch Sage alone.

"Did you need something?" she asked.

I shrugged. "I was going to see if I could borrow some of Lauden's books, to look for information for Maddox."

Sage's brows furrowed. "Didn't Evaline tell you that she and I finished going through them?"

Of course she had.

I shook my head. "No. No luck, then?" I asked.

Sage pursed her lips. "No."

I took a deep breath, mostly because I had no idea what to say now. I guess I hadn't completely thought this through when I'd told Dean I'd check on her. I barely knew Sage, what was I supposed to do, ask if she was feeling antsy lately? Gods, the rum had gotten to my head that night. How did I think this was a good idea, or that I'd even be able to hold a conversation with her long enough before she figured me out?

Luckily, she spoke for me.

"How's Evaline?" she asked, wringing her hands together.

I sighed. "Not well. She hasn't left her bed, essentially since you last saw her breakdown next door," Sage's eyes flashed at that. "She's lost hope."

She bounced her leg. "Evaline can't give up." Her words came out quickly. "If she does, what hope do the rest of us have?"

I took a step toward her. "What do you mean?"

She shook her head and waved a hand through the air. "If Evaline gives up on Maddox, then what? We've lost them both?" Tears were sprouting in her eyes now and I took another step closer. "She wastes away until she isn't herself anymore? The pain wins?" She scoffed and shook her head. "Absolutely not."

"Sage, are you okay?" I asked softly.

She threw her hands in the air.

"Obviously fucking not," she rasped as the tears fell. She brought up a hand and sloppily wiped some away. "I was just starting to fit in, Maddox and Evaline cared about me when no one else did. More than the most important—" She cut herself off before she could continue. "They were becoming my friends, and I don't have many of those," she finished quietly.

I took another step closer to the counter. "Cora and I care about you," I said, and her eyes flicked up to mine. "We're your friends. And Evaline isn't gone, she's just going through it. She'll be back eventually, she just has to find her reason to get up past the pain."

Sage's brows raised then, and realization seemed to flicker over her eyes. She nodded. "You're right."

"How are you doing?" I asked, resting my hands on the countertop a couple feet from her.

"I'm fine," she said quickly.

She and Evaline were so alike, and right now she reminded me of the Evaline that Maddox and I had found in Kembertus when we'd first met her.

"Okay." I nodded. She seemed about done with me for the day. "I'll get out of your hair," I said and turned back toward the door, but she rushed forward then and grabbed at my forearm.

"Wait, Wyott?" she asked.

I turned back toward her. "Yeah?"

She swallowed. "I haven't seen Dean at the training center. Is he okay?"

My heart did a fucking leap for my friend, but I hid the reaction. I only gave a slight nod.

"He's been quiet lately, but I'm sure he'll be okay," I said, and looked for any signal that she understood why she was feeling this way about him.

"Has he said why he stopped going?" she asked, wringing her hands again. "I used to see him there all the time and now he never goes."

I pursed my lips and shook my head. "He hasn't said why, just that he's been feeling a bit odd lately. Anxious."

Her eyes widened at that and she nodded, looking down at her hands.

"Wyott, you said you'd be my friend?" she asked.

I nodded fiercely, but her head was still downturned, so I spoke. "Yes. Of course."

She took a deep breath, and looked to the door as if she were waiting for Lauden to walk in at any moment.

"If I ask you something, do you promise not to judge me, and not to tell a soul?" She settled her gaze on me.

"I give you my word." Fuck. It would make it hard to relay to Dean, but I had to keep my promise to her.

She chewed on her lip. "Does Dean have a mate?"

I gave a slow nod, and her face fell.

"Oh," she said softly, and I realized immediately she thought it was someone else. Gods, she and Evaline had a lot more in common than I thought.

"It was recent." I added. "He said he met her recently."

Her brows rose at that, and I heard her heart rate increase. "Really?"

I nodded.

"Did he tell you who?" she asked.

"Do you have a different question you'd like to ask me, Sage?" I asked quietly.

She gave me a long look as she considered my words, and then sighed. "How do you know—how would a non-Kova—know if they found a mate?"

I explained to her what Evaline had said about her bond with Maddox. That she felt anxious, that she was drawn to him, that she could sense where he was.

Her heart seemed to beat faster with every piece of information I shared, until I finished.

She nodded for several seconds when I'd finished, and I didn't dare speak.

"Thank you," she finally said.

That's it?

"Did you need anything else?" I asked, hopeful she'd confess to me about Dean.

She shook her head. "No, thank you for everything."

I reached a hand out toward her arm. "Sage," I said softly. "You can tell me, if something's going on. If you feel something for Dean."

She scoffed and pulled away from me, and I saw that her wall was back up.

"Don't be ridiculous. I'm with Lauden. I have been for years. He is my partner, mate or not."

She seemed to realize her confession then, and her eyes widened at it. But she only shook her head and half turned away from me.

"Lauden will be home soon."

I nodded and headed for the door.

"You still promise to keep that between us, right?" she asked quickly before I turned the handle.

"Of course."

As soon as that door clicked behind me I was sprinting through the streets to get home to Cora. Talking to Sage, seeing the way she denied the bond, the way she doubled down on the man who treated her so poorly but clearly had some kind of hold over her, reminded me that I was so lucky.

Between Maddox and Evaline who were torn apart, and Dean whose mate was denying the bond, I was eternally blessed by the Gods.

My mate was the most amazing person I'd ever met, and I'd been thankful for every day I'd had with her all this time. But I'd pushed her away, I'd hurt her because I'd let my own fear get between us.

And I didn't want to do that anymore. I was so fucking lucky not only to have her but that she wanted me back. And I should've realized far sooner that she was right. We both wanted a family, and we couldn't—*I* couldn't—let Vasier get in the way of that.

She wanted children, desperately. And I did too. I wanted to have children with the woman I loved and be the father to them that my father was to me, before he was taken. I wanted to teach them to fight and to throw knives, and I wanted to put them to sleep at night and watch them grow up and find their own mates.

And the more I thought about it the harder my heart beat, and with each pump it seemed as if it reiterated the truth. That this was exactly what I wanted, that I'd pushed the thought away for so long I'd nearly forgotten how much I yearned to be a father. That my family was more important than my fear.

Vasier was dangerous, and he'd taken so much from me, but I wouldn't let him take this. And as the images of my father's death flashed through my mind, I realized that perhaps I'd never truly been afraid that Vasier would come for someone else I loved. That perhaps everyone was right, and my mother's death was a horrible mistake, bad luck. That perhaps Vasier hadn't turned Maddox to get to me, but to hurt his own brother. That perhaps all along, I'd taken all the evidence of Vasier's atrocities and applied them to my own life—that I took ownership of all that he'd done and what he may do down the line—because at the end of the day my true fear wasn't that Vasier would take my children from me, but that he'd take me from them.

Like he'd done to my father.

Maybe I was more afraid of leaving a child fatherless, like I'd been, than I could admit to myself before. But I understood now, and I understood Cora. She was right, we couldn't live in fear of something that may never happen. All we had was right now, and each other.

And the thought had my feet making a stop, had me ducking into the physician's shop and purchasing the item that I should've decades ago.

When I rushed home and threw the door open, Cora jumped in the kitchen where she was cooking.

"Gods!" she shouted, clutching her chest as I appeared in the doorway. "You scared the shit out of me," she hissed, but then she turned around toward the counter.

"Cora," I croaked, and I saw her spine straighten, knew she heard the change in my voice.

She turned around to face me again, but kept her distance with her back to the counter.

"What's wrong?" she asked, wiping her hands with a dishtowel.

I opened my mouth, and closed it again. Realized that I had so many things to tell her that I didn't know which one to say first, and that all the thoughts died on my tongue as I looked at her. As I saw her effortless beauty, how she looked ethereal standing in the dim lighting of the lantern she'd lit while she made dinner. I thought back to the very first day we'd met, when her father had sailed them here and I saw her swing off of the boat. We had just been kids, but I'd already known that she was my best friend the moment I'd seen her.

And all of that, the emotion and the excitement, was exactly what I felt now.

If only I could say it.

I pulled the vial from my back pocket and she watched with questioning eyes as I stood it up on the counter nearest me.

The dishtowel fell from her hands and crumpled as it hit the floor.

"What's that?" she asked, her voice breathless.

"You know what it is, Cor," I said softly. Of course she did, it was the tiny black vial with a green top. It was the twin of the vial I'd taken so long ago, except that one had a blue top to it. Blue for sterility, green for fertility.

She knew what it was.

She walked toward me, but stopped a few feet away and reached for it. Her hands shook as she brought it closer, felt the weight of it in her hand.

She looked up at me, tears in her eyes. "It's empty."

The desperation in her voice, in her eyes, had my knees hitting the floor.

"I'm so sorry," I said, tears of my own filling my eyes and my voice.

I placed my hands on her thighs and half expected her to step away from me, as she had been lately but instead she stayed.

"I'm so sorry that I've made you wait. I'm sorry that I was too selfish to give you what you deserve and what we both want." I shook my head as I stared up at her. "But, Gods, I'm so fucking sorry that it's taken so long that even when you see that the vial is empty, that you have such question in your eyes because I've made you wait so long that you've convinced yourself—that *I've* convinced you—that it'd never happen."

Tears streamed down my face, and I heard the vial hit the floor, felt her hands fall to my shoulders.

"What are you saying?" she asked, tears falling down her cheeks.

I blinked through mine because I wanted to see her face, I wanted to see it clearly when I told her, when I gave her what I'd kept from her for so Gods-damned long.

"I'm ready," I said and her chin trembled. "I want to have children. I don't care about Vasier. I don't care about any of it. You were right. Fear shouldn't hold me back. It should've never held me back, and I'm so sorry it di—"

I didn't get to finish the sentence before she was falling down into my embrace, before her lips crashed onto mine and I tasted the salt of both of our tears through our kiss and it was as if it was the first time, all over again.

I stood us up, dipped to catch her in my arms and walked down the hallway toward the bedroom as we both whispered *I'm sorry's* and *I love you's* down the bond and into each other's lips.

Chapter Sixty-Seven

Evaline

Another few days passed with each of them coming in and out. None of them stopped to try to get me up anymore, they just moved quietly somewhere behind me before reminding me that they were there if I needed them, before they left.

So when I heard the door creak open, I awaited the sound of soft footfalls and hushed reminders. Instead, I heard the footfalls stop behind me.

I tensed, awaiting the guilt I knew I'd feel after another lecture from Cora or Wyott or Rasa. But the voice that sounded through the air was raspier than the others, and the color drained from my face when I realized who it was.

"Enough. Get up," Sage said behind me.

I sighed and shook my head. "You're not my mother, Sage," I said, repeating the same words she'd said to me before she got on that ship and left for Merwinan.

"Someone has to be."

I rolled my eyes. "I don't need parenting, I don't want help. Leave me alone."

The bed sunk as she sat behind my back.

"You need to get up, you need to fight. And if everyone else has tried and failed to get that through your head, then it's probably because they've been coddling you." I heard her click her tongue. "I'm not here to do that."

I snorted. "No shit."

She sighed. "I get it, okay? I'm the bitch that everyone struggles to connect with. I push people away, I pushed *you* away, but do you know what happens when you spend most of your time alone? You learn to read people, and you get fucking good at it."

"How interesting," I said, my voice dull and even.

"You learn that some people are motivated by coddling," she continued, ignoring me. "That sometimes they need to feel someone hold their hand to be strong. And that's fine, nothing wrong with it." I heard her crack her knuckles. "Just not you."

"Please, tell me all the ways you understand me better than I do myself," I said.

"I will, actually," she said, ignoring my sarcasm. "I know you better than you might think." Her voice lowered. "Pain sees pain."

She took a deep breath and I had to fight back the tears that threatened to fall.

"I know that you're not the type that needs to be coddled. You're the second type, that doesn't need to be told that they're strong. They know they've survived the worst the Gods could throw at them before, and still got up every day. They know they hold their own fate in their hands, because they've cultivated their physical strength, emotional strength, and additionally for you, your magic. And they did all of that mostly by themselves."

I stayed silent as she talked, this lecture switching gears into a territory I hadn't expected.

"They don't need to be coddled; they need to be reminded."

I furrowed my brows, not that she could see it. I could tell she paused to hear any response I might have, but I didn't speak, so she continued.

"I don't know you that well, but I know a little. Your mother is dead, and she created the Kova and the Vasi. And you've lost your father. So you're an orphan, and you were stuck in a shitty kingdom, and they tried to marry you off to some asshole. That's all shitty, but you came out of it all on top. You survived."

I cut her off from continuing. "Listen, if this is a grand speech about how I'm strong and I've survived worse, save it. Surviving worse and persevering is one thing, but there's a limit to how many times it can be done." I shrugged. "I've hit mine."

"That's not what I came here to remind you." There was a pause. "But first I have to tell you a secret about myself." My ears perked up at that, but I didn't speak in fear she'd change her mind. "Lauden won't be happy," she said, but then quickly continued. "He thinks if people knew, it'd put me in danger. Will you keep this secret?"

My eyes widened in surprise, but I nodded. "Of course."

She took a deep breath. "You're not the only Sorceress on this island—or even in this room—with one of a kind magic," she said softly, and I furrowed my brows. "It used to be more common. There used to be four Sorcerers alive somewhere in the world, who could do it. One for each element. But slowly, they were killed off until the bloodlines that carried the trait went extinct." She paused. "Or they thought." I held my breath, waiting for her to reveal it.

"The other Sorcerers who didn't wield the ability, killed them. Not the humans, not Vasier, but the Sorcerers. The Sorcerers saw the gift as too dangerous. That no one should have that much magic. It could change kingdom politics, it could change the world. They didn't want that kind of ability to be gifted randomly through inheritance, to only four Sorcerers in a generation." She sighed, and I knew she was gathering up the nerve. "The ability to open portals is one the Sorcerers didn't want to gamble with. So they took it into their own hands, and extinguished the gift entirely. Until I was born, until my magic manifested, and I had the gift."

I whipped up into a sitting position, turning to face her. "What are you saying?"

She pressed her lips together and met my eyes. "I'm saying that I can open portals, and travel anywhere I want to, in a heartbeat."

I shook my head. "How does that even work?"

She wrung her hands in her lap. "If there is someplace I've been, I can picture it. When I open my portal with that image in mind, and step through it, I'm transported there and no time has passed. I can travel a thousand miles in one breath. Or if I haven't been there, and someone else has, I can touch them while they picture it, and it works the same way."

My mouth hung open as I thought about all of the possibilities she had in her life, how she could be anywhere, but she chose to be here.

I shook my head. "I don't understand."

She shrugged. "You don't really need to. I only told you because I have to remind you." I met her eyes. "And it's not to remind you that you're strong or that your love for Maddox will conquer everything," she said, and gave a slight roll of her eyes.

I ground my jaw at that, but her eyes caught mine again. And the ferocity of her sage green eyes, I couldn't look away.

"I have to remind you that impossibilities don't exist. There've been a thousand things we thought impossible that just aren't. The Kova and Vasi were created by one of us. You have more than one element, even though it should be impossible. I have the gift of portals, even though the Sorceresses who wielded them should've died out centuries ago. If nothing is impossible, if we—your mother and you and I—are all testaments to that, then what is left? Only possibilities. Only potential. If your mother could *create life* with her blood, Gods know what you could do."

She finished speaking and her eyes were wild, as if she begged me to understand. And it made sense, all of it. In some twisted way, I think she was exactly the person I needed to talk to in order to feel better. But all of my thoughts hushed as she said the last line.

"If your mother could create life with her blood, Gods know what you can do."

My blood.

The memories flashed in front of me so quickly that I felt stupid for not considering it sooner.

Wyott with his back against that tree in Neomaeros, telling me that Maddox could only feed from me after our bond settled into place.

Maddox telling me how it felt like molten metal to drink from a human after we met.

Maddox after he fed from me, and how the two of us always felt stronger after, rather than weaker.

If my mother's blood created life, who knew what mine could do.

If the Gods wanted the Vasi gone, if they wanted Vasier gone, and it was my fate to change it, then maybe I was not only the chosen one, maybe I was the *cure*.

I let out a sound and I wasn't sure if it was a cry or a laugh, but there was a smile on my face as I grasped Sage's arms.

"You're right!" I exclaimed, her brows rose in a look of relief. "You're right, everything you've said, it's all right. I just needed to be reminded," I said, and dragged her body into mine and gave her a hug.

"Gods," she hissed against my ear. "I'm glad I could help, but do we really need to hug?"

I winced at that, but she didn't pull away. We held each other there for a moment, and then I pulled back to look at her.

"I'll stay here and bathe and get dressed, and you need to go get Wyott and Cora." I shrugged. "Fuck it, get Lauden too. I'll need all the help I can get if something goes badly."

Her brow furrowed. "What do you mean?"

I smiled at her. "You're right, who knows what my blood could do." I shook my head. "I don't have time to explain, but I have an idea. I'm going to let Maddox feed from me."

Her eyebrows shot up and she waved her hands between us.

"No, no. That's a horrible idea. What if he kills you? This is not at all what I'd hoped when I came here. I just wanted you to get out of bed and feed *yourself*."

I pulled us both up off of the bed. "It'll be okay," I said, but as we stood I felt myself grow faint, saw black clouds shift over my vision, and had to hold onto Sage so I wouldn't fall.

"Evaline," she snapped, catching me and grasping my shoulders to steady me. "You can't even stand, you're so weak and hungry. You can't let him drink your blood."

I waved her worries away.

"It'll be okay. I'll stay here and bathe and while I do I'll eat as much as I can." I looked back behind me. "I'll drink that entire pitcher of water, if it'll get all of you on my side." I turned back to face her. "Please, Sage. You're right, only possibilities are left. Please, go get all of them and bring them back to the hallway right outside of where he's being held."

She opened her mouth to object but took another look at the hope that fell over my face. Then something flashed in her eyes, and she ground her jaw and nodded.

"I will. But you better eat."

I ran to draw the bath and while the water heated I sat on the side of the bed and guzzled down water.

Now that I was up, now that there was hope in my chest again, I realized I was parched. After bringing one glass of water to my lips, I drank it in only a few gulps. I thought I'd have to force myself to drink, and then to eat, but the more I did of each the more I realized I needed it. I was starved.

By the time I was done, the bath was ready, and I sank down into it. I scrubbed at my skin quickly while the shampoo sat in my hair. I finished in only a few minutes and then dried and ripped my brush through my hair to get out all of the tangles that remained from lying in bed for the last two weeks. Once it was combed, my fingers made quick work of weaving the barbed wire into my braid.

I moved to the closet and threw on pants and a linen blouse with a scooped neckline. I laced up my boots and headed for the door when I looked to the table that sat against the back wall of our room. All my weapons laid there, along with Maddox's, and I quickly grabbed my Rominium dagger and strapped it on. My mind flashed to the night when Maddox fed from me for the first time, when he fastened my holster on my thigh in case I needed to get away from him. The memory didn't cause pain, like every reminder of our time together usually did. Now, it only pulsed with the hope that beat in my chest. This was going to work. It had to work.

I was coming out of the hallway that our suite resided in and placing my foot on the first stair up the next flight when I heard steps on the landing behind me and then Wyott's voice.

"Take your foot off that fucking stair," he boomed.

I cringed. He was *not* agreeable to this plan. I took my foot off and turned to face him. He stood beside Cora, who shot me a worried glance. Lauden stood on his other side, looking absolutely inconvenienced, and Sage stood beside him, flicking her eyes between all of us. Wyott took a step toward me.

"If you think I will let you go and get yourself killed, you've got another thing coming."

I thought about what I could say to change his mind, even opened my mouth to speak. But instead I turned and started to run up the stairs. I didn't even make it up two whole steps before I felt his hand close around my wrist and he turned me around.

"Evaline!" he shouted.

I whirled to face him and he released me. He still stood on the landing, but we were at eye level.

"What?" I yelled, throwing my hands up. "You wanted me out of bed," I said, waving my hands up and down my body. "I'm up. I bathed, I drank an entire pitcher of water and ate that entire tray of food." I clasped my hands against my chest and lowered my voice. "I'm fine, Wyott. Please, I think this could be the key."

He narrowed his eyes at me and there was a moment of silence before he whirled around to look at Sage.

"What did you say to her?"

Her brows shot to her forehead and she shook her head. "I was just trying to get her out of bed, I was trying to help."

Wyott wagged his head. "By telling her to get herself killed?"

"She reminded me that there are so many things about this world, about the Gods, about my mother's magic and now mine that we don't understand," I said, and felt Sage's eyes on me.

I knew she was holding her breath to see if I'd out her secret. Of course I wouldn't.

"All of it should be impossible, but it's not," I continued. Wyott slowly turned back to face me, but didn't interject. "She reminded me that if my mother's blood could create life, who knows what mine could do," I said the last sentence slower, giving him a pointed look.

We didn't want Lauden and Sage to know that Maddox, and now the Vasi, couldn't drink from anyone else besides me. The less people who knew, the better. But Wyott's eyes widened only slightly, and only enough for me to see. They glazed over for a moment, and I knew he was discussing with Cora through their bond, but after a moment he gritted his teeth and nodded.

"Fine."

Sage scoffed. "Fine?" she questioned.

Clearly she'd thought Wyott would talk me out of it. I looked to Lauden, expecting him to also protest, but he remained silent. I looked back to Wyott and smiled.

"Great!"

I turned on my heels to head upstairs but his hand shot out again and he pulled my shoulder back around to face him.

"He will not be feeding from *you,* though," he said. "We will draw some of your blood, and feed it to him. While you are a safe distance away."

I pursed my lips. That wouldn't work.

Yes, maybe my blood was the cure. I hoped it was—prayed for it. But this exercise had two purposes. First was to see if my blood was the cure. Second was to see if, in the Vasi's daze of feeding, I could pull any sign out that Maddox was still there.

"Wyott," I started, my voice even but of course he knew my intent by the sound of it because he shook his head quickly.

"No."

"But—"

"No."

I ground my teeth and stomped a foot onto the stair.

"I am Evaline Manor. My mother created your species. I hold dominion over four elements. I can make the ground shake and the oceans rise. I can wage an inferno and fuel it by the gust of my wind. Maddox might be the son of the First, but I am the daughter of the Creator. I will do whatever the fuck I want, when it comes to saving my mate." My words grew rushed the more angry I became. "You can either get on my side," I said before raising my hand forward and pointing to the stairs behind him. "Or you can go."

This time when I turned around, he didn't stop me. Only cursed under his breath and followed.

I heard the rest of them follow and within a few minutes the lot of us were standing in front of the door. Wyott sent the guard on a break, and stood beside me as I stared down at the door knob. But as I thought more about my plan, I realized that I'd have to tweak it.

"Actually I don't—" I started, and Wyott expelled a sigh of relief that flitted over my face.

"Oh thank the Gods, you've seen reason," he said, placing a hand over his heart.

I cut my eyes up to him.

"*Actually,*" I started. "I don't think that the men should come in. I only want Cora and Sage in there with me."

I didn't know if Maddox's body would still respond to me the way mine did to him, but if it did then this feeding could get intimate very quickly. And I didn't want Wyott or Lauden in there to see it. It was already bad enough that Wyott had interrupted us when I fed from Maddox for the first time.

Wyott's brows furrowed. "You can't be serious."

Cora shot him a look. "We've got it covered."

He sighed and took a step back away from the door and gave us all a nod. "Be careful."

I could tell that he wanted to say more, to give further instruction, but Cora was right. The three of us were plenty capable of handling this on our own.

I looked between the two of them. "Sage, you stand near the door ready to open it and bring in Wyott and Lauden if needed."

Since they wouldn't be able to hear what was going on, she'd have to alert them.

"Be prepared to use your magic if you think necessary, but Cora should be able to get me away from him if it's warranted." I turned to Cora. "You'll stand a few feet back from us." I lowered my voice. "Both of you," I said looking between the two women. "Please try to avert your gaze."

When they nodded, I took a deep breath and pushed the door open.

The Vasi immediately swung his head toward me. "Hello, love."

I heard both Sage and Cora take in sharp breaths at the sight of him. He was malnourished, badly. It was obvious. Even worse than Maddox had been before he fed from me for the first time.

His smile widened. "And you've brought friends." His eyes flicked to Cora. "Hello, Cora." I saw her wince, knew it hurt to see her friend this way. She hadn't been to see him in this state. His eyes moved to Sage. "And the Sorceress who saw it all happen," Sage ground her teeth at that.

"Yes," I said, walking closer. Sage stayed at the door as instructed and I heard her close it behind us. Cora strode beside me. "Wyott told me you wanted to feed."

His brows shot to his forehead. "I do. I'm starved."

I nodded and stopped in front of him. Cora moved a few paces to the side.

"Well, here I am."

I could see the calculations he ran through, trying to guess at any hidden intentions, trying to figure out why I was standing here, instead of bringing him a glass of my blood to drink.

"If it's okay with you, it'd save me time to just let you drink from me now." I tilted my head. "It's less painful, as long as you don't intentionally try to harm me."

He nodded. "You have my word, I will only drink."

I pointed to the two women in the room with me. "They're here to prohibit you from killing me."

He inclined his head toward me and smiled. "Won't be necessary."

The hungry gleam in his eye had already taken over, and I knew he'd agree to anything I said now that he knew this was happening.

His eyes lowered to my neck, and I strode forward. Of course I could just give him my wrist, but if this was going to work, if I was going to be able to distract him long enough to try to communicate with Maddox, then I'd have to fully commit. If Maddox's body still reacted to me, then this should be plenty distracting.

I placed a hand on his shoulder and brought up the opposite knee to kneel in the gap between his hip and the chair. His eyes widened as he watched me intently until I brought up the other knee and was straddling him.

"Wha—" The Vasi said.

"You want the blood, don't you?" I asked, and tried to lower my voice to feign arousal.

He only nodded.

"Then don't ask questions," I said and lowered my hips until the two of ours met.

He sucked in a shocked breath at the contact and stared up at me as I pulled my braid to the other side of my neck.

"Ready?" I asked, searching for Maddox behind those red eyes.

He nodded and I took a breath before I tilted my chin to the ceiling and exposed my neck to him.

I didn't have time to finish the breath before his fangs were biting into me. The breath exploded out of me at the contact, and it felt as it always did with Maddox. Want started to beat through my veins. If I closed my eyes, I could almost pretend that this was Maddox. He smelled the same, his touch was just as warm and his lips just as soft. I had to lean forward into him so that he could reach, the neck brace limited his range of movement, which meant that my face was pressed against his temple and his curly hair brushed up against me just like it always had.

He bit down harder, but it didn't hurt. Just elicited a moan from my lips and my cheeks flushed. I was embarrassed that Sage and Cora were here, but if I wanted to distract him, I'd have to do whatever was necessary to pull his attention away.

I let my left hand fall down his chest and slip into the collar of his shirt, spreading my hand over his chest. He shivered at the contact and it only increased as I brought my right hand up his neck to tangle in the back of his hair.

He groaned, and I felt his cock twitch below me. I took the opportunity and ground myself against him, which only resulted in the both of us moaning. Mine wasn't completely fake.

It was hard to compartmentalize it all, when everything about him *was* Maddox. My body couldn't tell the difference.

He took another drag and I took a breath—and there it was.

Deep in my mind, that bond that had gone nearly silent started to pulse. I wasn't sure if it was my imagination, or if I was only experiencing what I wanted to be real, but it seemed authentic.

I didn't know if that was Maddox trying to reach out to me, but I knew that this was my chance. I tilted my head down toward his ear, and shoved as much strength and power as I could down the bond at the exact same moment as I spoke the words.

"Until the end of my days."

Immediately the Vasi took out his fangs and shoved my neck away with his chin.

"You stupid bitch," he hissed. "You were using me."

I pushed away from him and stood, shrugging. "You can try, but you will *never* be able to shame me. I will do whatever it takes to get him back."

His chest heaved as he tried to catch his breath. His eyes were wild, and my blood still coated his lips.

I waited to see any change in his demeanor, but he only stared right back at me. A wave of dread ran through me as I realized that if Maddox was still in there, he should've responded to me. The Vasi wasn't in control. He was distracted, and he was weak. I hadn't felt any response down the bond when I'd shoved the power through, but I couldn't tell if I felt the blockage down it either. Between the Vasi yelling at me and shoving me away, I couldn't tell in the moment. I tried again now, and felt the impact of that wall.

Cora moved to my side. "Evaline," she whispered. I looked over at her and she pointed to her neck. "You're still bleeding."

"Oh," I said, bringing my fingers up to prod at my own blood. I cut my eyes toward him. "You couldn't be bothered to heal it?" I snapped.

"Fuck off," he spat back at me.

I rolled my eyes and turned back to Cora, but as I did that same black fog flitted over my vision and I had to take a step back to catch my balance.

"You've lost too much," she said, wrapping an arm around my shoulders. Even though he hadn't taken much, I knew she was right. I felt weak, even just standing here. I knew it was because I hadn't been taking care of myself lately. Cora lifted her wrist to her lips and opened a wound, and then offered it to me.

I gave her a small smile. "Thank you," I said before putting my lips over the two pricks dribbling blood.

"You can let them in, now," Cora said, I assumed to Sage.

I heard the door open, and Wyott rushed in, his arms around both Cora and I in an instant.

"What happened? Is everything okay?"

I took another gulp and knew it was enough, before I pulled away.

"Everything's fine," Cora said and I nodded.

"It is."

"Fuck you all, no it's not." The Vasi said. "I didn't get enough, and even the amount I did get isn't helping. I still feel just as awful."

Hope sprung up in my chest at that. Perhaps it was working, perhaps this would change him.

His eyes settled on me again. "Stop looking for him," he hissed. "He didn't answer, because he isn't here."

Chapter Sixty-Eight

Maddox

Gods, she was strong.

I thought I'd lost her. I thought she'd lost all hope in me the last time she was here. But she came back for me, and with a plan.

The Vasi let me see her, for a time. He wanted to mock me, to make me watch as he fed from my mate. But he let me feel it, what it felt like to taste her blood. To have my lips on her warm neck.

And she was playing him, I knew she was. He was too hungry to notice, but I wasn't. And when she whispered those words, the vow, I'd launched myself forward and tried to scream it back.

And in the Night that follows.

But at the same time he pushed her away from us, he locked me down again. The world went black and quiet. He didn't let me see or hear anything else. I tried not to let it get to me.

She had faith in me, she was fighting for me, and I'd do the same for her.

My thoughts cut off as I felt the chains that held me in place disappear. My eyes widened and I stood, and stretched. Felt the way my joints cracked and my spine popped as I got out of the horrifically uncomfortable position I'd been in for weeks.

Her blood was working. I didn't know whether it was curing me or not—I knew that was her intention—but he was weaker now than he was when she walked in the room. I still couldn't hear or see anything, but I was standing.

I strode forward, just to test the limits, and walked straight into a barrier. I reached out in front of me and my hands flattened on a wall. As I pushed, I found some give, and I realized it wasn't a wall at all. It couldn't be a ward either, because when I pressed my finger into it, the material of the wall moved with it. Like I was poking through sheet instead of a wall.

Like a veil.

I thought back to everything I'd ever learned about the change. That there was a veil that protected our souls, and that feeding to kill tore a hole in that veil; marred it until it was irreparable, until the worst part of us took control.

We'd always been taught that it was impossible to come back, but we were also told that we would disappear. Who we were as Kova would be gone once the veil was torn.

But I was still here.

I looked up, but of course there was still only darkness. I reached my hands up, felt at the wall. Continued all the way around until I felt a break in it.

I followed my hands down the torn fabric until it met the floor I stood on. Followed the tear up until I couldn't reach anymore. I didn't dare move past it, unsure of what I'd find. I stayed in place and only moved to try to find the other side of the fabric. The other half of the tear.

It was wide, several paces away, but I found it. It laid on the ground as if it were a curtain that fell sideways once dismantled.

I peeked out through the gap, and saw it all. I saw everything that the Vasi saw. The room was dark and we were alone again. They must've all left. But I saw the windows that stretched to show the ocean below. I saw everything he was keeping from me, and I don't think he knew it.

I pulled my head back behind the barrier and couldn't help the smile that stretched over my face.

If the veil was torn, perhaps it could be sewn.

Chapter Sixty-Nine

Evaline

After we left the Vasi, Lauden quickly excused himself to talk to Kovarrin, and Sage, Wyott, and Cora left.

They all cast me pitying stares, but I didn't care. Where they saw failure, I saw hope. If my blood was the cure, we had no idea how long it would take to work. I didn't get what I wanted in the way of a sign from Maddox, but perhaps that was okay for now. Perhaps I had just enough hope to continue on, until we drew more of my blood for him, until he turned back, or we found more information to help us.

A mix of sorrow swirled with that hope through my chest as I opened the door to my suite.

"Evaline?" Sage said behind me.

I turned and moved out of the way of the door and let her into the suite before shutting it behind her. "Yeah?"

She strode to the middle of the room and turned to face me. "Are you okay?"

I pulled my braid away from where the Vasi had bitten me.

"Yeah, see? Cora healed me." I shrugged. "And the healing magic of it must've worked for my malnourishment too, because I feel like myself again."

She smiled. "That's good, but that's not what I meant."

I sighed. "I'm standing, and today that's enough." I waved my hand toward her. "Thanks to you."

Her brows furrowed and her chin quivered for one second before she locked her jaw in place to still it.

"It was nothing," she said softly, then looked down at her hands. "But I came because I know what that feels like, that hopelessness. When there's so much pain that you can't even feel it, and it just looms above you, always."

My heart ached for her, and I took a step closer. What had happened to her? What had Lauden done?

"I've been there, in that place, for so long now and you were the first person in ages who saw that. Who extended your hand to me, who tried to pull me out of it," she said.

Tears welled in my own eyes and when she raised her gaze to meet mine, I saw that they matched.

"And then Maddox, he cared too. And now you both are going through such horrible pain." She shook her head violently. "It's not right, and it's not fair. And I'm so sorry."

I took another step toward her. "You don't need to be sorry, Sage." I shook my head and my voice broke when I spoke. "It's hard, of course it is. But like you said, I've been through pain like this before. I know how to get through it, and the hope helps."

She clenched her eyes shut, then opened them. "Do you want to get away?"

I straightened. "What do you mean?"

She shrugged. "I mean that I want to help you, but there are so few ways that I can. But my gift," she said, motioning toward the floor. "I can give you a break. We can go somewhere fun, somewhere you'll be safe from Vasier. Maybe one of the Madierian Kingdoms. I can portal right into the wards."

My eyes widened at her words, at this offer. When she'd told me about her gift of portaling, it had seemed like something she wanted to keep secret, and here she was offering to show me.

"Are you sure?" I asked.

She nodded, a smile drawing on her face as she wiped her tears away. "Yes. Where would you like to go? I haven't been to all the Madierian Kingdoms, but if you've been there, we can go."

I knew at once what I wanted to do.

Sage was right, I'd been through pain before. I'd lost people I'd loved. And right now, the only place in the world I wanted to be, was with my father. I couldn't do that, but I could go back to Neomaeros, and finally sort through his belongings in the home we'd shared together. I could escape this pain, by falling into a different one. One that had closure.

"Yes," I said, "Neomaeros."

Sage smiled and nodded. "Let's go back to the loft to do it."

I ran to get my satchel, and flung it over my shoulder. We jogged down the hill and I was glad when we didn't pass any Kova outside of the training center on the way.

"Don't you need to warn Lauden?" I asked as I shut the door of the loft behind us.

She shrugged. "He'll see me when I return."

I nodded. I hoped she was finally starting to see who he was.

She stepped a few feet back and tilted her head toward me.

"Try not to panic. I've done this a thousand times."

I nodded and watched as she stared at the ground and brought her hands out in front of her. She flexed them and held them out wide, then clenched her hands into claws. The world around us rumbled, and it reminded me of the minor quakes we'd been experiencing, although I couldn't remember the last time I'd felt one. My eyes widened as I realized that she'd been the culprit.

How many times had she portaled in and around Rominia?

I looked back to the ground as the rumble grew worse and saw that there was a small circle of darkness opening in the floor. It grew until it was the size of a tabletop.

She turned to me and reached out for me to take her hand.

"Now you just have to picture it. Think of the last time you were there. What did it sound like, smell like?"

I closed my eyes and nodded. I pictured the way the dim light from the street lanterns filtered into our kitchen from the windows. The way the wooden floors sounded beneath our boots when I was young, and I chased him through the house. I imagined the smell of my home.

"Ready?" she whispered and I nodded. I saw a flash of light and opened my eyes to see her hand extended over the portal. There was a slight blue hue and I could hear the soft patter of raindrops. "Now, we just step through."

I nodded and took a deep breath.

We looked to each other one last time, and then took a step into the darkness.

My boots landed on wood. I opened my eyes, didn't remember when I closed them, and saw that we weren't in the loft in Rominia anymore.

It was dark, but the lantern light from the street cast a glow over the kitchen. I could see that sheets had been thrown over the furniture to preserve it, but this was home. It still smelled the same way I'd always remembered. Like my father.

"Where are we?" Sage whispered, letting go of my hand.

I smiled and turned to walk toward the fireplace.

"This is where I grew up. The Lord and Lady left my father's home here for me to return to, whenever I wanted."

My hand swept out toward the fireplace, and a fire roared within a second. I turned back to Sage, and her face had fallen.

"What?" I asked, rushing to her side. "Is that okay? Did you want to go somewhere else?"

She shook her head and wiped a lone tear from her eye. "No. I'm fine." She took a deep breath. "It just seems like you and your father were very close."

I nodded, and pulled a sheet off the chaise for her to sit. "We were. He was my best friend." I moved to the cabinet where he kept all his weapons, and threw the doors open. "We were a team. He believed in me, always."

Sage sniffled.

"I'm sorry about the dust," I said, waving some out of my own face as I saw the cabinet's contents. My father's weapons were still hung up on their displays. Daggers, big and small, and an assortment of swords.

I reached forward and dragged my fingers down them. I remembered each and every one of them, especially if they were pieces I'd picked out for him during one of our trips to the market.

Sage remained in the living room while I went about the house. My hands trailed over the walls as I walked, but there weren't any tears.

I didn't feel the same sorrow that I did the last time that I was in Neomaeros, with Maddox and Wyott. I didn't feel the usual ache that sat in my chest when I thought about my father. Being here felt like being with him, like he was standing right here with me, like everything was going to be alright.

My bedroom looked just as it had when I left it. I smiled as I stepped into it and shuffled through some of the books on the shelves. I sat on the bed and swiped my palm over the blankets covering it.

I'd brought my satchel, in case I wanted to take anything with me, but I left my room without a thing. It looked like the room of the girl I'd been so long ago. But that girl had grown, and she'd changed. She'd hurt, she'd loved, she'd lost. But she'd also gained so much; she gained a mate, a family, gained Gods-damned magic beyond anything this world had seen before.

I wasn't the same woman who had left Neomaeros with my father, and maybe that's why being here didn't hurt so bad. Maybe everything that hurt me, had also built me into the person I was destined to become. Maybe losing Maddox was a part of that, but maybe it wasn't the end.

My smile grew as I moved to his room. It looked exactly as I always remembered—boring.

It was all brown; the lone bed, the single dresser, and the wooden walls around me. I looked over the bed that could fit two people, that bore two pillows, but only had one with a head indent in it.

I sat and scooted closer to the top of the bed, to see if his pillow still smelled like him, when I noticed a lump in the mattress.

My brows furrowed as I knelt to the ground beside it and lifted the mattress from the frame.

I snickered as I saw a holstered sword lying there. Of course he hid swords beneath his mattress.

Sage must have heard me laughing because she appeared in the doorway.

"What's so funny?"

I sat back off my knees and onto my feet, holding the sword up for her to see. "My father had this hidden under his bed."

She laughed. "Why did he have all the other weapons in that cabinet?"

I shrugged as I stood and pulled the sword out of the sheath. "I don't know, probably just being extra cautious."

I pulled the sword from its holster and a slip of paper popped out. I furrowed my brows and wedged it out from between the metal and leather.

I tucked the re-holstered sword beneath my arm and opened the note. It was dark, so I pulled one hand back and lit a small flame from my thumb.

Sage leaned against the door jamb as I read it aloud.

"Evaline, if you are reading this then you've gone ahead and ruined another surprise for yourself."

I snorted at that, and turned to Sage, pulling the note back for a moment.

"My father was always horrible at finding hiding spots for my presents." I waved around the room. "Small house and all. I always stumbled upon them accidentally."

She gave me a small smile, and I went back to the note.

"But since there's no proper way to wrap a sword, it's obvious to see what your birthday gift is this year—a silver sword for my silver haired girl. Every year you grow older is another year I'm so Gods-damned proud of you. I love you."

My chin trembled as I read the last bit and the paper shook in my hand.

I didn't look up to see Sage, but heard the soft gasps she let out. I let my hand that held the note drop by my side and looked to the ground, brows furrowed.

When we'd left Neomaeros, my birthday was just over four months away. He must've worried that he wouldn't have time to get me a gift if he waited until after we got back from our trip in Kembertus.

I swallowed and dropped the note onto the bed. I unholstered the weapon. With one hand I held the sword to examine it, and with the other I lit a flame to cast some light.

It was a gleaming silver, the perfect length for my height, and perfectly balanced. It took a moment for me to realize that this was a replica of his sword that was sitting in Rominia right now.

I gave a small laugh through the tears. My father had a sword made for me, an exact replica of his, to match. We *were* a team.

I re-holstered the sword, and then grabbed the birthday note, and tucked it safely in my satchel.

I straightened then. A birthday note. And this was a birthday present.

The numbers flew through my head as I did the mental math. Gods, how had I not realized it before? But I knew that it was because I hadn't been paying attention to the calendar lately, and nothing had mattered to me since Maddox turned. Least of all, this.

I laughed and lifted my head to meet Sage's.

"My birthday is in a week."

Sage and I left my childhood home shortly after that. We didn't portal out, just walked the streets. Sage had never been to Neomaeros and wanted to explore.

It was night, and it was raining, but I created a shield of air above us, preventing the rain from soaking our clothes while we explored. I showed her where the markets were usually held, we looked up at the ornate castle, and walked back down the main road.

"We'll come back during the day." I told her. "When all the shops are open and you can see more of Neomaeros."

She nodded. "I'd like that." She smiled, and a soft glow lit her face. Her eyes flicked to something behind me, and light reflected in them, too. "Is that store open?" she asked, and I turned around.

A gasp flew past my lips at the shop. At the window, of the shop. The inside was lit, and it was easy to see the interior with the dark of night all around us. There were boxes everywhere, and two women standing in the center of it all, dresses piled high in their hands.

"Oh, Gods," I whispered.

I blinked away the tears of joy that sprouted at the sight of Aurora and Jacqueline inside the shop, late at night, preparing it to open for business as quickly as they could.

"What is it?" Sage asked.

I didn't dare move closer to the window, in case they saw me. I just stood in the middle of the desolate street, and watched as my friends laughed with each other and sorted through the dresses they were unpacking.

"Those…" I said, and trailed off. "They're my best friends, from Kembertus."

Gods, they looked so healthy. So happy. Aurora's wide smile was bright on her face and Jacqueline's green eyes were squinted in laughter.

"Do you want to say hello?" Sage asked quietly beside me.

I shook my head. "No, they were compelled to forget me."

And it wasn't until then, that my tears of joy turned to sorrow. Because it wasn't until then that I remembered.

The only person who could compel them to remember me, was Maddox.

Chapter Seventy

Evaline

Sage and I portaled back shortly after I'd explained to her why Aurora and Jacqueline were compelled to forget me.

"Do you want me to stay with you?" she asked when she portaled us into the loft again.

The ground still shook beneath me as I answered. "No, it's okay. I'll be fine." I reached forward and touched her arm. "Thank you for today, Sage. Thank you for everything."

She nodded and smiled, but the bed in the loft above us stirred and Lauden called out. "Sage, is that you?"

I left and headed back for the mansion and when I reached my bedroom, I stopped and looked around it. There were blankets and pillows on the floor that I'd thrown from the bed and tissues strewn about that I'd used for my tears.

I grabbed the trashcan from the bathroom and started cleaning. By the time I finished, I realized that I also desperately needed to change the sheets.

I cleared the bed and ducked into our closet where the extra linens were stacked on the back wall.

When I pulled the comforter out, it was far heavier than I would've imagined for a piece of cloth, and it fell down and knocked me sideways.

I caught myself in Maddox's clothes to keep from falling, knocking a few things from his hangers, and cursed under my breath before carrying all of the bedding back to the room.

After I made the bed and placed the last pillow on top I went back to the closet to hang up his jackets again. Only a few had fallen. As I bent down to gather the last piece, I noticed it was a heavy leather jacket. It was so warm on the island that Maddox must've only worn it if he traveled to colder regions.

I straightened to add the jacket to a hanger and something fell from the pocket of the coat, thudding on the carpet.

I looked down and squinted in the darkness to see a small shadow on the floor. I hadn't bothered to bring a lantern with me, and the light from the room didn't reach the corner of the closet. I gathered the jacket in one arm and bent to grab whatever had fallen out.

My eyes widened as I felt my hand close around a small box. My chin trembled as I stood and walked into the sitting room. The fireplace lit as I knelt in front of it to see the box better. I folded the jacket onto my lap before resting my hands on top of it. The box trembled in my shaking hands.

It was small and black, and exactly the size that would fit into a pants pocket.

I gritted my teeth, afraid of what would happen if I opened it. A shaky hand moved to the top of the box, and slowly lifted the lid.

A sob worked its way out of my mouth when I saw what was inside. And for a moment I reflected on this moment. Because this was not the first time I saw an engagement ring meant for me, but this was far from the reaction I had to Bassel's.

The ring was silver, or perhaps white gold. Maybe platinum. It was simple, and I knew that was because Maddox understood me. But my lips pulled up into a smile, despite the tears in my eyes, as the pad of my finger prodded the diamond that sat in the middle of the setting.

It was a round diamond, much smaller than the one Bassel had given me but still quite large. And I knew this ring was custom made. That

Maddox gave the jeweler plans for it, just as he had my Rominium dagger. And the way I knew, was because the diamond wasn't set in a traditional way. It was reversed, just like the Madierian Sea Blue Topaz on the top of my dagger. The flat side of the diamond was what was pressed into the silver metal that held it in place, leaving the sharp point of the gem facing up.

It was the most Gods-damned beautiful ring I'd ever seen.

I ran my thumb over it. Up one side of the ring, over the point, and down the other.

I considered putting it on, wearing it. I'd been married once, but only as a means to an end. This marriage, with Maddox, this was the one I wanted. But I wouldn't wear it until he slipped it on my finger.

I closed the box and put it back where I'd found it, and then began pacing in front of the fireplace. My breathing hitched, and I knew a panic attack might come on if I didn't calm myself down in time.

We'd gone through all the books we possibly could and had found nothing. I couldn't just sit here and wait for Maddox to come back to me, I had to *do* something. I huffed out a sigh as I slammed down onto the chaise by the fire.

What good were these powers if I couldn't use them to bring my mate back?

I thought of my mother, about the magic that I was given because of her. Surely, there had to be some way she could help me. But I never knew when I would see her, I desperately wanted to, but it wasn't as if I could control what I drea—

My thoughts cut off as I heard a sound around me. It was a gentle hum that started off quiet, almost indistinguishable, and then grew louder. Not loud enough to drown out the fire, but loud enough to be noticed among it.

I turned behind me, and noticed that the shadows around me seemed bigger, darker. I straightened as I recalled where I'd heard the humming before.

"Evaline."

As if thinking about her summoned her, I heard my mother's voice beside me. I jumped up from the chaise and saw her standing beside it, in that same birthing gown she always wore.

I shook my head and looked around. "I don't understand. I didn't think this was a dream," I said, trying to remember exactly how I'd gotten here.

She smiled at me. "You aren't sleeping, I'm really here."

My brows furrowed, before I realized what had happened. "My gift from Mortitheos?"

Her smile widened. "Yes." She nodded her head to the chaise. "You were thinking about me, you created the tether. If the spirit on the other side is cognizant enough to hold onto that, then you bring us to you."

My eyes widened. "Can I do that with father, too?"

She gave a small, sad smile. "I don't think so. I've tried to find him since the day he passed. I haven't been able to."

"What does that mean?" I asked, my heart painfully pumping in my chest.

She shrugged. "Some souls take a while to get used to being in the Night. For some, it takes years. For others, decades. I've been gone for over twenty years, so I've become coherent to my surroundings. It may just take him time."

I nodded, but then was reminded why I wanted to talk to her in the first place.

"Where have you been?" I asked. "I've needed you."

"I've been trying to help you," she urged. "I've been searching, trying to find you answers for Maddox."

"You've what?" My voice wavered.

She nodded. "I've searched all over, talked to all the souls I could along the way." She raised her brows. "Not an easy feat when you don't know what you're searching for."

Hope fluttered in my chest until it felt like it was suffocating me. "Did you find anything?"

She smiled. "Yes."

CHAPTER SEVENTY-ONE

Evaline

Rage had become an emotion I was too familiar with. And the reasons I had felt it lately had been completely justified. But never would I have thought that Kovarrin would be the source of it.

Actually, I would.

I'd been growing more and more frustrated with him for not helping our attempts to save Maddox, but this... This was unforgivable. This was unimaginable. This was not how a father was supposed to act.

My mother told me what she had found and I kept going through the information over and over again in my head as I made my way downstairs.

It wasn't easy to communicate with souls, especially if you didn't know who they were. But she was able to find some that wandered the Night, and each person she'd talked to led her to another. Until she crossed through several different regions and found what she was looking for.

Two Kova, mates who'd died separately; one in a Vasi attack a few decades ago and the other when she tried to avenge him. I couldn't help but think that it was beautiful that they'd found each other in the Night, just as Maddox and I always promised we would. The two Kova she'd found were friends with another couple, and that's the information she was bringing to me.

I'd shaken my head at my mother. "What do their friends have to do with helping Maddox?" I'd asked.

She'd smiled at me then. "This isn't just any couple." She'd grinned. "They're both Kova, too. They live in Correnti. His name is James and her name is Charlotte."

I'd wagged my head. "I understand, but what did—"

She'd cut me off. "Charlotte was a Kova, but she turned."

My brows furrowed. "Willingly?"

She tilted her head. "Stories differ. But the one from her friends is that she got too intoxicated one night and fed on a human without realizing that they were already wounded. They'd lost some blood the day before, and by the time she realized they were dead, it was too late."

Realization flooded through my mind then. "You're not saying…?" I trailed off and my mother's smile widened.

"She was a Vasi, until she wasn't."

Now, I was running. Straight down the halls to the exact place Maddox had taken me when we arrived in Rominia.

My steps didn't slow and I didn't wait to be let in. I threw the door open and let it slam behind me.

Kovarrin looked up with wide eyes from whatever document he'd been reviewing. "Evaline, what in the Gods?"

I strode forward and slammed both palms on the top of his desk. "Who the *fuck* is Charlotte?"

And Gods, it was clear he was centuries old. Because as I said the question, even though I tried to put as much venom into it as I possibly could, he didn't waver, his eyes didn't flicker, his expression didn't change at all.

He'd been waiting for this.

He let out a sigh, and I realized how drained he looked. His eyes looked tired and bloodshot, and I wondered if he'd been crying. But as he leaned back in his chair, crossing his arms in front of him and looking up at me, I noticed his skin was sallow and how hollow his cheeks were.

He was grieving, too. Just like the rest of us. Even if he hardly ever showed it.

My tone softened then, but I only felt mildly guilty for the way I'd stormed in here. I leaned back from the desk. "Why would you keep that a secret?"

He dragged a hand over his face. "Because it's all bullshit."

I stepped back and crossed my arms. "What do you mean?"

He nodded his head toward a chair in front of his desk. "Take a seat."

I ground my teeth and sank into the chair as he bid.

He leaned forward over the desk and rested his elbows on top of it, clasping his hands together.

"Charlotte never changed; she was never a Vasi. They were banished from Rominia because during one of our wars against the Vasi, they deserted. Their absence caused the death of most of their troop. After the war, when everything settled, their troop came back home, and we found out. A few centuries later they came back to live among the Kova again and I banished them."

I swallowed at his words, at the fact that there had been a time when Kovarrin had to make difficult decisions for his people.

"You just left them out there?" I asked.

His eyes pinned me in place. "When you are responsible for the care and safety of hundreds of thousands of people and they look to you as their leader, you do what best suits the whole, and not the few," he said. "It's not pretty, and it's not nice. But it's leadership. They deserted. Gods knew when it would happen again. If the Vasi came knocking, ready to tear us down, would they go and help them? I couldn't chance it."

I shook my head. "What does that have to do with Charlotte not being a Vasi?"

He rolled his eyes.

"Another century later James and Charlotte wrote, begging me to let them come back. They said she'd become a Vasi, and then changed back to a Kova. They feared that if the Vasi found out, they'd hunt her down. They were afraid the Vasi would never let the secret to changing back be known. But they also wanted to bring the information to our Kova, to help anyone who might've turned accidentally like she did."

My brows furrowed. "So she did change back, and you ignored them."

He groaned. "Evaline, it was clearly a lie. No Kova has ever come back from being a Vasi. Of the only two Kova I ever had to banish, one of them is the one who miraculously turned and returned? They weren't strong enough to stomach war, but she was strong enough to come back from being a Vasi?" He shook his head. "No, absolutely not. They were lying, they would've said anything to get back in."

"If they wanted to come back that badly, wouldn't they have spread the word?" I asked.

He shrugged. "I think it was a combination of things. They didn't want the Vasi finding them, and telling others would've risked that. Besides, I threatened them. I told them that I'd tell their families what they'd done, that they'd deserted, if they continued their pursuit and if they told any other Kova what they were telling me."

"But you never saw them," I said. "You never saw her eyes, you never saw her as a Vasi, you never saw her change back. So how can you say that it didn't happen?"

"Because it's impossible. The Gods have their laws for a reason," he snapped. "If the Gods had a way for the Vasi to come back, then they wouldn't need to help end the reign of the Vasi. They would just give them the information."

My fists balled at my sides and I let out an exasperated breath. "How do you know that me finding this information out, and being the chosen one, isn't the way that the Gods chose to give the Vasi this information," I hissed. "How do you know that this thing you say is impossible because it hasn't happened yet, how do you know that it isn't happening right *now.* How do you know that this isn't the work of the Gods? That this isn't their plan?"

He opened his mouth and shut it, and there was a pause before he spoke again.

"I'm a leader," he said, his voice low. "And I have to do what is best for my people. And part of that means not bouncing silly ideas into their heads. If Kova heard a lie that someone changed and was able to come back, they might be less careful with how they feed. Think about the consequences of that. More humans would die, more Kova would turn. And what if it didn't work? What if there was no way to bring them back? There'd be far less humans and far more Vasi. *That* is not a sustainable system," he said. "*That* is not what the Gods want. And *that* is not their will."

I stood up. "You speak of the Gods as if you are one, as if you know what they want. Your people may have thought you were a creation of the Gods, but you weren't. You were created by a Sorceress, *which I am.* I am the only person in this room, in this world, for all we know, who was touched by the Gods. The only one of us who has any plans gifted to them by the Gods. You can call it a curse; I will call it my fate. You may not care to find them and figure this out, but *I do.* I'm going to go to Correnti, and I'm going to bring them back here. And you will allow them in."

He rolled his eyes and I could tell he was growing angry.

"There is no reason you should be leaving Rominia. If you leave, you will be in danger."

I scoffed. "I don't care. I can't do anything to help the Gods end the Vasi if Maddox is gone. I don't care if I have to spend my entire life fighting for him, but I will if that's what it takes."

"If you leave," he said. "And the Vasi take you, or kill you," he said slowly and lifted his eyes from where he'd been looking at his hands. "Then Maddox turned for nothing. His attempts to keep you safe, and the consequences of those attempts, will be for nothing."

I sighed and leveled my gaze at him. "Maddox has fought for me since the moment we met. Since before I ever reciprocated his feelings. Now, it's my turn to fight for him."

I turned to leave.

"Evaline if you go, and are abducted, I will not send a team to save you."

My hand halted above the doorknob, but I didn't dare turn around.

"I loved my son, and I love you for everything you've done for him, and even for this passion you have to help him. But I *cannot* start a war over one person's life," he said. "I cannot start a war to avenge Maddox, it's why we haven't done anything. I can't start a war to save his mate, either. I loved your mother, and I respected your father, but I cannot protect you once you leave these wards. If you leave, and are captured, you're on your own."

A ghost of a smile played at my lips as I dropped my hand to the doorknob and turned it.

"I'm quite used to that," I said, before opening the door and letting it slam behind me.

I planned to storm all the way to my room and figure out what to do from there, but as I left his wing of the home and my boots thudded over the tile that made up the entrance to the mansion, I looked to the large double doors that led outside. My feet stopped, still facing toward my destination, but my head turned to stare at the door.

I knew in an instant where I needed to go, and as I trudged down the hill and away from the estate, I became more and more sure with each step.

After a few soft knocks on the door, I started to knock harder. I was already waking them up, what was the point of trying to be quiet about it? Besides, it hadn't been long since Sage and I had portaled back in, she might not have even fallen asleep yet. I heard some thumps in the loft before Lauden whipped the door open with Sage standing behind his shoulder.

"What's wrong?" he asked.

I shook my head. "Nothing."

His brows rose. "What do you mean nothing? You can't just come here in the middle of the night and bother us if nothing is wrong."

I managed to suppress an eye roll and turned to Sage. "I need your help."

Her brows furrowed and she looked back toward Lauden before looking to me, and Lauden widened the door to let me in.

I didn't move. "Actually," I said. "I need to talk to Sage privately," I said to Lauden, then turned to her. "Could you come out here?"

Lauden scoffed as Sage slipped past him. "It's fine," she said to him as she pulled her robe tighter and came outside.

She was barefoot, and we walked away from the loft and directly into the sand, down to the beach where the waves would dull the sound of our conversation.

"What's wrong?" she asked.

"Do you want to go to another Madierian Kingdom?"

Her brows furrowed. "What do you mean?"

"I've learned that there are two Kova living in Correnti, one of whom was a Vasi who changed back."

Her eyes widened. "How did you get this information?"

I bit my lip. "I can't tell you," I said. "Not quite yet, I don't understand it myself."

Her eyes flashed at that and the wind shifted through her hair as she shook her head. "I can't portal you into Correnti."

I nodded. "You're right, I shouldn't have asked that of you. I just thought that since we'd already done it tonight, it wouldn't be an issue. I'm sorry I asked."

Sage rolled her eyes. "If you'd let me finish," she said, with a twinge of annoyance in her voice. "I can't portal you into Correnti because I've never been. Have you?"

I pursed my lips. "No."

She shrugged. "Okay then, I can't portal us there."

I looked toward the sea, thinking of all the people who'd been to Correnti that could help us, but immediately realized that I couldn't ask her to reveal her secret to more people.

I nodded and looked down at my hands. "Okay," I said. "I'm sorry I woke you up. I was just excited. It was the best chance we've had in weeks."

"I'll still go," she said, and I looked up from my hands, my brows furrowing.

"What do you mean?"

She shrugged. "Portaling isn't the only way to travel, or have you already forgotten after doing it once?"

"You mean you'd still go?" I asked. "Even if it took more time and put you in danger?"

She rolled her eyes. "I've lived this long, haven't I? I am powerful. Just because the Vasi got the jump on us once doesn't mean it'll happen again. And you're powerful as fuck, too."

My eyes flicked between hers. "You're really willing to go?"

She nodded. "Of course."

I nodded, a small smile growing on my face. "Thank you so much," I said, and she tensed up.

"You're not going to hug me again, are you?"

I laughed. "No."

She nodded. "Good, because once in one day is enough."

We parted ways and this time when I got to my suite, and back to the freshly made bed, I flopped onto it and didn't wake for hours.

Chapter Seventy-Two

Wyott

When I woke up, my spirits were still low from the day before. I'd let Evaline convince some part of me that her blood was the trick. And it was only when she'd said the words, that I realized that she could possibly be the cure. I'd known that was what she was going for, and all it'd taken was a look to relay the message. And when her blood hadn't been the cure, when he'd still sat there as a Vasi, it was as if my stomach fell all over again. But I still hoped, like Evaline did, that it would just take time.

Perhaps it would take a few weeks of feedings. I didn't know what cadence we should feed him at. On one hand, it could make him stronger. And it would only give the Vasi strength to take complete control, if there was a chance Maddox was still in there. But on the offhand that it was weakening him, and it seemed as much from his reaction after, then perhaps feeding more frequently would make Maddox come back faster.

Before the thoughts could plague me through lunch, a letter was slipped beneath our door; a summons to appear at Lauden's loft. Cora and I just looked at each other and finished eating.

As we entered the loft, I raised a brow as I looked up only to find Sage, Evaline, and him standing in discussion over a piece of paper spread out over a worktable in his office.

My brows rose as I approached. "What's this?"

Evaline's head popped up and her eyes brightened. "Oh! Thank you for coming."

Immediately, her tone was too sweet, and I knew something was wrong.

"What are you looking at?" I asked, dread slithering through my stomach.

Cora and I walked closer and looked down to see a map. It was of the waters between here and Correnti. I ground my jaw.

"No."

Evaline let out an exasperated sigh. "You haven't even heard the idea yet."

I shrugged. "Don't have to. You're not leaving."

She furrowed her brows. "How do you even know the map was for a trip for me?"

I cocked my head to the side. "It's not?"

She rolled her eyes. "Well, I mean no, it is, but—"

I cut her off. "No."

Cora snickered at my side.

"Why don't you just hear her out?" Sage said from the other side of the table where she stood beside Lauden.

I lowered my lashes at her. "Because then we'll waste time before I tell her, again, that she's not going."

"Wyott," Evaline said, her tone a warning.

I sighed. "Fine, go ahead and tell me your plan."

Evaline turned back to face the table and spread her palms over the map. "I've received knowledge that there is a Kova in Correnti that was a Vasi and changed back."

I crossed my arms and furrowed my brows. "And you know this, how?"

She turned toward me and flashed her eyes. "Someone reliable told me."

It dawned on me that she likely meant her mother. She must've come to her in another dream. Gods knew how she had any information about the living world, but Evaline trusted her.

Begrudgingly, I nodded. "Okay, continue."

She nodded. "There's a Kova in Correnti, two of them actually. They're mates. The woman changed into a Vasi and came back. I have to go follow up on this," she urged.

I weighed the options in my mind. We could stay here and continue feeding her blood to Maddox and hope that it was the cure. Or we could try this option.

"Okay," I said, shrugging. "But you're not going."

She clenched her jaw. "I'm the only person who *has* to go," she said. "I'm going. The last time people ventured out to protect me, they ended up hurt. They were tortured, and Maddox became a Vasi." Her eyes blazed. "That will not be happening twice. Besides, I can move the wind through the sails and help us get there faster."

I took in a long breath, let it huff out even longer.

"Fine," I said, my voice gruff.

I was already considering who we could take with us, and how long it would take to get it all together.

Wyott, Cora said, her voice was soft through the bond.

My eyes had dropped to the ground in thought, and at the sound of my mate's voice I looked over at her and saw that she was looking to Evaline with furrowed brows. I turned to see that she, Lauden, and Sage were all looking at me with a knowing look in their eyes.

Immediately, I understood.

"Oh, fuck off," I groaned. "You're not leaving me behind twice. Maddox already did and look at how that turned out."

She shook her head. "I don't care. I need you to stay here to protect him."

I opened my mouth to argue, but she was faster to rebut.

"Wyott, don't argue," she snapped. "Maddox was right to leave you behind the first time. He trusted you the most and needed you to protect me. I feel the same. I trust you and Cora the most and need you to stay here and protect him."

I rolled my eyes, wondering what she thought could possibly happen to him while he was locked up. But then, I understood.

We hadn't heard outright rumblings that the kingdom wasn't happy about a Vasi living here—aside from Foster—but it was only a matter of time before the citizens started to feel unsafe in a kingdom where a Vasi was allowed to remain alive, even if he was the son of the First. And Kovarrin, Gods knew what he would do to put his son out of his misery.

I shook my head and struggled to swallow past the lump of frustration in my throat.

"Is this because I didn't let you go with Lauden and me before?" She shook her head but didn't respond. "You can't do this to me again," I said, my voice a low growl.

She looked at me and I could tell she felt guilty. "It's what's best for him, and us. When Maddox and Sage and the others went the first time, I nearly took three Kova away from their mates," she said, and the look that flashed through her eyes was one of pain. "I will not be risking that again. I refuse to take someone from their mate."

I wiped a hand over my face and put my hands on my hips. "Fine, but that really limits who can take you. Most of the best trained Kova here are mated."

She pressed her lips into a line and looked down at the table, tilting her head toward the two Sorcerers who stood on the other side.

I scoffed and turned to Evaline. "You'll let Lauden go, but not me?"

I could see Lauden's scowl in my peripheral, but Evaline only pursed her lips and nodded. I couldn't believe she'd trust him to go, but by the way she and Sage looked down at the same time, I had a feeling that Lauden invited himself on this trip.

Lauden crossed his arms. "Sage and I are strong enough to protect Evaline, but with how strong her magic has grown, she doesn't need protecting anymore."

I knew he was right. But it would only take a moment for a Vasi to get an upper hand on her. One moment for a Vasi to move faster than her mind could process before she could use her magic to protect herself.

"The three of us together are powerful, we can protect ourselves," Lauden continued.

I jerked my head toward him. "Well, you'll forgive me if I don't believe that," I snapped. "Maddox went out with a powerful Sorceress, and four of our best Kova. And they were *still* taken."

Evaline straightened and turned to me. "Unfortunately, this is not a debate. I didn't ask you here for your opinion, I just wanted to tell you myself."

I ground my jaw and looked to Cora, who spoke down the bond.

She's going to do whatever she wants. And look at what happened to Maddox when he tried controlling her safety.

My face paled at that, because of course she was right. I took a long breath and looked to the ground, before looking back up at Evaline.

"At least one Kova has to go with you. Not just you three." She opened her mouth, I'm sure to dispute, but I continued. "Dean isn't mated, he can go with you," I lied and made sure I didn't look at Sage, but even out of the corner of my eye I saw Lauden straighten, and Sage wring her hands together. No one else knew their situation, and Dean would want to be there with Sage. Evaline shrugged.

"I'm not going to make anyone go with me."

I rolled my eyes. "Of course not, Evaline. But he'll say yes."

He said yes.

Cora stayed with Lauden and Sage to instruct them on how they could help Evaline sail the boat with her wind, since the three Sorcerers had never run a boat before.

They planned to take a small sailboat that could be manned by just the four of them, with sails flown by Evaline. They didn't have a choice, they needed something quick. Vasier would know where she was as soon as she used her magic, and we could only hope that they'd be in and out of Correnti before he had time to send any Vasi their way.

Evaline and I went to Dean. I'd barely gotten the words out before he was nodding.

"Of course, yes."

Evaline shook her head. "You haven't even heard the plan."

He shrugged. "I don't care, I don't need to hear the rest." His jaw was set as he looked to the ground. "Maddox is my friend, and I failed him." He looked up to meet her eyes. "If I get a chance to right this wrong, I'm going to take it."

I clapped my hands. "Great. Can you leave tomorrow?"

His brows rose but he nodded. "Of course." Then he turned to Evaline. "Just you and I then?"

She shook her head. "No, we'll have Lauden and Sage with us too."

His eyes widened and he shook his head. "I don't think—"

But Evaline cut him off. "No, it's okay. The three of us are strong enough to fight any Vasi off. Then, if any slip past and get too close, that's where you come in."

"Trust me, I already tried to talk them out of it. You're the best I could think of when they wouldn't budge," I said, meeting his eyes.

He slowly shut his mouth and nodded.

"I'll meet you at the docks at dawn."

I nodded. "Thank you."

The rest of the day was largely spent gathering supplies, while Cora ensured that the skiff was brought out of storage for them.

As Evaline and I walked I turned to her. "Weapons… You should have your Rominium dagger, your father's sword, your throwing knives," I said, ticking them off on my fingers in a list. I tried to think of any other weaponry that I could strap on her that wouldn't weigh her down too much, but thought that was enough. "And then your magic."

She nodded. "I know, I know."

I looked forward as we walked. "And I shouldn't have to tell you this, but just as Maddox told you once before, you don't hesitate. You act first."

She nodded. "I know, Wyott."

A moment of silence passed between us, the only sounds were the waves in the distance and the soft thud of our boots across the cobblestones.

"I'm sorry that I'm asking you to stay behind, again," she said.

"Don't be."

Chapter Seventy-Three

Evaline

We met everyone at the loft to go over the plan a final time. Cora had done a great job to inform them of our projected route and had prepared a map for us. They'd gathered together some food for our trip, even though we only expected it to take us a day to get there, whereas it would take a normal ship a few days.

I didn't know how strong my magic was, if I could last an entire day using it, but Wyott instructed me to go for as long as I could and then rest. It was better than nothing, and we all just hoped that by the time Vasier knew where we were heading, we'd safely be there. And by the time he could send anyone after us, we'd already be back.

It was fading into late evening when we wrapped up, and I knew that Wyott was going to make me turn in early to ensure that I was as well rested as possible before we left. But we still had a lot left to do.

Wyott, Cora, and I went back to the mansion to draw my blood, so that they could continue feeding Maddox while I was gone.

I winced at the pain of the cut, and as they drew it, I looked up at them. "Will this be enough?"

Wyott stood over us with his arms crossed. "Not sure, hopefully you won't be gone long enough for us to use all of it." He shrugged. "But we also can't risk taking too much and then having it spoil by the time we can give it to him."

I nodded. "True."

Wyott shrugged and gave a chuckle. "Unless you can create ice to store with it."

Cora and I laughed, but then I looked to the glass of water beside me. I'd never tried before, but if I could manipulate water, I didn't see why I couldn't turn it into a solid. I turned to the cup of water and raised my free hand toward it. With barely a thought, the cup was freezing until the ice expanded and the glass cracked.

The two Kova jumped. Cora looked up at Wyott with wide eyes and he nodded.

"I'm going to go get more water."

Cora finished drawing my blood in his absence and when she was done, she bit her wrist and offered it to me. I still didn't like drinking from anyone besides Maddox, but I knew it was out of necessity.

"You know you have to," she said. "You have to go into this trip as strong as you possibly can."

I just nodded and drank. But only a few gulps until I saw the wound on my arm heal and felt a renewed strength coursing through my veins.

Wyott came back after and I froze a few large blocks of ice, and while he took the ice and the blood down to the cellar, Cora helped me pack.

Finally, I had to go say my goodbyes.

We went to Rasa first. She was surprised by the adventure, and concerned for me, but she smiled anyway and pulled me in for a hug.

"May the Gods give you answers," she whispered in my ear. "And thank the Gods for you."

Then we went to Kovarrin's study, and he shot disapproving glances at Wyott.

"You're not going," he commanded, but there was a question in the lilt of his voice.

Wyott set his jaw. "No, I'm not."

I'd told Wyott what Kovarrin had said, the threat he made. And I could tell it made Wyott angry. Of course, we knew we couldn't start a war based on the few, but it still hurt to know that he wouldn't do anything of the sort, even for his own son.

"I would've," Wyott said. "If duty commanded that of me." Then he paused, as if deciding to reword that phrase. "If Evaline had commanded that of me."

Kovarrin and I cringed at that, at the same time. It was the first time I'd ever seen Wyott counter Kovarrin, and here he was, taking a side. And making it clear.

"I would've gone. Because I will do anything for Maddox. It just so happens that the best thing I can do for him, is to stay here."

A question flickered over Kovarrin's eyes as Wyott said that, then he turned his gaze on me.

"You do whatever it is you think you need to do, Evaline," he said. "I just pray to the Gods that you come back from it."

I nodded. "Lauden and Sage are also coming."

He scoffed. "You can't take the Arch Sorcerer with you."

I turned my head. "Are you going to forbid him? Because best I see it, three Sorcerers and a Kova are our greatest chances."

He sighed and I knew he didn't have it in him to argue with me anymore. He just nodded and dismissed us, and I couldn't help the feeling that his worry over this trip would age him a few years.

Then we went to go see Maddox.

I didn't even say goodbye to him; I didn't want the Vasi to know I was leaving. If he knew, and then knew where I was going, then Gods knew what he could do internally to Maddox to make him disappear forever.

He was snarky, as usual. But he seemed tired, and I hoped that meant that my blood was working.

When we left him, it was time to sleep.

What felt like moments later, I woke. I looked toward the window and saw the last remnants of night start to fade into morning.

Sleep slid away quickly; I was ready for the day.

I pulled on black leather pants that clung to me. The thickness of the leather would protect me better than linen from blades, or fangs. I dressed in a fitted long sleeve black top, which would keep me warm on the waters of the Madierian as we traveled north. Then pulled on a leather top that covered the length of my torso and reached up to cuff around my neck and cap over my shoulders. The leather helped protect my midsection, and the corseting on the back of it hung low enough for me to reach back and tighten it myself. I didn't want to risk any chafing of the material against my skin as we bobbed over the waters. As I pulled at the strings on the back, I marveled at the front of it in the mirror. Three black roses were embroidered on the lower belly, and their stems and thorns stretched up until the three blossoms sprouted over my chest and under my collar bones. I pulled my boots on and laced them tightly over my calves, up to my knees.

I strapped on my thigh holster, where my Rominium dagger would sit. On my opposite calf, a dagger I'd taken from my father's cabinet in Neomaeros, to replace the one I purchased in Kembertus. I swung on the holster that held my father's sword and tightened it until it felt comfortable.

I didn't put the matching sword on, only because I didn't know how to explain how I'd gotten it to Wyott. I pulled on the bandolier that Wyott had gifted me last, displaying its six silver rose-engraved throwing knives.

By the time I was finished, I could tell the difference in the amount of weight I was carrying. Gone were the days of just hiding a single dagger, and when I looked in the mirror I smiled at how I looked like Maddox had the first time I saw him. Now, I was the one carrying an arsenal.

I moved to the bathroom, because there was only one thing left for me to do. I twirled my braid together and picked up the sparkling silver barbed wire, weaving it into my braid.

By the time I made it to the entry way, Wyott and Cora were just walking into the front doors. I smiled and adjusted the black leather pack I had looped over my shoulder.

"I thought you said we were meeting at the docks?"

Cora smiled and shrugged. "Maybe all the rest," she said. "But not family."

She looped her arm through mine, but the concern that crossed her eyes gave her away.

We made it down to the docks, and Wyott was quiet the entire walk. When we got there, I saw that Sage stood with Lauden on one side and Dean on the other. I'd never seen three people look so uncomfortable.

We all listened as Cora explained how the ship worked. It was small, the size of only a few lifeboats put together long, and a few less wide. Not large enough to house many more than the four of us. She showed us how the short mast worked, and how the sails opened.

"It's not going to protect you from much, but it'll get you there the quickest."

"Are you ready?" I asked everyone, and the three of them nodded.

Dean stepped up to shake hands with Wyott. "See you in a few days."

Wyott nodded and grabbed Dean's shoulder. "Yes, you will," he said, as if he could urge fate to follow his orders. "Keep safe."

Dean nodded before hugging Cora goodbye and hopping into the boat. He offered Sage his hand, but she ignored it and jumped in on her own, followed quickly by Lauden.

I turned to Cora and she was wrapping her arms around me before I even had time to open mine completely. I laughed against her shoulder and ignored the way her hair tickled my face as I returned her embrace.

"It's only going to be a few days," I said.

"A few days too many," she said, but then her tone grew more serious. "Be careful, Evaline. Come back to us. Come back to him."

We gave each other one final squeeze, and I tried to ignore the lump in my throat growing more painful by the moment.

I expected Wyott to give me a pointed look or ignore me completely because he was angry that he couldn't come, or to nudge my shoulder like he usually did. But instead, he wrapped me up into a hug so tight that I had to remind him to ease up on his strength.

"Sorry," he said, chuckling. But then he grew serious. "He will fucking kill me if you don't come back."

I laughed. "At least that'll mean that he's back, huh?"

He shook his head. "No. Not 'at least' anything. This family won't be complete until both of you are back with us."

Tears nearly broke through but I swallowed them back and nodded my head, unable to speak.

He pulled away and held my shoulders to look me in the eyes.

"No hesitation," he reminded, and I nodded. "No mercy." I nodded. "And no deviating from the plan." I nodded. "Okay," he said, before letting me go and wrapping an arm around Cora.

I turned away from them and joined the others in the boat. Dean opened the map, Sage held the compass, and I unfurled the sails.

I twisted the air until it expanded and the sheets grew to three times the size of the boat, and we were off.

Chapter Seventy-Four

Maddox

I was still living off the high of seeing Evaline the night before when I heard Wyott enter the room. Now that I had access to this tear in the veil, I had a far better grasp on time through the rise and fall of the sun.

The Vasi tried to keep me in the darkness, but there was nothing he could do to keep me from viewing and hearing everything through that seam.

I was sitting against the back wall when some noise filtered through, and when I neared it, I knew it was Wyott. I peered out, but kept the rest of my body behind it.

I saw hope flash across Wyott's eyes, and I knew it must've been from the looks of us. I felt the Vasi's fatigue, the way he could barely keep our eyes open. But by the look on Wyott's face, I knew we looked the part, too.

He opened his mouth to speak, and I knew what he'd say.

You look like shit.

But he didn't, and I knew why. If he or Evaline, or any of the others, thought that her blood was working, they wouldn't let the Vasi know.

"What the fuck do you want?" The Vasi asked, and Wyott lifted the cup of blood he held in his hand. The Vasi hadn't even noticed there was blood in the room with us, that's how off he was.

"Is it hers?"

Wyott nodded.

The Vasi hesitated, and I knew it was because he thought Wyott might be lying. That maybe he'd take a swig and it would be the molten metal. But he must've decided it was worth the risk, because he nodded.

Wyott strode forward and the Vasi tilted our head back so that Wyott could tip the cup back into our mouth.

Wyott was staring down at us, right into our eyes as the Vasi gulped it down hungrily. I knew he was analyzing any changes, to see if her blood was doing anything. But a part of me also thought that perhaps he was looking for me.

Immediately the taste of her sweet blood bloomed across our tongue, but something was wrong.

The Vasi must not have noticed, likely because he'd only ever fed from her once and it had only been a few sips. But I knew the taste of her blood, and not only was this colder than it should've been, even if they drew it a few hours ago and let it sit out, but it tasted wrong. It tasted *old*. As if the air had gotten to it. It wasn't fresh.

Without realizing what I was doing, I was reaching for the bond, only to remember that it was gone. Just as it had been when I woke up from the change.

But this time, it wasn't gone. When I searched it out, I felt the pulse of it slow and low in the depths of my mind. My brows furrowed, and I pushed harder for it, worried this was a trick. An awful prank my mind was playing on me.

It was fainter than it used to be, but it was unmistakable. And I realized that the Vasi had been blocking it away from me. All these weeks he'd been silencing it so that I didn't know it was there, so that I'd lose hope.

I felt for it again, let it slither through my mind until it cemented there. The more I did, and the more the Vasi drank, the more I realized that it didn't feel the way it was supposed to. The way I'd grown used to it feeling.

Because for that month with her, before I'd left to go to Merwinan, I'd lived and breathed each day with the feel of the bond in my head. With the feel of her on the other side, of her reciprocation and presence. But this didn't feel that way. This was full of static, hardly discernible, and I knew what that meant.

I remembered the first time I felt this, when I found that Gabriehl had taken her far from me. I'd felt it again when I went to Merwinan, when I was too far to feel her the way I was used to.

It meant only one thing. And that had me forgetting the boundaries I'd set for myself, it made me forget that I was hiding from the Vasi. It had me sprinting through that tear, into the full presence of myself, until I felt the control of my own body—my *physical* body—slip back into my grasp.

I looked up and saw Wyott standing above me, with no tunnel to separate us. I jerked forward and felt the pain of the Rominium digging into my neck and chest.

"Where is she?" I growled, and Gods if it wasn't for the look on his face, I would've thought that the words had fallen where all the other words I'd try to speak in here had, within my own mind.

But Wyott's eyes widened, and he bent forward, grabbing at my shoulders.

"What the fuck did you just say?" he gasped.

"Wyott," I choked out as the Vasi began to fight back.

Maybe he was weak, but I think I was weaker, simply from lack of use of my own body, as if I had forgotten what it felt like and the muscles I used to control it were fatiguing.

Wyott grabbed my jaw in one hand then and tilted my head up toward the light of the windows behind him. He was looking directly into my eyes, and I wasn't sure what he saw, but there were tears in his.

"Maddox?" he asked, and the tone of his voice brought me right back to when he'd gotten off of that ship as a kid, when he was crying and we'd collapsed together.

I opened my mouth, ready to say that yes, yes it was me. That I was here the entire time and Gods I'd just been waiting for them to notice.

But before I could, I let my emotions get the best of me. The Vasi gripped the back of my neck, and I was ripped back into that black cell.

Turn the page for a sneak peek of...

Sewn & Scarred

The Fated Creations

Book Three

Chapter One

Evaline

Sage's hair had been down and free, but it wasn't a few minutes into our trip before she had to pull it back with a tie to keep it from flapping around her face.

I held my hands up to guide the gusts into the sails, but eventually had to lower them and only will my magic to do as I bid.

I breathed a sigh of relief when the air through the sails remained strong. Sure, it was still tiring. But it was far less taxing than holding my arms up the entire time.

It'd been a few hours, and Dean handed me a canteen of water and urged me to drink it. I started to decline, but he pushed it closer.

"Wyott and Maddox would have my head if I didn't keep you hydrated and nourished."

I laughed and grabbed the canteen to take a few gulps to appease his prying stare. I closed it and offered it to Lauden and Sage, but they shook their heads.

Dean looked to Sage, and it almost seemed as if he was preparing to urge Sage just as he'd urged me, but he instead quickly snapped his gaze back to mine.

He acted almost shy around her, and I wondered if it was because he found her attractive. She was beautiful, and it wouldn't surprise me at all if the Kova had noticed.

By the time the sun was its highest in the sky, I had to take a break. It felt as if we'd slammed to a halt with how weak the natural winds were, but I didn't have a choice, I needed to rest. I leaned back against my seat and breathed a sigh.

When I stopped using my magic and had no distractions, fatigue set in.

"You can sleep," Dean said, nodding to his shoulder. "It's more comfortable than the wooden post."

I shook my head and smiled at him. "No, I'm okay," I said. "I just need to wait awhile. Maybe I should eat something."

He nodded, opening his pack and pulling out dried fruits, hard meats and cheese.

We all munched on that and after, silence fell over us as we sailed without my help for the next couple hours. It was incredibly awkward. I never wanted Lauden to come on this trip in the first place, but didn't have much of a choice after he invited himself. I supposed it was better to have more Sorcerers than less, for protection, but I couldn't help but feel his presence was the source of the tension that curled between the four of us.

Perhaps I was being paranoid. My nerves *were* lit for every moment that we were vulnerable on the water. My eyes darted around with each second that ticked by, waiting for that same pirate ship that I'd sent to the bottom of the Madierian to come speeding over the horizon.

"Okay," I said, straightening and looking up to the sails.

Dean turned to me. "Are you feeling up for it?"

I nodded. "I'm tired, but it's okay, I can rest when we get there."

He pursed his lips and I saw his hands in his lap twitch. "If you need to feed," he said lowly. "To regain some strength…" he said, and the blush on his face was deep.

I couldn't tell whether he was embarrassed to be asking or scared that I'd scream at him like I had that time at Wyott.

Sage swore as she dropped the compass and bent to retrieve it from near her feet.

I looked back to Dean and gave him a small smile but shook my head. "I appreciate the offer but, really, I'm okay for now. I will tell you when I need it."

The sails expanded like a set of lungs and we were skimming across the water again.

The rest of the day passed without issue and only a few course corrections from Dean and Sage who were working the map and compass.

I breathed a silent sigh of relief when I saw the snowcapped mountains of Correnti rise into view.

Dean whistled and looked at me out of the corner of his eye. "You just turned a three-day trip into one."

I smiled at him and nodded.

As we grew closer to shore I lowered my wind from the sails. I didn't want anyone watching to know that a Sorceress was on board.

When we landed, Dean paid the docking fee and we all grabbed our belongings and exited the vessel. As soon as we did, the dockhands lowered the sails and tied them up.

When my feet were on dry land again, I looked at the shore before me. This beach was not made of sand, but gravel. Small pebbles rounded from hundreds, maybe thousands, of years of being rocked against the ocean floor and caressed by the waves until their edges were as smooth as silk.

I looked up at the castle. It sat high up above the water, built into the mountain. The walls that surrounded the kingdom looked to be made of the same stone. From here, you could barely see the spires behind the walls, but as we drew closer, the castle started to rise into view.

The guards let us into the kingdom and we aimed for the castle. Wyott had briefly considered sending a raven to warn Lady June and Lady

Harper of our arrival, but decided against it when he realized that while the white ravens were less likely to be intercepted than the black birds, because they camouflaged into the clouds, he didn't want to risk anyone finding the message.

When we got to the castle doors and the guards asked what we wanted, I spoke.

"Please inform Lady June and Lady Harper that Kovarrin Vicor's daughter-in-law is here."

He nodded and sent another guard inside. We all stood outside the doors for only a few minutes, fidgeting and looking to one another.

When the door opened then, we were escorted to a private sitting room. One woman sat in front of the fire and turned to smile at us. Her lips were coated in red which contrasted sharply against her porcelain white skin and light blond hair.

Another woman stood near the fireplace. She rushed forward aiming directly for me, her hand outstretched.

"Welcome," she said, and then cocked her head which caused a few strands of her long walnut hair to fall away from her face. Her skin wasn't as fair as her wife's, but it wasn't far off.

"Evaline," I offered.

She nodded with a smile. "Welcome, Evaline. I'm Lady June." She turned to wave an arm toward her wife. "And this is Lady Harper." June turned back toward us and clasped her hands together. She looked to Sage, then Lauden, then Dean before looking back to me. "You're Kovarrin's daughter in law?"

She didn't have to voice her real question for me to understand it.

"Yes, I'm Maddox's mate."

No doubt she noticed that the only pair of gray eyes that stood before her were Dean's. He spoke then, reaching his hand forward to shake hers.

"It's true. We've run into an incident, and Maddox was unable to travel. We're here to gather some information that we're hoping your kingdom can provide us."

Lady Harper spoke from the chaise. "Of course, we're happy to help. As long as this information doesn't require any violence?"

Dean looked to her and shook his head. "Of course not."

She nodded. "Good to hear."

"This is Lauden and Sage," I said, introducing the other two. "They're also friends of Kovarrin."

The Ladies nodded, and June moved aside and cast her arms out toward the chaise that stood across from her wife.

"Please," Lady June said. "Take a seat."

Sage, Lauden and I sat while Dean stood on my other side.

"What can we do to help you, while you're here?" Lady June said as she sat beside her wife.

"I'm aware that two Kova live here. Charlotte and James?" I spoke.

Their brows furrowed for a moment as they looked to each other. They nodded.

"I think they live up in the mountains. Almost at the edge of the wards."

There were no walls on that side of the kingdom, I'd noticed. But there didn't need to be. The land was a fortress, on the other side a sheer cliff that no army could traverse.

"I haven't seen them in years," June said as she shrugged. "To be honest, I forgot they were there at all until you said something. They keep to themselves, I haven't seen them since I was a girl." She looked to Dean then. "I've never formally met them, only discovered what they were after my father passed on the knowledge of the Kova and Vasi to me before he passed, and I took control of Correnti. They don't come to any castle events, but I think they're still up there. Do you need us to make introductions?"

I shook my head. "No, thank you for the offer though. We'll make do," I said, not wanting to inconvenience them any further.

"Please, feel free to stay in the castle," Lady Harper said, and I would've objected so as not to impede, but since we were only staying for hopefully one night, maybe two, it made more sense to stay here.

Lauden spoke then. "I'm the Arch Sorcerer of Rominia. Please, allow me to maintain the wards while I'm here. It's the least we can do for your hospitality."

Lady Harper smiled and nodded her head. "That would be lovely. The last time they were maintained was nearly a decade ago. We haven't seen Ankin since then. He's retired?"

Lauden shook his head. "Unfortunately, Ankin passed away this year. Of old age."

Lady Harper's brows pulled together as she muttered her condolences and hopes for his restful peace.

"Please let us know if you need anything to help in your ward maintenance," Lady June offered.

Lauden waved a hand. "Thank you, but I won't need anything. I'll run the spell after we've talked to James and Charlotte."

Soon after we thanked the Ladies for hosting us, they handed us over to their house manager who showed us to our rooms and asked how many we'd need.

"Three, please," I said, and Dean stiffened beside me.

She nodded and led us through the castle. All the guest rooms stretched down one hallway, which made me feel even safer since it appeared we were the only guests here and could all stay close.

She opened the door to one, and I turned to Sage and Lauden. "Go ahead," I said, nodding to the room. "Rest for a bit."

They nodded and went in, Lauden's arm curling around Sage's waist in the process, and I felt Dean tense beside me.

"Are you okay?" I whispered up to him. He jumped as if he had forgotten I was standing there and nodded.

"Yes, I'm sorry."

The house manager showed us to the next room, and Dean urged me to take it.

"He'll be in the next," the house manager said, nodding to the door beside mine.

I smiled at Dean and closed the door behind me. The room was gorgeous and unlike anything I'd ever seen before. The walls weren't smooth, but jagged, and it was clear that this room butted up to the mountain. That the wall I stood across from *was* the mountain. The floor was darkened hardwood and covered in fur rugs. The bed was big and also had a fur blanket tossed over it. Gods, it was summer and still they needed this much protection from the cold.

I threw some logs into the fireplace and my magic ignited them. I moved to sit beside the hearth, stretching my hands closer and letting the warmth settle into my skin. We'd reconvene in a few hours, right now I needed to let everyone rest. I should've rested, too, but I couldn't. I only stared into the flames and pictured what it would look like when Maddox's eyes turned gray again.

Please. I prayed, to no God in particular. *Please, let this be real.*

Acknowledgements from the Author

I'm not sure what I could possibly say that would sufficiently describe how much of a whirlwind this last year has been, and how utterly thankful I am for it. The response to Bound & Barbed has been incredible and far more than I could've ever dreamed. So first and foremost, thank you, Reader, who took a chance on an Indie author and changed my life. Every email, message, post, and video I received or was tagged in was so sweet and I'm so grateful for the book community and for everyone who reached out. You're the reason I decided to publish, you're the reason I want to keep writing all the new stories in my head, and you're the reason I'm able to continue publishing!

My husband has been a rockstar since the moment I decided to write Bound & Barbed, and that hasn't changed for Made & Marred. Thank you, Paul, for dealing with my endless random questions, for re-enacting fight scenes with me, and for listening to me talk a million miles a minute about the new plot idea I have or the characters I love.

As always, thank you to my family for continuing to support me in everything I do. Thank you for sharing this series, even if you aren't allowed to read it (Dad). Thank you to my sister for going to school to be a Physician Assistant just to be available for all my sword and dagger injury-related medical questions (that's why you're going, right?).

After the success of Bound & Barbed, it was a lot of pressure to write its sequel! So I found myself second-guessing my instincts a lot. This book really, *really*, depended on a lot of character development and character relationships. And writing it was challenging. Thank you to my mom, who is a therapist and stayed on the phone with me for hours as we discussed the different characters and their development. This book is absolutely better because of your help.

Ari Annachi, editor and owner of Padma Katha Press, is the greatest mentor and friend I could ask for. Thank you for listening to my podcast-length audio messages (only a slight exaggeration), for hyping me up for new story ideas, and for always pushing me to be a better writer.

Since Bound & Barbed has released, the entire Fated Creations series has been picked up by the audiobook publisher Dreamscape. Thank you to the entire Dreamscape team for being so amazing to work with, and thank you to the narrators Auri Alden and Tor Thom for doing such an amazing job of bringing this story to life.

Thank you to Saumya, Bianca, Aamna, and Daniel for helping make this book look beautiful on the inside and out. Thank you to my amazing ARC and Street teams, for whom there are too many to list. Thank you to everyone else who helped Made & Marred along the way; Carolann, Alisha, Ruthie, Reese, Jessica D., Jessica L., Lilly, Casie, Tayler, Victoria, Julie, Mayhanna, Baylie, Candace, Ayla, Madeleine, Aryn, Andrea, Jodi, and Melissa.

Until next time.

About the Author

Samantha R. Goode is an author from Cleveland, Ohio. She's been an avid reader and writer since she was young, and has a bachelor's degree in Creative Writing from The Ohio State University.

She spends her free time reading, writing, re-watching the same few shows countless times, and spending time with her husband, corgi, and collie.

Find out more about her or her works on www.samanthargoode.com or @samanthargoode on Instagram and TikTok.

Milton Keynes UK
Ingram Content Group UK Ltd.
UKHW042020021123
431836UK00005B/14/J